M

6, 8, 9, 10,   34,

37, 38, 40,

52, 53, 54, 73, 75, 88,

91, 92, 93, 100, 112

113, 115, 123, 128, 136,

144, 146, 149, 153

156, 169, 176, 179,

182, 184, 186, 187,

188, 192, 194, 196, 200,

202, 204, 206, 209,

212, 217, 218, 226, 228,

229, 234, 235, 236,

242, 249, 251, 254, 255,

258, 263, 269, 272, 275,

294, 296, 298, 301, 303,

305, 306, 307, 313, 314,

318, 320, 321, 325, 326

330, 331, 338, 345, 347

349, 353, 354, 362, 368,

370, 373, 374, 375, 376, 378

381, 387, 389, 397, 399

400, 401, 405, 409, 410, 414

422, 423, 426

A Book of
Girls' Stories

A BOOK OF
GIRLS' STORIES

HAMLYN
LONDON • NEW YORK • SYDNEY • TORONTO

First published 1964
Sixth impression 1973
Published by
The Hamlyn Publishing Group Limited
LONDON • NEW YORK • SYDNEY • TORONTO
Astronaut House, Feltham, Middlesex, England
© Copyright 1964 The Hamlyn Publishing Group Limited
ISBN 0 601 07057 7
Printed in Czechoslovakia by Tisk Brno
51105/6

CONTENTS

Illustrated by Alison Reid

PONY MAD

by

Barbara Ker Wilson

Jenny Hodges sat at the table in the living-room, writing a letter to Ingrid, her Swedish pen-friend. At least, she was trying to write a letter: but concentration was difficult because Jim, her young brother, was crouched in front of the television set, watching his favourite cowboy programme. He had insisted on drawing the curtains across the window, although it was only five o'clock on an evening in early summer.

'How anyone can be expected to write letters in the pitch dark I don't know!' Jenny exaggerated crossly — but Jim took no notice. He was far away, riding the range. His right arm flicked an imaginary lariat. 'C'mon, c'mon, ride 'em, cowboy!' he muttered. The room was filled with the drumming of horses' hooves.

Finally, Jenny could stand it no longer. She retreated upstairs to her bedroom and finished the letter there. '...must stop now,' she wrote, 'darling Suntan will be looking for me. If I peer out of the window I can see her grazing in the field below. She deserves an extra lump of sugar today for clearing the 3ft jump. Only a week to go till the next gymkhana! Write soon — Love, Jenny.' She folded the blue airmail form, wrote Ingrid's address on the front, and her own on the back: *Miss J. Hodges, Rosedean, Laburnham Avenue, London S.W.17.* Then she sat quite still for a moment, gazing out of the bedroom window.

What did she see? What *was* there to see? Only a maze of red-roofed, semi-detached houses and bungalows, each with a pocket-handkerchief size garden, and all neatly arranged into the pattern of a housing estate: the suburban avenues, crescents, and closes of S.W.17. But Jenny, like Jim, could use her imagination. And now, as she looked, the red roofs with their television aerials and the back-gardens with their ornamental gnomes and lily-ponds and creosoted fences just melted away. In their stead, she saw, as plain as daylight, a green field bordered by chestnut trees, and grazing in the field a bay pony with a white forelock...her pony...Suntan.

The imaginary feats of Suntan had filled Jenny's letters to Ingrid for over six months now, ever since the little mare had 'arrived' one day in an imaginary horse-box, to live in the imaginary stable at Rosedean. During the past six months, Jenny had schooled Suntan, taught her to jump, won third prize in an imaginary bending race at an imaginary gymkhana, and had once had to spend all night in the stable looking after her when she had colic. She had chosen the name Suntan because the pony's coat was the gorgeous deep honey colour of a really super suntan.

Jenny, quite simply, was crazy about ponies — pony mad — and, since there was not a pony to be seen in S.W.17 (even the milkman made his rounds in a motorised float), she had invented one for herself!

'Whatever do you find to write about in all those letters to Ingrid?' Jenny's mother used to ask. She was a comfortable sort of mother, very good at cooking things like roast beef and Yorkshire pudding, and sensible about not fussing if you felt poorly.

'Oh — things,' Jenny answered vaguely. She had an inkling that her mother wouldn't approve of all the make-believe about Suntan. But all the same, Jenny told herself, it was much more interesting to write about Suntan than about the dull sort of things that happened at school, and her humdrum life at home. Ingrid always wrote back and said she enjoyed Jenny's letters, anyway. So she should, Jenny thought. Why, it was like receiving a continuous pony story in weekly instalments! Ingrid wrote her letters to Jenny in English, too,

10

of course. Jenny often thought this was unfair, but then English was taught at Swedish schools, and she had never heard of anyone in a British school learning Swedish.

With a sigh, Jenny turned away from the window. There were more ponies all over her bedroom — not imaginary ones, these, but pictures and photographs of ponies, arranged in a frieze around the walls. Her bookshelf, too, was filled with a row of pony stories that she had read over and over again. And on top of her tallboy was a group of blue pottery ponies, kicking up their heels in play. Jenny knew perfectly well that her chances of actually riding a real live pony were more than remote. Children in S.W.17 just didn't ride ponies — there wasn't a riding-stable for miles, and in any case her parents could not afford riding-lessons. The nearest she ever got to being on horseback was when she and Jim took donkey-rides along the sands, during holidays at the seaside.

Now she shrugged on her school blazer, slipped the letter for Ingrid into her pocket, and went downstairs.

'Supper's nearly ready!' her mother called. 'Dad will be home any minute now.'

A tempting smell of sausages and chips wafted from the kitchen.

'Shan't be a sec., Mum — I'm just going to post a letter,' Jenny called back.

'Not *another* letter!' she heard her mother exclaim as she ran out of the front door and set off for the pillar-box on the corner.

The summer went by. Jim learned to swim a length and a half at the local swimming-baths. Jenny's mother went to the sales and bought a hat for fifty pence. At school, there were exams and then the results: Jenny did well in English, her best subject, but was near bottom in algebra and geography, which she disliked. The only country she really knew anything about was Sweden. Ingrid, who lived in a flat in Stockholm, had sent lots of postcards with views of the

Swedish countryside. Ingrid's life in Sweden did not seem all that different from Jenny's life in Laburnham Avenue — except, that is, for the winter, when Ingrid went skiing in the mountains, and skated on the frozen lakes. Jenny thought that sounded marvellous. She had often wished she could learn to skate at the local ice-rink — but, there again, boots and skates and lessons cost too much money.

It was at the very beginning of the summer holidays, during breakfast one morning, that Jenny saw the competition advertised. Her mother brought a fresh packet of Scrunchy-Puffs out of the larder, and put it on the table. Jenny found herself confronted by lines of bold black type printed on one side of the packet.

BOYS AND GIRLS — WIN A VALUABLE MYSTERY PRIZE! WRITE A STORY — THAT'S ALL YOU HAVE TO DO!!! ENTER TODAY — DON'T DELAY!!!

And below this, in smaller type, were details of the competition. It was open to children under fourteen — well, that was all right, Jenny thought; she was twelve. What you had to do was, simply, to write a short story about anything you liked. The idea appealed to Jenny at once. She sat dreaming over her bowl of Scrunchy-Puffs, wondering what her story should be about. She didn't wonder for long. Of course, what else could it be about but Suntan — dear, darling Suntan, at this moment sheltering under the chestnut trees in the field. (It was raining outside).

'Rotten old Scrunchy-Puffs!' Jim was complaining. 'Crunch-Snackerels are much better — there's a plastic helicopter in every packet this week.'

His father looked up from the daily newspaper. 'You look at the goggle-box too much, son,' he remarked reprovingly, recognising in Jim's last sentence the echo of a television commercial.

Dreamily Jenny helped her mother wash up the breakfast things; absent-mindedly she said goodbye to her father when he left for the office. Her mind was wholly absorbed in working out the details of her story. She spent the entire morning in her room, busily scribbling, and emerged for lunch in a daze; the heroine of her story had just ridden a clear round on Suntan in an international show jumping contest at the White City. The story wasn't exclusively pony-minded, however; there was an enemy secret agent in the plot, who was trying to kidnap one of the other show jumpers... Still sorting out the rather complicated events in her mind, Jenny ate her lunch without really noticing what it was. (As a matter of fact, it was fish pie followed by strawberries and cream.)

'And what have you been doing all the morning, dear?' asked her mother.

'Writing a story,' Jenny told her.

Jim was quick off the mark. 'Huh,' he said, 'I know what you're doing, Jen — you're going in for that Scrunchy-Puffs competition. Waste of time, if you ask me — those competitions are always rigged,' he added knowingly.

Jenny scooped up her last strawberry. 'What d'you mean, they're always *rigged*?'

Jim looked a bit abashed. 'Well — I dunno 'xactly. But that's what all the chaps at school say. I think it means that they always give the prize to the daughter of the man who owns Scrunchy-Puffs, or something.'

'Rubbish,' Jenny retorted scathingly. All the same, she hoped it wasn't true.

'Anyway,' Jim went on, 'who wants to go in for a competition when you don't even know what the prize is? "Mystery prize" might mean anything.' He grinned. 'It'll probably turn out to be a plastic helicopter, that you could have got for nothing if Mum had bought Crunch-Snackerels instead of rotten old Scrunchy-Puffs!'

'Now that's enough, Jim,' his mother said firmly. 'If Jenny wants to go in for the competition, that's her affair, and we must hope she wins it.' She sighed reminiscently. 'I remember, when I was a girl, I won a consolation prize in a painting competition... they sent me a propelling pencil, but it

13

never worked properly. Still, I wore it clipped inside my school tunic just the same.'

Jenny and Jim looked across at their mother, trying to imagine her as a schoolgirl in a gym tunic.

After lunch, Jenny escaped upstairs again. By tea-time, she had written the last word in her story. The heroine — and Suntan — were triumphant. Thanks to their united efforts, the wicked spy had been forced to flee the country. She spent a long time trying to think of the right title for the story. Inspiration came at last. *Suntan and the Spy*, she wrote with a flourish at the top of the first page. Now it only remained to copy it out in her neatest handwriting and then post it off, together with the top off the Scrunchy-Puffs packet.

'You must wait until we've finished the packet before you can have the top off it,' her mother told her when she went downstairs. 'Otherwise the Scrunchy-Puffs will go all soft and un-scrunchy.'

Jenny was very eager to get her story sent off, now that she had finished it. For the rest of that week she took extra large helpings of cereal for breakfast, and the packet of Scrunchy-Puffs was emptied in record time. On Saturday, she walked to the corner of Laburnham Avenue carrying a large envelope.

'Now I shan't hear anything more about the competition for ages and ages,' she told herself, as *Suntan and the Spy* slithered through the mouth of the pillar-box and landed with a soft thud inside. 'But how super — how absolutely *super* it'll be if I win it!'

Two more months slipped by, and Jenny actually forgot all about the competition. After the first month she had in any case given up all hope of winning the prize. Secretly she was disappointed — *Suntan and the Spy* was a jolly good story!

The autumn term began at school, and Jenny went up into a new class. For a while, using the classroom and the text-books that the girls in the form above had used last year, she felt much older and rather important... but quite soon the novelty wore off, and she got used to the idea of being in the Upper Fourth instead of the Lower Fourth. Then, one morning at Assembly time, the Headmistress announced a startling piece of news.

'I know that some of you have been corresponding with Swedish pen-friends,' she began in what Jenny thought of as her 'good news' voice — quite different in tone from the 'bad news' voice she reserved for talking about misdemeanours, or reading out lost property lists.

'All these Swedish girls are pupils at a Stockholm school, as you probably know,' the Headmistress went on plummily, 'and I am sure you will be very interested when I tell you that three of them are coming to spend the second half of this term with us, to improve their English and find out what life at a British school is like.'

Jenny, sitting in a back row of chairs between Linda Marsh, who always sang the hymns at Assembly very loudly and out of tune, and Christine Renford, her best friend, gasped and swallowed hard. Surely Ingrid couldn't be coming to England. *Please* don't let it be Ingrid, she thought desperately. Into her mind flashed all those fantastic tales she had made up, week after week, about Suntan, gymkhanas, mucking out stables, pony-treks... Oh, it would be just *awful* if...

'Now I will read out the names of the three girls who are coming,' the Headmistress was saying. She paused, and picked up a piece of paper from the table in front of her. Jenny waited breathlessly.

'Elisabeth Neilson, Anna Lingard and Ingrid Carlson.'

Jenny closed her eyes for a split second. She felt a jab in her ribs from Christine's sharp elbow.

'Ingrid's *yours*, isn't she?' Christine hissed.

'Yes,' Jenny said. Her reply sounded more like a groan.

'Aren't you pleased?' Christine whispered. 'What's the matter, then?'

But Jenny just shook her head. She couldn't tell anyone — not even her mother, not even Christine — about her

15

imaginary pony, and all those letters to Ingrid, and the things she'd made up and pretended were true! This was her very own personal problem, and somehow she must find a solution.

Later that day, the Headmistress called Jenny and the two other girls whose pen-friends were coming to England, and gave them notes to take home to their parents, asking whether the three Swedish girls could stay with the families of their pen-friends' during their visit.

Jenny's mother thought this a splendid idea. 'We'll clear out the box-room and move the spare divan in there,' she decided as they were having supper in the kitchen. 'It'll be nice to see this pen-friend of yours at last, Jenny! Goodness knows you should have plenty to say to one another when you meet, judging by the amount you think up to write about in your letters!'

Jenny smiled wanly, and tried to appear enthusiastic about Ingrid's visit. Actually, one part of her *was* enthusiastic and excited about it. It would be jolly nice to see Ingrid, and be able to talk with her instead of just reading her letters... at least, it *would* have been nice if... And Jenny bit her lip anxiously. What on earth would Ingrid think when she found out there was no Suntan, no stable, no field with shady chestnut trees and red-and-white jumping stands...

'Well, Jenny, you'd better write a letter now to Ingrid, and tell her that we're looking forward to having her to stay with us,' her mother went on.

That evening, when she had finished her homework, Jenny pushed aside her exercise books and began a letter to Ingrid, as her mother had suggested. She sat for ages chewing the end of her Biro, trying to pluck up courage to confess that Suntan was only an imaginary pony after all. For she had quite decided she must make a clean breast of the whole thing before Ingrid found out the truth for herself — which she would as soon as ever she arrived at Laburnham Avenue. But somehow, Jenny just *couldn't* do it. How should she

16

begin? Should she say — 'Oh, by the way, about Suntan...'
— or, 'There is something I ought to tell you!...'

'No I'll tell her when I go to meet her at the station, face
to face!' she decided at last. 'And if she thinks I'm the
world's biggest goon, well, that's just too bad, for there's
nothing I can do about it. The damage is done now!'

As she sealed the envelope, she reflected that this was the
first letter she had written to Ingrid that never once mentioned Suntan! Yet the funny thing was that in spite of this,
she had managed to fill up all three sides of the paper quite
happily! Maybe it wouldn't be so difficult to write about
ordinary, everyday things after all.

It was dusk now. Jenny switched on the light in her room
and went over to draw her curtains. As she looked out of
the window, by force of habit she conjured up a picture of
a little bay mare in the gloaming, 3 years old, 12 hands high,
with a white forelock. But tonight it seemed strangely
difficult, almost impossible, to do so. Instead, Jenny saw only
the roofs of the other houses, yellow squares of windows,
and someone's line of washing still flapping in a back garden
like a row of white signal flags in the gloom. It was as though
the green field and the waving boughs of the chestnut trees
had faded away for ever.

Ingrid wrote back at once to say how thrilled she was at
the thought of coming to stay with Jenny and her family.
'This will be most nice,' she wrote, 'and I am looking up to
it always.' (Her English was often a bit shaky, especially
when she tried to use colloquial phrases.) Then, at the end
of her letter, she added a postscript: 'You write nothing of
your pony Suntan in your letter. Why is this? I am hoping
the pony is not unwell!'

Jenny smiled grimly as she read this. Little did Ingrid
know that Suntan had, quite simply, vanished into thin air!

A fortnight flew by, and now it was the day of Ingrid's
arrival. In the afternoon Jenny and her mother set off for
the airport terminal at Victoria, travelling by Underground

train. The three Swedish girls arrived together, and the other two were collected by their respective 'families'. Jenny spotted Ingrid at once, recognising her from a photograph she had sent. Ingrid was tall and fair-haired. She was wearing a blue raincoat, and looked a very gay sort of person, with smiling blue eyes. She and Jenny greeted each other joyfully, and in the excitement Jenny almost forgot the crushing weight of the 'confession' that lay on her mind.

She remembered it, however, as soon as they struggled on board the tube train for the journey home. It's now or never, she told herself firmly. It was lucky, she thought, that it was the rush-hour, and the train was so crowded. Her mother had managed to find a seat farther along the carriage, and Jenny and Ingrid were strap-hanging. People going home hemmed them in on every side: bowler-hatted men balancing brief-cases between their feet and reading evening newspapers; secretaries in high heels, teetering from side to side every time the train lurched; and shoppers who had lingered for a cup of tea before starting for home. Strange, Jenny thought, that it should seem easier to carry on a difficult conversation in the midst of a crowd!

She took a deep breath. 'There is something I must tell you, Ingrid,' she began.

'What is that something?' Ingrid inquired smilingly, tearing her gaze away from the advertisement placards above the carriage seats.

'It is about my pony — about Suntan,' Jenny went on bravely. She faltered for a moment as she met Ingrid's clear-eyed gaze, then went on slowly and clearly: 'All those letters I wrote to you about Suntan — they were not true; the things I wrote about did not really happen!'

Ingrid stared at Jenny incredulously. 'What do you mean Jenny — your letters, they were all make-up?'

Jenny flushed and nodded her head. 'I thought it would be more interesting. I have no pony, Ingrid.'

Quite suddenly, Ingrid's look of amazement gave way to

a wide grin. 'You mean — there is no Suntan?' she chuckled, 'no stable — no meadow with trees?'

Jenny nodded again, and now her lips too began to twitch into a smile. Ingrid's good-humoured laughter was infectious.

'No gymkhanas?' Ingrid persisted, her voice wobbly with mirth.

'No gymkhanas,' Jenny giggled.

'No colic!' Ingrid spluttered as the train roared through the tunnel.

'No colic!' Jenny echoed, shaking with uncontrollable laughter.

'No jumping!' Ingrid shrieked above the rattling of the train. She pronounced it 'yumping', which made Jenny giggle even more.

'No yumping!' she shouted merrily. Then a fresh spasm of laughter welled up inside her, and as the train gave a sudden lurch, she weakly let go of her strap and collapsed sideways on to a bowler-hatted man with a handlebar moustache.

'Sorry!' Jenny gasped.

The bowler-hatted man grunted in reply and rattled his newspaper in an irritated way. This sobered Jenny up, although for the rest of the journey she and Ingrid nearly began laughing again whenever they caught each other's eye.

Jenny felt happier than she had done for days. 'I've told her! She knows! It's all right!' she thought triumphantly.

From where she was sitting, Jenny's mother caught glimpses of the two girls every now and then. They seemed to be getting along together splendidly, roaring with laughter over some joke. Smiling sympathetically, she turned her mind to planning the meals for the coming week. She wondered if Swedish food was very different from English food...

By the time the train reached their station, it was fairly empty, and Jenny and Ingrid had found seats.

'Now I will tell you something,' Ingrid confided, leaning across to Jenny. 'I was not looking up to meeting with your imaginary pony — no, not at all! You see, I am a small bit scared of horses: they are so big when one is beside them, and I am a city girl and have never been doing things with them every day. I have been thinking you would expect me to ride and yump on your Suntan. But now —' she spread out her hands in an eloquent gesture '—now all is well!'

'The only thing is,' Jenny said thoughtfully, 'you'll find my letters awfully dull from now on, now that Suntan has — er — evaporated.'

'Evaporated? What is that?' Ingrid asked.

'Gone — pushed off — vanished,' Jenny translated.

'Oh,' Ingrid shook her head. 'You know, Jenny, I should say that really I grew a small bit tired of reading about that pony of yours! What I was liking most in your letters were the bits when you have told about your home and your school. In those bits I was feeling I knew you much better as a person than when you were winning all those gymkhanas!'

Jenny felt rather pleased when she heard this. 'That's all right, then,' she said. 'I promise I shan't invent any more imaginary quadrupeds... er, four-footed animals,' she explained hastily as she caught the puzzled expression on Ingrid's face.

They took a taxi from the station, and as they turned into Laburnham Avenue, Ingrid exclaimed with pleasure at the neat rows of well-kept houses on either side of the tree-lined street.

Jenny's mother had hoped they would be home before Jim got back from afternoon school, but he had beaten them to it: they saw him rushing down the garden path to meet them as the taxi drew up outside the house. He looked very excited, and began talking even before they were all out of the taxi.

'Hold your horses a minute, Jim,' his mother said, paying off the taxi driver.

'Horses!' Jim shrieked, 'that's just it, Mum — that's what I am trying to tell you! There's a *horse* in the garden!'

'What are you talking about?' his mother said. 'How can there be a horse in the garden? There aren't any horses in

A Shetland pony looked up at them

Laburnham Avenue... Only that Alsatian puppy of the Williams'. He sometimes roams into other people's gardens. Are you sure it isn't the Williams' Alsatian?'

Jim cast a glance of scorn upon his mother. 'Honestly, Mum, I do know the difference between an Alsatian and a horse! This is definitely a horse... well, a pony really... a shaggy sort of pony.'

Jenny and Ingrid did not stop to argue with Jim. They ran round the side of the house into the back garden. And there, sure enough, with its four feet firmly planted in the rose-bed, stood a Shetland pony! It looked up at them, gazing soulfully through the thick fringe of hair that hung over its forehead.

Jenny clasped Ingrid's shoulder for support. 'It's true!' she gasped. 'A pony in our garden! How on earth did it get here? She's rather sweet, isn't she?' And she went up to the pony and spoke to it softly.

Ingrid laughed. 'So your dream has come true after all, is that not so?'

Jenny looked round. She looked indignant. 'This one is rather different from the pony I imagined! This is a little child's pony — not my show-jumping mare!'

At that moment her mother appeared, followed by Jim, who was still talking. When Jenny's mother saw the pony, her jaw dropped. 'Just *look!*' she wailed, pointing at the garden. 'Hoofprints all over the lawn! The rose-bed a trampled mess! The herbaceous border ruined! Whatever will your father say?'

Jenny looked grave. Her father spent all his spare time looking after the garden, which he kept as neat and tidy as the ledgers in his office. The pony, as though sensing their dismay, whinnied and blew through her nose. Then she stretched her neck up to the laden branches of an apple-tree, and began ravaging that.

'Now, Jim,' his mother went on, 'tell me again exactly how that pony got here.'

22

'Well, there was this man with the horse-box.' Jim looked round at his audience, feeling important. 'He drove up to the gate, and then he got out and rang the front-door bell. He asked if Miss Jenny Hodges lived here, and I said yes, and then he asked me to sign my name on a delivery form, and then he unloaded the pony from the horse-box...'

'Did he say where it had come from?' Jenny demanded.

'Oh yes. From Cereal Products Limited. And there's a letter for you too, Jenny.'

'Cereal Products?' Jenny and her mother repeated the name together and together they realised what it meant.

'That blessed Scrunchy-Puffs competition!' said Jenny's mother.

'My story!' cried Jenny.

'The mystery prize!' Jim exclaimed, catching on to their train of thought.

Only Ingrid looked puzzled, so while Jenny ran to open her letter and his mother went in to make some tea, Jim explained what it was all about.

A few minutes later, Jenny came into the kitchen, where everyone had assembled for tea. She held the opened letter in her hand, and read out disjointed sentences: ' "... happy to inform you... best entry in the opinion of our panel of judges... hope you will appreciate your mystery prize... compliments of Cereal Products Limited, the makers of Scrunchy-Puffs." Well!' she looked round at them all. 'I'd given up all hope of winning that competition ages ago!'

'That pony,' her mother said firmly as she cut the chocolate cake, 'is going back tonight. As soon as your father comes home, he can telephone the Cereal Products people and ask them to send another horse-box to take it back where it came from.'

Jenny nodded. 'I know. She'll have to go back. We just can't have a pony here... there isn't room. And anyway, she's almost too small for Jim to ride, let alone me!'

Then she dipped her hand into the sugar-bowl and went

out into the garden. 'You are rather a darling, though,' she told the pony, as she grazed Jenny's outstretched hands with her lips and crunched up the sugar-lumps.

Ingrid, sipping her first cup of English tea, watched Jenny through the window. Poor Jenny, who had wanted a pony of her own so badly!

'What will Jenny get instead of the pony, Mum?' asked Jim practically, gulping his bread and butter so that he could go on to chocolate cake.

'I daresay they'll give her something else instead — maybe they'll ask her what she'd like,' his mother answered.

Jenny came in from the garden. 'Well,' she remarked, sitting down in her chair, 'what with one thing and another, I'm really cured of my pony-craze now.' And she looked across at Ingrid and grinned.

There isn't much more to tell. Jenny's father was very angry when he got home to find the mess his garden was in, and he spoke to the Cereal Products people so severely on the telephone that they sent a horse-box to collect the pony straight away. They sent Jenny a cheque instead, and with the money she bought a pair of ice-skates and boots, and paid for a course of lessons at the local ice-rink. This was really Ingrid's idea: she thought it would be more fun for Jenny if she could join in the skating parties when she came back to Sweden for the Christmas holidays. The invitation had come from Ingrid's mother, and Jenny looked forward tremendously to spending Christmas in Stockholm.

Jenny was quite right: the day of Ingrid's arrival did mark the end of her pony-craze. She and Ingrid spent one evening tearing down all the horsey pictures in Jenny's room, and Jenny gave all her pony-books to the classroom library at school. Only the blue pottery ponies still kicked up their heels on top of the tallboy. Now Jenny has a frieze of skaters gliding gracefully around her walls, and her bookshelf is filled with skating books. You see, she has become skating-mad instead, and dreams of becoming a world figure-skating champion!

COME TO THE FAIR

by

Lois Lamplugh

N etta leaned from her bedroom window and listened to the fairground music blown on the wind from the level ground near the river. Over the roof-tops she could see the flags on the big switch-back and the Dodgem car rink. It was Saturday: a mild, blue October Saturday.

Every year, for three days in late autumn, the fair came to the same pitch, between the park and the quay. Every year, for as long as she could remember, Netta had been taken to it by her mother and father, or sometimes her father only. This year her father was in bed with a bad attack of 'flu. As he could not take her, and her mother did not want to leave him alone in the house while he had a high temperature, Netta had been told she would have to miss the fair for once.

'I could go alone,' she said. 'I'm old enough. I could take Jamie. He'd love to go on the little ones' roundabout.'

Jamie was her brother. There was nine years between their ages; he was only three.

Her mother looked worried. 'Better not,' she said. 'I don't like the idea of you going without us. There are odd people around fairs, sometimes.'

Below her, in the garden, Netta could see Jamie standing quite still, his head tilted as though he was listening to the fluty steam-organ music. She did not know the tune it was playing; she had only heard it once before. It wasn't any modern tune, she was sure of that. It sounded like something that might have been written centuries ago. It fascinated her; it twisted and jumped and turned back on itself. Last night, when she was in bed, this same music had come floating in through her open window. She had had a dream. Suddenly she remembered it, a strange, frightening dream of people in masks dancing by lantern light, and a voice singing words she couldn't quite hear. She began to hum the tune, leaning far out to catch the sound as it ebbed and flowed on the light wind.

The front doorbell's abrupt jangle made her start. She glanced round. On the bed lay her school blazer, and her purse with this week's pocket money in it. On the mantelpiece stood her money pig. She wrenched the loose stopper from the pig's tummy and tipped out a little pile of onepence, and twopence pieces. Picking up her blazer she thrust the coins into one pocket, took her purse and ran downstairs.

The bell rang again. She opened the door. It was the doctor. Netta asked him in, and at that moment her mother came from the kitchen and took him upstairs to see her father.

Netta ran out into the garden. 'Come on, Jamie,' she said. 'We're going to the fair.'

'Fair,' he repeated eagerly. 'Go to fair.'

They followed the sound of the music, which grew louder and louder as they left their own road and followed the one leading to the park and the riverside. They cut across one corner of the park, where the well-kept beds were still bright with late dahlias, Michaelmas daisies and chrysanthemums. Overhead, orange clusters of berries flowered on the branches of mountain ash trees, which Netta's mother, who was Scottish, called rowan, and said were regarded by Scottish people as a protection against witches. Some of the berries were scattered on the ground, and Jamie wanted to eat them. He was disappointed when Netta told him he mustn't, or he would get a pain.

An autumn haze was drifting in from the river. At home it had been sunny, but in the fairground, coloured lights were already burning. Among the booths and stalls it seemed almost dusk.

28

'You can ride on the roundabout,' said Netta

Netta held Jamie's hand. She must take care of him. Just for a moment she wondered what she was doing here. Would her mother notice they had gone, and be worried? Well, they wouldn't stay long; just enough to see the fair, and have a ride on something.

Jamie tugged her towards the Dodgems. He had seen them last year, but then he had been barely two; surely he couldn't remember?

'Cars,' he said. 'Cars whizz.'

They stood at the side of the boarded rink and watched the Dodgem drivers speed around or thud into one another. Purplish sparks flickered across the wire mesh overhead as the little curved metal pieces on the tops of the rods attached to the cars travelled over it.

Electricity, Netta thought. It made the cars work, she knew, although she did not understand how. She wondered why the sparks were not dangerous.

Out of the corner of her eye she saw Jamie make some movement. He seemed to wave and nod his head.

'Who did you wave to?' she asked.

'The lady,' he said. 'Over there.' He pointed to a little window in the wooden wall at the end of the Dodgem building. Netta saw a woman sitting there, looking down on the cars. She had black hair piled high, and wore a crimson blouse with some kind of sparkling beads or sequins sewn on it.

'Why did you wave to her?' Netta asked.

'Because she waved to me,' Jamie said. 'The fair belongs to her.'

'Oh Jamie, how do you know? You've never seen her before. Anyway, she's only the person who works the switches to make the cars start and stop.'

'I saw her last night,' Jamie remarked. 'When I was asleep.'

Netta did not argue. He was at a fanciful age, her mother said. 'Let's go over to the roundabout,' she suggested. 'You can have a ride.'

'I want a car ride,' he said.

'You can ride a car on the roundabout. Or a boat. Or an aeroplane.'

He wavered. She thought that if he started a tantrum she would have to take him on the Dodgems, but she felt a little nervous of them. She couldn't remember how you made them work. Was there a foot pedal to push? And what about Jamie? Would he be safe beside her? She wouldn't be able to hold him and steer.

'You'd like to go in an aeroplane, wouldn't you, Jamie?' she wheedled.

He considered; then nodded. As they turned away, she saw him wave again towards the woman in the window. Netta had the impression that the woman's eyes were black, hard and glittering — yet she knew this was absurd. At this distance, how could she tell what anyone's eyes looked like?

Jamie wanted to stop and gaze at everything: the coconut shy, the stalls where you tried your skill at rolling pennies on to numbers or throwing hoops over pegs, the rifle range with its targets rows of little white tin men which had to be shot down to win a prize. He stared up at the big switchback as it thundered round with girls shrieking excitedly in its plush seats. Netta was relieved to see that this frightened him a little; it frightened her too.

They came to the quiet corner where the toddlers' roundabout revolved gently. On its staging were several painted wooden cars, aeroplanes and boats, a coach with seats inside and on top of it, two motorcycles and a single steam-roller.

'That one!' Jamie exclaimed. 'I want to go on that one!' He pointed to the steam-roller.

It certainly stood out among all the others, its red, black and gold paintwork gleaming. It had a little driving wheel and levers that looked as though they moved. No child was riding it, however; Netta thought this odd.

'Run to it when the roundabout stops,' she said. 'Someone else may want it.'

'No, they won't,' said Jamie. 'That one's for me.'

Again Netta did not answer. He was in a fanciful mood this afternoon. For all that, he turned out to be right; when the roundabout stopped, no other child dashed to get on the bright steam-roller. Jamie climbed into its seat and began to work the levers to and fro and spin the wheel. The roundabout filled up and the attendant leaned down from his central perch to collect fares from the children or the older people with them.

As Netta handed over five pence she was startled to see that the attendant wore a mask — the sort of crude pink grinning mask that boys wear on Guy Fawkes night.

The roundabout began to move, and at the same moment, from somewhere across the fairground, came that mysterious, twisting, old-sounding tune. Jamie gave his sister a delighted smile and swung the steam-roller's wheel vigorously. She watched for a while, and waved to him as he came past her. He waved back once, and then did not look at her again. She supposed he was lost in a make-believe world of driving steam-rollers.

From the stalls around, more and more coloured lights glowed. Overhead the mist grew thicker. Netta noticed that the flags on top of the highest fairground buildings, that she had seen earlier from her bedroom window, had vanished into the dimness. It could not be long since they had left home, yet it felt like evening already.

Suddenly, from the rifle range, came a fusillade of sharp cracks and shouts of laughter. She glanced that way. A row of youths were leaning on the high counter that formed an armrest, apparently competing to see how fast they could fire and re-load.

She watched them for a few moments. When she turned back to the roundabout, fear, sharp as a pain, shot through her. The steam-roller had no driver. Jamie had gone. Frantically she looked about her. There must be another steam-roller; she must have missed it. But no, there was only one, and it was unoccupied, just as it had been when she and Jamie first saw it.

She turned to the woman next to her. 'Did you see a little boy get off the roundabout?' she asked. 'He was on the steam-roller. It's my brother. I only looked away for a minute, but he's gone.'

'No, dear,' the woman said indifferently. 'I didn't see any one get off.'

Netta called up to the attendant on his little stand in the middle. He leaned towards her and she saw his eyes shining behind the silly, ugly mask.

'No, ain't seen nothing,' he said vaguely.

What could she do? Where could she look? She pushed her way through the people clustered near the roundabout. Had Jamie fallen off? She searched the trampled ground, but no small boy lay there.

The roundabout slowed and stopped. All the children got off; others climbed aboard. But none of them, anywhere, was Jamie. Netta looked about her desperately, at the stalls and sideshows and the crowds moving among them. Could he possibly have jumped off and gone over to the Dodgems? She began to make her way there. The fairground was very full by this time, and she was jostled this way and that.

Now she saw that the attendants on all the stalls were wearing masks, some red and bulbous, some green and mournful, some white, painted like skulls. When she came to where she thought the coconut shy had been she stopped, aghast. The coconuts had gone. Instead, a row of hideous faces, lit from inside, grinned at her. Her skin prickled with gooseflesh. Then she realised that they were turnips, hollowed out, with faces cut in them.

She hurried on, feeling bemused with anxiety. The Dodgems were just whining to a stop as she reached them. Eagerly she scanned each car as it came to rest, but it was soon plain that Jamie was not here, either. From somewhere high in the roof came the strange, twisting, old-fashioned tune once more. Netta glanced across at the woman who worked the switches. It gave her a shock to see that the woman appeared to be staring straight at *her*.

Netta joined the people standing on the raised side of the rink. Was that Jamie, getting into a car with a young woman? As she leaned forward to see better she lost her balance and had to step down to the rink floor. The attendant came past and said, 'Get in quick, then, they're just starting.'

Netta began to say, 'I don't want to,' but he pushed a car beside her and she scrambled into it.

'Put your foot on the pedal,' he told her, and she obeyed, and was away, steering cautiously along the low board wall. She looked for the woman with the little boy, and presently managed to come alongside their car — only to see at once that he wasn't really at all like Jamie.

She gazed up at the watchers lining the wall. Two boys in another car drove straight at her, shouting, 'Dreamy!' Her car spun round so that it was moving widdershins. Others thudded into it, and she was jolted on all sides and jammed against the wall. There came a last little thump, and she saw someone small jump down into the seat beside her.

It was Jamie.

'Jamie, where have you been? How did you get here?' she asked, ready to cry with relief and yet angry at all the worry he had given her. 'I thought you were lost. I've been so frightened.'

She looked at him. He seemed wildly excited. He bounced up and down on his seat and said, 'Drive, drive, go on!'

The attendant had come over and pushed the blocked cars apart. They were all gathering speed again. Netta pressed down on the pedal and steered for an open space.

'Where have you *been*, Jamie?' she asked again, shouting above the roar of the car wheels and the yells of their passengers as their buffers collided.

'Over the river,' he said. 'With the lady.'

'What lady?'

34

'That one.' He pointed to the black-haired woman.

'How could you have been with her? She stays here all the time.'

'She took me over the river,' he insisted. 'She wants you to come too.' He laughed up at her, a gleeful and somehow malicious laugh. He looked different. She felt cold as she saw how different. A word from some story that had been read to her long ago, when she was very small, came back to her. Changeling. Fairies stole a baby and put a spiteful elf baby in its place. That was a changeling.

Overhead the purple sparks fluttered and flashed across the wire mesh, seeming to grow brighter and brighter. Jamie made faces at the black-haired woman, and all the sequins on her crimson blouse glittered in the lights as she leaned forward and shook her fist at him. But she was laughing, and to Netta her laughter sounded terrible; mocking and shrill.

'She's a witch!' Jamie shouted. 'She's got a little house, with a toad, and bats, and a black cat, and a big black pot that steams.' He pointed up at the mist that hung so thick over the fairground. 'There, look, that's it. That's the steam. It all comes from her house. You come and see. You've *got* to come, she says.'

A witch! That was it, Netta thought, panic-stricken. The whole fair was bewitched. She must escape, and run to the park, and pick bunches of rowan. Then she must face the witch-woman and make her release Jamie — the real Jamie, not this changeling.

The cars slowed with their usual whirring whine. She climbed out the moment it was safe, jumped the barrier and ran. But almost at once she was caught in the crowd and had to dodge and twist to get through.

The fair seemed to stretch on and on into the mist. She could not see where it ended. She remembered that the big switchback stood on the fringes, listened until she could hear its roar, and pushed her way towards it. Masked faces seemed to be jeering at her from every stall — and suddenly she heard a voice behind her calling, 'Here, dearie, come back, you didn't pay your fares. Ten pence for the Dodgems, dearie, two fares. Come on, pay up!'

Netta glanced over her shoulder. It was the black-haired woman, and she had Jamie — the strange, changed Jamie — by the hand. 'She mustn't catch me too,' Netta thought. She ducked around a group of young men in black jackets — and saw ahead of her the tops of the oak trees on the edge of the park.

Behind her the shrill voice called, 'Stop that girl! She hasn't paid her fare! Stop her!'

But Netta had passed the great switchback and was out of the fairground, and ahead of her lay one of the gateways to the park. Still the witch-woman ran after her, very close now, but she reached the first of the rowan trees and leaped up to a branch. Twigs snapped and she fell back with a cluster of berries in each hand just as cold sharp fingers gripped her shoulder. She swung round and pushed the berries into the witch's face.

There was a flash and a shriek, and the witch, and the mist, and the fair had gone. Someone was gently holding her hand and talking softly.

'Jamie!' she cried. 'Jamie, where are you?'

'Jamie's at the fair with Daddy,' her mother's voice said.

'But he can't be. Daddy's ill,' Netta protested.

'He was, but he's better. Don't you remember? You're the one who is ill now — it looks as though you've caught the bug from him. You've got quite a fever. I think you've been having frightening dreams. Here's the doctor to see you.'

Netta tried to push herself up in bed. It was difficult to believe she was here, in her own room. But she could remember now, beginning to feel ill yesterday, and going to bed early, shivery and sick.

Then the terror of the fair rushed over her again. 'Don't let Jamie go on the Dodgems!' she pleaded. She saw her mother and the doctor glance understandingly at one another, and went on quickly. 'I'm not dreaming now. The fair's horrible this year.'

'But darling, how can you know?' her mother said. 'You haven't even seen it.'

'I have. I did. It's horrible, I tell you. Jamie must come back.'

'Lie down, dear, it's all right. I know you've had wretched dreams with this high temperature.'

The doctor added cheerfully, 'I don't think you need worry about Jamie. He'll be safe with your father, after all. I hear it's a rather special fair this year — it's under new management. Some remarkable dark gipsy-ish lady has taken it over, and they tell me she has had the idea of putting up turnip lanterns and making the attendants wear masks. It's Hallowe'en today, you see.'

PORTRAIT OF JULIETTA

by

Anne Barrett

'**O**h you are lucky, Juliet Appleby!'
Was she? Sitting down on the locker to pull on her outdoor shoes, as the others chorused all round her, Juliet sighed.

'Wish I were you!' said Susan Shaw.

Juliet pulled up the laces with a jerk. She was lucky, yes of course she was, she told herself fiercely, to have a mother who had been an actress and to go home every evening to a house full of her well-known and glamorous friends. To see them close to, listen to them talking about their books, pictures, plays; to go to the premières of their films and be able to do all the while a lively business with their autographs oh yes, it was lovely, but... Juliet sighed again.

The trouble was that you never quite knew what you were going back to. The trouble was — and Juliet felt ashamed of thinking it — that everyone, her mother included, was always having new ideas and always got so very enthusiastic about them. Going back from school every day was like going out of a sheltered alley into the full force of a gale and you never knew which way you were going to be blown next.

Not that she would have changed it, she told herself with fierce loyalty, as she tied up the bows, of course she wouldn't. Her mother was the most wonderful, the most exciting person in the world. It was that just sometimes, instead of all the fizz and froth, she would have liked to go home to a good old wodge of stodgy peace. She wanted to be like the others.

Susan, she knew, and Jane and Sarah, all went back to the same things every day. The same large tables with goodly piles of bread and butter on them, the same comfortable families and gardens untidy with babies and dogs and toys; the friendly old climbing trees. But she... their garden at home was lovely, but you couldn't really play in it, at least not in the way that Juliet liked to play. It was all so beautifully arranged that you could imagine people walking there and talking, or having their portraits painted, as Juliet's mother was doing at this moment, but not turning cartwheels, or standing on their heads.

If there was bread and butter for tea it would be in thin wavering slices which trembled over when you held them up, but more likely it would be some sort of rugged health bread which looked like bark. In her mother's Nature Food periods there might be nothing but bowls of fruit, which looked lovely but only filled you in a watery, unsatisfying kind of way, and on one or two horrible occasions, when Mrs Appleby looked at Juliet and decided that she was getting too podgy for the dancer or actress she wanted her to be, there was nothing at all until supper.

The real trouble was, she decided, getting her coat down from its hook, that she never ought to have been called Juliet. If her name had been Jane or Susan it might not have been so bad, but people somehow expected Juliets to be light and artistic and airy-fairy, and she was none of these things. Taking after her father, instead of her mother, she was solid and tough and square. And not all the white muslin dresses with cherry coloured bows on them in the world could hide her cheerful knobbly knees, nor all the bright Italian clothes and quaint coats, such as this one, could make her look anything but thoroughly matter of fact. With tough brown fingers Juliet buttoned its scarlet scallops disgustedly and longed for a shabby duffle like Patsy's as they went off together down the road.

They stopped at Juliet's gate.

'Coming out after tea?' Patsy was Juliet's particular friend and knew her difficulties. She lived only next door, with their two gardens between them, but Juliet's mother thought her family dull and so they might have lived in different worlds.

'If I can.'

'By the Route?'

Juliet nodded. They made their secret, crossed-finger sign to each other and then went their ways. Outside the door of her house Juliet paused to listen. She wondered who would be there today and what she might be expected to do? Sometimes it was fun and the visitors laughed and joked with her, but sometimes they would be feeling serious and make her play her latest piano piece to them, to see if she was developing any talent. On one or two miserable occasions, when they had given up hope of her as a pianist she had even had to stumble through some poetry, standing all alone in the middle of the room. Mrs Appleby and all her friends thought it was very important for children not be self-conscious.

This evening, to her relief and surprise, she thought at first that there was nobody there. An evening all alone with her mother, telling her stories about the theatre, about romantic foreign places that she would one day take her to, would be wonderful, and happened all too rarely. But then, as she started to go in and made out a low murmur of voices, Juliet realised what was happening. It must be a Hush Day. These didn't occur often, because the bubbling enthusiasm of her mother's friends, like steam lifting the lid of a kettle, wasn't easy to hush. But sometimes, when one of them had a special bit of work to finish, like writing an article or learning a part, her mother would put them in a special room, shut the door and wave a warning hand at the other visitors, who would then try to keep silence, smiling and nodding at Juliet when she came in as though their mouths were shut with clothes-pegs.

Today, sure enough, as she tiptoed into the drawing room, her mother came forward with her finger on her lips. As Juliet hugged her, rubbing her face against the silk and getting a whiff of delicious scent, her mother hugged back again for a minute and then bent down to whisper.

'Mr Serelman!' she said dramatically, pointing upwards. 'In the studio! Finishing my portrait for next week's exhibition!' And, miming a few brush strokes with one hand, she put the other round Juliet's waist and led her into the room.

Mr Serelman! Then it really was important. Even among all these famous people his name stood out and when he said he wanted to paint a picture of Juliet's mother she had been tremendously pleased and flattered. The sittings had all taken place while Juliet was at school, first in the garden and then in the old attic which had been rigged up as a studio, and to Juliet, who longed above everything else to see this portrait of her mother in the making, the attic had become forbidden territory.

Forbidden, that is, by the usual ways of getting in, such as doors, but what her mother didn't know about was the Route. Their light and attractive house had been built to a Spanish design and the blue-tiled roof was much lower than those of the houses next door. A large skylight over the hall made a completely flat bit in the middle, along the bricked edge of which someone of Juliet's size could easily walk if they were careful, and to each side of it there was the gable of an attic room with a safely balustrated little balcony outside. One of these was Juliet's playroom and the other was the attic, and both had French windows. Long ago she had discovered that if she came out of her room, crossed the edge of the skylight and then went past the window of the studio-attic it was only a step or two more round the corner to be in sight of Patsy's garden.

As though the early gardeners of the house, as well as the builders, had been on Juliet's side, there wasn't even any real danger of falling, certainly not getting more than a scratch or two if you fell, for they had planted fat-trunked leafy climbing creepers at all the main points of the Route and sown thick soft grass down below. Sometimes Juliet, who longed for adventure, wished it had all been more difficult, but there was no doubt it was very convenient when she wanted to get across to Patsy quickly.

There were difficulties of a sort, too, in not getting noticed. Many a time when she had been crossing the skylight she had seen people come into the hall down below and had to flatten herself against the brickwork; once, when there had been people in the studio, as she was passing the window she had to lie down flat on the balcony and even had some warm cigarette ash tapped on to her out of the window before she could go on her way.

Patsy, a faithful ally, would always be patiently waiting, and as Juliet dropped down from among the leaves of the magnolia which grew against the house she would dash across the last few yards of thicket to join her friend.

Once they had made the return journey together but had to smuggle Patsy into Juliet's toy cupboard when they heard Miss Grassman, the Swedish housekeeper, outside the room which had been chalked up as number one of their Roll of Glorious Deeds of Honour. Fired by this, Juliet had done the journey by moonlight, which was wonderfully exciting, not so much the rooftop journey itself as getting from her bedroom to its beginning. It had been the night of one of the Mother's grand parties and Juliet had to keep dodging guests and bobbing little curtsies to them if she couldn't, pretending she was on her way to the bath. Curtsies were one of the things on which her mother insisted — 'So charming!' said her friends — but by now Juliet, who loathed curtsying, had managed to get them down to the smallest possible jerk of the knee.

Ever since Mr Serelman's portrait had been in the attic Julliet had been trying to get a glimpse of it on her way along the Route, but he always left the window fastened and the easel and its canvas at an angle which made it impossible for her to see. If only he would move it a little! Juliet longed to see it, partly, of course, because it was of her mother but partly because she specially liked Mr Serelman, and of a conversation that she had overheard.

45

'Little pitchers have big ears!' people were always saying brightly in front of her, but really, she thought disgustedly, if you made little pitchers stay in rooms full of chattering grown-ups how could you expect their ears not to grow to elephant size? Feeling, on this particular day that hers were flapping like sails and as sensitive as telephone receivers, Juliet had overheard two guests talking about Mr Serelman's paintings.

'Slipping a bit nowadays, isn't he? His work doesn't seem to have its old quality.'

The other had nodded his head.

'This portrait of Julietta ... ,' (Julietta was Juliet's mother).

'Yes. This will be his chance to show he can still do it. If he misses this ...'

Oh, but he mustn't, Juliet had only once met Mr Serelman, but she felt that he was her friend for life. It had been on one of the days when she most hated curtsying and when there was a particularly tiresome collection of visitors, the sort who would leave their heavy hands lying about on her shoulders and keep twisting up little bits of her hair. Furious, she had done her bob in front of Mr Serelman, looked up sulkily at this little man whom she knew to be so famous, and seen one of his very bright eyes closing in a most enormous wink. He knew what she felt! Not only that, but he had got her to lead him across to the tea table so that she could stuff herself under his cover, and when she had done this and explained to him how she was longing to get out and go over to Patsy he had loudly asked her to show him the garden and then let her make her getaway. Oh, he mustn't slip! Not anyone as nice as Mr Serelman!

From that day onwards Juliet had been fierce in her devotion to the strange little bushy-haired artist; she wanted him to be the most famous and successful painter in the world. And now with this portrait of her mother ... as Juliet looked up at her this afternoon, so bright and so lovely, she felt that he couldn't possibly fail.

Still in the Hush, her mother squeezed Juliet's hand.

46

'He doesn't want me up there any more,' she whispered. 'The face is finished, he's just touching in the trees behind. Now come in dear...' and Juliet went forward and through her usual bobbings. They seemed even sillier than usual with everyone so silent and she thought longingly of Mr Serelman and his wink. Then she looked hopefully through the window towards the edge of the garden and Patsy's trees.

Luck seemed to be with her for her mother realised that it would be awkward for Juliet to munch her tea in the midst of all that silence.

'Take a plate out into the garden and play there,' she said, and Juliet thankfully piled one.

'She's happy to play out there for hours by herself,' she heard her mother say fondly to the others, 'such an imaginative child! I often wonder what she really will be in the end.'

The bold and reckless Captain of the Roof Climbers, determined upon a career as a steeplejack, made one awkward goodbye bob to the whole room and escaped, loaded with sandwiches, into the garden. From there she skirted round the house again and went in through the back door to reach her own play room and the beginning of the Route.

Out of her cupboard she took the old pair of jeans that Patsy had given her, put them on, and stuffed the remainder of the sandwiches into the back pocket. From its tin she took the Roll of Glorious Deeds of Honour. It was divided into two columns, headed Juliet and Patsy, and at the moment they had two Deeds each. Hers were the cigarette ash and the Moonlight Flit, Patsy's was the Toy Cupboard Hide and an encounter with an angry gardener. It was time Juliet did another.

But of course! Today was the very day, for Mr Serelman would be in the studio and she would have to get past without him noticing. Wild and splendid thoughts of clinging to the balustrade with her finger tips and edging along, like on the wall-bars at school, came into her mind, but then she remembered that there were some uncomfortably wide gaps. Never mind, she would get as far as the attic and then make her plans. Mr Serelman might have turned his back for a moment or gone out of the room. She climbed out of the playroom window and set forth.

From beneath the skylight she heard the sounds of a piano being played softly — to keep the other guests hushing, she supposed. There was no danger there, she knew just how they would all be sitting with their hands in their laps and far-away expressions. She walked along the brickwork and climbed up the coping to the studio gable. She came to the window. This was the moment and with her hands on the woodwork she leant forward as far as she dared and cautiously pushed the tip of her nose and one eye forward to look in.

At first she thought the room was empty, then, in a chair at the back she saw the figure of Mr Serelman. Was he asleep? She stared curiously; he was slumped forward with his hair coming through his fingers in spikes. Then, as she saw him gently rocking himself backwards and forwards, she realised that he wasn't. His position was all too familiar, he was doing just what she did when she couldn't work out a maths problem or think what to say in an essay. Oh dear, poor Mr Serelman! Were things going as badly as that?

As she looked across from him to the easel she saw that he had changed its angle at last, so that it was facing more towards the window. If she moved forward a little more and leant right up against the glass, she could probably get a glimpse of the painting, see what his worry was all about.

Yes, she could. The edge of her mother's cheek, the highlight on her pearl earrings... but it was the eyes she wanted to see. Those were the most important things about anybody's picture. Juliet pressed further forward. Unlatched for once, the French windows swung inwards and sent her flying, to land with a tremendous crash and lie spreadeagled among bottles and paints and brushes.

She lifted her face from a rag covered in turpentine just in

She landed with a crash among the bottles and paints

time to see Mr Serelman take his head out of his hands. Oh dear, what would he do? To have disturbed someone as important as he was, on such a special work! Juliet scrambled nervously back on to her hands.

The painter stared at her distractedly for a moment, opened his mouth, so that Juliet trembled for what he might be going to say, and then suddenly started to laugh.

'Ah, my friend Juliet! Zis is another of your — how you say — curtsings?' Juliet had now got awkwardly to her knees in front of him, and he held out a hand to help her up.

'Well, I'm ver' pleased to see you,' he looked at her closely for a moment, as though searching for a likeness to someone, then he looked towards the easel, 'But tell me, my friend, vy you no fall through that?'

Fall through the canvas? Through her mother's portrait? Juliet stared back at him shocked.

He watched her. 'You look,' he said.

Juliet went over and stood in front of the portrait. There was a long pause.

He was still looking at her, his eyebrows raised.

'Well,' began Juliet miserably, for she suddenly knew that with Mr Serelman you could only be honest, and not polite, 'The shape's very like her, but...'

'I know,' said Mr Serelman, 'You don't have to tell me. She is not inside.' He looked at the picture gloomily for a moment, then suddenly his mood seemed to change. He took the canvas briskly off the easel and stacked it with its face towards the wall.

'Ach was!' he said cheerfully, 'It cannot always go right, no! Anozzer day. Tomorrow I come back, perhaps...' then he looked at Juliet and saw how longingly she was looking at his brushes and paints. Far better than maths, far better than essays, and almost as much as roof climbing she liked painting, but at school she was always made to draw dreary things like towels and drawing boards and seldom got a chance.

'You like to try?'

Juliet swallowed hard, then nodded, and her friend put a new canvas up on the pegs.

'What will you do? Portrait of Julietta? Now you show me how *you* would begin.'

This was easy! Juliet knew just exactly what she wanted to do. She looked for a colour, loaded the brush and then splashed it across the canvas, a lovely bold upwards line that ended in a spluttering burst of blobs. That was her mother! She knew she could never manage to copy people's faces but she didn't want to, what was the point? They wore their faces, anyway, for everyone to look at; what she wanted to paint was what they made her think of. And this lovely rose red and those exploding sort of stars and fireworks — yes, that was her mother all right. But then she suddenly remembered; she was painting with Mr Serelman, she ought to be doing all the things that they told her to do at school. She looked up nervously, and saw that the painter had taken up another brush.

'Good. Yes,' said that astonishing man, 'That is exciting like she is, but she is ver' kind too, no?' and he filled in a pattern with a gentler, softer swirl, which was exactly right.

'And smells nice...' Remembering the things that you first noticed about her mother Juliet tried out something which was meant to be a branch of white flowers. With enormous yellow middles, she thought, making them so with satisfying splashes of paint, and then, to show that it was summer, she added a bee. And some rustling leaves and...

'She laughs a lot,' she said to Mr Serelman, baffled, but he only leant forward and picked out two colours and lo and behold when you put them together they made you laugh too.

'And she moves...' there was something like a bird flying, '...and speaks... but'... as they looked at each other and remembered the curtsyings Juliet added a small brown squiggle of disapproval. Then, as they got really going, shouting out one thing after another that they wanted to put into the portrait, they darted backwards and forwards snatching the colours from the palette and brushes from the table till the canvas was so full that there was no room to put anything more. Panting and exhausted, Juliet and the famous Mr Serelman stood back in front of their picture and looked at the results. Oddly enough, although it did look rather as though someone had ridden a bicycle over it at speed, the portrait had come out swift, laughing and exciting and did give a very strange feeling of Juliet's mother.

'It's a masterpiece,' said Mr Serelman. 'We shall sign it,' and he handed Juliet a brush.

It had purple paint on it and she wrote JULIET in large straggling letters, with a flourish at the end. In the opposite corner, in small and modest white, Jules Serelman put the long tailed J, with an S across it, for which dealers were willing to pay hundreds of pounds.

'It's yours,' he said to Juliet, 'This nice picture we paint together and which make me feel so much better. When it's dry you can take him away. Now please, is there a back way I can go away from here?' As he lifted his bushy eyebrows once again in question and they heard the strains of the piano playing coming upwards, Juliet realised that he didn't want to meet the visitors any more than she did.

'We can go by the Route!' she said, and shortly afterwards they dropped down in front of the patiently waiting and astonished Patsy, after which they all sat down on the grass together and divided the sandwiches. They told him he could go back that way whenever he wanted to finish the portrait.

'No, I'm not going to look at it!' Juliet heard her mother saying gaily to a friend, as she got back from school a few days later. There had been a van pulled up in the road, with men in baize aprons getting out of it, so she guessed that they had come to collect the portrait. 'Jules Serelman didn't want me to look at it while he was painting it and now I'm going to wait for the exhibition and see it there with him for the first time. He's away for a couple of days, you know and he's asked me to send it there for him. I've told the men to bring it down and see that it's labelled "Portrait of Julietta". She turned to Juliet.

'Ah, there you are, dear! Did you ask Miss Butterworth for tomorrow afternoon off?'

Juliet nodded. Her headmistress was a great admirer of her mother's glamorous world and had gladly given permission for Juliet to go to this exhibition of such a famous painter. Juliet was glad. Usually she hated going to picture shows because she always felt like a very small fish in a sea full of enormous whales, and wouldn't see anything but people's backs. But this one was different; Mr Serelman was her friend and she was longing to know what he had done with her mother's portrait and to hear everyone praise it, for she felt quite sure that he must have been able to make it splendid and quite right.

As she saw the carrier's men come down the stairs, the covered canvas between them, she realised that now the attic was empty again she would be able to go in properly through the door and take away her own picture, the one Mr Serelman had given her. She waited till the men were out of the door and then darted up the stairs.

The easel stood there empty, bringing back memories of that glorious afternoon and the canvas which must be hers was propped with its face against the wall. Juliet hurried across to turn it round, then gave a small startled squeak and let it fall back. It was still her mother's portrait, unaltered! Had he painted another, quite different one, then? Astonished that he could have done it so quickly, and without her mother, Juliet looked round for her own picture. But there was nothing else there and suddenly the dreadful truth dawned on her. The men from the van must have taken the joke picture away. Juliet turned out of the room and ran full speed down the stairs.

Halfway down she stopped. How could she tell her mother about the picture, when she shouldn't have been in the attic at all? She would get into the most dreadful trouble, the Route would be closed; she would never be able to use it again. But if she didn't tell? She thought of poor Mr Serelman, their silly picture hanging there and everyone knowing that he had really slipped and wouldn't be a famous artist any more, and then of her mother's face when she saw every one laughing. No! She must stop them hanging up the picture, whatever happened, even if it meant that she could never meet Patsy any more.

'Mummy!' But the delay had been fatal. Juliet got down to the hall just as the front door closed and as she plucked round the stiff handle she saw the tail of a taxi vanishing down the road.

'Why are you staring, Chuliet?' said Miss Grassman, 'Do you not remember that your mother she go down to Sussex this night? We are to meet her tomorrow at the picture show.'

Juliet stared at her in dismay. She started to try and explain, but what was the use? Miss Grassman hardly understood about the most ordinary things in English, how whould she ever know how to stop a picture getting to an exhibition? In despair, Juliet moped round the garden until bedtime, slept fitfully, with dreadful dreams of disgrace, and lived woodenly through the next morning's school.

'Oh aren't you lucky, Juliet Appleby!'

The familiar cry rang round Juliet as she got ready to go home at lunch time, but she only scowled back. If only they knew! If only they knew how lucky they were to be staying at school and doing peaceful geometry!

'...please to stand still, Chuliet!' After her knees and hand had been scrubbed Miss Grassman buttoned her into her hated white muslin. 'Now are you ready? We will go to meet your mother,' and having got Juliet into a taxi and then to the picture gallery, she led her up to the doorway and then gave a rough but affectionate push.

'There is your mother...' and Juliet ran straight towards

her, through all the people at her side. There might still be time to tell her, to do something.

'Mummy...'

'Oh there you are, Juliet dear, we'll go straight up and see the portrait, shall we? I waited for you so that we could see it together. Now let's see...' She studied her catalogue, 'Its number twenty-three. Twenty, twenty-one... oh look, there's an enormous crowd round it! Oh Juliet, don't hang back now, dear — whatever are you doing? Come along.'

If only she could run forward, throw herself across the picture, tell them it was her fault! But there was nothing she could do. As though she were still in last night's nightmares Juliet was tugged forward, someone turned round and the crowd parted as they saw Julietta, making a lane to let them go in. Right up in front of the picture Juliet saw Mr Moseby, who she knew was a critic; the one who had been so beastly before.

'Julietta!' Juliet shut her eyes; this was it; now they were going to laugh. She gripped her mother's hand.

'But this is wonderful! Why didn't you tell us! A completely new style — how clever of you both to keep it dark!'

Could she be hearing right? Juliet opened her eyes again — had the picture been changed by a miracle? She looked up and shuddered, the blobs and dots and squiggles were still there. She felt her mother start and saw her look wildly round the room in search of Mr Serelman while the chorus of praising voices went on.

'The colour!' they were saying, 'the depth and the balance! So like you, Julietta dear — just look at that touch there!' This was the brown curtsy mark and Juliet looked up apprehensively again. Her mother first stared at the familiar shape of the sprawling letters beneath the picture, then down at her daughter; then her lips began to twitch. She was laughing! She knew, and she thought it was funny! In her relief Juliet clung hard to her hand.

'Those two colours Mummy...' she began, 'Those funny

ones there...' then everyone stopped talking for a moment and there was another stir at the edge of the circle.

'Allow me to congratulate you, sir!' Mr Moseby was bustling forward to shake Jules Serelman's hand. 'This is something totally new, the most exciting bit of work I've seen for a long, long time!'

Now surely he would have to say something? Mr Serelman looked at the picture, looked at Juliet, and her mother, then at Mr Moseby again. 'Thank you,' he said, 'I am most touched by your praise,' and he gave to Juliet one large, swift wink.

THE LITTLE WHITE ASS

by

Maribel Edwin

Now and then, in camp or market-place, when the talk is of beasts and the prices they fetch, men still speak of Moonshine, the little white ass. What became of the wonderful animal, they ask; did Sulaiman really sell her, as he said he would, to a wealthy prince for a large sum of money? There follows an argument about Sulaiman, the rug-vendor. Some admire him. They call him a traveller and believe him to be welcome in palaces and among collectors of rare goods. Others scoff at him, knowing him as a boaster, a liar and a cheat, and say that the only customers for his rugs are the wandering herdsmen of the steppes. Nearly all agree, however, that there was something exceedingly strange about Moonshine.

It was not only that she was white. White asses, though rather uncommon, were not unknown. There was something stranger: the way her white hide glittered at night, when she sped like a wayward moonbeam through the town — as silently as a moonbeam, too, even on the cobbled streets; that was another queer thing! — and the dogs ran away from her, howling, instead of chasing her.

Wild as the wind at nights, Moonshine was... and yet, and yet, did she not come home without fail every time? Truly Sulaiman is a remarkable man, with a strange power over animals, and that ass was a marvel, worthy of the notice of princes. Doubtless Sulaiman sold her in the end to someone who could afford the price.

Nobody in the camps or bazaars knows the whole story, and it is useless to expect Sulaiman to explain the mystery.

But one other person knew the truth all along and could, if he chose, tell even more about Moonshine than is known to Sulaiman himself. That person is Tashi, the orphan boy whom the rug-seller picked up somewhere on his travels and adopted.

It was on the last day of their stay at a herdsmen's camp on the steppes that those two first saw the little white ass. Tashi was lying on the ground beside his master, who sat crosslegged on a mat outside their tent, when a troop of wild asses came into view. One of the animals, which lagged behind the others and limped a little, was much paler than the rest. Indeed, it was white.

'A white ass,' murmured Sulaiman. 'A *white* ass.'

The gloating expression on his master's face was well-known to Tashi. He had seen it whenever Sulaiman made what he called a good bargain. This often meant tricking somebody into paying a big price for something of little value. Wondering what his master was plotting now, Tashi looked at the wild asses again and felt sorry for the small white one.

A dog barked. Instantly the troop stood still. The leader moved again, wheeling sharply towards a nearby ridge, and in a few moments the asses were out of sight — all but one. Among the boulders near the skyline a small patch of white could still be seen.

There was a sudden bustle in the camp. The day was nearly over and evening tasks had to be hurriedly done before the short twilight was followed by darkness. Tashi was called to supper and while he ate his meal and listened to the herdsmen's talk he forgot the wild asses. Later on, when he was rolled in his blanket and half asleep, he saw Sulaiman leaving the tent. The moon was up and he could see his master clearly. On one arm Sulaiman was carrying a coil of rope. Tashi heard him chuckle and speak softly to his dog, Brindle. Next, he heard him mount his horse and ride away.

Long before his master came back, the boy was asleep. Yet in the morning, when he went to help with the loading

'She is frightened,' murmured Tashi

of the pack-animals for the journey, it was no surprise to find beside them an extra beast, a small white ass. All along he had guessed that for some reason Sulaiman meant to capture that wild ass.

'The beast is lame, master,' he objected. 'It will be of no use to you.'

'Not so much talk, boy!' commanded Sulaiman. 'The less you talk about this beast, and how we came by her, the better it will be for you. As for being lame, that is not a serious matter. Look at this sharp stone. I gouged it out of her hoof this morning.' Recovering his good humour, he laughed and patted the trembling captive. 'My beauty! My little Moonshine!'

'She is frightened,' murmured Tashi.

Sulaiman laughed again, unkindly, and said: 'She will learn all the more quickly to do what she is told.'

Tashi stroked the ass's white back. 'Will she become darker when she grows up?' he asked.

'She is already full-grown,' replied Sulaiman. 'She is not a foal; just an unusually small beast. Very small, very neat — and pure, pure white! Is she not beautiful, Tashi?'

'She is frightened,' repeated the boy.

Moonshine stood with drooping head. The sun was bright, and, like many white animals, she had weak eyes. Besides, Sulaiman had put a halter on her head and was holding it tight. She trembled all the time and now and then gave a violent start. Close to her was the dog, Brindle, big and fierce as the wolves that hunted on the steppes. To have to stand there, a captive beside the huge dog, hearing him growl and pant and feeling his hot breath, was torture.

'Let her go, master,' begged Tashi.

To his astonishment Sulaiman agreed and tossed the end of the rope away, crying: 'Run, foolish one, run!'

Moonshine was off like a flash, limping only a little and tossing back her head. But her freedom lasted no more than a moment. At a word from his master, Brindle bounded after her, caught the rope in his teeth and pulled her up short. Terror-stricken, she stood there, sagging and shivering, a pitiable object at the mercy of a cruel man and a cruel dog.

'Let that be a lesson to you, little Moonshine,' said Sulaiman. 'And to you too, Tashi,' he added warningly. 'Do not interfere.'

Tashi said nothing. He himself had been bullied so often that he guessed rightly what would happen on the journey to the market town. Again and again the same trick was played on Moonshine, and Tashi could do little to help her. He could only pat her and talk to her gently, trying to make her understand that he was her friend.

To tame the wild ass, by winning her trust, would have been too dull for Sulaiman. He set himself instead to break her spirit; and at the same time he was planning to create a legend that would give the animal a value far beyond that of any ordinary ass.

Tashi did not understand the second part of this plan until they had been living in their town dwelling for some time.

When Sulaiman began his game of rousing people's interest in the beast, he did most of it by talking. He was a good storyteller and seldom lacked listeners in the market-place. Only once did he let Tashi lead the ass through the town, and then the people had only a glimpse of her, for she was draped in a gorgeous red and gold shawl and wore a fringe slung from her ears to hide her eyes.

Then queer things began to happen at night. The white ass was seen, without trappings, racing through the moonlit town all by herself. Rumours sprang up, just as Sulaiman desired, and soon news of the wonderful white ass spread to other places. In the bazaar a story never loses in the telling, and before long the legend became fantastic. Sulaiman had tamed a white ass that could fly! Sulaiman was a magician! Sulaiman had refused a fabulous sum offered by a rich merchant for the beast. He would sell it to no one less than a royal prince.

Tashi did his master's bidding, but his tender heart was torn by Moonshine's sufferings on moonlit nights. After those midnight expeditions she used to tremble for hours and cringe every time Brindle came near her.

In the dark stable Tashi groomed his charge, preparing her for her ghostly run. The final touch was a dressing of shining powder, rubbed over her hide. Tashi dipped his hands into a bag and did what Sulaiman had told him. Tiny flakes floated down to the ground and lay shining in the lamplight. Moonshine shone, too, and looked whiter than ever. Tashi thought her beautiful. When he opened the stable door and the night air blew in, she began to tremble, not with fear but with eagerness.

Sulaiman, who had been watching, laughed softly and said: 'Run, foolish one!'

She darted off, with only a light halter to show that she had been a captive, and Tashi went and lay down in a corner. The palms of his hands were still shining and felt greasy when he rubbed them together. He shut his eyes and lay there waiting for Moonshine's return.

Out in the street Moonshine pawed the ground uneasily for a moment. Her hoofs made no sound. She tossed her head and felt no restraining pull on it. It dawned on her that she was free. Wildness stirred in her and she began to run. She ran, as she had run on moonlit nights before, up the middle of the street, towards the outskirts of the town and the steppeland that was her home.

A wakeful woman, peeping from a dark house, saw the gleaming ass speed silently by. She did not see another form, a dark one slinking along in the shadow at the side of the street. She could not know that a stray dog that fled yelping was running not from a harmless little ass but from the most vicious dog in the town, Sulaiman's Brindle. He was keeping pace with Moonshine as she ran, and listening all the time for the signal his master had taught him to expect. When it came (it was a weird call, like the hoot of an owl) the dog leapt towards the ass, snatched at the trailing rope and tugged it savagely.

Moonshine's freedom was at an end. She gave in without a struggle. Sulaiman had done his cruel work so well that she had not the spirit to try to escape, and so the dog led her back as usual to her prison.

If ever a dog was like his master, that dog was Brindle. He enjoyed tormenting Moonshine as much as Sulaiman did. When they were back in the stable, where Sulaiman sat rocking to and fro with laughter, Brindle fawned on him and demanded praise for his work. Tashi was glad when both of them retired to the dwelling-house. Then he could soothe Moonshine with his hands and try to comfort her.

'Why do you not give in, little one?' he whispered. 'Why do you run? You will never be free. Sulaiman will not let you go. Keep still and stay with me and then, perhaps, he will grow tired of the game. There... there... it is over. You are safe with Tashi.'

He stooped and unbound her hoofs, for they had been padded for the ghostly run, and then he began to brush her coat.

'There, my little Moonshine, that is better. Stop shivering. No one will hurt you. Some day, somehow, I will find a way to help you.'

For a while the performance went on. Sulaiman invented new tricks to excite the people's curiosity. Once he sent Moonshine out with a little bell tied on to her tail. Another night she had to wear false ears, twice as long as her own. But Sulaiman was growing anxious. He was afraid that he might miss the market, if he did not sell the white ass before his trickery was exposed. And so, hearing that a rich merchant, named Hafiz, was journeying in these parts, Sulaiman decided to waylay him and see whether he would buy Moonshine.

It was the time of the full moon and Sulaiman was confident that Moonshine would be cleverly displayed. Brindle had brought the 'cat-and-mouse' trick to perfection, and learnt to keep out of sight so skilfully that the ass appeared to be alone during her moonlight runs.

The caravans met on the steppes and Sulaiman at once approached Hafiz. By evening they appeared to be on the best of terms. Hafiz was interested in Moonshine. He stood looking at her for some time and spoke to Tashi.

'The fame of this white ass has reached me,' he said. 'Is she all that your master says she is? She looks ordinary enough as she stands there. True, she is white — so far as can be seen. You certainly keep her well covered with shawls and fringes!'

'She is a beautiful beast,' said Tashi, in a low voice. 'And she is pure white all over.'

'I will decide tonight,' said Hafiz. 'Will the strange wildness come upon the beast then?'

Sulaiman shrugged his shoulders. 'How can I tell? But the moon is full. She may feel like dancing! We must wait and see.'

Throughout the performance Hafiz said nothing. He sat with Sulaiman just inside a tent and looked out at the steppe. The moon was high in the sky, but a storm was gathering and cloud after cloud crossed the moon's face. The fitful light was excellent for Sulaiman's purpose. When Tashi set Moonshine free, she darted out like a sprite and began to race to and fro. At one moment she was in full view, brilliant white; at the next she was half-hidden by the cloud shadows. As for Brindle, he was just a shadow among shadows.

Tossing her head, plunging, capering, Moonshine ran on. Her movements had a dancing grace. Surely, thought Tashi, Hafiz would wish to possess this lovely creature. He would, of course, discover before long that she was not worth very much, for she was not strong enough to carry heavy loads and had no magic about her at all. But, even so, Hafiz would surely be a kinder master than Sulaiman.

Tashi was so thrilled and hopeful that he nearly forgot to

give the signal. Pulling himself together, he gave a wavering imitation of Sulaiman's owl-call; and Brindle did the rest.

'Tashi! Tashi! The coffee, boy, quickly!'

The boy hastily tethered Moonshine and ran to his master's tent.

'Well, my son,' said Sulaiman, smilling, 'have we lost our pretty pet? Has she fled back to the moon, where no doubt she belongs?'

'No, master. She has come home. The wildness has gone from her,' answered Tashi.

Sulaiman glanced sidelong at Hafiz and waited for him to speak. Hafiz was looking at Tashi.

'What strange hands the boy has,' he remarked. 'The palms shine with a silvery light.'

Tashi started so violently that he upset the coffee, and Sulaiman swore at him.

'And there are little flecks that glitter on his clothes,' went on Hafiz relentlessly. 'Once I saw a pretty toy in a bazaar. A little house it was, covered with frosted snow...'

He was interrupted by an angry outburst from Sulaiman.

'Out of my sight, bungler! And take this with you!' He flung the coffee-pot at Tashi, narrowly missing the terrified boy's head. 'Get out! Get out, I tell you!'

A moment later Tashi was outside the tent, listening to what Hafiz had to say.

'No, Sulaiman, I will not buy the beast from you. I have no use for an undersized ass with weak eyes. Do you suppose I did not notice how she blinked in the light and hung her head? I am not blind; no, nor easily duped. Your trickery may fool the simple-minded of the market-place, but...'

'That boy...' began Sulaiman angrily.

'You need not blame him,' said Hafiz. 'It was not the stuff on his hands that revealed the trickery. Ah, here comes that dog of yours, sneaking in again! A clever dog, Sulaiman, well trained in rounding up animals!'

Sulaiman cursed Brindle in his turn for clumsiness, but

Hafiz went on calmly; 'Let the dog be, Sulaiman, it was not his fault. I did not see him. But I knew that he must be there. It was plain that the ass was trying to escape from some pursuer. Tell me, is she a wild ass? You will not answer? No matter! As I said, I do not want the ass. But,' he added firmly, 'I will take the boy.'

Outside in the darkness Tashi gasped.

'The boy?' Sulaiman was amazed and indignant. 'I do not understand.'

'I will take the boy away with me,' repeated Hafiz. 'I will not buy him from you, Sulaiman, for it is not right that human beings should be bought and sold like animals. But this I will do — *I will forget about the white ass.* Sell her, if you like, to some credulous fool. I do not grudge your fun. And now I am going to my tent. We leave at daybreak and the boy travels with my caravan. Is that understood?'

Tashi did not wait to hear Sulaiman's reply, but stumbled away in a daze towards the spot where Moonshine was tethered.

A hand fell on his shoulder. He looked up into Hafiz's face, which looked grave but kind in the moonlight.

'You were listening, boy,' said Hafiz. 'Well, will you come with me?'

Tashi nodded vehemently. 'Oh, yes — master!'

'Good! At daybreak, then. Why, what is troubling you?'

'The little ass, master... oh, buy her, please!'

Hafiz shook his head. 'I do not want her. Besides, I made a bargain with Sulaiman,' he said. 'You will forget her, Tashi. I will give you a better pet. A dog of your own and, perhaps, some day a pony. Good night, boy, you must get some sleep, for tomorrow we travel far.'

The following day Hafiz's caravan had gone only a little way when Tashi turned back. Slipping away unseen, he ran to Moonshine and set her free. His fingers shook as he removed the halter, and his chest was heaving.

'Now go, Moonshine,' he panted. 'Run fast! It is your

only chance.' He tore the peg from the ground to make it look as if the ass had dragged it away, and rolled up the rope to take with him. 'Oh, run, run! What are you waiting for? Sulaiman will wake and set Brindle on you. Run, Moonshine, run!'

At last she seemed to understand. After another moment of hesitation, she set off, and as Tashi began to run after his new master's caravan the sand-cloud hid Moonshine from his sight.

It was foolish of Tashi to imagine that he could set the ass free without Brindle's knowledge. But the dog had been punished unjustly and was still sulky. Though he opened one eye and watched Moonshine go, he did not immediately lift his muzzle from his paws. By the time he did decide to give chase, the ass was well away from the camp.

Moonshine began to realise that this run was different from the others. There was no rope dangling from her head. There was at first no dog lurking near her. Though she had not grown in size, she had grown in strength, and as she raced over the ground she began to enjoy the exercise. In spite of the sand pricking her eyes, she tossed back her head and cantered.

But now Brindle was at her heels, snapping and panting. His blood was up. He was determined to catch her. There was no rope for him to grip, and he had not heard the usual owl-call signal, yet he meant to triumph once again over the little ass he had tormented so often. For an instant Moonshine checked in her stride, seized by the old terror; then she recovered. Out shot her hoof and Brindle yelped with pain. He was so enraged by the unexpected blow that he would have mauled Moonshine savagely, if he had caught her. But he could not catch her. Filled with a new spirit, the wild ass careered on across the steppe at an amazing pace, and the dog was left to slink forlornly back to his master's tent, where he was beaten again.

It so happened that that last race between Moonshine and

Brindle took the two animals close to Hafiz's caravan. A sound made Tashi stand stock still. It was Brindle's bark. He was sure of that. Brindle must be chasing Moonshine. How Tashi longed to know the result of that chase! But the swirling sand clouds blotted everything out. With an aching heart the boy plodded on, trying to forget. He had done his best for Moonshine; there was nothing more he could do.

Hafiz was a kind master, and Tashi realised that a new and happier life lay ahead of him. Yet at night, when he curled himself up and tried to sleep, he still felt sad. The hours passed. The storm clouds had rolled on, the wind had dropped and the moon shone bright. Everyone in the camp was asleep except Tashi, and he was drowsy. Suddenly he was wide awake. Something had touched him. He started up and saw what it was.

'Oh, Moonshine!' he faltered.

There in the moonlight stood the little white ass, free and unafraid. She nuzzled his shoulder again. He put his hand out and stroked her face. He was at the same time happy and sorrowful.

'Oh, Moonshine,' he repeated, 'you should not have come to me. My new master will not let you stay. Besides, you are a wild ass, Moonshine, you should be free.' He flung his arms round her neck. 'I want you! I want you, my little friend!' he sobbed.

Moonshine moved restlessly and he let her go. She stood beside him, hesitating. Freedom was still strange to her. She had felt drawn back to the boy who had been kind to her. And yet she was restless and Tashi knew it.

'Go, Moonshine,' he whispered, 'go and learn to be a wild ass again.'

He looked across the steppe, and Moonshine looked too. Something was moving out there. Dim shapes were crossing an open space not far off. One, two, three... a dozen or more... a whole troop of wild asses. Instantly Moonshine knew where she belonged. Her head went up, her nostrils quivered and her ears were pricked. Even her feeble eyes were alert. One hoof struck a stone as she started off, but after that she sped as quietly over the sandy ground as she had run through the streets with muffled feet. The leader of the troop came to meet her. He was suspicious, but only for a moment. This was no rival, he discovered, and so she was welcomed to his troop.

Tashi watched the troop go. Some of the asses had pale coats, but none so white as Moonshine's. She was the last to disappear.

THE MONSTER

by

Janet McNeill

The wheels of the pram made an important purring noise on the gravel and the rims winked back at her as they revolved. The handle was the right height, not like the handle of her doll's pram, to which, even before she had stopped using it, she had had to stoop. She held her head high, proud of the new pram, of her own position at its helm, of the fresh-frilled pram cover — yellow with blue rabbits — and overwhelmingly shy of the baby that lay back on his pillow, watching her. His eyes were amost circular and so widely open that the white — which was itself palely blue — was exposed all round the deep blue of the iris. He never shifted his gaze from her, and never blinked.

Does he know that this is the first time I have wheeled him out? He likes me. Aunt Lily said he likes me, and she would know.

'You'll help Aunt Lily with the baby, won't you?' her mother had said, seeing her off at the station.

'But I don't know anything about babies,' she cried, already faintly disturbed at the idea.

'It will be good for you to learn.'

'I mightn't like him.'

'Of course you will.'

And she did, if 'like' was the right word. She had never lived in a house with a baby before. It was surprising how much of the house was taken up with the baby; the garden path always overshadowed with blowing clothes, the kitchen on wet days steamy, like a greenhouse, the bathroom cluttered with his gear, special white soap and a hairbrush with bristles as soft as satin threads, like the tail of a Christmas tree bird. Then there was the nursery, a froth of pale colours and pretty fabrics, with teddy bears still in their first fluffiness waiting their turn on a shelf. Everything in this room was light and soft and pretty, and all through the house you could smell the smell of baby powder, sweet, like flowers.

It was surprising how much of Aunt Lily's time the baby needed. Between sink and clothes-line and ironing basket and cot and pram and the saucepan of milk on the stove that rose perpetually in a threatening white pyramid, Aunt Lily moved, her mouth full of pins or pegs or baby talk. How clever she was with the baby. Peg sat where she would not be in the way, admiring her aunt's dexterity. She spread him on her lap fearlessly, plundered his clothing for small buttons or ribbon bows, turned him over without ceremony while she changed him, bathed him, dressed him, fed him, in a communion of intimacy.

The first time Peg saw the baby naked on his mother's knee her eyes had misted up with an unaccountable excitement and her hands trembled. His body was very small and very pink. It was not pretty. It was creased and wrinkled unexpectedly where it seemed that no wrinkles were called for. 'Even the soles of his feet,' Aunt Lily said, holding one of them up for her to see, 'though he hasn't used them yet.' The baby's arms and legs moved all the time in an amiable jerky fury. He snatched at things that were not there and was puzzled when he couldn't reach them. Aunt Lily's hands moved over him, plucking, sorting, smoothing, putting him to rights.

This was the first time that Peg had wheeled him out. 'To the crossroads and back,' her aunt declared, pushing her hair up off her forehead. Her hand was slow when it wasn't concerned with the baby. 'Keep to the side all the way, and don't go too quickly. If you wheel smoothly, it's likely he'll fall asleep.'

He showed no sign of sleeping. He was still watching her.

A beast ambled within a foot of the pram

Presently they came to a place where the flag-paving gave way to an earthen pavement, rough with the roots of trees that spread under it. The springs of the pram joggled and the baby laughed and Peg laughed and joggled the pram again and they both laughed. She let the pram run ahead of her a little way, bouncing the palms of her hands against the polished handle.

They tightened suddenly at the turn of the road, and she stopped with a jerk. There were cattle ahead, straddled right across from hedge to hedge, a moving jostling mass of tawny and white, of horns and staring eyes and steamy breath. Moving from side to side in little rushes, on the pavement and off it again, sliding and barging they approached. Away at the back of them she saw the head of the driver.

It would have been easy for Peg to shin up a tree, dodge in behind a gate, clamber up the grassy bank and squeeze through the hedge. Easy — if she'd been walking by herself. With this fearful charge it was impossible. The baby and herself were chained together. Her whole body was filled with terror. She held her breath, for if she had breathed she would have screamed. The animals were almost abreast of her; they eyed the pram sideways, tossing their heads, snorting. They were level with her now, were passing her. Rigid she endured an infinity of shaggy flanks, the smell of their bodies, and felt herself drown in the confusion of their hoofs.

A beast ambled within a foot of the pram, stopped, cocking its head, eyeing the baby. The baby laughed and shook his doubled fists in the air. The beast prolonged its scrutiny. Peg could see the several hairs of its thick eyelashes. Then the man who was following behind beat it a skelp on its angled rump and sent it scuttering past.

'Out with the child, are you?' the man said good-naturedly, 'indeed you make the grand wee nurse.' And he followed after his beasts.

She was angry because he had been unaware of her ordeal. The baby was still laughing. 'Stop it! You're silly, do you hear, you're silly!' she cried, bending low over the handles. His face stiffened. Slowly, elaborately, his lip thickened and he opened his mouth and began to shout. She took no notice but pushed on furiously, feeling her clothes sticking to her and her hands sliding on the handle with the sweat.

The baby was still crying when they reached the water-trough where boys were crouched over a game of marbles on the ground. They looked up as she paraded past, quickening her pace, her face scarlet.

'What have you done to the child?' one of them called out. He turned to laugh, the marble nursed in the crook of his thumb. She hated him blackly and hurried on with a self-conscious stalk, hearing their amusement kindling behind her.

The baby's rage was frightful. He drew in his breath until his face was red, and after a moment of terrible silence he opened his mouth and shouted. His eyes were brightest blue and tears from them ran out over his cheeks and fell in a continual stream on the yellow pram cover, but for one that lodged on the shelf of his cheek. The fact that he made no attempt to wipe his tears was alarming and strange. His clenched fists shook and battered the sides of the hood.

'Be quiet,' she cried, 'oh please be quiet!' but he took no notice, and in his own good time, little by little, at last was quiet, falling asleep midway through a howl, waking to finish it, stirring again to a whimper, making another effort to recapture his rage, and finally surrendering to sleep, lying crookedly back on his pillows with an open pouting mouth.

Cautiously Peg stopped the pram and went round it to bend over the baby. Tears from her own eyes dripped on his face. She wiped them away and bent again, smelling the smell of his skin, feeling his breath against her cheek and the moisture of his open mouth. She tried to straighten him, but her hands had no confidence and she let him lie.

She had turned now for home and her spirits lightened.

The boys had left their game, there was a group of girls there. She heard the smack, smack of a rope and saw it rise in an arc above the bobbing heads. A skipping-match! And Peg could skip.

She stopped to watch them. Still the baby slept. The chant that the girls used was different from the one she used at home.

One-two-three-killivey,
Four-five-six-killivey,
Seven-eight-nine-killivey,
Ten-killivey-postman!

It wasn't the kind of skipping Peg did at home on the smooth city pavements, but even on a country road she could have done better than this. Her fingers itched for the rope.

The girls had stopped skipping and were looking at her.
'Hallo.'
'Hallo.'
'Is that Mrs Patterson's baby?'
'Yes.'
'Can you skip?'
'Yes.'
They smiled, mocking. 'It's easy saying.'

She didn't know into whose hands she thrust the handle of the pram, whether she snatched the rope or if it was given to her. The first thing she knew she was skipping, taking a little while to get used to the rope's texture and weight and to the roughness of the road. Her skill came into her fingers and feet. The rope swung over her head, across her eyelids and smacked the road and rose again. Though it was a heavy, generous length of rope it answered easily to the flick of her wrist. She tightened it in and showed them every step she knew.

At the end of it she threw down the rope. 'There!' she panted and looked round at their admiring eyes, 'did you think I couldn't skip?'

No one had time to answer her for the bus came swinging

up the road. It was on them before they knew. They hardly heard the scolding horn, and flung themselves against the bank below the hedge. The pram bounced and bucked as Peg sprang to wrench it from the fingers that held it. There was no need of this, but panic at her own neglect made her do it. The pram had been safe where the other girl held it.

'It was all right where it was,' she told Peg, but Peg was angry with herself and had to be angry with someone.

'He could have been killed,' she cried, 'you might have had more sense.'

'Who's talking, showing off their skipping when they're out minding the baby?' jeered a girl with red hair.

Peg had no breath or stomach to argue. She set off down the road with the pram at a hasty pelt, trying to work the shakiness out of her knees. He's quite safe, the girl was right, he was quite safe the way she had him, there was nothing wrong with what I did. They couldn't skip, any of them. I was only showing them.

The baby, who had woken miraculously fresh and amiable, lay back against his pillow, seeming to smile. He knew. He knew all about it, her sin of pride, her boasting, her neglect of him, the danger he might have been in, her trembling and mortification. He knew.

'I hate you,' she said to the baby, 'I hate you. It is all your fault. What do you do but cause trouble and work and worry and what do you give for it? It isn't right for anyone to depend so much on anyone else. It isn't right. No one ought to be asked to do it. I could have been trampled by those cattle, couldn't I? What did you want to start yelling for when it was all over? And when I was frightened by the bus you were glad. If you think I love you, you're wrong. Why would I love you? You're not a baby — you're a monster.'

The monster lay and smiled at her until they reached home. Aunt Lily lifted him out of his pram in the hall, clucking over him absurdly. He cooed and snatched at the untidy pieces of hair that hung down from her forehead on to her face.

'He says thank you for his lovely walk,' Aunt Lily interpreted, 'are you coming to watch him having his bath?'

'No,' she said, and went away quickly into the yard. The floor was evenly flagged. She found a piece of rope. The water was running in the bathroom, she heard a jug set down and her aunt's voice singing the ritual nonsensical vespers. She began to skip, going through every single step from start to finish, smacking the rope down on the flags with unnecessary emphasis, feeling relief and satisfaction in it, skipping till she had a stitch in her side, till her ankles ached and her wrists were sore.

When she stopped there was no sound at all from the house. The curtains were drawn close across the nursery window. Peg went indoors slowly. Aunt Lily was sitting hunched at the table in the kitchen. She was still wearing the apron she wore when she bathed the baby. She was doing nothing, just sitting there with her hands lying empty, fingers up, on the top of the table. She stared at Peg for a moment as if she were remembering who she was. Then she smiled.

'He's in bed as good as gold,' she said.

'You're tired,' Peg said.

'Yes.'

'I'll make you a cup of tea.'

Neither of them spoke while the kettle quickened over the flame and began to sing. Silence was beautiful. When the kettle boiled Peg made the tea carefully. She stirred it and poured out two cups, sweetening them both with the same spoon. She carried a cup over to Aunt Lily and lifted her own. They sat with the hot cups in their hands, drinking the tea slowly, not talking.

Presently in the room upstairs the baby whimpered. Aunt Lily drew in her breath and set down her half-finished cup at once. She rose, beating her knuckles gently against the table.

82

'You stay here,' Peg said suddenly, 'let me go.'

She went upstairs and into the darkened room where among the pale draperies of his cot the baby's fists threshed and waved. With confidence and no fear at all she turned the blankets back and scooped her hands under him to lift him. His body beneath the flannel nightgown was warm and firm. She held him against her for a moment. Then she put him in the crook of her arm.

'You be quiet,' she told him, 'we're tired, both of us. That's enough for one day. You stop it and go to sleep, and let us have a rest.'

In the dimness she could see his large eyes looking at her uncertainly. Then with an air of confidence and respect he turned his face in towards her body and his lids closed. Before she had laid him down again he was asleep.

She went down to the kitchen and picked up the teapot.

'He's asleep,' she said to Aunt Lily, 'and there's another cup in the pot.'

WITH LOVE FROM JENNY

by

Kathleen O'Farrell

T he letter lay on the mat. It was small and white and oblong, with the name and address neatly typewritten, and Jenny knew what it was about before she even picked it up. Her throat felt suddenly dry; the early morning rosiness left her cheeks. 'It's come,' she whispered, in a ghost of her normal voice. And because its contents meant so much to her, more than anyone would ever know, she wished, desperately that it hadn't.

'Well, open it, silly,' said Barbara, close behind her. 'I'm just as keen to know as you are. Simply bursting, in fact.'

It wasn't true, of course. Because it couldn't possibly matter as much to Barbara as it did to Jenny. Barbara never really worried about anything, least of all about lessons or passing examinations. At thirteen, she was tall and pretty and gay, all sparkle and fun and bubbling energy, besides being quite astonishingly clever — she was all the things which Jenny, two years younger, secretly yearned to be. Barbara had passed her examination with seemingly little effort and now she was one of the most popular girls at Whitfield Grammar School, shining not only at lessons, but also in the school plays and on the tennis-courts. One day she would be a Prefect, maybe even Head Girl...

And Jenny longed to be like her.

If only she could make Mum and Dad as proud of her as they were of Barbara. If only she could go to the Grammar School too, and wear the violet blazer emblazoned with a silver crest, and the hat with its striped ribbon of violet and silver! She wouldn't expect to shine there, as Barbara did.

She wouldn't even ask to share in her sister's popularity. Just to be a pale reflection of Barbara would more than satisfy her; indeed, just to be under the same roof in that wonderful, immense, red-brick building — the doorway to all the most fascinating careers — would be enough.

If only it could be...

With shaking fingers Jenny opened the letter, and while she read it there was a full minute's silence.

'I've failed,' said Jenny.

There wasn't any expression on her face or in her voice only a queer sort of blankness, of emptiness.

They crowded round to console her, Mum, Dad, Barbara, and even young Tim, who, at seven and a half, couldn't be expected to understand. His jolly brown eyes were full of concern.

'Goodness me,' cried Mum, large and fat and wrapped in a floral overall, as she clutched a panful of baked beans. 'Whatever does it matter? The Secondary Modern is a lovely school, too. All those polyanthus in the flower-beds! And a beautiful orchestra they've got there, besides winning the sports' cup for the whole district. Why, you'll be much happier there, Jenny, my love, than if you went to the Grammar School and couldn't keep up.'

'Come on, pet, and have some breakfast,' said Dad, small and rather shabby, with gentle, kindly eyes behind the big spectacles. 'Mum's right, you know. It's silly to take it so much to heart. Why, I've never passed an examination in my whole life — not for a single thing!'

It was quite true. Dad had never been one for book-learning, and he was far from clever — judged by most people's standards. But he had a good job, and was very well thought of at Bryce and Nicholsons, where he had worked for nearly twenty years. At first he had worked in their factory in Bermondsey, but when the firm had moved all its premises to the New Town of Whitfield, Joe Patterson and his family had moved too. They had come to this brand-new, modern

They crowded round to console her

little house in Blackbird Close, with its small neat square of garden that was Dad's great delight, and its shiny, up-to-date kitchen that was Mum's.

Jenny thought it a lovely idea, the way all the streets and closes and crescents in Whitfield New Town were named after flowers and birds and animals. And Blackbird Close seemed a perfect name for their own little corner of it, with the blackbirds singing their heads off from morning till night. Little glossy black creatures with bright yellow beaks, they hopped to and fro among Dad's daffodils and wall-flowers, trilling away like mad, and even the April showers didn't stop them.

Mum worked at Bryce and Nicholsons, too, in the canteen. She scooped the eyes out of potatoes — sacks and sacks and sacks of them — before putting them in the peeling machine. Jenny often thought what a boring job it must be, but Mum never complained. She had a cheerful, happy disposition, and such a loud laugh that sometimes, in the street, people turned round to stare at her. 'Give over, Mum,' Dad would say beseechingly. 'You don't want people to think you're common, do you?' And Barbara would get quite cross if Mum laughed like that when any of her Grammar School friends were around.

But everyone liked and admired Mum, and the folk in Blackbird Close came to her as a matter of course, if their babies were poorly, or their jam wouldn't set, or they ran out of sugar or milk.

'Such a nice, hardworking woman,' Mrs Simmonds next door would say of her. 'The children are a credit to her, and as to her house — why, you could eat your dinner off the floors.'

Jenny tried so hard to act normally at breakfast that morning, if only for the sake of Mum and Dad, but somehow the baked beans and fried bread stuck in her throat. If only she had got through that exam! She had been so determined to do so, swotting for months beforehand, and giving up all her favourite programmes on the television so that she could spend more time on her homework. It was her Arithmetic that was weak, of course... not English — she loved English even more than Barbara did; in fact, it was her very best subject. But Arithmetic was important, too, and when it came to problems, especially the tricky sort, she knew that she was downright stupid.

Well, she had tried her utmost, and she had failed. There was nothing she could do about it now. But she would never be able to follow in Barbara's footsteps. The way was barred to her, the door was closed...

'I think I'll go and change my library books,' she announced after breakfast. It was a Saturday, so she was quite free. 'It's a nice morning for a walk, so I won't hurry home, I'll come back the roundabout way, through Old Whitfield.'

That was the charm of living in a New Town, thought Jenny as she set off a little later. You could enjoy the best of both worlds, the new and the old. Her way into town, down Hawthorn Avenue, took her past rows and rows of trim new houses, all sparkling clean and brightly painted, and surrounded by beds of spring flowers and neat, low hedges. Every now and then she came to a green open space, where children could play, or a little belt of trees, carefully preserved, to break the monotony of brickwork. It was like a toy town, so well set out, so deliberately arranged, that it very nearly didn't seem true.

But when, after a happy twenty minutes or so in the splendid new library which was the pride of the Town Centre, she took the little by-road which led to Old Whitfield, Jenny Patterson told herself that it was here that real beauty lay.

Jenny loved Old Whitfield. It was so close to the New Town it almost rubbed shoulders with it — and yet it still kept its own personality, its atmosphere of a friendly old Sussex village. There was a pillar-box of moss-covered stone, which still bore the letters V.R., and Jenny had been quite puzzled by it until Dad had explained. 'V.R. — Victoria Regina,' he had chuckled. 'Don't you see — no one's ever bothered to change it, and the old Queen, bless her, gone all these many years ago.' Dad and Mum were great ones for royalty. Sometimes, thought Jenny, when they spoke of them so affectionately you'd think they were talking about their own relations, the really near and dear ones.

Old Whitfield boasted one little shop, a dark, cramped place, which sold everything, and which was presided over by a funny old woman in carpet slippers, with a broad Sussex accent. Sometimes Jenny and Tim went there to buy their sweets or iced lollies — it made a change from The Parade, with its plate-glass windows and glittering chrome, and the old lady always seemed so pleased to see them.

There was a church in Old Whitfield, too, small, but quite the most beautiful that Jenny had ever seen. It went right back to the Middle Ages, and had a Crusader's tomb in it.

Later on there would be wild roses in the hedgerows, and gorgeous golden twists of honeysuckle, but now there was only the new outburst of green leaves, and the stray dandelion shining in the undergrowth. Jenny strolled along slowly, until a bend in the road brought her to Fern Cottage, and then she stopped, remembering a very special dream that might never now be realised.

Fern Cottage was old, very old indeed, with tall slender chimneys and lattice windows, and grey walls dappled here and there with yellow lichen. Fruit trees grew all around it, and in summer the little patch of grass in front was snowy with daisies. It was far and away the dearest little house that Jenny had ever seen, and one day she was going to own it... No one else knew about it. It was Jenny's own secret dream, and one she couldn't possibly share with anyone, not even Mum. At least, it *had* been her dream. Until this morning...

This morning's letter had spoilt the very special dream, as well as everything else. Because now Jenny wouldn't be going to the Grammar School, and she wouldn't go on to the

University, and she would never qualify for a career that would make her rich and, possibly, famous. And, unless she went away from New Whitfield, and returned rich enough, she would never be able to buy Fern Cottage and live in it and love it right till the end of her days. She had planned it all so beautifully. The old gentleman who now lived in Fern Cottage was lame and rather fierce-looking, and Jenny's conscience didn't prick her at all at the thought of taking over his home one day. He couldn't just go on for ever, and besides she was sure he didn't really appreciate it — not with that cross face and those great bristly eyebrows! She wondered how the daisies dared to show their little faces on his lawn.

With a deep, tragic sigh she turned away. It had been a lovely dream while it lasted, and now it was over. Perhaps it was silly to have dreams when you were only very ordinary, and not clever enough ever to do anything important or really worthwhile. She would just have to face it — she wasn't any different from Sandra Benson or Marilyn Cook or Betty Tyler, three girls in her own form at school whom she had always secretly despised. Sandra and Marilyn and Betty hadn't even *wanted* to pass for the Grammar School. All they wanted was to leave school as soon as possible, and earn high wages in one of the factories in New Whitfield. Sandra could hardly wait to join her sister at the sweet factory — she had a simply wonderful job, Sandra declared, rolling out great big slabs of pink and white nougat, just like pastry, and every Friday was allowed to take home a large parcel of mixed sweets at a special cut-price rate.

Perhaps, thought Jenny, a shade bitterly, these other girls were right and she was wrong. If you didn't dream dreams and make wonderful plans for the future, then you couldn't be disappointed.

And then she came to the field of lambs, and all unhappy thoughts left her. If only she had Tim with her! How Tim would have revelled in this breath-catching sight.

93

There seemed to be dozens and dozens of lambs. So small, so sweet, so heart-breakingly helpless-looking. They skipped about beside their mothers on the wobbliest little legs, so that Jenny longed to rush and put her arms around them.

'Oh, the darlings,' she breathed. She leant over the gate, all her troubles forgotten, her brown eyes glowing with love and tenderness.

No matter what happened, there would always be such things as lambs.

There were two little ones with black faces, nestling close together, as pretty as a pair of china ornaments. They returned Jenny's stare, gazing back at her with gentle, innocent faces. And, she thought, with a sudden rush of thankfulness: 'Just fancy, if Dad's factory hadn't decided to move down here, I'd never have been here now. I might never have seen baby lambs, or honeysuckle, or wild roses — or Fern Cottage either!' What a wonderful idea these New Towns were! Why, she wouldn't go back to Bermondsey for anything at all! Of course, some people found it a bit quiet here — Mrs Simmonds, nice enough neighbour though she was, was always saying that if it wasn't for her Bingo twice a week she'd go potty. And other people complained it was deadly dull just because they missed all the noise, and the hustle and bustle of the traffic and the scurrying crowds — but then, as Mum said, some people would grumble when they got to Heaven. Jenny, herself, had no patience with them. If they got bored, why didn't they walk out to Old Whitfield sometimes? So many of them had just never bothered to go and see how lovely it was.

But time was getting on, and Jenny went on home to lunch, her library books tucked under her arm, feeling a good deal happier than when she had set out. Besides taking out *Wuthering Heights* for the second time, she had found a Mary Webb book she hadn't read before, and a delightful anthology of poems, so she was well satisfied with her outing.

And when she got home there was sausage-toad for lunch,

and her favourite syrup pudding which Mum had made specially.

That afternoon, Jenny took Tim to the pictures. There was a Western on, and a slapstick comedy which Mum said would do her a world of good. Mum herself was going to start the spring-cleaning.

'But the house looks so clean, dear,' protested Dad. 'Why, it's spotless!'

'Ah!' retorted Mum darkly. 'It may *look* clean but it still wants a thorough Going Over.' The way she said it was so ominous that Dad quickly retired to his garden, while Barbara hurried off to see a school-friend. Barbara, who hated any form of housework, wasn't going to be roped-in to help.

And Jenny and Tim set off to go to the pictures, debating whether to buy a quarter of toffees or a quarter of fruity-chews to eat when they got there. Tim was a nice little boy — as boys went, thought Jenny. He had a pleasant, rather ugly face, with a big freckle that sat in a surprised sort of way on his snub nose.

It was amazing how Jenny enjoyed that afternoon. The keen disappointment she had suffered that morning was still with her, and would be for many weeks to come, but she found that she was still able to laugh helplessly at her favourite comedian, especially when he disguised himself as an old lady. As to Tim, he laughed so much that he fell off his seat, while the Western, which followed, kept him goggle-eyed with excitement.

'Do you think *I* could be a cowboy when I grow up?' he asked, as they walked home up Hawthorn Avenue. Jenny said she didn't see why he shouldn't, although the thought of him going so far away was a dreadful one. Jenny didn't want to see her family break up — not ever. Each member of it was much too precious to her. She linked her arm through Tim's, thinking happily of the eggs and chips they would soon be having for tea. They always had eggs and chips on Saturday.

But as they turned into Blackbird Close they both stopped, frozen with sudden terror. A large white ambulance stood there, and two men in uniform were just closing the doors at the back.

'It's outside our house!' gasped Tim. He burst into tears.

Jenny had a choking feeling in her throat. She stared, as though unable to believe her eyes, as the ambulance moved swiftly away. Someone had just been taken away from their house. But who could it be? Not Mum! Oh, please, *please* God, don't let it be Mum!

But is *was* Mum.

'She fell downstairs,' Dad said brokenly, as Jenny and Tim rushed in. 'It was all to do with this spring-cleaning nonsense. She was coming downstairs all loaded up with boxes and things — trying to carry far too much in one go — when she tripped, and of course she didn't have a free hand to save herself. I took one look at her and sent Barbara to 'phone for the doctor, and he had the ambulance here in no time.'

'But I didn't even say goodbye to her,' whimpered Jenny, tears streaming down her face. 'Oh Mum! Poor old Mum! Is she very bad?'

'We don't know yet,' Dad answered. He put his arm around Jenny, trying to comfort her, while Barbara cuddled the sobbing Tim. 'She — she knocked herself out. Concussion, that's what they call it, and besides that, Dr. Lorimer says, she's broken some bones. You see, Mum's so heavy...' He paused, stroking Jenny's hair with a work-roughened yet gentle hand. 'I'm to 'phone up the hospital later on this evening, so perhaps the news will be much better then. Your Auntie Flo went with her — she said it was only right that I should be here when you children came in.'

'Auntie Flo?' said Jenny weakly. 'Don't tell me Auntie Flo has started coming round again?'

Auntie Flo — she was really Mum's auntie and the children's great-auntie — lived only a few streets away, but they sometimes saw nothing of her for weeks at a stretch. Relations between her and the Pattersons were always a bit uncertain, owing to Auntie Flo being very sensitive and quick to take offence. Time and time again she had walked out of the house in a huff, either because of Dad's teasing or Mum's outspokenness. You had to be so careful with Auntie Flo. But she was, as Dad always said 'a nice old duck underneath,' and the first to help you out in an emergency.

'Yes,' answered Dad, and he smiled feebly at the look on Jenny's face. 'She arrived just after it happened — when we were waiting for the doctor to come. I expect she'll be back presently, so you *will* all be nice to her, won't you? She's not a bad old stick at heart, and she'll be falling over herself to try and help us out.'

The children promised, though somewhat dubiously. Auntie Flo was such a funny old biddy, and it was very hard to keep on the right side of her, but they knew they would have to try their hardest if only for Dad's sake.

'Will she stay here and look after us?' asked Tim anxiously.

'She's sure to,' nodded Dad. 'To tell the truth I think she's going to revel in it. Still, it will ease Mum's mind.'

That evening was the very worst, the most frightening, that Jenny had ever known. Dad 'phoned the hospital twice, but the news he received: 'Fairly comfortable,' and then later on: 'As comfortable as can be expected,' told them very little. Jenny lay awake all that night, crying in the darkness. She had never wanted Mum quite so badly before.

Next day the news was more definite, though still not very reassuring. Mum was being moved from the local hospital, which was only a very small one — the big new one was still being built — to a hospital in London. 'She's come round, anyway,' said Dad. 'They say I can go and see her for a little while this afternoon, but only me, as she's still suffering from shock. They're moving her tomorrow.'

Meantime, Auntie Flo had moved in, and had taken over the entire running of the house. Her cooking was dreadful

— not a patch on Mum's — but no one dared complain, and all the food was eaten up, whether enjoyed or not. She was a tiny woman, with shrewd yet kindly eyes, and could be very lovable when she wasn't in a huff. She had grey hair that was always falling out of its bun, and she wore pastel twin-sets and lots of old-fashioned jewellery. 'Bossy old thing!' grumbled Barbara, when Auntie Flo asked her to help with the washing-up. But Jenny, to her own surprise, found that she got on with Auntie Flo very well indeed. This was just as well, because it soon grew evident that Mum was going to be away for several weeks.

Dad went to visit her regularly, and once he took Barbara and another time Jenny, but it was a long way to go and very expensive, so Jenny had to content herself with writing letters instead. Not that she minded, because she enjoyed writing letters, especially to Mum, and into them she poured everything she could possibly think of to cheer Mum up and make her laugh her jolly old noisy laugh.

Mum was getting better, and nothing else really mattered. It was a long, slow, tiresome business, and they were all dreadfully impatient to have Mum home again, but at least she was growing better and stronger with every passing day. The broken bones had mended, the wound in her head had healed, and rest and good nursing would soon complete the cure. And all this time Auntie Flo was ruling the roost in the little house in Blackbird Close.

Her cooking was still deplorable — they would never forget the day she turned out a steamed syrup pudding and it collapsed like a mound of porridge — and her mending wasn't much better, but underneath it all Auntie Flo was really very kind — particularly to Jenny.

'I hear you'll be starting at a new school in September,' she remarked one day, when they were turning out a room together. 'What a fine big school that Secondary Modern is!'

'Yes,' agreed Jenny. And then, because all her disappointment had come rushing back, 'Oh, Auntie, I'm so miserable about it! I *did* so want to pass my examination! And I tried my very hardest — I honestly did.'

'Then it wasn't meant to be,' Auntie Flo told her firmly. 'And it's silly to upset yourself about it. Why was it so important, anyway?'

'I wanted to go to the Grammar School, with Barbara,' said Jenny. 'Mum and Dad are so proud of her, and she's doing so well — she's hoping to go to the University. Why, she might be *anything* when she grows up; a teacher, or a doctor, or a scientist, or... or anything she wants to be. But I'm just a duffer. My Arithmetic is dreadful, and my Geography isn't much better — all those beastly trade winds and things. I expect I'll finish up in a factory.' The thought was so frightful that she choked over the last words.

'I never heard such a lot of nonsense,' said Auntie Flo. Privately, she thought Jenny was worth six of Barbara — Barbara, who always disappeared when there was work to be done, who was so much in demand for netball practice and drama rehearsals that she scarcely found time to write to her mother. Jenny was kind and gentle and sensitive — she was the only one of the Patterson family who never, even in the smallest way, upset Auntie Flo's tender feelings.

'Shall I tell you something?' went on Auntie Flo. 'When I was a young girl I was disappointed over something too. And my mother told me of an old saying — a very true saying indeed. "When a door closes, another opens." So just you remember that, Jenny. Before very long another door will open for you.'

At the time Jenny wasn't much comforted. She went on dusting china ornaments — how Mum loved her ornaments! — and told herself that it was all very well for Auntie Flo to talk, But, as the days wore on, and summer came to New Whitfield, all golden and fragrant and full of the drowsy hum of bees, she began to wonder. Would another door open for her? And, it if did, where would it lead? It was a fascinating thought, and one that gripped her with its wealth of possibilities. She waited, patiently.

And, in the meantime, she wrote to Mum.

She wrote almost every day. There was so much to write about, so many funny, lovely, and interesting things to tell her. She wrote about Auntie Flo, and how she'd had words with Mr Briggs the butcher about not trimming the lamb chops — Jenny had heard him whisper to his assistant afterwards that Auntie Flo was a Real Caution! She wrote about Dad's roses, and said what gorgeous colours they were, and about Mrs Simmonds winning a prize at Bingo at last — a lovely red plastic bucket and a bowl to match — and about the baby over the road, who was growing so pretty and so knowing, and about Tim joining the Cubs. She described the new milkman, and the dear little budgie one of their neighbours had just bought, and she told Mum all about the films she saw and the books she read and what happened at school. But most of all she wrote about their home-life, and the hundred and one little everyday things that went to make up the pattern of it, like a gigantic jig-saw.

Then, one summer evening, Dad took Jenny up to see Mum.

She was almost well enough to come home again, and was sitting up in bed, looking simply enormous in a fluffy pink bed-jacket. She greeted Jenny with laughter that wasn't far from tears.

'Oh, ducky,' she cried, 'How lovely to see you! You just don't know how I've missed you all. And how can I ever thank you for all those wonderful letters? Do you know, they've made a world of difference to me. They brought Blackbird Close right into this very ward. We've all read them — I passed them all round the ward — and every single person here has enjoyed them too.'

'Oh, Mum, how could you?' Jenny blushed scarlet.

'But we've loved them.' Mum's eyes shone with pride. 'Oh, Jenny, you're such a clever girl! More clever than I ever dreamed. Would you believe it, the lady who used to be in the next bed — she only went home last week — was the wife of a publisher, and *she* said you've got a gift — a real gift. I told her all about you, and she said that you'll be able to learn shorthand and typing at your new school. She said it will be awfully useful to you, if you're going to be a writer when you grow up.'

'A writer?' Jenny's face was suddenly radiant. 'She — she though I might become a writer? Like Emily Brontê?'

'Well, I don't know about *that*...' Mum's laughter, as loud and just as raucous as it had ever been, rang through the ward. 'But she said that you've got the gift of self-expression, a real feeling for words, and oh, lots of other things besides. It seems as if, because you make things sound so real and so vivid, you must be a *born* writer. And this lady said, if you work hard at English...'

'Oh, but I will! Of course, I will! I've always loved English.' And then Jenny said something which puzzled Mum very much indeed. 'It's the door — the door Auntie Flo told me about — she said another door would open. And now it has.'

NIGHT OF TERROR

by

Alan C. Jenkins

Jane frowned as she sat with the family on the veranda of the bungalow, while the fireflies flickered in the darkness of the garden and jackals wailed like lost souls in the distance.

'Jane, darling, don't imagine I don't sympathise with you,' said her mother, for the dozenth time, as her knitting-needles clicked. 'It's only because you've been away so long. After all, it's nearly three years since you came out to India the last time and you've grown a lot.'

'It's jolly bad luck,' murmured Jane's father, drawing on his cheroot, the tip of which glowed like a fat firefly. 'But you'll probably feel a lot better down at Kodi and we'll pop down and see you as soon as we can.'

'I don't want to go,' Jane said impatiently, stroking Laska's head until the black labrador looked up at her sympathetically. 'I'd so looked forward to coming out again. I'll be perfectly all right if you don't fuss me.'

'There must be something up,' pointed out her brother Robin, with fraternal brutality. 'After all, you've passed out three times in a week. It must be either the heat or the height. Not everyone can stand it, you know.'

'Robin is quite right, darling,' continued Mrs Rawson. 'I really am anxious about this fainting. The best possible thing, as Daddy says, is for you to go down to Kodi for a few weeks. The Radcliffes will be delighted to have you and it will give Dr Kirwan a chance to give you a check-up.'

'But I'm perfectly all right, Mummy,' Jane protested, glowering fiercely into the darkness of the garden that was fragrant with the scent of tobacco-plants. 'It's simply that I haven't got acclimatised yet. After all I've scarcely been here ten days. I haven't had a chance. Besides, what may have upset me was that prawn curry Schriedram made the other day.'

'Funny, we all had it and we are O.K.,' said Robin unhelpfully.

'You're an absolute beast, Robin.' Jane rounded on her brother. 'Anyone would think you wanted to get rid of me.'

'There's some splendid riding down at Kodi, darling,' Mrs Rawson said encouragingly. 'And the gymkhana...'

'But I don't want to go,' wailed Jane, while the jackals responded faraway. 'I want to stay here at Manavurrai.'

That night in bed, while the fire of blue gum logs crackled in the white hearth (for the nights were cold at that height, despite the heat of the day), Jane stared miserably at the flickering shadows on the ceiling. She had looked forward for months to going out to India again after all this time. It seemed ages since she was last at Manavurrai; in fact, she'd been quite a kid when she began school in England. She admitted to herself that she had felt a bit whacked since her return, but she knew it was merely because she'd been rather excited about the flight out and also the sudden change of climate had made her feel a bit odd. But it was nothing to worry about. She'd fainted once or twice — or passed out, as that beast Robin kept saying — but if only the family wouldn't *fuss* her.

And she just didn't want to leave Manavurrai so soon after she'd got back. It would be so *feeble*, she told herself as she drowsily watched the flickering shadows.

How long she slept she didn't know. But when she woke up with a sigh and turned over on the other side, the flickering shadows had ceased and the fire was a sullen ember. For a few moments she lay there enjoying the various familiar sounds.

'That's the old rat-snake,' she murmured, as she heard

a bumping and rustling in the roof overhead. He was quite harmless; in fact, he did a lot of good, living up to his name.

'That's a muntjac deer in the tea,' she thought, as she heard a sharp barking cry in the distance.

Down in the village where the estate workers lived, pariah dogs dolefully answered the dirge of the jackals. Somewhere a porcupine was gnawing at the roots of a tea-bush. Jane identified all the nocturnal comings and goings and settled down to sleep again.

But as she closed her eyes she heard another sound. An unsteady, distant drone which seemed to come and go uncertainly, reminding her of somebody who wasn't sure of his way.

'It's an aeroplane,' Jane said to herself. She sat up in bed, hands clasped round her knees. 'What's an aircraft doing near Manavurrai? They never come this way normally, unless things have changed. It sounds awfully lost, poor thing.'

Impulsively she sprang out of bed, switched on the light, and put on dressing-gown and slippers. She'd creep out to the veranda and perhaps she'd be able to spot the aeroplane.

As she went out into the corridor, other bedroom doors opened and her father and Robin emerged, also in dressing-gowns and slippers.

'You heard it too?' asked Robin, blinking in the light.

'Sounds in trouble doesn't it?' said Jane, as they hurried out towards the veranda.

'Jane, go back to bed at once,' grunted her father, though without much conviction, for he knew very well his daughter wouldn't miss any excitement if she could help it.

Accompanied by Laska, who had been alerted by the sound of people moving about, they hurried into the garden and stood listening anxiously on the lawn.

'Two-engine job,' muttered Robin, knowledgeably, scanning the sky and trying to spot the aircraft's navigation-lights among the brilliant tropical stars. 'And it sounds as if one of those is misfiring.'

'I certainly don't like the sound of it,' agreed Mr Rawson. 'She's in trouble and losing height. It the pilot doesn't know these hills he's had it.'

'There she is,' screeched Jane eagerly, pointing heavenwards as the tiny port and starboard lights, pinpoints of red and green, showed up almost directly overhead.

Her engine coughing and stuttering, the aircraft continued on her course and there was no disputing now that she was losing height. In helpless horror the watchers in the garden stared and listened. To Jane, the wail of the jackals in the distance seemed to take on an even more sinister note.

'Poor devils,' muttered Mr Rawson. 'What a ghastly time they must be having up there, knowing they're going to crash.'

'Can't we do something, Dad?' asked Robin. 'We can't just stand around doing nothing?'

'Be sensible, my dear chap,' his father replied. 'There's nothing we can do except wait for the crash. By the look of it they'll come down somewhere on the Animulli Hills. The worst bit of jungle country they could possibly have chosen.'

'It probably won't worry them very much if they crash, Dad,' said Robin, grimly.

With tears in her eyes Jane stood on the lawn, staring at the beads of light receding in the distance as the doomed aircraft continued to lose height.

By the time the sudden tropical dawn was burnishing the petals of the flame-coloured forest trees and the bougainvillaea hedges, Mr Rawson and Robin were busy getting the shooting brake ready. It was fairly certain that the crippled 'plane had been forced down somewhere in the hills and as soon as any news was received Mr Rawson intended to set off to do what he could for the pilot and any other occupants there might be.

'Not that we're likely to be of much use, I'm afraid,' he admitted to Robin. 'Those poor chaps have had it by now, surely.'

'We'll be able to pick up the bods, anyway, Dad,' said Robin with his usual brutal frankness.

While Schriedram the house-boy was bringing them a hurried breakfast of chappattis and paw-paws, Laska started barking urgently. Down the dusty red estate road a weary hillman came loping, a crowd of excited estate-workers chattering to him as he ran.

The newcomer confirmed Mr Rawson's fears. He had come nearly ten miles through the night to report that the aeroplane had indeed crashed in the jungle, a few miles from the fishing bungalow at Crystal Water.

'How many people?' demanded Rawson.

'Pilot, he get to bungalow, master,' the man explained, the sweat trickling down his forehead under the dirty puggree.

'He's alive, then?'

'Very ill, master, badly smash up.'

'The boys at the fishing-bungalow are looking after him?'

'Yes, master. But he very ill and...'

Without listening to the rest of the messenger's news, Rawson began to shout orders to Schriedram. There was no time to lose.

'I can come as well, Daddy, of course?' said Jane, though she knew full well there was no 'of course' about it.

''Fraid not, Jane,' her father answered hurriedly and turned aside to tell Robin to get a couple of rifles.

'But, Daddy, please...'

'Now, don't argue, Jane,' her father's tone was sharper. 'This isn't a picnic. It's matter of life and death. You'll have to stay at home. Besides, your mother would have a fit. I haven't woken her yet. You'll have to tell her what's happened when we've gone.'

He slipped into the bungalow to fetch something and Jane, disconsolately, wandered across the courtyard.

Five minutes later the shooting brake went churning off along the estate road in a cloud of dust, with Mr Rawson at the wheel and Robin in the passenger's seat.

Though the Crystal Water bungalow was only some twelve miles away from Manavurrai, it was a three or four hours drive. Once you left the tea estate, the road into the hills degenerated rapidly. Monsoon rains had gouged great scars in the soil and a car journey was a lurching, painful endurance test. On the one hand you needed to keep all the windows open because of the heat; on the other hand, if you did so, you were choked and blinded by the smothering dust which billowed relentlessly over the car in a never-ending wave.

'Certainly no joy-ride, Dad,' observed Robin, his voice thick.

'You're telling me,' agreed his father, forearms tensed as he battled with the steering-wheel, while the heavy vehicle crashed and slithered over the tortuous road. 'Driving this thing is like driving a tank again. Just like old times!'

'About as hot in here as it is in a tank, I should think, isn't it?' croaked Robin.

Huddled uncomfortably under the covering of rugs and blankets in the back of the vehicle, Jane listened impatiently to the muffled voices. She liked that, indeed! No joy-ride, said Robin, and there he was comfortably ensconced in the passenger-seat. How would he like it if he had to lie sweltering under those blankets, while the dust seeped up through the floorboards and some part of him was bruised and jarred every time the car crashed over a pothole.

Well, of course, she admitted to herself it was her own fault. Nobody had asked her to hide in the back of the brake.

Now she regretted her impulsiveness. She was feeling ghastly and began to wonder whether the time had come to reveal that she had stowed away. Her father would be furious. But by now they had perhaps gone too far for him to turn back.

Cautiously she began to push her way out from underneath the rug that hid her. But it was too late. Everything seemed to

110

be going round and round, not merely up and down as the car bucketed its way. Her head swam and then with a stifled gasp she sank back on the floor of the brake.

Jane had blacked out again.

When Jane came to everything seemed completely silent. At least comparatively so. The tropics are never really silent. The endless chizz-chizz-chizz of cicadas sounded like an electric current gone haywire. Racket-tailed drongos were kicking up their usual fuss. Langur monkeys were vaulting through the stinkwood trees, their curiosity evidently aroused by the car...

The shooting-brake! It was this that gave the illusion of silence. As she pushed the blanket away and sat up, somewhat shakily, Jane was astonished to realise that the car was no longer lurching along the dusty track. Not only was it stationary, but the engine wasn't running, either.

And, what was more, there was no one else in the car. Her father and Robin had vanished.

'Oh dear,' she murmured, rather blankly, as she combed back her tousled hair with her fingers. What on earth could have happened? They had not reached Crystal Water yet.

She decided they must have got out to have a breather or perhaps they had met someone with news of the 'plane crash. But when she got out of the car there was nobody in sight.

'Daddy?' she called. 'Robin?'

The cicadas kept up their frantic chizzing. The langur monkeys leapt in the branches. Otherwise there was no response to Jane's shout. Uneasily she went back to the car and sat in the passenger seat. She'd have to wait; they were bound to come back to the car eventually.

She spent the time reproaching herself for passing out again. What a booby she was! It was all so feeble, she told herself, for this temporary frailty irked her considerably. She might have been some Victorian maiden swooning or getting the vapours!

111

The minutes passed and there was no sign of Robin or Mr Rawson. It was sickeningly hot in the car even with doors and windows open and presently Jane got out again restlessly. She walked along the track into the shade of some feathery bamboo trees and all at once she guessed what must have happened.

The shooting-brake had been parked a little distance from the edge of a shallow ravine spanned by a wooden bridge. It was obvious at a glance that the bridge was unfit for a vehicle to pass over. Some of the central timbers had been damaged and were dangling underneath the structure.

While Jane surveyed the bridge she recognised where she was. The stream that ran through the ravine was part of Crystal Water that passed near the fishing-bungalow.

'Of course, I remember it now,' she said to herself. 'We often used to come this way for picnics. It's not very far from the bungalow. Daddy and Robin must have seen the bridge was unsafe, left the car here and crossed on foot.'

If two men (or at least a man and a boy) could cross the bridge safely, it would certainly stand up to her weight. All the same, she was considerably relieved when at last she had made her way to the other side of the ravine, across the creaking, swaying timbers of the derelict bridge.

She stumbled hurriedly along the track, while the eternal noise of the cicadas clattered around her. The tall, graceful, many-stemmed bamboos closed in on both sides, for the track was little more than a footpath now. Only a few vehicles a year came this way when planters wanted to do a bit of fishing. Otherwise, the only traffic was an occasional convoy of pack-donkeys, and the jungle was steadily creeping in.

At last the little bungalow at Crystal Water came in sight and Jane was so glad, she started to run towards it. It seemed ages since she had seen a living soul.

'Daddy?' she called eagerly and from the bungalow she saw a white-clad figure run out. It was old Sarjoo, the Hindu 'boy' who had acted as ghillie and caretaker at Crystal Water

112

for donkey's years. She remembered him carrying her on picnics when she was very small.

'What you do here, Missie Jane?' the old man asked anxiously when they met.

'I went to sleep in the car, Sarjoo,' Jane explained airily. 'But where is big master, my father?'

'They not here, Missie. They go into hills to seek other airman,' Sarjoo told her. 'They patch up pilot but he say other passenger up there badly hurt, so they go look.'

'Is the pilot here, then?' asked Jane, as she and the Indian went into the bungalow.

'Is here, Missie. Very sick. Cattlemen, they carry him down to bungalow. Big master send runner for doctor Sahib.

'You know how to nurse, Miss Jane? Pilot he get fever maybe...'

'I'll try,' said Jane, a little unsteadily. Her head was throbbing and she felt more like having a bit of nursing herself. All the same, it looked as if she would have to take charge of things until her father and Robin arrived.

Sarjoo had not exaggerated when he said the pilot was a very sick man, despite Mr Rawson's first aid work. He was obviously in considerable pain, though he contrived to put a cheerful face on things for Jane's benefit.

'I'm Jane Rawson,' Jane introduced herself, as she stood by the camp bed. 'I'm terribly sorry this has happened.'

'How d'you do, Jane?' the pilot smiled wanly. 'My name's Martin Kinnsale. Sorry I can't stand up for a lady.'

'Is there anything I can do?' Jane asked, feeling rather helpless. 'My father and brother have apparently gone to search for your passenger. Sarjoo says there was news he was still alive in the hills.'

Jane made him as comfortable as she could. He was suffering from shock and multiple injuries, and one of his legs looked as if it had been broken in several places.

For some time she was too busy to wonder when her father and Robin would return. Apart from looking after the injured pilot she made Sarjoo prepare a meal. There was plenty of food in the bungalow, for one or two planters had been fishing there recently and others were expected at the week-end. In addition, Kamalia had caught a large mahseer that morning. It was full of murderous bones, but otherwise was good eating and Jane realised she was famished.

Having coaxed Martin Kinnsale to eat a little food, she sat down herself to eat the curry Sarjoo had made. Only then did she have time to think — and at once her heart sank apprehensively.

'Where on earth have Daddy and Robin got to?' she wondered, as she sat there, staring out into the strident jungle beyond the river. 'I hope nothing's happened to them.'

'Don't start fussing,' she told herself severely. Robin and Daddy were perfectly capable of looking after themselves. It would probably take them hours to get the injured passenger down, even supposing he was fit to be carried.

But as the hours passed and the brassy sun began to curve down towards the jungle horizon, the frown above Jane's blue eyes began to deepen. She knew only too well how quickly the tropical night came down once the sun had gone. Robin and Daddy might be forced to spend the night out in the open with the injured man and she would be stranded here alone, with old Sarjoo and Martin Kinnsale to look after. Outside, the noise of the cicadas seemed to clatter to a frenzied crescendo as if they were mocking her.

Hurriedly she left the veranda and went in to Martin Kinnsale's bedside for company.

'Sorry I'm being such a confounded nuisance, Jane.' The pilot managed to grin, but Jane could see that he was still in considerable pain.

'Don't worry, you'll be all right,' said Jane, unconsciously bracing her shoulders.

'I light lamp, Miss Jane?' old Sarjoo asked presently, padding in on bare feet and suddenly, with a shock, Jane realised that night was indeed upon them. Moths were beginning to

114

flutter into the bungalow; the chik-chak lizards were beginning to scuttle about the walls.

In the next hour or so Jane must have gone out to the veranda at least a dozen times in the hope that she would hear Robin and her father returning. Hostile and dark, the jungle confronted her, as if a hundred pairs of eyes were furtively watching. The clatter of the cicadas had given way to a chorus of frogs down by the river and the screaming, rending cries of unknown night creatures.

All at once as she stood there staring into the velvety darkness she heard another sound, a peremptory, trumpeting cry which she recognised immediately. Her heart almost stood still as she went on listening in case she had been mistaken.

But the trumpeting squeal rang out again and was accompanied by the crashing of branches and the movement of heavy bodies. Elephants! Somewhere out there in the jungle, not very far away, elephants were on the move.

She gasped as something moved behind her, but it was only old Sarjoo.

'Elep'ants, Miss Jane,' the old ghillie said nervously, his brown face gleaming.

'There's nothing to worry about, Sarjoo,' Jane said, with a firmness she didn't altogether feel, for she knew that although she was only fifteen she was in charge. The Indians were always afraid of elephants and it was up to her to keep calm.

Though she couldn't help feeling apprehensive and wished fervently that the elephants would go away, she wasn't unduly alarmed at first. She knew that nine times out of ten the elephants would be perfectly harmless, in fact, they wouldn't want to come too close to the bungalow. She knew also that there would be no question of a 'rogue' elephant; a rogue would have been rampaging on his own, whereas she could tell that there were two or three elephants out there, probably stuffing themselves with bamboo fronds.

115

She decided to go and talk to Martin Kinnsale in case he had heard the elephants and was feeling anxious.

'We've got visitors, eh?' he said, lying there on the camp-bed, his cheeks hollow in the feeble light of the kerosene lamp.

'Oh, that's nothing,' Jane assured him. 'We often get elephants round these parts. They'll soon go away.'

The words were scarcely out of her mouth when she heard a violent crash from the direction of the little go-down or storehouse that was connected to the bungalow by a covered passageway. Jane and Kinnsale stared at each other in aghast silence for a moment.

'I guess you spoke a bit too soon, Jane,' the pilot murmured.

'Missie, Miss Jane!' old Sarjoo came padding in breathlessly. 'Elep'ant in go-down...'

'That's impossible, Sarjoo!' Jane frowned. 'How could an elephant possibly get in there?'

'Baby elep'ant, Miss Jane,' Sarjoo told her. His eyes were round and his hand was trembling. 'He push his way in through the double doors.'

A series of bumps and crashes punctuated Sarjoo's words. They were followed by an angry squeal from the go-down. Having in youthful curiosity forced his way into the storehouse, no doubt attracted by the smell of rice or sugar, the baby elephant was evidently finding difficulty in getting out again.

Jane's heart sank. She knew enough about elephants from her father to realise that it was most dangerous to have a baby elephant on the premises. Normally elephants are fairly harmless, except for their occasional raids on plantations and fruit-gardens. But a mother elephant will go almost berserk in defence of her young.

Jane hurried to the veranda and glanced out. She could see nothing, but her ears told her only too well what was going on. A peevish trumpeting came from nearby. The ground shook as a mighty body strode past somewhere outside in the inky darkness.

116

Jane caught a glimpse of an adult elephant making its way towards the buildings. She drew back into the bungalow, her mouth dry, her heart working overtime.

Meanwhile, the hullabaloo in the storehouse increased in volume, as the panic-stricken young elephant barged his way here and there, trying to get out. The mother elephant trumpeted again and now her angry noise was echoed by a second adult elephant, the inevitable 'aunt' elephant who invariably accompanies a female elephant with young.

The din was unbelievable. The more panic-stricken the baby elephant became, the more frantic the two female elephants grew. They trumpeted unceasingly and trampled to and fro around the bungalow and the adjoining storehouse. Jane felt sick with fear. Had she been on her own she would have fled into the jungle, anywhere to get away from these vast creatures who were so terrifying in their anger.

But she had to stand fast. She knew everything depended on her. A frightened old Indian servant and the helpless pilot — she was responsible for them both. Yet what could she do? Trying to do anything about these rampaging elephants was rather like trying to halt a tidal wave.

Nobody who hasn't heard a furious elephant squealing can have any idea of the nerve-racking time Jane endured that night. Nearly eight tons of elephant were stomping round the bungalow, while volley after volley of ear-splitting squeals made the air tremble. If it had only been a question of noise, it wouldn't have mattered. But after a while, when they realised that their anger was not helping the baby elephant to escape, the two cow-elephants took more drastic action.

Suddenly Jane realised they were tearing at the roof of the bungalow with their trunks. They tried this for a while and then the whole place shuddered as one of the animals evidently leaned against the flimsy wooden wall with its forehead. Again and again the bungalow rocked and all the time the storehouse rang with the violent caperings of the young elephant.

'Miss Jane, we have to go, we run for it!' yelled old Sarjoo, his normally dark brown face grey with fear. 'The elep'ants, they destroy the bungalow, trample on us. Come! We go...'

'You'll do nothing of the sort, Sarjoo,' Jane shouted back, (she had to shout anyway because of the noise). 'We can't possibly leave the pilot.'

'Maybe if you and Sarjoo help me, I could hobble along,' suggested Kinnsale. 'Those elephants are just about going to tear the place apart.'

'No!' said Jane. 'It would be hopeless if we left the bungalow. The elephants would simply trample us to pulp, they're so angry.'

'Please, I go,' quavered Sarjoo, as the bungalow shuddered again and the angry trumpeting continued.

'Shut up, Sarjoo!' Jane ordered and grabbed the old Indian by the arm. Jane was becoming angry herself and, ironically, it helped her to think more clearly. 'I've got to think. The thing is, we've got to get rid of the baby elephant. Get him out of the go-down.'

But that was easier said then done! As she tried desperately to think, Jane began to sniff. Something was burning in the kitchen.

'Have you let something boil over, Sarjoo?' she asked him accusingly.

'I make coffee when elep'ants come,' confessed Sarjoo and hurried out to the little kitchen. Jane followed him and as soon as she caught sight of the flame of the primus, the idea came to her.

It seemed a daring plan but it was their only chance. At least it was better than doing nothing and waiting while the berserk elephants battered down the place.

'Sarjoo!' she commanded. 'Get me a piece of wood. Dry and long. Look, one of those billets in the corner. Dip it in kerosene and light it. I want a really good flame going.'

In considerable bewilderment Sarjoo did as he was told.

118

She opened the door and rushed in

His eyes stared wonderingly as he handed the flaming brand to Jane. Jane knew she was taking a terrible risk. But she was going to chance it. Otherwise it was only a matter of time before the elephants smashed their way into the bungalow. Once they got within range of any human beings they would almost certainly kill them in their frantic anxiety to protect the baby elephant from harm.

Cautiously Jane hurried along the covered way to the little storehouse, praying harder than she'd ever prayed in her life before. If only her scheme would work.

Almost deafened by the row, she halted at the little door into the storehouse. Fortunately the young elephant had been concentrating his efforts on the double doors on the other side. Provided he was still facing that way, all might be well.

That moment while Jane paused, grasping the flaming brand and preparing for action, seemed longer than a century. Then, biting her lip — and not noticing till afterwards that she'd drawn blood — she opened the door of the passageway and rushed in. She thrust the burning, oil-soaked stick straight at the baby elephant's hindquarters.

It was an undignified and somewhat unsympathetic treatment but it worked. With a squeal of rage and pain even more than before, the young elephant hurled himself at the double doors in a frantic effort to escape from this new threat. There was a sound of splintering wood and to her infinite relief, Jane realised that she had been successful.

The pain from the burning brand had given the young elephant the extra impetus to crash his way out of the godown. Jane ran outside to fling the stick away, in time to see the two cow-elephants, still trumpeting, shepherding the squealing baby elephant to safety.

There were a good many explanations all round when, at dawn the following day, Robin and Mr Rawson eventually turned up, together with Kamalia and a couple of cattlemen who were carrying the injured aircraft passenger through the jungle on a charpoy.

Jane's patent method of getting rid of elephants came in for a deal of hilarious comment, though Martin Kinnsale was more sober.

'All I can say is thank goodness you did pass out in the car,' he said with a wry smile. 'I would probably have had it if I'd been on my own while those elephants went on wrecking the place.'

The 'Night of Terror', as they laughingly called it, was to have one, last, striking after-effect. Jane's fainting spells stopped as inexplicably as they had begun.

THE GINGERNUTS

by

Lilias Edwards

When Penny's cousin bought a new guitar and offered to sell his old one for £ 1.25, it gave Penny a wonderful idea.

'I'll buy your guitar,' she said eagerly, and she did. It took all she had in her money-box, plus two postage stamps and an I.O.U. for ten pence but it was certainly a bargain.

'What are you going to do with that thing?' asked her mother in surprise, when Penny showed her precious new possession.

'I'm going to start a guitar group,' said Penny, happily strumming discords. 'It will be such fun! Can I ask some friends round tomorrow evening?'

'How many?' asked her mother warily.

'Only three,' said Penny. 'Janice and Brenda and Chris.'

'Mm — those redheads!' said her father, from behind his newspaper.

'You know we sing well together,' Penny pointed out. She strummed again and sighed dreamily. 'With guitars, we'll be fabulous!'

Her father laughed. 'Is that so?' he asked, looking over the top of his paper. 'Well, just you tell me when you're about to start and I'll buy some earplugs.'

'Oh Daddy!' grumbled Penny, 'You are awful!'

Penny's friends loved the idea from the start.

Janice said. 'Oo, smashing!' and before the week was ended she owned a shiny black guitar with glittering decorations. It was easy for Janice; her parents were quite rich and she could have most things she wanted.

It was not so easy for Brenda, however, and she puzzled over her problem for days. At last she decided to do without the camera she had been promised for her birthday, and to have a guitar instead.

That left Chris, and after the first excitement she decided not to join the group after all.

'You'll have to find someone else,' she said regretfully. 'My parents can't buy me a guitar. I'd have to save for it myself, and I've got exactly five pence.'

'We *must* have you in the group,' said Penny. 'We need you to sing the alto parts; no one else can do it so well. You'll have to get a Saturday job and save up.'

'But it would take years!' exclaimed Chris.

'We'll all help,' said Penny. 'Yes, even Janice! We'll run errands and weed gardens and do baby-sitting.'

Alas! such work was not easy to find. Parents wanted older, experienced baby-sitters, and most people did their own gardening and shopping. At the end of the first month, when they met at Penny's house to compare notes, there was only about fifty pence in their collection.

'It's no use,' said Chris dolefully. 'I'll never have a guitar at this rate. Why don't you ask someone else?'

'Because we want *you*!' said her friends together.

Chris went home, comforted by her friends' affection, but still puzzling 'ways and means'. As she passed a neighbour's garden she saw the owner busy among his rose bushes.

'Hello, Mr Brown,' said Chris. She leaned on the fence and looked meaningly at a clump of dandelion leaves. 'Would you like to hire me to weed your flower beds?'

Mr Brown looked at her over the top of his glasses.

'That's the third time this week you have offered to work for me,' he chuckled. 'What's it all about? Or is it a secret?'

Chris shook her head. 'I'm saving to buy a guitar,' she explained, and told him all about it.

'Now, that's very interesting,' said Mr Brown. 'My nephew is a music teacher, and he has several guitars. In fact, he

126

makes them — it's his hobby — and very good they are, too. Perhaps I could persuade him to part with one.'

'Would it — would it be very expensive?' asked Chris, rather timidly.

Mr Brown stood silent, stroking his chin and thinking hard then he smiled.

'You leave it to me,' he said. 'I'll pay for it, but I shall want you to do something in return.'

'Oh, what?' asked Chris eagerly.

Mr Brown pointed along the road.

'See that little cottage down there? It belongs to an old couple called Morrison. I want you to mow their lawn for them once a week till the end of the summer. Is it a bargain?'

Chris was hopping with excitement.

'Oh *yes*!' she said. 'Oh, Mr Brown, you *are* good! I'll give them the best lawn in the country. I'll start tomorrow.'

The following day, on her way home from school, Chris called at the Morrisons' cottage and rapped loudly with the old-fashioned brass knocker. A little old lady came in answer.

'I'm Chris Wilson,' said Chris shyly. 'I've come to mow your lawn.'

The old lady beamed a welcome. 'Mr Brown told me about you,' she said. 'Are you sure it won't be too much for you, my dear? No, I'm sure it won't; you look a strong, healthy girl. Come round to the back, love, and I'll show you where we keep the mower.'

Soon Chris was pushing a small grass-cutter round the garden. It was a blunt old-fashioned machine and squeaked horribly, but the lawn was not much bigger than a tablecloth and the job was soon done.

The old lady and her frail little husband came to look at the result.

'How clever of you, my dear,' said Mrs Morrison admiringly. 'It's too much for Tom and me now, and we get so worried when the garden looks untidy.'

'I'll do some weeding for you too,' said Chris impulsively.

'I'll do that little border, shall I? And next time I'll do the other border.'

'My dear young lady, that *is* kind of you,' quavered the old gentleman.

'Not at all,' murmured Chris, turning very red, but feeling pleased and happy. She weeded the border quickly and carefully, and remembered to put away the lawn mower.

'I really enjoyed that,' she thought with surprise, as she started home again, the old couple leaning over the gate to wave goodbye as she went. 'I'll keep it up whether I get a guitar or not.'

She sat down to tea that evening with an even bigger appetite than usual, and was just starting on a second helping of apple tart when Mr Brown arrived with an enormous brown-paper parcel.

Chris forgot her apple tart immediately.

'It this the guitar?' she asked, almost breathless with excitement.

'Yes, it is,' said Mr Brown, ripping away the brown paper. 'Rather a nice one, I think. Look!'

'Ooh! It's beautiful!' Chris exclaimed.

'It's on loan to you,' said Mr Brown, 'but if you keep the bargain we made it will soon be yours. Agreed?'

'Oh *yes*!' said Chris.

Janice lived in a bigger house then the others. It was rather old-fashioned in appearance, but it had a big garden with a summer-house, and two big attics which were used only as lumber rooms.

'I've had a super idea,' Janice told the others when they met again. 'I've asked Mum if we can have one of the attics for our practices, and she said yes. We'll have to throw out the rubbish and clean up a bit, but we won't be a nuisance to anyone there and Penny's Dad won't have to buy those earplugs.'

'That's marvellous!' said Brenda. 'When do we start?'

'Tomorrow?' suggested Janice. 'Come along after tea, and remember — wear your oldest clothes.'

On the following evening, therefore, they met at Janice's house and went upstairs to the attics. They decided to use the one which looked out on the quiet back garden, and began to move the lumber to the other attic. They intended to do this very quickly, but it is extraordinary how interesting old furniture and books can be! And when there is a box of 'dressing-up' clothes...

'Look at me, girls! Aren't I gorgeous?' simpered Penny, strutting about in a long trailing skirt and a huge hat with feathers.

'See this!' cried Chris. 'A real Japanese umbrella! And here's a fan to go with it.'

'I've found some music sheets,' said Brenda, kneeling by an open box. 'Just look at these! *Alice, where art thou? Soldiers of the Queen. Beautiful Dreamer.* There's stacks of them. Can we use them?'

'Why not?' said Penny. 'We'll try everything.'

'In the meantime,' Chris reminded them, 'we've got to get the rest of this stuff out of here. Come on, you slackers!'

It took several evenings to get the attic just as they wanted it. They brushed down the ceiling and walls, scrubbed the floor and washed the paintwork. Then they furnished it.

Brenda supplied the curtains. 'They belonged to my brother's room when he was a baby,' she giggled, opening them out to show a gay pattern of toy soldiers and teddy bears. 'They'll be too long for these windows, but I'll soon shorten them.'

Chris brought a tray she had made in the basket-work class at school, and four tumblers. 'We'll be sure to want refreshments sometimes,' she said happily.

Janice, who had arty ideas, painted a frieze of black crotchets and quavers round the walls, finishing with a big treble-clef sign in the space between the windows. She also put a label, MUSIC ROOM, on the door.

Penny's contribution was a small plaster bust of Beethoven. 'I know he's not exactly right for guitar music,' she admitted, 'but I couldn't get anyone else.' She put him carefully on the mantelshelf. 'He's our mascot.'

Janice's parents supplied a rug, and allowed the girls to borrow the folding chairs from the summner-house — and the 'Music Room' was complete.

And so — at last! — they held their first rehearsal. They sat down in a circle, rested their guitars across their knees, and looked at each other.

'How do we begin?' asked Brenda.

'I've bought a book', said Penny. 'It's called *How to Play the Guitar,* in Six Easy Lessons.'

'Oh, that's fine,' said Janice. 'You read it out and we'll listen.'

However, it was not so easy as they had hoped. They had lots of fun but made little progress.

'I know what's wrong,' said Janice. 'We need someone to explain things first. How about your cousin, Penny? He *ought* to help us, really, because it was his guitar that started all this. Do you think he'd come along some evening?'

'I'll ask him,' said Penny, but she looked doubtful.

Penny's cousin, as she had feared, was not at all anxious to help.

'I'm too busy,' he said.

'Oh *please*, Jonathan,' coaxed Penny. 'Just one teeny-weeny little lesson. Please. If you do, I'll clean your cycle for you.'

Jonathan burst out laughing. He knew how much Penny disliked cleaning her own bicycle.

'I can see you're really desperate,' he chuckled, 'but I'm not weakening.'

'There must be *something* I can do for you,' Penny wheedled.

'Yes, by golly, there is.' Jonathan rubbed his hands together in sudden glee. 'It's Mum's Jumble Sale on Saturday. You know I always have to help with it—collecting jumble, sorting jumble, selling jumble! Ugh! But I'm not going to do it this time.'

Penny was listening with growing horror.

'You don't want *me* to do it for you?' she wailed.

'Why not?' grinned Jonathan. 'You want a guitar lesson, don't you? I think it's a fair bargain.'

'I think you're dreadful,' said Penny. 'But... I'll do it...'

They kept their bargain, and Jonathan came to the next meeting of the group, bringing his guitar with him. He admired the 'Music Room' and tried the girl's instruments. Then he demonstrated a few chords.

'I never thought it would be so difficult,' sighed Janice. 'I wish I had two or three extra fingers.'

'You'll soon get the hang of it,' said Jonathan encouragingly. 'What do you want to play? Pop songs? Negro spirituals? Folk songs?'

'We don't know yet,' said Penny, 'But we've got some old music here. Will you look at it?'

Jonathan rummaged through the box, then held up a large, shabby book.

'Here you are!' he said. '*Old-Time Songs, with Music for Piano and Guitar*. Exactly what you want! Now, see all these little 'squares' of music on the pages. These are the guitar chords. Do you understand them?'

'No!' chorused the girls, all together.

Jonathan sighed. 'Gather round,' he invited. 'I'll give you Lesson One tonight and I'll come again next week and give you Lesson Two.'

The weeks went by and the lessons went on. Jonathan was delighted when he heard the girls sing together, for they harmonised really well and had a good sense of rhythm. Soon they were singing to their own guitar music, and it was a real thrill when they found themselves able to swing into a song and to go straight through without a hitch.

Penny was suddenly fired with ambition.

'Let's enter the Saturday Club Contest,' she suggested, her eyes shining with excitement.

'Oh, no!' cried Brenda, looking horrified. 'We're not nearly good enough.'

'I think we are,' said Penny.

Chris turned to Jonathan. 'They're talking about the Saturday Morning Cinema Club,' she explained. 'They're holding a Talent Contest at the end of the month. Do *you* think we're good enough to enter?'

Jonathan shrugged. 'I've never been to the Saturday Club,' he said. 'It's for kids like yourselves, isn't it? I expect you'd be as good as anybody there.'

Penny didn't like being described as a 'kid', but she decided to overlook it.

'I'll put our names down for the contest,' she said firmly.

'Oh no!' cried Brenda, Chris and Janice in a panic.

'Why not?' argued Penny. 'What's the use of being a guitar group if we never *do* anything?'

'But we daren't! wailed Brenda.

'I should die of fright,' announced Chris.

'We're not ready for a public performance,' declared Janice.

'You can save your breath,' laughed Jonathan. 'When Penny makes up her mind, it's useless to argue.'

'That's settled then,' said Penny happily. 'Next thing is, what shall we call ourselves? We must have a good name.'

'Penny and her Stooges,' said Brenda gloomily.

'The Four Flops,' suggested Chris.

'The Green Guitarists,' said Janice, and added, by way of explanation, 'we'll be green with fright.'

'Don't be so silly,' said Penny. 'We'll probably be a huge success. In the meantime, we must practise often, and we *must* think of a really catchy name.'

Chris was at the Morrisons' cottage on the following evening. She was now a great favourite with the old couple, and they knew all about the guitar group and had followed its adventures with interest.

'We're entering a Talent Contest at the end of the month,' Chris told them. 'I'm scared. I'm sure we'll be a flop. I go hot and cold all over when I think of it.'

'Just do your best, love, and I'm sure you'll be very good,' said little Mrs Morrison kindly.

'We've got to find a name for ourselves,' said Penny. 'It's ever so difficult.'

'Penny's Guitar Group,' suggested Mrs Morrison.

'That's too ordinary,' said Chris, shaking her head.

'Have you any nicknames?' asked Mr Morrison.

'We-ell, Penny's Dad calls us the "redheads",' said Chris, 'because of our hair, you know. But none of us is *really* red.' She shook back her hair. 'You wouldn't call *me* a red-head, would you?'

'No,' said Mr Morrison. 'You're more of a gingernut, I'd say.'

'That's it!' cried Penny, in sudden excitement. 'Ginger-nuts! That's our name. We're *The Gingernuts!*'

On the morning of the Talent Contest, the four girls, with their guitars, met outside Penny's home.

'I feel awful!' said Chris. 'I couldn't sleep a wink last night.'

'I couldn't eat any breakfast,' said Brenda.

'Let's not go!' said Janice.

'Oh, fiddlesticks!' said Penny. 'Look at me! I'm not n-n-nervous.' She cleared her throat quickly. 'As for you, Brenda, you must eat something. Suppose you go fainting with hunger right in the middle of our song?' She felt in her pockets. 'I've got some nuts here.'

'I don't like nuts,' Brenda objected.

'They're better than nothing,' said Penny.

'Here comes the bus!' said Penny, as Brenda took the nuts and began to chew.

'Come along, then,' said Penny. 'And do cheer up, girls! This is going to be *fun.*'

Brenda ever afterwards declared it was the nuts that caused it, though Chris said it was probably stage-fright — but,

133

whatever the cause, Brenda suddenly began hiccupping. She hiccupped all the way to the cinema in the bus, and all the way through the travel film and the Mickey Mouse cartoon that started the programme.

'Hold your breath and count a hundred,' advised a distracted Penny.

'Try sucking this peppermint,' offered Janice.

'I've had three peppermints already,' whispered Brenda. 'It's no use, girls. When I — hic! — get hiccups, I sometimes go on for hours. Hic!'

But at last the attack died away and she seemed quite cured when at last the Talent Contest began and they were lined up with all the other contestants in the wings.

'Our turn soon!' whispered Janice nervously, as they kept moving forward.

'And now,' said the Compère, 'we have a guitar group. The Gingernuts!'

'That's us!' said Penny with a gasp, and led the way forward.

The stage seemed enormous, and it was quite frightening to think that hundreds of eyes were watching.

'Come along, young ladies,' said the Compère heartily. 'Come closer to the microphone. Now, who is the leader here? Will you please tell us what you are going to sing for us?'

Penny took a big breath and spoke into the microphone.

'*Oh, dem golden slippers,*' she announced.

'Off you go then,' smiled the Compère. He waved his hand and stepped back.

Penny struck a chord, and she and Janice began together but Chris, who had paused to clear her throat, missed her cue completely. Penny and Janice slowed down as though to wait for her, and at that moment Brenda gave a tremendous hic. She was close to the microphone and the sound went round the hall like a small explosion.

There was a ripple of laughter from the audience, and

134

Penny and Janice speeded up and sang as loudly as possible. Chris found it impossible to join in; she simply could not find the right note at the right moment, so she put on a stagey smile and strummed her guitar furiously. Behind her, Brenda gave muffled hiccups.

They finished amid a scatter of applause, whistles and boos.

'Thank you, girls' said the Compère, coming forward. 'Quite a good effort,' he added, smiling politely.

The Gingernuts knew he didn't mean it. They made a brief bow and hurried offstage, and left the cinema without waiting for the rest of the show.

'We were a complete flop,' said Penny, as they walked home in a cloud of gloom. 'Oh, I do feel a fool!'

'I didn't even get started,' lamented Chris.

'I said we weren't ready for a public performance,' said Janice. 'We needed more practice.'

Brenda was looking thoughtful. 'My hiccups have gone, she said suddenly.

They stopped and stared at her.

'Well, isn't that just lovely!' said Penny in a sarcastic voice.

Janice began to giggle.

'It's ever so comical, really,' she choked out.

'Huh!' said Penny, and stalked off.

Chris went round to the Morrisons' cottage that evening. The old couple were waiting for her impatiently.

'Did you win a prize?' they asked, almost before Chris had time to say 'Hello!'

Chris groaned. 'No,' she said mournfully. 'Everything went wrong. It was awful!' She poured out the sad story of the Gingernuts' misfortunes, while her two old friends held up their hands in dismay and tut-tutted in sympathy.

'That was just bad luck, my dear,' said Mr Morrison kindly. 'Don't let it discourage you.'

'You'll do better next time,' said Mrs Morrison.

Chris shuddered. 'No more contests!' she cried vehemently.

'I never want to touch a guitar again,' said Penny

'Never, never!' She paused, thinking about the disaster. 'There was another thing, we chose the wrong kind of song. Everyone was doing 'pop' stuff except us. I think everyone wants 'pop' songs these days.'

'No, dear, not everybody,' said Mrs Morrison firmly. 'I'm sure I don't. Tom and me, we like the old songs best; don't we, Tom? You must bring your friends to play for us, Chris. Ask them to come with you next Saturday. I'll make one of my gingerbreads and we'll have a little "do".'

'That will be lovely,' said Chris, cheering up. 'I'm sure my friends will be delighted to come.'

To her surprise, however, the others were not in the least delighted with the idea.

'I never want to touch a guitar again!' said Penny, still smarting from the group's failure.

'No more public performances!' declared Janice and Brenda with one voice.

'But this won't be a public performance,' said Chris. 'Just Mr and Mrs Morrison. They're a sweet old couple, and you can't let me disappoint them.'

In the end, of course, they all agreed to go, and when the time came the evening was a huge success. Mr and Mrs Morrison knew all the old songs and they listened with such pleasure that the girls went on and on, singing and playing everything they knew.

'That was wonderful!' said Mrs Morrison, when they came to an end at last. Her face was rosy with delight. 'Oh, I wish you would come and play for our Darby and Joan Club.'

'Ah, they would love to hear the old songs,' nodded her husband. 'That would be a real treat for everybody.'

'We'd love to play for your Club,' said Chris, full of enthusiasm. 'Wouldn't we, girls?'

Janice nodded, but Brenda looked doubtful and Penny shook her head.

'No,' she said. 'I'm sorry, but I couldn't play in front of a crowd, not ever again!'

'Oh, Penny!' said Chris.

Penny remained stubborn. 'I wouldn't like to be such a flop again,' she said. 'Everyone has been pulling my leg about it. You know that awful Jones boy in our street? Every time he passes me he whistles *Oh, dem golden slippers*. He makes me wild!'

She tried to finish with a laugh, but there were tears in her eyes. Her friends looked at her in surprise, then Mrs Morrison quickly changed the subject.

'Let's have a cup of tea,' she suggested.

The girls laid aside their guitars and gathered round the table to enjoy their tea and big slices of home-made ginger-bread, and the Darby and Joan Club was not mentioned again that evening.

Chris, however, could not forget the suggestion. She wanted to please her old friends, and she felt sure that Penny would change her mind if she were coaxed. She waited for the next practice evening, hoping that Jonathan would back her up.

'About the Darby and Joan Club,' she began, when they were all together. '*Do* let's play for them. The old people would love it. We could ask them to join in and sing with us. It would be lots of fun, and a good deed at the same time.'

'You can count me out,' said Penny firmly. 'I'm not going.'

'Oh, why not?' asked Janice. 'I'm willing.'

'Me too,' said Brenda.

'No!' said Penny.

'Now then, Penny,' said Jonathan. 'Stop brooding about that wretched contest. After all, you went into it just for fun, so why let it upset you like this? Don't be so silly!'

Penny looked huffy.

'I'm not silly,' she said crossly. 'We disgraced ourselves once, that's enough for me.'

'Oh, what stuff!' said Jonathan crossly. 'Stop acting like a tragedy queen!'

Penny was furious.

'You needn't be so rude,' she flared. 'And you don't have to give us any more lessons. You meant to give us just one, remember? It's a shame for you to waste your time with — with *kids* like us!'

'Penny!' exclaimed her friends in horror.

Penny knew she was behaving very badly, but she went on recklessly.

'Anyhow, I can't come to practice every week. I'm going to be busy with — with other things.'

'Oh, indeed!' Jonathan stared at Penny's hot, angry face, then he smiled and shrugged. 'All right,' he said. 'No hard feelings! But let's have one more practice over at my house. I want you to hear some new records.'

Penny looked as though she would like to refuse, but her friends gave her no chance.

'Of course we'll come!' they said quickly.

'Good!' said Jonathan. 'Now, let's go on with our lesson, shall we?'

The girls picked up their guitars, and as they did so Jonathan looked over at Chris — and he winked!

It was a pleasant change to go to Jonathan's house. He had some interesting things to show the girls, and he let them try his mandolin and drums.

'Now, let's have our practice,' he said at last. 'As it may be the last, I'd like you to play and sing everything you know. Let's start with *Beautiful Dreamer*.'

He seemed rather solemn, and the girls settled down to their music without any fuss. They sang and played for over an hour, then Jonathan's parents (who, of course, were Penny's uncle and aunt) brought in tea and cakes.

'How about those records you wanted us to hear?' asked Brenda, as she sat back with a big cream doughnut clutched in her hand.

'You can hear them now,' said Jonathan, turning to a

cabinet at his side. 'You will know all the songs, I'm sure. The first one is *Beautiful Dreamer*.'

There was a little silence, then the record began.

'Girls and guitars — just like us,' said Janice, looking interested.

'They harmonise awfully well,' said Chris, with a sigh of envy.

The girls listened in silence till the music ended and Jonathan switched off.

'That was lovely,' said Penny. 'Really super!'

'That was a very special guitar group,' said Jonathan. 'Four girls and guitars. They call themselves the Ginger-nuts.'

The girls looked puzzled and Jonathan burst out laughing.

'You've been listening to yourselves,' he chuckled. 'Look, I've got you on my tape recorder. I've been recording you all evening.'

Penny looked quite stunned.

'I'd no idea we sounded like that,' she said. 'We're quite good, aren't we?'

'I think so,' said Jonathan.

'Good enough to play for other people!' cried Chris excitedly. 'Good enough for the Darby and Joan Club!'

'Yes, we are,' agreed Penny. Suddenly she looked happy and excited. 'Oh dear, I've been ever so silly, and I'm sorry! We'll play for the Darby and Joan Club whenever they like to ask us.'

Chris could hardly wait to tell the Morrisons the good news. As soon as she was free from school next day, she went round to the cottage. To her surprise she found Mr Brown leaning on the gate, admiring the neat well-kept garden.

'You're doing a good job here,' he said, waving his hand towards the smooth grass and bright flower borders.

'I like doing it,' said Chris. 'It's quite easy, really, because it's such a little garden.'

'All the same, it was too much for the old folks,' said

Mr Brown, 'and you're a great help to them. I think you can call that guitar your own now. You've really earned it.'

Chris was too happy for words. She simply threw her arms around Mr Brown, almost knocking his hat off, and gave him a warm hug.

'Bless my soul!' he exclaimed clutching at his hat... but he looked very pleased.

About three weeks later the Gingernuts met outside the Darby and Joan Club. A smiling W.V.S. lady led them into a big cheerful room full of people. There were old gentlemen reading, or playing chess or dominoes, or just having forty winks behind a newspaper. There were old ladies, too, knitting or sewing or gossiping together. They all turned to stare as the girls entered.

'These young ladies have come to give us a little concert,' said the W.V.S. lady, and the old ladies and gentlemen pulled their chairs round and prepared to listen.

The Gingernuts felt very nervous, but they were determined not to make a false start this time. Penny struck the first chords and all together they swung into *Little Brown Jug*.

Long before the song finished, the old people were joining in the chorus. There was a loud burst of applause at the finish and a voice called out, 'Let's have *When Irish Eyes are Smiling*.'

They went from song to song. The old people joined in everything. They nodded and swung to the rhythm of the music, and one old lady beat time loudly on the floor with her umbrella; and when they sang *Three o'clock in the Morning* a sprightly old gentleman pulled his wife to her feet and waltzed her round the room.

The concert ended amid loud applause, and the old folks gathered round the girls, eager to talk.

'When I was a young lad,' said one, 'we had a sing-song in the parlour every Saturday night. Mother played the piano and we all sang. You should 'ave 'eard me Uncle Charlie sing *Nirvana*. Beautiful, it was!'

'I've heard Marie Lloyd and Nellie Wallace sing some of these songs,' said another, with pride.

Penny looked at the happy old faces, some still flushed and beaming, others grown thoughtful with memories. She felt a big lump in her throat.

'Come again,' said the old people. 'You *will* come again, won't you?'

'Yes,' said the Gingernuts. 'Indeed we will!'

As they walked home together, Penny was very thoughtful. Suddenly she gave a sigh of sheer delight.

'It's wonderful to be able to give such pleasure,' she said happily. 'You know, I don't care about the contest now. It wasn't important.'

'It was tonight that mattered,' said Chris, nodding wisely.

'I don't suppose we'll ever be famous,' said Brenda, 'but who cares? We'll be the pin-up girls of the Darby and Joans!'

'It was a lovely evening,' said Janice. 'We must play for them again soon.'

They walked on, hugging their guitars, deep in plans for the next concert.

LOB
by
Joan Aiken

S ome people choose their dogs, and some dogs choose their people. The Pengelly family had no say in the choosing of Lob; he came to them in the second way, and very decisively.

It all began on the beach, the summer when Sandy was ten and the twins six. Sandy was really Alexandra, because her grandmother had a beautiful picture of a queen in a diamond tiara and high collar of pearls. It always hung by the kitchen sink and was as familiar as the doormat. When Sandy was born everyone agreed that she was the living image of the picture, and so she was called Alexandra and Sandy for short.

On this summer day she was lying peacefully reading and not keeping an eye on the twins, who didn't need it because they were occupied in trying to see who could wind the most seaweed round their legs. Father — Bert Pengelly — was out in his fishing-boat after pilchards and Mother — Jean Pengelly — was getting ahead with making the Christmas puddings because she never felt easy in her mind if they weren't made and put away by the end of August. As usual, each member of the family was happily getting on with its own business. Little did they guess how soon this state of affairs would be changed by the large new member who was going to erupt his way into their midst.

Sandy rolled on her back to make sure that the twins were not climbing on dangerously high rocks or getting cut off by the tide. At the same moment a large body struck her forcibly in the midriff and she was covered by flying sand. Instinctively, she shut her eyes and felt the sand being wiped off her face with something that seemed like a warm, rough, damp flannel. She opened her eyes and looked at it. It was a tongue. Its owner was a large bouncy young Alsatian, or German Shepherd dog, with topaz eyes, black-tipped prick ears, a thick, soft coat, and a bushy black-tipped tail.

'Lob!' shouted a man farther up the beach. 'Lob, come here!'

But Lob, as if trying to atone for the surprise he had given her, went on licking the sand off Sandy's face, wagging his tail so hard meanwhile that he kept knocking up more clouds of sand. His owner, a grey-haired man with a limp, walked over as quickly as he could and seized him by the collar.

'I hope my dog didn't give you a fright?' he said to Sandy. 'He meant it in play — he's only a puppy.'

'Oh no, I think he's *beautiful*,' Sandy said truly. She picked up a bit of driftwood and threw it. Lob, whisking easily out of his master's grip, was after it like a flash of light. He came back with the stick, beaming, and gave it to Sandy. At the same time he gave himself, though Sandy was not aware of this at the time. But with her, too, it was love at first sight, and when, after a lot more stick-throwing, she and the twins went home for tea, they cast many a backward glance at Lob being led firmly away by his master.

'I wish we could play with him every day,' sighed Tessa.

'Why can't we?' said Tim.

'Because Mr Dodson, who owns him, is from Liverpool, and he's only staying at the Fisherman's Arms till Saturday,' Sandy explained.

'Is Liverpool a long way off?'

'Right at the other end of England from Cornwall, I'm afraid.'

It was a Cornish fishing village where the Pengelly family lived, with rocks and cliffs and a little round harbour, and palm-trees growing in the gardens of the little whitewashed stone houses. It was approached by a steep, narrow, twisting

146

hill, and guarded by a notice that said 'Low Gear for 1 mile. Dangerous to cyclists.'

The Pengelly children went home to Cornish cream and jam, thinking they had seen the last of Lob. But they were strangely mistaken. Their father came home after supper, and the whole family was playing Beggar-my-neighbour in the front room when there was a loud thump and a crash of china in the kitchen.

'My Christmas puddings!' exclaimed Mrs Pengelly, and ran out.

'Did you put gunpowder in them, then?' said her husband.

But it was Lob, who finding the front door shut, had gone round to the back and bounced through the open kitchen window, where the puddings were cooling. Luckily only the smallest one was knocked down and broken.

Lob stood up on his hind legs and plastered Sandy's face with licks. Then he did the same for the twins, who shrieked with pleasure.

'Where does this friend of yours come from?' inquired Mr Pengelly.

'He's staying at the Fisherman's Arms — I mean his master is.'

'Then he'd better go back there. Find me a bit of string, Sandy, to tie to his collar.'

'I wonder how he found his way here,' Mrs Pengelly said, when the reluctant Lob had been led whining away, and Sandy had explained about their afternoon's meeting on the beach. 'Fisherman's Arms is right round the other side of the harbour.'

Lob's owner scolded him and thanked Mr Pengelly for bringing him back. Mrs Pengelly warned the children that they had better not encourage Lob any more, or it would lead him into trouble — after all, he was only a puppy. So they dutifully took no notice of him on the beach next day — until he spoiled their good resolutions by dashing up to them with joyful barks, wagging his tail so hard that he winded Tess and knocked Tim's legs from under him.

They had a happy day, playing on the beach.

The next day was Saturday. Sandy had found out that Mr Dodson was to catch the half-past nine train. She went out secretly, down to the station, nodded to Mr Hoskins the stationmaster, who wouldn't dream of charging any local twopence for a platform ticket, and climbed up on the footbridge that led over the tracks. She didn't want to be seen but she did want to see. She saw Mr Dodson get on the train, accompanied by an unhappy-looking Lob with drooping ears and tail. Then she saw the train puff away out of sight, leaving a melancholy plume of smoke that drooped, like Lob's tail, down on to the line.

Sandy wished she hadn't had the idea of coming to the station. She walked home miserably, with her shoulders hunched and her hands in her pockets. For the rest of the day she was so cross and unlike herself that Tess and Tim were quite surprised, and Mrs Pengelly gave her a dose of senna.

A week passed. Then, one evening, Mrs Pengelly and the children were in the front room playing ludo. Mr Pengelly had gone out with the fishing fleet on the evening tide. If your father is a fisherman he will never be home at the same time from one week to the next.

Suddenly, history repeating itself, there was a crash from the kitchen. Mrs Pengelly leapt up, crying, 'My blackberry jelly!' They had spent the morning picking and the afternoon boiling fruit.

But Sandy was ahead of her mother. With eyes like stars she had darted into the kitchen, where she and Lob were hugging one another in a frenzy of joy. About a yard of his tongue was out and he was licking every part of her that he could reach.

'Good heavens!' exclaimed Mother. 'How in the name of all that's wonderful did *he* get here?'

'He must have walked,' said Sandy. 'Look at his feet.'

148

They were worn, dusty, and tarry. One had a cut on the pad.

'They ought to be bathed,' said Mrs Pengelly decisively. 'Sandy run a bowl of warm water while I get the disinfectant.'

'What'll we do about him, Mother?' said Sandy anxiously.

Mrs Pengelly looked at her elder daughter's pleading eyes and sighed.

'He must go back to his owner, of course,' she said, making her voice firm. 'Your father can get the address from the Fisherman's Arms in the morning and send a telegram. In the meantime I should think he needs a long drink and a good meal.'

Lob was very grateful for the drink and the meal, and made no objection to having his feet bathed. Then he flopped down on the hearth-rug and slept, in front of the fire they had lit because it was a cold, wet evening, with his head on Sandy's feet. He was a very tired dog inded. He had walked all the way from Liverpool to Cornwall, which is more than four hundred miles.

Next day Mr Pengelly sent the telegram, and the following morning Mr Dodson arrived off the night train, very cross, to take his pet back. That parting was worse than the first. Lob whined, the twins' burst into tears, Sandy crept up to her bedroom afterwards and lay with her face pressed into the eiderdown, feeling as if she were bruised all over.

Mrs Pengelly took them all into Plymouth to see the circus next day and the twins cheered up a little, but even the hour's ride in the bus each way and the Liberty horses and performing seals could not cure Sandy's sore heart.

She need not have bothered, though. In ten days' time Lob was back — limping again, with a torn ear and a patch missing out of his furry coat, as if he had met and tangled with an enemy or two in the course of his four-hundred-mile walk.

This time Bert Pengelly rang up Liverpool. Mr Dodson,

when he answered, sounded weary. He said, 'That dog has already cost me two days that I can't spare away from my office — plus endless time in police-stations and drafting newspaper advertisements. I'm too old for all these ups and downs. I think we'd better face the fact, Mr Pengelly, that it's your family he wants to stay with — that is, if you want to have him.'

Mr Pengelly gulped. He was not a rich man. He said cautiously, 'How much would you be asking for him?'

'Good heavens, man, I'm not suggesting I should *sell* him to you. You can have him as a gift. Think of the train fares I shall be saving. You'll really be doing me a kindness.'

'Is he a big eater?' Mr Pengelly asked doubtfully.

By this time the children, breathless in the background listening to one side of this conversation, had realised what was in the wind and were dancing up and down with their hands clasped beseechingly.

'Oh, not for his size,' Lob's owner reassured Mr Pengelly. 'Two or three pounds of meat a day and some vegetables and gravy and biscuits — he'll do very well on that.'

Sandy's father looked over the telephone at his daughter's tremulous face. He came to a decision. 'Well, Mr Dodson,' he said briskly, 'we'll accept your offer and thank you very much. The children will be delighted and you can be sure Lob has come to a good home. They'll look after him and see he gets plenty of exercise. But I can tell you,' he ended briskly, 'if he wants to settle in with us, he'll have to learn to eat a lot of fish.'

So that was how Lob came to live with the Pengellys.

Four years went by, and each summer Mr Dodson came back to stay at the Fisherman's Arms and called on his erstwhile dog. Lob always met him with recognition and dignified pleasure, accompanied him for a walk or two — but showed no signs of wishing to return to Liverpool. His place, he intimated, was definitely with the Pengellys. He was devoted to all of them but there was no doubt that he loved

Sandy best. He followed her wherever he was allowed to, sat by her chair at meals, and sneaked out of his box in the kitchen to sleep by her bed at night — until an evening in late September when Sandy was fourteen.

It was a wet, windy dusk. All the summer visitors had left and the little town looked empty and secretive. When the children came home from school Mrs Pengelly said, 'Sandy, your Aunt Rebecca says she's lonesome because Uncle Will's gone out trawling, and she wants you to go and spend the evening with her. Wash your face and put on a clean dress.'

Sandy looked far from enthusiastic.

'Can I take Lob with me?'

'No, dear, you know Aunt Becky can't stand dogs. Lob terrifies her. He'll have to stay home for once.'

Slowly and reluctantly Sandy tidied herself up, put on her damp raincoat again, and set off to walk through the dusk to Aunt Becky's cottage, which was a quarter of a mile up the steep hill above the village.

Lob, left inside the front door, whined and cried and pleaded to be let out. He scratched and scrabbled on the paintwork, standing up to look out of the little glass panel set high in the door.

'It's no use, Lob,' said Tess firmly, 'you can't go, so you may as well make the best of it — anyway it's a horrible night to go out.'

But Lob still whined pitifully and Mrs Pengelly, making chutney in the kitchen, called: 'For goodness' sake, quiet that dog somehow, or turn on the radio to drown him, the noise is driving me frantic. I nearly chopped my finger off.'

'Come on, Lobby, sit by the fire,' Tim urged. But as Lob preferred to sit whining with his nose pressed against the front-door crack, Tim found some cheerful music on the radio and turned it up loud. And on account of this music the Pengelly family did not hear the motorbike roar through the village a few minutes later.

Dr Travers was driving through Cornwall with his wife,

taking a late holiday before his patients began coming down with winter colds and 'flu. He saw the notice that said 'Steep Hill' and dutifully changed into low gear.

'We must be nearly there, dear,' said his wife, looking out of her window. 'I noticed a sign farther back that said the Fisherman's Arms was only one mile. What a dreadfully dangerous hill! But the cottages look pretty... Oh, Frank! Stop, stop! There's a child — I'm sure it's a child — by the wall over there!'

Dr Travers jammed on his brakes and brought the car to a stop. A little stream ran down by the road in a shallow stone culvert, and half in the water lay something that looked, in the dusk, like a pile of clothes — or was it the body of a child? Mrs Travers was out of the car in a flash, but her husband was quicker.

'Don't move her, Emily!' he said sharply. 'She's been knocked down — can't be more than a minute or two ago. Remember that young fool who went careering down the hill past us on his motorbike? Here, quick, run to the first cottage with a 'phone and get an ambulance. She's in a bad way. I'll stay here and do what I can to stop the bleeding. Fast as you can.'

Doctors are expert at stopping dangerous bleeding, for they know all the right places to press on arteries, and so this Dr Travers was able to do, but he didn't dare to do any more; the girl was lying in a queerly crumpled heap and he guessed she had more than one bone broken, and that it would be dangerous to move her.

Mrs Travers was very quick. She had seen a lot of accident cases and knew the importance of speed. The first cottage she tried had no 'phone, but the woman told her where to find a call box. In two minutes she was back, and in five an ambulance was screaming down from the hospital at the top of the hill.

They lifted the child on to a stretcher, as carefully as if she were made of fine thistledown. The ambulance sped off

152

to Plymouth — for the local cottage hospital did not take serious accident cases — and Dr Travers went down to report the accident to the police-station.

At half-past nine that night Aunt Rebecca was sitting by her fire thinking peevish thoughts about the ingratitude of nieces who were asked to supper and never turned up when she was startled by a neighbour who burst in, exclaiming, 'Have you heard about Sandy Pengelly, then, Mrs Pearce? 'T'is a terrible thing, then, poor little mite, and they don't know if she's likely to live. Police have got that wicked young Rawley boy that knocked her down, ah, it didn't ought to be allowed, careering through town like that at umpty miles an hour. They ought to jail him for life — not that that would be much comfort to poor Bert and Jean Pengelly.'

Horrified, Aunt Rebecca put on a coat and went hotfoot down to her brother's. She found the family with white, frozen faces; Mr and Mrs Pengelly were just about to be driven to the hospital where Sandy had been taken, and the twins were crying quietly and miserably. Lob was nowhere to be seen, but no one thought about him at that time.

'Thank goodness you've come, Becky,' said her brother. 'Will you stop the night and look after the twins? Dear knows when we'll be back.'

'Oh, if only I'd never invited the poor child,' lamented Mrs Pearce. But Bert and Jean hardly heard her. They jumped into the village taxi and were whisked away.

The night passed slowly. The twins cried themselves to sleep. Bert and Jean sat outside the door of Sandy's room in the Western Counties Hospital, but she was unconscious and remained so. All that could be done for her was done. The broken bones were set, her arm was put in a splint and her leg slung in a cradle.

'Is she a healthy child — has she a good constitution?' the hospital doctor asked.

'Aye, doctor, she is that,' Bert Pengelly said. The lump in

Jean's throat prevented her from answering, she just nodded.

'Then she has a chance. But I won't conceal from you that her condition is serious, unless she shows signs of coming out of this coma soon.'

But Sandy did not show any signs of recovering consciousness. Day followed day, and still she lay with her eyes closed, hardly moving. Her parents spent every minute of the day at the hospital; at night they stayed with Grandma Pearce, Jean's mother, who lived in Plymouth.

Every day Dr and Mrs Travers went along to the Pengelly cottage to inquire about Sandy, and the report was always the same, 'Still very serious.' The twins were dreadfully unhappy. They forgot that they had sometimes called Sandy bossy, and remembered only how often she shared her extra ten pence pocket money with them, how she read to them and took them for picnics and helped them with their homework. Now there was no Sandy, no Mother and Father, and, worse still, no Lob! Lob would have been some comfort (which Aunt Becky was not) but he had been missing since the night of Sandy's accident.

Aunt Becky could not be bothered about a dog. 'Go out and look for him — it'll keep you out of mischief,' she said, 'but if you ask me he's gone back to his other owner, and good riddance too. That dog eats as much as a human!'

Looking for a lost dog is a miserable task, specially if you don't succeed in finding him. Everybody in the village sympathised with the twins, but nobody had seen Lob. Aunt Becky refused to bother their parents with the report that the dog was missing. 'They've got worse than that on their minds,' she said grimly.

Bert and Jean certainly had. They were numb with worry, spending day after day in the hospital, hardly eating, speaking to nobody. They did not hear, paid no attention to hospital gossip.

The Western Counties is an extremely large hospital, with dozens of different departments and at least fourteen or

Lob strained towards the door

fifteen entrances. After a few days it was common knowledge among the hospital staff, and a subject for many jokes, that a dog seemed to have taken up residence outside the hospital, with the fixed intention of getting in. Patiently he would try first one entrance and then another, all the way round. Sometimes he would get a little way inside, but animals were, of course, not allowed, and he was always kindly but firmly turned out again. Sometimes the porter on the main entrance threw him a couple of his dinner sandwiches, he looked so gaunt and hungry. Nobody seemed to know where he came from, or anything about him; Plymouth is a big town and he might have belonged to anyone.

And then one day Grandma Pearce came to the hospital to bring some lunch and a flask of hot coffee to her daughter and son-in-law. Just as she arrived at the entrance the porter was gently but forcibly shoving out a large, agitated Alsatian dog.

'No, old feller, you can *not* come in here. Hospitals are for people, not dogs.'

'Why,' exclaimed Mrs Pearce, 'that's Lob! Here, Lob, Lobby boy!'

Lob ran to her, whining and wagging his tail. Mrs Pearce walked up to the desk.

'I'm sorry, madam, you can't bring that dog in here,' the porter said.

Mrs Pearce was a very determined old lady. She looked the porter in the eye.

'Now, look here, young man, that dog has walked twenty miles to get to see my grand-daughter. Heaven alone knows how he found out she was here, but it's plain he knows somehow. And he ought to have his rights! He ought to get to see her! Do you know,' she went on, bristling, 'that dog has walked the length of England — *twice* — to be with that girl? And you're going to keep him out with your fiddling little rules and regulations?'

'I'll have to ask the Medical Officer,' the man said doubtfully, and went off to find him.

'You do that, young man.' Grandma Pearce sat down in a determined manner, and Lob sat at her feet.

Presently a tired, clever-looking man in a white coat came downstairs, with a grand, silver-haired man in a dark suit, and there was a low-voiced confabulation. Grandma Pearce caught the words.

'... frankly ... not much to lose.' She sat up straighter and grasped her umbrella firmly. The man in the white coat approached her.

'As it's a serious case we're making an exception,' he told her quietly. 'But only *outside* her bedroom door — and only for a minute or two.'

Without a word Grandma Pearce rose and stumped upstairs Lob followed close to her skirts, as if he knew his hope lay with her.

They waited in the white-tiled corridor outside Sandy's door. Bert and Jean were inside. Everything was very quiet. A nurse came out. The white-coated man asked her something and she shook her head.

The door was now open a little and through it could be seen a high, narrow bed. Sandy lay on it, very flat under the bedclothes, very still. Her head was turned away. All Lob's attention was riveted on the bed. He strained towards it, but Grandma Pearce clutched his collar firmly.

'I've done a lot for you, boy, now you behave yourself,' she whispered grimly. Lob gave a little whine, anxious and pleading.

At the sound of that whine Sandy stirred a little. She sighed, and moved her head just a fraction on the pillow. Lob whined again. And then Sandy turned her head right over. Her eyes opened so that she was looking at the door.

'Lob?' she murmured sleepily. 'Lobby boy?'

The doctor by Grandma Pearce drew a quick, sharp breath. Sandy moved her right arm — the one that was not broken — from under the covers, and let it hang down,

157

feeling, as she always did in the morning, for Lob's furry head. The doctor nodded slowly.

'All right,' he whispered, 'let him go to the bedside. But keep a hold of him. We don't want him to jump up at her.'

Grandma Pearce and Lob moved to the bedside. Now she could see Bert and Jean holding hands tensely on the other side. But she didn't look at them. She looked at the smile on her grand-daughter's face as the groping fingers found Lob's ears and gently pulled them. 'Good boy,' whispered Sandy, and fell asleep again.

Grandma Pearce led Lob out into the passage again. Her old face was working, but she spoke to Bert fiercely.

'I don't know why you were so foolish as not to bring the dog before!' she snapped. 'Leaving him to find the way here himself! Do you know what I'm going to do now? I'm going to take this dog and buy him the biggest steak in Plymouth — and then I'm going to put him on the bus and tell the conductor to take good care to see that he gets home. You'd better telephone those children.'

Aunt Becky was out when the phone rang. Tess leapt to answer it. She heard her mother's voice — joyful, tearful, half-choked.

'Sandy's all right! She's going to be all right! It'll be a long time still, but the doctor's not worried about her any more. And Tess — both of you — go off now — hurry — and meet the half-past two bus from Plymouth. Someone you know will be coming on it. Don't forget now — start right away!'

And so the twins started off to meet the bus. They couldn't think who might be on it, but somehow the nearer they got to the bus stop, the more excited they grew, until by the end they were running full tilt, hand in hand. Somehow they knew that whoever they were meeting must be the most important person in the whole world.

SITTING ON THE FENCE

by

Mary Steward

J essica looked at the twins and her heart sank. 'If I take you with me to the studio, you'll have to be very good, promise to behave.' She mistrusted the innocence on their ten-year old faces.

'Of course we'll be good,' said Prue, who liked a quiet and orderly life. 'We can play thieves quietly anywhere.'

'The things you children think of!' Jessica was almost shocked.

'There's been a lot in the papers recently — especially about that big robbery at Thorsen Castle.'

Pippa believed in saying what she thought. 'You haven't got much choice,' she pointed out. 'We can't stay here alone all day, can we?'

Jessica was tempted to say they could, but she knew it was impossible. It was unfortunate that everything had happened at once: their father was away, Aunt Jane had hurt her leg and was being looked after by their mother. But it was not only the twins that worried Jessica. Something was seriously wrong with the cast of the play, there was a tension and uneasiness which disturbed her.

Feeling every hour of her eighteen years, Jessica said, 'Come along, then. We don't want to be late for rehearsal, or Hugh'll snap my head off.'

'That's Hugh Galloway, the producer?' Prue almost always listened, even when people thought she was dreaming, and stored away tiny pieces of knowledge and unexpected facts.

'Course it is,' said Pippa. 'And Julia Bellemy's the leading lady, and Niven Turner's the leading man...'

'Appearing in a weekly television serial entitled "And They All Lived Together",' chanted Prue, as she skipped up to the bus stop.

'Aren't you a clever pair!' said Jessica, but she was rather pleased that her familly showed some intelligent interest in her career when they looked in on Friday evenings.

'What exactly does a Production Assistant do?' asked Prue, innocently spoiling the effect.

Jess sighed. 'Don't you ever listen?'

'Sometimes,' confessed Prue, and her school mistresses would have recognised the expression on her face.

'I help Hugh generally. I'm a sort of secretary. It's my job to see that the scripts have come from the typists, that they're given to the cast each week. Halfway through the week, Hugh prepares a camera script, showing what the television camera's got to do when a certain character speaks, how it must move round. Then there are forms to be filled in; letting the studio know what props — furniture and so on — we'll need, the changes in the cast and so on. We're all down at the rehearsal hall now, because we've got to time everything exactly. We go over and over the script, time each scene with a stop watch so that it'll take exactly twenty five minutes. That leaves time for the credits, which show the cast and the director, and the commercials.'

'I see,' said Prue, gravely, although their father had explained all this long ago.

'Will Beth be there?' broke in Pippa. Beth Croxley was a child actor, who lived not far from the Stone family. Jessica had asked her back to tea several times and the twins had found her surprisingly nice.

'Yes. She plays Julia and Niven's daughter, and she's home from school in this episode.'

'But she really goes to an acting school, doesn't she?'

'Yes,' said Jessica. 'But for heaven's sake don't ask so many questions, and don't bother people at rehearsal. You're to sit quietly...'

162

'Or?' Pippa could not let the threat pass unchallenged.

'Or... I'll get Jeremy to beat you!' Jessica frowned, and retired to her own private worries. She would not admit it but these always seemed to stem from Jeremy Thorp. What on earth had upset people so much recently? The cast had been a particularly happy one, no quarrels nor petty jealousy. Yet in the last few weeks Hugh had treated everyone as if he were a particularly acid teacher. Niven had contributed to this attitude; he either would not, or could not, learn his lines, was unpunctual and, when reprimanded, had been extremely rude. But it was Jeremy Thorp who frightened Jessica, although she could not have explained why. He was the floor manager at the studio and, because he worked directly with Hugh at transmission, appeared at rehearsal in the middle of the week to get Hugh's instructions to see how the episode was shaping. Because Jessica could not explain her feelings, she said nothing to the twins. Had she done so, however, they would instantly have understood what she meant when they met him.

Rehearsals took place in an old school hall, and Jeremy was parking his car as the Stone family arrived. He was a very tall man, with thick dark hair and heavy eyebrows which met over a big, hooked nose. But it was the expression in his eyes, a look of secret laughter, as if he alone knew a rather unpleasant joke, which made Pippa stick her chin in the air and Prue hang behind Jessica.

'Ah, your small sisters,' he said, and although his mouth smiled his eyes did not change.

'We've got two brothers away at the moment,' volunteered Pippa, then blushed because Jeremy laughed. She turned, took Prue's hand. 'Come on, we'll go and sit down!'

'There's good kids,' said Jessica, opening the door and walking to a card table set up halfway down the big room.

The twins might have been invisible for all the notice anyone took of them. They sat down on the hard bench running round the walls and watched the rest of the cast slowly

163

assemble. They recognised Julia Bellemy, doing a crossword with two other women. Hugh was talking to them, and Julia said something which made him laugh. The stage manager was busy on her hands and knees going over the blurred chalk lines on the floor. A broken down sofa, another card table and a cane chair with no bottom, represented the sets as they would appear in the studio. The rooms were marked by pieces of coloured tape, pinned down, but obviously in rehearsal yesterday Hugh had asked for chalk marks, showing the actors where to stand.

'What's Jess doing?' whispered Pippa, her bright eyes everywhere.

'Getting out the scripts and the stop watches.' Prue spoke softly. 'They have two; one to time each scene with, one which runs from start to finish so they know if the programme is running too long and must be shortened, or if it's too short and they must fill it out.'

Pippa said nothing. Prue was reliable about facts. She stiffened as Jeremy walked up the room towards them, followed reluctantly by Niven. He spoke quietly, but his actor's voice was trained to carry and they heard him say, 'I've told you, not again! I can't do it!'

Jeremy turned round. It looked as if he were only offering Niven a cigarette, but the twins heard him say, 'I don't think you've any choice, have you?'

Absent-mindedly Niven took the cigarette. 'It was the sparklers last time, and that was final! You said so!'

Jeremy murmured something they could not hear, but Niven's face was turned towards the twins and they saw a look of hopeless despair. Suddenly he saw them, and as clearly as if he had spoken aloud that they were a refuge, an escape from Jeremy, he walked over.

'Hallo twins!' He smiled down charmingly. 'Now wait a minute. You're Prue ... and so, you're Pippa.' He had got their names right, which amazed the twins because, while they were not identical, people often confused them. He

164

laughed at their surprise, and the girls smiled back at him. 'Jess has told me about you, you see. You must be very bored. Why not come on down to the others? You can read my script if you like, and then you'll know what's going on.'

It was usually Pippa who decided what they did, but before she could speak, Prue stood up, slipped her hand into Niven's. Normally cautious, if Prue liked someone there was nothing more to say. Pippa also saw Prue glance nervously over her shoulder. They heard Jeremy laugh, unpleasantly, and say, 'It's all right, I don't eat little girls.'

Hugh was talking the cast through the opening scenes. He called Julia, Niven and the elderly woman who played the part of a neighbour in the serial. They spoke their lines, walked back to their seats and took up their previous conversation as if it had been uninterrupted. Pippa began to yawn, because after a scene had been repeated four times, on each occasion timed by Jessica, she began to get bored.

A voice behind them said, 'Hi kids!' Turning, the twins saw Beth Croxley. She was tall for her age, wore her red-gold hair hanging to her waist. When they had first met Beth, the twins had been suspicious, but they found she put on no airs because she was an actress. As Pippa was about to speak, Beth put her finger to her lips, whispered: 'Shush, I want to talk to you. Privately. Come on down here.' They followed her to the other end of the room and, still in a whisper, Beth said: 'Talking disturbs Hugh and he gets mad. But, listen, I want you to do something.'

Pippa could smell excitement a mile off. 'Of course.'

'Something funny's going on...'

'That man Jeremy... and Mr. Niven Turner,' said Pippa.

'My goodness!' Reluctantly Beth was admiring. 'You pick things up quickly. That's it. No one knows what it is. Niven's not working properly — all nervy, can't give any sort of performance, that sort of thing.' She spoke professionally. 'The company may break his contract and sack him. And once he's got a bad reputation, bang? No work. It's got to stop.'

'And?' prompted Pippa. 'What do we do?'

'What you've done. Stick around. Keep your ears open. You see, I've got a chaperone, it's not so easy for me.' She nodded her head and they saw a grey-haired woman sitting against the wall, knitting, and chatting gently to the stage manager. 'She comes from school — it complies with some law or something.'

'Got anything to go on?' asked Pippa briefly.

'Not much. Jeremy gets at Niven in some way, by calling him Nick. That's one thing.'

'Doesn't seem much.' said Pippa.

Prue said softly, 'It can mean prison, you know.'

'Niven!' scoffed Beth. 'No one'll ever convince me *he's* a crook. But you two snoop round. After all, kids can go anywhere. They're not noticed, they can hear all sorts of things. Especially bright youngsters like you two!' The stage manager had seen Hugh's expression, caught Beth's eye and frowned warningly. 'Shush, we must be quiet. See what I mean? It never used to be like this. Something's going to blow up soon. Unless we can act quickly!' She wandered off, swinging her script and banging it against her thigh.

Hugh was saying, 'All right, all right. We'll break. Niven, for heaven's sake go away and study your lines for fifteen minutes. You're not here to write the script, that's been done for you by the expert. Your job is to speak his words — unless you're thinking of changing your profession!'

To her surprise, Pippa suddenly found that Prue had vanished, gone up to Niven and said: 'Would you like us to hear you?'

The embarrassed and worried look vanished from his face. He rubbed his hands across his eyes and said: 'Bless you, but no! I know the lines, it's just that I can't concentrate somehow. I get worried, and then everything vanishes from my mind.' As he said something about fresh air, the twins followed him into the front courtyard.

Prue said, 'I know!' She then added, apparently innocently,

'I don't think I like that Mr Thorp very much. He's in charge of the actors and cameramen and Hugh talks to him from a microphone, from the production room, doesn't he?'

'That's about it,' said Niven. 'And if you could tell me how he manages to live as he does on a floor manager's salary, I'd be very much obliged!'

'He must do something on the side!' said Pippa wisely.

'Well, don't you have anything to do with him. Nothing at all, do you hear?'

'You don't want to have anything to do with him either, do you?' Prue produced a phrase from the back of her memory. 'Couldn't you tell him to 'publish — and be damned?'

Niven shook his head. 'It'd ruin my career, my wife, my home. It's nothing very serious, but ...' Suddenly he realised that he was talking rather freely. He looked at the girls, gave them an actor's smile, crinkling and insincere. 'You'd better run along, you two, or you'll have me telling you all my secrets!'

'We didn't find out much!' complained Pippa. 'I wonder if Jessica knows, though.'

'I shouldn't think so!' said Prue. 'Grown-ups are too busy working and pretending to be important to be like us ...'

Pippa understood. 'Just like Beth said. We can watch and listen. Come on.'

They wandered back into the room, to find most of the cast enjoying the coffee break. Jeremy was standing just inside, talking to Hugh.

'Come off it, Hugh. You know he's finished. Just a back number!'

Hugh Galloway's face was red with anger. 'I don't know what you know, Thorp.' It was not a pretty expression when Jeremy frowned. 'But I've known Niven for twenty years. I don't like to see him going to pieces, throwing up a good career. And I may say, if you don't watch your step, you might be looking for another job, too.'

Prue shivered behind Pippa, but all Jeremy said was, 'Well, I don't suppose that'd break my heart, if it came to it.'

'There's such a thing as having more money than sense,' said Hugh, darkly, and walked off, coffee cup in hand.

Jeremy watched him, fingering expensive gold cufflinks thoughtfully. He did not notice the twins, standing behind him against the wall. 'Fools!' he muttered, and it was not a pleasant thing to hear. 'Fools! If they knew... but then they don't know, do they?' At that moment Niven pushed open the door and could not avoid Jeremy, who blocked his path, calling him softly. 'Nick!'

Niven hesitated, came over reluctantly. 'My name's Niven!'

'Of course it is! What can I have been thinking of?' Niven made no comment. 'We're to go down to the studio this afternoon, for a camera rehearsal — so aptly called a stagger through. This is a good time, isn't it?'

'I've told you, no.'

'But there's more stuff, still. Can't be helped!'

'I can't do it again.'

'Of course not, old chap.' Jeremy's eyes gleamed. 'But how are you going to avoid it?'

Niven shrugged his shoulders, turned away as Hugh called him.

'Niven, sorry I snapped earlier on.'

'That's all right!' But Niven hardly seemed to hear him.

'We'll break for lunch, then go to the studio. O.K.?'

'Sure. Sure. I'll just have to stop off at my flat for a moment, but it's on the way...' His voice trailed away before Hugh's frown.

'Now, look here, Niven, I may be a bit hasty, but I've been very patient. God knows what you're up to, but if you cut rehearsal once more, or are late, you're out! You may be the star of this serial, but we can write you out of the script as easily as if you'd really broken your leg!'

'We'll go with him, we'll see he gets to the studio on time.'

Both men looked at Pippa in surprise. Only a member of her family could recognise the bright and shiny expression on her face meant that Pippa was frightened, and was trying not to show it.

Hugh laughed. 'Jessica's little sisters! Well, well. Excellent idea, eh, Niven? All right, you're in charge!'

Prue pulled his hand. 'Come on!'

Despite himself, Niven smiled. 'Haven't got much choice, have I?'

Jessica came up. 'Now, you two, don't make a nuisance of yourselves. You promised to behave.'

'And so they have,' said Niven. 'We'll have lunch, and they'll bring me down to the studio.'

'If you're sure it isn't too much bother...' said Jessica.

'Come on!' shouted Hugh, but the irritation had gone from his voice. 'Don't gossip all day. I want one complete run through, then we'll break early for lunch.'

Because it was convenient, they ate in a café next to the hall. Beth sat between the twins at the end of a long table. 'Well?'

'It's nothing much...' said Prue, sadly.

But Pippa broke in, eager to tell her story, to air her views. 'I'm sure there's nothing really wrong with Niven,' she ended. 'But Jeremy knows something, it's given him a hold over Niven.'

'Could be. It adds up!' said Beth, thoughtfully. 'But I don't quite see what we do about it!'

'We'll snoop round the flat, report later,' said Pippa, confidently.

'Come on, you two kids,' called Niven, and he was actor enough to appear quite cheerful. 'We'd better get a move on!'

'Don't forget the tomfoolery,' called Jeremy, apparently with considerable humour, 'while I'm sitting on the fence.'

Niven ignored him. 'I'll start the car up. Now, where's Prue gone?' Pippa looked after her sister, who had rushed back to the table and was whispering furiously in Beth's ear.

'She'll come.'

'I can't hang about for children all afternoon,' said Niven with irritation.

But he didn't have to wait, because while he was warming up the engine, Prue came running out to join Pippa on the back seat.

She hissed at her twin, 'Beth's going to try to tell Hugh this afternoon...'

'Shush!' Pippa was not paying attention, but was sitting up very straight, looking out through the windscreen.

Rather hurt, Prue fell silent and Niven said, 'Are you two whispering secrets?'

'We haven't got any secrets to whisper,' said Prue. 'I think the only person to have secrets is Mr Thorp.'

'No doubt. But not very nice ones, so I shouldn't enquire too closely into them,' said Niven, grimly.

'Do you know what they are?'

But he would not answer. 'Young lady, you'll soon learn that there are things it's better not to know,' and Prue found nothing to say. 'I don't think perhaps I'll need to go into the flat, but we'll have to go there just the same...'

They did not understand what he meant, but both girls realised that Niven would not explain. They recognised the block, small and modern, with every convenience, including a telephone door bell. As they parked, Niven's face changed again. He ceased to be their gay companion, once more looked grey and hunted. As if he had forgotten the twins he muttered: 'Got to keep the kids out of this!' He put his arm over the back seat and looked at the girls. 'You two sit here, I've just got to do something...'

They watched him walk across the road, between two small shops and disappear down a narrow lane. Immediately Pippa said, 'Come on, Prue. Up to the flat. Now's our chance!'

'Pippa! We can't!'

'Why not? This is a golden opportunity. Remember what Jeremy said? We might even catch him red-handed.'

170

Prue uttered a scream

'But...' protested Prue, frowning because she did not understand. 'And what if we're caught?'

'We wanted the bathroom. Something. Anything. Come on! We'll worry about that later.'

'How will we get in?' Prue's breathless voice reached her sister as they rushed up the stairs. 'The flat'll be locked...'

Pippa did not pause. 'Don't fuss!'

The door was unlatched. Automatically Pippa pushed it open, automatically Prue followed her. It was a small flat. The hallway ran down the middle, a bathroom then a kitchen were on the right, to the left the sitting-room overlooked the street and there were two bedrooms at the end. They could see the foot of a bed through a half-open door. Behind the other there came sounds of movement, a thump and then a bang.

Prue clutched Pippa's arm. 'There's someone here! I'm sure it's that man Thorp. Oh Pippa let's go!'

But her sister stood her ground. 'No, we're not babies, we can't run away, just because it's a bit scarifying.' But for all her brave words, her freckles were standing out like bruises because her face was so white.

There were a couple of suitcases standing in the hall. Creeping past, they went into the sitting-room, hid behind the half-open door. After a moment the bedroom door opened, there were faint noises, and presently there was silence.

'Let's go and have a look round,' suggested Pippa.

Prue, who would have given anything to have gone downstairs, followed her along the passage. Gently they turned the bedroom door handle, tiptoed in.

There was nothing to see. The room was obviously disused. The bed was stripped, some winter coats lay piled across a chair, empty paint pots stood on the chest of drawers.

'He must have shut the front door jolly quietly,' said Prue, voicing something which had been worrying her.

'Oh no he didn't,' said a voice behind them. Prue uttered a scream, and both girls swung round to face Jeremy. 'And just what do you think you're doing here?'

172

Pippa found words first. 'We... we came up with Niven, and then we heard something, so we thought we'd better investigate... and...'

'You little liar!' he hissed. 'Niven doesn't walk so quietly. You came up alone — to spy. Well now, just you buzz off and wait in the sitting-room. And if you don't do what you're told...' He made a twisting movement with his hands. Instinctively Prue touched her neck.

They were too frightened to disobey. In a moment Jeremy joined them and Prue was so scared she thought she was using up a lifetime's ration of fear.

'Now, where is he?'

Obediently Prue said: 'He went across the road...'

'Oh yes, to the café where we sometimes meet. I thought he'd have the sense to take *you* there, to keep you out of this business. He can't have imagined I didn't mean what I said. However, you needn't worry. I often come here. Niven and I are good friends.'

'To watch you, no one would guess it.' Pippa recovered from her fright more quickly than her sister.

'Wouldn't they? Well, well, young lady, what sharp eyes you do have to be sure!' He paused. 'I think you'd better wait here for a moment.' He turned on his heel and they heard the front door shut.

Pippa glanced out of the window. 'Look, there's Niven! I suppose they'll meet on the pavement. I wish we could warn him. Prue wait here a sec., there's something I want to look at.'

She popped back after a moment. Prue had moved, was watching the people in the street. The two sisters exchanged looks. They understood each other, almost without words.

'This is a case for the police.'

'Beth?'

'And Hugh? Perhaps Jess — you know how she worries!'

'It's her age,' said Pippa, and had anyone been there they would have remembered her eleventh birthday was still some months away.

It was Prue who telephoned the studio, and Pippa who greeted Niven. They had expected him to be angry, but he was obviously more frightened than anything else. Indeed, the two girls had to reassure him as they all sat in the living room, waiting.

They did not have long to wait. Hugh came first, with Jessica and Beth.

Jessica, worried and afraid, was inclined to be bossy. 'What on earth have you two been up to?' she demanded, and was not pleased when the twins chorused, 'It's a case for the police, I'm afraid.'

Beth looked enquiringly at Prue. 'So you were right?'

'I'm afraid so.' Prue might have been a woman, three times her age.

'Children!' Jessica sat in the big chair, flouncing her skirts.

'Niven, you must tell me, old chap. I've guessed there was something.' Hugh was pleading. 'I've known you for what, twenty-five years? I know when something's wrong. You wouldn't tell me! What was his hold? Not that old business about the money?' Miserably, Niven nodded and Hugh smiled. 'But, my dear fellow, I knew all about that! We all did, we all knew you took the blame for that wretched brother of yours. It was a tragedy, of course, that he should have been found out just before his car accident. I understood you didn't want your parents to know what a rotter he was, just when they were mourning his death. Afterwards, we just thought you didn't want to talk about — about a distressing incident. You'd paid the price for a crime you hadn't committed and we decided you wanted to forget, to regard the matter as closed.'

'If only I'd known! If only I'd known!' was all that Niven could say.

At that moment Inspector Hunt, who was an acquaintance of Hugh's, arrived with two constables. 'Now, what's all this?' he demanded, in that time-honoured phrase.

Hugh shrugged his shoulders. 'It's these two,' he indicated the twins. 'It's their affair!'

'Well?'

'Well!'

They took a deep breath and the Inspector said, hurriedly, 'One at a time, please!'

Pippa put in her word first. 'I think it's that robbery — the big jewel robbery up north. It was in the papers a month or so back. You'll find some of the takings in a suitcase in the hall.'

'Indeed!' The Inspector did not sound as if he believed Pippa, but he motioned to one of the constables to investigate. 'And what makes you think that?'

'Jeremy — Mr Thorp — was in the flat when we arrived. He made us wait in here alone. But after he had left the flat, I saw one of the suitcases had been moved. When we first came in, the initials were facing us, but now you'll find them facing the wall.'

'Well!' exclaimed the Inspector. 'And what makes you think it's jewels? Did you look?'

'Certainly not!' exclaimed Pippa, '*I* thought of finger-prints.'

'Good girl!' he was obviously impressed. 'But...'

It was Prue's turn. 'I listened.' She blushed, because everyone looked at her and she tried to explain. 'He went out and met Mr Turner on the doorstep. He said 'It's the last load of the Thorsen rocks. Look, I can show you.' She lifted up the white telephone on the sitting-room wall. 'It's part of the doorbell,' she explained, as if he had never seen one before. 'When the bell rings, you lift this up and ask who it is. The caller hears your voice down in the street through a sort of grid microphone thing. You then press the button, which opens the door. But if you lift up the receiver, you can hear people talking outside.'

Glancing at her, the Inspector took the receiver. 'She's quite right, you know. There are two women sheltering from

175

this shower, discussing the price of fish!' He laughed. 'And where is this Mr Thorp?'

Hugh explained who he was and Niven, rather white but not so unhappy as he had been, said, 'I think you'll find him in Dino's café, round the corner.'

Inspector Hunt caught the eye of the second constable. Hugh saw the movement and said, 'I'll come with you. I know the fellow, so it'll make things easier.'

Niven looked up as the door closed. 'I think I've got some explaining to do, Inspector.'

'That's as maybe, sir,' said Inspector Hunt, comfortably. 'But I shouldn't worry too much about that. We can go into all this later. I'd just like to finish hearing the story from these two young ladies first, if I may; the twin who keeps her ears open, and the one that keeps her eyes open.'

They went rather pink, and it spoke much for the Inspector's intelligence that he managed to piece the story together from the two excited girls. 'But what I don't quite understand, if I may say so, is why you suspected it was jewels before you even got to the flat.' Pippa looked as mystified as the rest. Realising he had said something odd, the Inspector looked round. 'I understood this from the young lady here,' and they all looked at Beth.

She was quite unruffled by all the attention. 'Yes, I thought I'd give you some warning when we heard from the twins, and Hugh rang you from the sudio. But it was Prue. She picked up the hint that a threat involving prison was being used on Mr Turner. She also said it was probably jewels that were being hidden here — she told me as they left the café.'

'Well, young woman?'

'It was something Mr Thorp said. I'd heard it before, and I just remembered what it meant.'

'She does,' explained Pippa, as if Prue suffered from a rare disease.

'So I gather!' said the Inspector, with feeling. 'And very grateful we all are, I must say. But what was it?'

'I knew what a fence was, you see — when it's not the kind round a garden. And then Mr Thorp called out something about 'tomfoolery', I knew this was thieves slang for jewellery — you know, the rhyming sort of slang!'

'I've heard of it,' admitted the Inspector, and no one could have sworn that he was smiling.

At that moment, Hugh returned, followed by Jeremy and the constable. Obviously the Inspector did not like him, any more than did the others. Jeremy was rude and truculent, but he listened to the Inspector in silence.

Eventually, he said, 'but this is ridiculous. Are you seriously telling me that you'd take the word of these two half-witted children — and heaven knows why they were creeping in here, either! Mr Turner's a friend and colleague. There's no reason why I shouldn't call round to see him. As a matter of fact I met him on the doorstep. I quite often look in...'

'Then why did you follow us, race ahead to sneak in here first?' demanded Pippa, her temper showing in her flaming cheeks.

'I don't know what you mean!' Jeremy sounded as puzzled as the others felt.

'I saw your car. And I expect Niven'll remember it, won't you?' Did she turn and look at Niven rather deliberately? At any rate, he seemed surprised, but said quickly, 'Yes, yes, certainly.' 'You can check on the registration number. It's YAV0188!' added Pippa triumphantly.

'There!' said Jeremy. 'That's proof the child's lying. The registration on my car begins with a V and an 8!'

'But...' Pippa's clear voice cut across everyone else. 'But I was looking at it reversed, in the driving mirror!'

'And I want to make a statement!' said Niven, suddenly. 'It doesn't matter any more Jeremy.' He smiled, in a sad, tired kind of way as Jeremy frowned. 'Hugh knows all about that old trouble — so do my friends. You haven't got any power over me, and I want to tell them all about it!'

Jessica pulled the twins away, so that they should not

watch Jeremy's struggles as, having completely lost his temper, he was removed by the two constables.

Wiping his face with a handkerchief, Niven said. 'It's the jewels, of course. The twins are quite right. He made me take them — act as some sort of go-between. They were put into a suitcase of mine. I took it to a left luggage office, posted the tickets to a given address. It was different every time, and I imagine it was a false name at an accommodation address. Then the case was collected, left somewhere else, the ticket again mailed back to me, so I would go and retrieve it again!'

'We'll go into all this at the proper place and at the proper time,' said the Inspector. 'But don't worry too much, sir. We're not fools, and we understand what are called 'extenuating circumstances'. I think you've probably paid very heavily for your unwilling part in this business already. And if I may say so, I've very much admired your acting. The wife's a great fan of "And They All Lived Together". She'll be tickled pink when I tell her I've actually met you!' Niven brightened considerably, and the Inspector turned to the twins. 'Before we go, I'd just like to thank these two young ladies again, and to congratulate them on their powers of observation. If everyone kept their eyes and ears open as much as you do, our jobs would be much, much easier!'

When they were all at home, with Beth, tucking into a well-deserved, but much delayed tea, and they had discussed the case from every angle, Jessica suddenly said, 'Pippa, did you really see the car following you while you were driving to Niven's flat? Or did you hope to make Jeremy lose his temper, give himself away. I know you, you see. You could easily have seen it parked outside, remembered the number, and made it all up!'

But Pippa wouldn't answer. She and Prue began to giggle, and Jessica sighed. She knew that there are some things that twins only ever tell each other.

THE DOOR TO NOWHERE

by

Elizabeth Stucley

When Lily was ten years old her parents were both killed in a bus crash, and she and her brother Dan went to live with Mr and Mrs Carter, their uncle and aunt.

Mr Carter was the schoolmaster in a large village in Dorset. It was called Queen's Caundle and was a pretty place on a clean, shallow river that flowed over a bed of flints right through the middle of the village street. Small bridges crosed the stream to every house and one led to the Carter's cottage which was built of flint. This house was solid and comfortable and Lily should have been happy there, but she was not.

Mr Carter believed, like many other schoolmasters, that he was always in the right and his wife believed it too, because she did not dare do otherwise. When Lily crossed the little stream and saw her uncle standing there, she knew from the first that she did not like him. He had a large dead white face splotched with a few yellow freckles, a bully's chin, and pale red hair that was smarmed down on his head but which jutted out as very bristly eyebrows. These eyebrows were already raised when he saw the untidy, bundly luggage the children were carrying over the bridge to his neat house.

Mrs Carter stood behind her husband on the garden path and looked anxious. She was a timid little woman who always appeared worried and this was not surprising as she was married to Mr Carter.

'What a lot of miscellaneous objects you have brought,' were Mr Carter's first words, spoken in his acid voice. Lily was not sure what 'miscellaneous' meant, but she knew he used it disagreeably, so she clutched the bird cage, the yellow kitten and her mother's old work bag even more tightly.

As soon as she stepped inside the flint house, polished all over like an advertisement for furniture cream, she knew that none of her treasures would be welcome there; and sure enough they were disposed of one by one. The canary sang too loud, the kitten made messes, and both were given away. The tidiness of the flint cottage was more important than the happiness of its inmates.

After two weeks, Lily realised that her uncle would have liked to give her away too. He did not like her any more than he had liked the kitten and canary. He had never had any children himself and did not really care for them. He was schoolmaster only because his parents had said he must be, and his behaviour was always so correct that the school could not think of any reason to get rid of him. Mrs Carter was secretly kind to Lily, but she was too terrified of her husband to be able to protect the child properly.

Unluckily, Lily was just the sort of girl who must annoy Mr Carter. Bright, energetic Dan who was thirteen, would fit into any home. He worked hard and was very willing and quick. But Lily trailed. Even when she talked, she drawled. Her looks annoyed Mr Carter too, because she was exactly like those thin, pale angels carrying one lily. Her hair was a pale yellow and dead straight. It hung to her waist without a ripple. She had a pale, pointed face and huge green eyes, set far apart, that gazed vaguely out from between the two curtains of yellow hair. Her hands and feet were long and slim like an angel's, floating in mid-air, and neither hands nor feet were very practical. She moved in a dream as though she were really somewhere else, carrying an immense amount of rubbish with her: flowers, books, small animals. She was so unconscious of the real world and its furnishings, that she bumped into tables and let things fall that were put into her hands. Consequently, she was not the slightest use in the house, and if she washed up, she broke a great deal of the china.

At school, she sat in a daze, and anything she wrote was a queer muddle of beautiful words set down on the page, but not strung together to make much sense. She loved certain figures like five and seven, but hated four and nine. She thought four and nine smug, and would leave them out of all her sums, so that none of her arithmetic gave the proper answers. Although Lily seemed so gentle and spoke in a soft voice, she was really very determined and always did what she wanted.

She should have easily passed her school examination because she was really clever, but on the day of the exam she was in one of her dreams and drew pictures on the paper instead of answers. In the general papers, she drew kings and queens, and instead of writing an essay on 'A Day in the Country' she ornamented her pages with fine pencil sketches of snails crawling on flowers.

As she did not pass this exam, she had to stay in the village school, which meant that Mr Carter had her under his eyes all day. It poisoned the school for both of them and Lily used to hide whenever she saw him coming.

The only place where Lily found happiness was in the water meadows that surrounded the village. Kingcups, yellow flags, rare orchids, celandines and wild peppermint grew there. Little streams ran everywhere in and out of the willows and there were great clumps of glossy watercress. Here, she wandered endlessly. But there was one place that intrigued her most. Long ago, someone had built a small square of wall, ten feet high and six feet wide. It was of rough stone and there was a door in it, an ordinary house door. When she opened the door, she had expected to find a little house or shed, but there was nothing behind the wall, nothing at all but a green path that led to a small bridge.

Lily was entranced by this wall and door and invented hundreds of stories why they had been built. Each time she went through the door, she knew she would find only the green path, the willows, a grassy peninsula jutting into the stream and the bridge, which was just a tree trunk on which a plank was nailed. But each time she half expected to find that a tiny house had grown up during the night, at the back of the wall... but it never had.

She would sit for hours on the bridge, gazing down at the clear water. Shadowy fish forms were poised above the sandy bottom, quivering as gently as the water weeds. In the back waters, where the current slowed down, grew water lilies. They were white and yellow and sprang above the flat leaves on india-rubber stalks. Amongst them the bog buttercups fluttered like night moths.

When it was time to go back through the door, Lily always felt sad. She would shut it very carefully and trail across the meadows to arrive muddy and bedraggled at the spotless flint house.

'Lily,' said Mr Carter, one morning in late May, 'I am ashamed of you. Your aunt and I are giving you a happy, comfortable home, and what do you do?'

Lily stared at him with her great, green eyes. She did not think her home either happy or comfortable, and so she abstracted her mind and pretended that she was back through the door that led to nothing. 'You do not take advantage of your good fortune,' went on Mr Carter, who always talked like a copy book. 'You do not work at school. Your room is always in a muddle. Your life is one long failure.'

The girl bent her head so that the long, yellow hair covered her face, and Mr Carter longed to slap her. 'Sit up! Look at me when I am speaking, and take that hair back from your face,' he shouted angrily. 'What will become of you, Lily? You've no money. I can't be expected to keep you for ever. Frankly speaking, I can't imagine how you will ever earn a living.'

Lily did not take her eyes off him, but in reality they were

184

seeing not the angry man sitting at a breakfast table, but the dim forms of fish in clear water, the writhing, stripped roots of trees and the birds' nests of rubbish that had collected between them.

'Your brother Daniel is doing very well,' went on the harsh voice, but it was so hateful that she concentrated on bird calls and grasshopper chirpings. 'He had excellent reports from school and will probably get a scholarship to the University. Why can't you be like him?'

Dan kicked her gently under the table to tell her not to mind, but she was not minding. She was changing the harsh voice into the sound of water bubbling through stones.

'And I'll tell you what,' cried the schoolmaster, made yet more furious by her inattention. 'This summer there is to be a cruise on a ship going to Spain, a special, cruise of schools. I am arranging for Daniel to go, and I would have sent you, too, but what is the use when you will not benefit from such a voyage? Unless you achieve success in some field during the next few weeks, you will stay here and do extra lessons with me during the holidays.'

The words 'ships' and 'Dan' did come through her consciousness. She looked up and saw the cruelty in her uncle's face, and she knew for certain that he had never meant to send her on the ship. It was just a fresh form of bullying. He was quite safe with his promises, because she would never achieve success of any kind.

Mrs Carter opened her mouth to say something, but she shut it again. She knew argument would be useless. The thought of Dan going away and the horror of extra lessons with Mr Carter made two large tears fall out of Lily's eyes. If Mr Carter had wanted to hurt her, he had chosen the right way, because she had always wanted to go for a voyage on a ship. Water in any form attracted her. The first time she had been shown the sea, she had run straight into the waves with a cry of delight. Her mother had often said laughingly that this child must be a mermaid or naiad.

Now she looked up under her yellow hair at her uncle and hated him. She hated him with all her heart because she knew he was paying the money for Dan so as to revenge himself on her. It was wicked to hate people, but she could not quench her feeling. It leapt like a hot, bright flame out of her heart. When the meal was over, she escaped quickly and Dan ran after her to whisper, 'I won't go without you Lily. I wouldn't leave you alone with him.'

'You must. You must.' She clutched his arm. 'Think of it, Dan, going over the huge waves and arriving at places, great cities, early in the morning. If only I could do anything properly, make a cake, anything, but I can't. My hands don't seem to know how. Or I start thinking and forget... but if I am left alone here with him... I shall have to run away.'

Dan rubbed his head angrily. 'You will be a success one day,' he promised. 'I know it's just shut up inside you... like... like the kernel of a nut. It's being here with him. We could both run away out of this beastly, flint house, but we've no money and no place to go...'

Lily almost told him then about her doorway to nowhere, but Mrs Carter called the boy, and the girl trailed upstairs to make her bed. As always, the blankets and sheets seemed to wrap themselves around her, and she got smothered in their folds. This morning she found the bedclothes wickeder than ever, because she was not concentrating on them. She was thinking all the time; 'I must be a success, I must. If I don't go in the ship with Dan, I'll die of sorrow.'

'Dear, dear, what a muddle,' cried Mrs Carter coming in briskly, 'Come along, child, I'll give you a hand.' In a moment the sheets and blankets became docile and lay down on the bed without a wrinkle. Lily stood in the middle of the floor and spread out her tapering fingers. 'Aunt, why can't I do things?'

'Your head's always in the clouds,' said Mrs Carter, but she smiled kindly because she was sorry for her dead sister's child, and thought her very beautiful.

186

'I do try,' sighed Lily.

'You are like the lilies in the Bible,' murmured Mrs Carter. 'They toil not neither do they spin...'

But Lily was still considering. 'Would any success do? Any prize at all? If I win any sort of prize would that count?'

'I suppose so,' her aunt spoke hesitatingly because she knew that Mr Carter would never let Lily go.

That evening, as soon as school was over, Lily ran across the water meadows to the door in the wall. She turned the handle, shut the door behind her and felt safe. The other three walls were still missing, but here was her fortress of peace filled with the sound of running water and birds singing. She sat down under the wall and, presently, worn out by emotion, fell asleep.

It was quite late when she awoke, and the daylight only touched the tops of the trees. She was surprised to find herself there for in her dreams she had been far away. Still swaying with sleep, she stood up, and was amazed to find that the door in the wall had opened, although she remembered closing it carefully.

The landscape enclosed within the door frame was like a picture — the water meadows, the distant blue hills and a great arch of sky. Suddenly, she knew that the door in the wall did not just lead to nowhere. From the other side, it could lead into the wide world, to the far off hills — and success. She had only to walk through it, and the world beyond was free, all hers, and no Mr Carter could really spoil it.

This new knowledge was so exciting that she stepped over the threshold of the door. Suddenly, she felt wildly happy. There seemed to be no reason for this great upsurging of hope. She no longer trailed through the rushes. She began to walk quickly towards the village, her head held high.

When she came to the first houses, the setting sun shone on some of their windows and the whole village seemed made of burnished gold. She felt she must run fast, faster than she had ever run in her life. Her mind was still dazed, only her feet seemed to know what to do. She kept on running as though she was late for some meeting.

It was in the village square that she saw the notice stuck up on a barn. The words QUEEN'S CAUNDLE VILLAGE SHOW leapt out at her as though printed in luminous paint. She stopped to read. There were to be pony races, a dog and a baby show, prizes for the best vegetables, a tea and a concert party. Slowly, she moved her finger down the whole list of classes and competitions. At the bottom of the notice, she came to the words, 'Silver Cup'. A silver cup was presented every year for the best arrangement of wild flowers. As this cup was held only for the year, the winner also received a money prize.

A silver cup! Lily stood in the village street and imagined the silver chalice used in the communion service. Her face tilted up her long hair blowing in the evening wind, she read and re-read the notice. If she could win a silver cup, if all the village knew her success, not even Mr Carter could deny her the voyage.

Already, there seemed to be a strange power moving in her. She wanted to go at once to the meadows to search for the right flowers. She would arrange them as if they were still growing. They should not wilt in jam jars. This was her plan, this would be her success, she knew it, but she would keep her idea a secret so that scorn should not kill the new power in her.

One evening, when her aunt and uncle had gone to a meeting, she began to search the flint house. At first, she hardly knew for what. She opened all the kitchen cupboards and drawers, but the unknown object was not there. It was as though the strange, new power directed her search. She looked in the shed, and under the stairs, but the Thing was not there. Then she climbed up to the bedrooms and peered into all the wardrobes and climbed on chairs to look at top shelves. She peeped into cardboard hatboxes, and under the

She pulled three perfect water-lilies

beds. All the time she felt it was urgent, there was no time to waste. At last, she lit a candle and went up the top, steep flight to the unused attic. She had never been there before, but she felt certain the Thing was in the house and she must keep searching. Then she saw It!

It was on the floor amongst all the queer throwouts: her aunt's dressmaking judy, a tin bath, cardboard boxes, old bottling jars. She recognised it at once — the wide, shallow dish of clear green glass. It had a corrugated rim and was very dusty. She did not feel surprised to find it there, ready for her, waiting, and she carried it downstairs and washed it carefully, polished it until the glass shone, and hid it amongst her underclothes.

Now that she had found the green dish, her power drove her to the river bed. For hours she walked slowly along the crystal clear river, gazing down into it, pouncing sometimes, but always drawing back disappointed. Yet, at the end of the week, she had found the three perfect flints she needed. Their forms were strange and sculptured, the yellow and blue and white of them were magnificent. She washed these too and hid them.

Once, she had seen a green frog sitting near the river, and she knew that she must have a frog too, not a live one, but a china creature that would stay still. On Saturday, she took her small savings and walked to the nearest town, but there was no such frog in any of the shops. On the way home, there came a roll of thunder and heavy rain fell, soaking her, so that she begged shelter from a wayside cottage. When the woman opened the door, she thought it was a queer fairy who stood there in the green, thundery light, for the wind and rain had whipped Lily's long hair into flying strands about her head.

The woman was kind and brought the girl milk to drink as they sat in the dark little kitchen across which the lightning slashed and slashed. In one of these bursts of jagged light, Lily saw the frog. He sat on the high mantelpiece, his head

190

cocked up. She did not feel at all surprised to find him there, for she had known all along that the power which had led her to the green vase and the three perfect flints would show her the frog.

'There he is,' she cried leaping up and she stretched carefully to lift him down from the high shelf. He was smooth and cold in her hand. 'I've looked for him everywhere. I knew I should find him. Now I must go home. I will bring him back, I promise.'

And the woman, bewitched by this strange child who had come out of the storm, let her go, taking the frog with her. She followed her visitor to the door and saw the girl walking away through the lightning, down the long straight road to the village.

The night before the village show, every one was buzzing with excitement. Down in the meadow, men were hammering. The great marquees shook out their folds and ascended trembling into the air. It was very warm, and all through the evening, people moved towards the meadow, carrying their exhibits. The caterers had brought baskets of thick white china and trestle tables, and the Vicar's son was setting up the Bowl for a Pig and the old Aunt Sally.

When the sun rose and the day was growing warm, Lily went down to the meadow to pick her water-lilies. She pulled the three perfect ones that she had been watching for days, and their stems were ice cold. She coiled up the stems and laid the lilies and their leaves in the bowl of water she had brought with her.

After dinner, she made two journeys to the show tent. On the first trip, she carried the green glass dish, the three flints and the china frog, all wrapped in a basket. On the next trip, she brought the lilies still in their bowl of water.

It was very hot in the marquee that smelt of crushed grass, sweet peas, mint and hot people. Everyone was there, busy putting last touches to their exhibits. Lily brought her entry card for a five pence, and then, paying no heed to the crowd, went straight to the trestle table, that was covered with a clean sheet. She did not want to talk, because the power was moving strongly in her and she was afraid of it being disturbed. She knew, without reflecting, just what she must do. Into the shallow, glass dish, she poured water and the marquee roof and poles were reflected there. Then she took the three flints, dipped them in the water so that their yellow was deepened and the whites and blues shone brilliant and pearly. On these flints, she poised the green frog that looked so real as if he might jump out of the dish at any moment. Then, lovingly, carefully, she lifted the lilies and their leaves out of the kitchen bowl, and poised them, stems tucked beneath the leaves, so that they floated around the flints. Each lily was a pure white casket encircling a golden coronet of stamens.

For days, she had dreamed of this moment, and now her great creation was ready. She stood there gazing at its beauty and was so entranced that she did not notice the group of women who had gathered behind her. They had stopped their chatter and stood silently, awed by the beauty of this thing created by a child in a white frock.

''Tis beautiful, my dear,' breathed one of the women, and they all marvelled that Lily had known how to arrange her flowers.

'She's like a lily herself,' muttered another woman, and so she was in her white frock.

It was two o'clock now and Lily must go home to change into her best clothes. The famous lady who wrote about flower arrangement in the newspapers would not be coming to judge the exhibitions until seven o'clock.

When Lily reached the flint cottage, her uncle and aunt were all dressed ready to start for the show, but the girl refused to go with them. In spite of angry orders from her uncle, she went up to her little room and sat there looking at the tops of the marquees, imagining her flowers and the green frog guarding them.

At last it was time for her to go down to the judging. Her heart was beating fast and her hands felt hot, but she brushed her long hair and washed her face and hands. She walked sedately down the empty village street and her freshly starched frock gave her importance. In the distance, she could hear the blaring of the roundabouts and the thud thud of galloping ponies.

She went straight to the marquee and cut through the crowd to her table. Already the grand lady judge had arrived, and was walking about with a pencil and notebook as she examined the various flower pieces. Members of the committee and anxious exhibitors were circling round her. Like a swallow, Lily flew across the tent — and then she saw what had happened!

She was too stunned to cry out. She just stood there, frozen with horror. On the table was a cheap glass dish, three stones, a tangle of rubbery stalks, some limp leaves, and amongst these lay three reddish, greenish, ugly buds. The lilies had closed up tightly and there was no sign of the frog at all.

For a second, it looked as though he had been stolen; but then Lily noticed his leg. He had somehow been jerked from his stones and had fallen under the water, amongst the closed buds.

Lily tried to force open the buds, but they stayed closed and it was then that she must have wailed out her despair, for suddenly, the judge lady in her grand clothes, and all the other women, came hurrying forward. 'What is it, oh, what is it?' the judge lady asked the girl with long yellow hair.

But Lily could not speak. She only pointed and then she ran away, right out of the tent, across the field, into the clover meadow beyond.

Somewhere there must be a place where she could hide her shame. The door that led to nowhere would have been best, but that was too far, because the storm of tears was upon her, and must break soon.

As she reached the clover field, she fell down amongst the high, green trefoils, and with a shuddering breath, she began to weep. The power, the wonderful exciting power that had filled her, that had forced her along for so many days, was gone. This power had so possessed her mind that she had forgotten her other reasons for wanting success. She had forgotten about the sea voyage, and her hatred of Mr Carter, in the delight of creating a thing of such beauty. Now the beauty had gone, and all the village would be laughing at a girl who put three stones and some tangled weeds into a glass dish, a girl who did not know that lilies closed in the evening.

'How could I know, how could I?' she moaned over and over again, and she pressed her face into her hands, and hid her head deep in the clover, wishing that she could vanish away. Everything she had done for weeks, the finding of the dish, the borrowing of the frog, the searching for the stones, all now seemed foolish.

Already her ears burnt as she imagined Mr Carter's sarcastic, cruel jibes.

At last, the first spell of sobbing ceased and she lay still. Presently, she managed to sit up and saw that her best frock was streaked with green. There would be more trouble about that, but she did not care. Dimly, she considered running away, following the stream along its course to the sea. Then she leapt up, because the grand judge lady was coming through the gate into the clover field. Lily was caught. There was no escape.

'Lily,' called the lady, in a clear, high voice.

The girl stayed poised in mid flight, like a wild doe trapped in the clover.

'Lily?' The lady came slowly through the green leaves, holding out her hand, as though she was afraid to frighten a wild creature. All the time the girl looked at her with large, frightened eyes. The lady judge was so grand, so famous and so beautiful. Her curling hair was black and shining and on it was perched a coronet of lilac flowers. Her dress was grey and she wore a brooch of amethysts.

'Lily,' said the lady. 'I came to find you, to tell you that all the women — the women in the tent say that your lilies were beautiful this morning. And I met the lady who owns the green frog. She told me how you came to her house in the thunderstorm, and how the frog was there, waiting for you on the mantlepiece.'

Lily could not speak. She only nodded.

'And the green dish that you found in the attic...'

'Who told you that?' whispered Lily.

'Your aunt. She has taken the dish home with her.'

Lily bowed her head. It was all over then. Everything had gone... the frog, the dish, had been swept away. Someone would take the limp flowers and throw them into the rubbish.

'I wish I could have given you the prize,' went on the lady, 'but it wouldn't have been fair, Lily, would it? The other women wanted you to have the prize, but I couldn't give it to you. Your lilies will be lovely again tomorrow, but the time of the judging was seven o'clock...'

Lily took a step forward. 'I just didn't know about lilies — that they closed at night,' she said. 'How could I know?'

'One can't know everything,' agreed the lady.

Lily gave the ghost of a little sob. 'I thought I might win a prize at last. You see I'm no good at anything. Uncle says I'm hopeless. He's always shouting at me, so I drop the cups. Now he won't pay for me to go in the ship. Danny'll go, not me. All this week, I thought I could do something at last.'

Tears fell from her eyes as she thought of the long search for the dish, the stones and the frog.

'But your flowers were beautiful,' said the lady. 'Everyone says so. Lily, you have the power to make a lovely thing.'

'But I didn't win the cup, the silver cup. So it won't count. I'm still a failure.'

The lady shook her head. 'I don't think the cup matters so much. The cup is just an extra. What is important is that one day you will give the world something beautiful because you have the power of creation in you.'

Lily stared at her, the last tear trembled and fell. 'The power of creation? Me? But what shall I make?'

'I don't know yet,' said the lady, 'but I'm sure you will.' And she held out her hand, and led the child back across the field.

In the early morning, when the Rector went to open his front door, he drew back with a cry of surprise and delight. A wonderful garland of wild flowers, vetches and campions, bog peppers, creeping jennies, pink willow herb, orange loosestrife, comfrey and yellow flags were arranged fantastically and lay upon his doorstep in a bed of damp moss. In the centre of the garland lay one great, white water-lily, its petals full open to the rising sun.

On a piece of paper was scrawled in Lily's uncertain writing: 'FOR THE JUDGE LADY WITH LOVE FROM LILY.'

THE CHAMPIONS
by
Monica Edwards

John Thatcher and his sister Tess were running down the track to Manor Farm. It was not to see the farmer, who wasn't the sort of man anybody would see on purpose, or to see his wife, who was chronically sad. They were looking for Walter Pooley, the horseman.

'If only it hadn't been for school,' John was saying as they ran, 'we could have watched the ploughing match ourselves. I wonder why they always hold it in term-time?'

'I'll bet Walter won his class, anyway,' Tess said. 'and the championship, too. He nearly always has, as well as dozens in other places.'

'But it gets more difficult every year, with all the modern hydraulic-lift tractors. Walter's almost the only horse team left.'

They climbed the gate into the farmyard and crossed a stretch of concrete to the stable. It was quite clearly a stable, because of the halter thrown over the open half-door, and the sounds and smells of horses coming out of it. The powerful brown hind view of one of its inhabitants filled the doorway like a picture in a frame.

'Oh, hullo, young uns,' said Walter Pooley. He had one hand, with a curry comb in it, resting on a grey horse's rump, and the other was grooming its flank in long, strong strokes that sent the fine dust floating in a shaft of low sunlight.

'Hullo, Walter!' Tess and John glanced round at once to look at the shining bridles where they hung on pegs along the wall. On one of them a crisp, red rosette was tied, but, far more important than this, there was a new card at the end of the row of prize-cards that were tacked underneath the bridles, and it said on it, 'Champion; Finkley and District Ploughing Match.'

'Walter! You've won it again!'

'That's right, Flower and Captain's won it again. Dah! those stinking tractors haven't got nothing on a real good pair of horses,' said Walter proudly, but there was a kind of sadness in the pride in his voice. John supposed it was sadness for the passing of the heyday of great horses, and said, 'Well anyway, there'll always be a real horse-team while you and Flower and Captain are around,' to cheer him up.

'Ah,' said Walter non-committally, and then, 'This one makes the 99th prize and the eleventh championship, all with Flower and Captain. Pity it's the last match this year, ain't it, Flower, old girl? I'd like to've made the century; and even better, the dozen.'

'You'll easily do it next year,' Tess said. 'May I give them a sugar-lump each, for winning? And one for Prince, to make it fair.'

'Carry on,' said Walter, moving over with his brushes and curry comb to Captain, who was a perfect match for Flower except that his dappling was a little darker, and his build a little heavier. 'But as to next year who's to know where me and the horses'll be? Manor Farm's been sold, just like that, over all our heads and no warning.'

'Walter — no!' Tess and John stared at him.

'I seen the new man down here two or three times, never dreaming what he were here for. But the boss he tells me they clinched the deal this morning, while I were ploughing.'

'But can't you stay on with the new man — you and the horses?' John asked. 'I should think he'd be glad to have a champion ploughman and a team like this.'

'That's just where you're mistaken, son.' Walter was brushing out Captain's silver mane, still crinkly from the morning's festive plaits. The 'new gents' mechanical. He don't hold with horses and that — like most of 'em, today.'

'Perhaps whoever buys the horses will take you on with them,' John suggested. 'They aren't likely to have a better ploughman, whoever they are.'

Walter looked up at them starkly, over Captain's broad back. 'No one buys horses much, these days, least of all old horses. Prince, there, he'll likely go to some smallholder chap — he's young and useful. But Flower and Captain, they're fifteen now, and they never worked for nobody but me. They wouldn't go kindly for a new horseman now, at their time of life.'

Tess wiped her sugary-slobbery palm on a handful of straw. 'But surely someone will pay something for Flower and Captain? Someone who sees what fine, beautiful horses they are, and who would be proud to have champions like them.'

'Ah. Someone'll bid, you bet. And that'll be the slaughter merchants. Fine, big horses is what they like above anything.'

John and Tess simply didn't believe what Walter said. They supposed he was exaggerating out of bitterness for what was going to happen. But Walter shook his head sadly. He brought his large hand down with a tender slap on Captain's rump and said: 'We got about one month, me and the horses. Me to find another job — who wants a horseman, nowadays? — and the horses... well... Anyway,' he added firmly, 'they've had a good life. A good, long, useful life, and all the while they carried flying colours.'

'But it mustn't happen!' Tess said. 'We'll have to do something — I don't know what, but there must be something. If they're too old to work for anybody but you, Walter, what about the Homes of Rest for Horses? Couldn't Flower and Captain retire? They jolly well deserve it, if any horses ever did.'

Walter nodded solemnly. 'I daresay. I thought about that, myself, but I reckon you got to pay to put horses in retirement. And another thing, even supposing some Home did offer to take 'em can you see the guv'nor letting, 'em go, and not getting anything back, when those slaughter gents'll put up forty or fifty quid apiece?'

The slant of sunlight had gone from the stable window and soon it would be dusk. John and Tess patted the horses and picked up their satchels. 'Cheer up, Walter! Something will happen, I'm sure it will. We'll let you know the moment we've thought of anything.'

But they couldn't do that, because when they thought of it they were in the bus on the way to school, the next morning. 'What we've got to do,' John said, 'is collect money for buying the horses and paying for their retirement.'

'But how much? And who from?'

'We'll find out how much. I'll write to one of the Homes. Then we'll just have to try everyone we know, and start a proper *Save the Horses Fund*.'

For the next few days they had no time at all for visiting the farm, except for one brief dash in and out to tell Walter the wonderful news that the Horses' Home had written to say that they would accept Flower and Captain for nothing at all, if necessary, so that everything was surely going to be all right.

'Oh dear, it simply must be, now we've said so,' Tess said anxiously.

But by the end of the first week the Fund stood at only £15.10. John and Tess went up to the farm on the Saturday morning to tell Walter that they were still pushing on.

'We must reach £80 somehow, and we're going to, however unlikely it looks now.' Walter looked at them gravely over Captain's steaming back. The horses had just come in from the fields and were being unharnessed for the dinner hour.

'Look young uns,' he said gently, 'you better forget that Fund, see. You can't make it, now. The guv'nor he fixed up with the slaughter men; £45 for Captain, here, and £40 for Flower. Saturday noon.'

'Oh, Walter! But that's only a week.' Walter nodded, saying nothing. But after a minute he said suddenly and fiercely; 'I won't let 'em have my horses, though. My horses go through their murder-sheds?' He looked at the three of them, the brown and the greys, lovingly. 'That Prince, he's all right! going to the brewery. But my greys...'

'What are you going to do, Walter?' Tess looked at him half hopefully, half apprehensively.

'I got me own gun,' said Walter, with a strange kind of dignity. 'I won't let 'em suffer. Sooner put 'em down myself merciful, I would, than let those pirates get a hand on them. And they can do what they like to me, afterwards. My horses 've served me all their lives, and now I stand to serve them.'

John and Tess were very shaken. Their chances of raising enough money to outbid the slaughterers before the following Saturday were so small as to be almost hopeless.

'There must be a way,' said John, 'if only we can think of it.'

But no one they knew seemed to be any better than they were at thinking of it. And the next two days at bob-a-jobbing only added a further £ 3.50 to the Fund, though everyone at both John's and Tess's schools had done their best.

Then suddenly, during breakfast on Tuesday morning, the children's mother said, 'You could try writing to the paper perhaps.'

'The paper? Gosh, yes, I suppose we could!' John said. 'But do you think they'd put it in? Or that many people would help us if they did? I mean, Walter and the horses would be strangers to them.'

But when they met in the bus, coming home again that evening, John said to Tess; 'I wrote that letter to the paper. If they put it in, and anyone answers, we'll get the letters on Saturday morning.'

'But Saturday morning is...' Tess began uncertainly. Then, 'John! Listen! We must go to the farm at once and tell Walter to wait until after the post before — before...'

her voice failed.

'At least an hour after the post, to give us time to get to the farm,' John said. 'But of course, the paper might not print my letter.'

The paper did print it. John and Tess could hardly concentrate at all on Friday's lessons, because of wondering whether enough people could possibly, at that moment, be writing out enough cheques and postal orders to save the horses.

On Saturday morning the postman came up the path as usual and pushed two letters through the letter-box. They were both ordinary business circulars. John and Tess simply couldn't look at each other. Finishing breakfast was quite out of the question. Neither of them had felt so awful in all their lives. The morning began its heavy footed, slow progress, until it was nearly three-quarters of an hour after the postman's visit. Tess wouldn't look at the clock, but John was looking at it all the time. Tess just stared hopelessly out of the window. And that was why she saw the red van first. It pulled up outside their gate, behind the hedge, and she could see a postman's cap bobbing along towards the doors at the back of the van.

'John — it's a post office van!' She hardly dared hope. But John, dashing across to the window, felt that he had known all along that help must be coming — if only it came in time.

'A whole sack! Look, Tess. A sackful of letters, just for us!' They tore through the room and down the hall and opened the door.

'Too many for the postman's bicycle,' grinned the man with the sack. 'What've you started, then? A mail order business?'

It was fifty minutes from the time of the first postman's visit. John's usually slow brain jumped to the only answer. 'I say, sir! Could you possibly take the sack, and us with it, straight to Manor Farm? Now, sir? You see, it's matter of life and death.'

'Walter! We've got a whole sackful of letters!'

'We can explain everything on the way,' pleaded Tess.

The driver looked at them. 'Right. Hop in,' he said. 'It's against regulations, but with life and death you've got to make allowances, eh?'

In less than two minutes John had him breaking a further regulation, because he had never driven that van so fast, in all his twelve years at the post office, and even up the bumpy track to Manor Farm they hardly slowed down. In the farmyard they threw themselves out as the van came to a stop and raced across the concrete to the stable.

'Walter!'

He was tying a white cloth round Flower's eyes.

'Walter! We've got a whole sackful of letters here, and probably every one with money in it. They came late, because there were so many. We brought them as quickly as we could.'

Walter turned towards them with a slow, incredulous look; and then he slipped the bandage down from Flower's eyes. 'A sackful, you said, eh?'

'We've got to count up and see how much there is, Walter. We'll need you to help.'

It took them more than an hour and a half to make even a hurried, rough calculation. Every letter had to be opened, and the sum inside noted on the envelope for sending letters of thanks. Then all had to be quickly added up: and the time was ticking on towards noon in a way that made Tess's heart jump. The total was £ 94.35. And the time was 11.45.

'God bless us all, let's take it to the guv'nor, quick!' said Walter.

'It's enough for buying the horses and paying their fare,' said John, as they hurried to the farmhouse, 'and with our own Fund added we'll be able to send quite a lot to the Horses' Home, too, towards their keep.'

And that, exciting though it was, was not quite the end; because one day in the next autumn, when Walter was visiting his horses, the Manager of the Horses' Home said to him: 'I suppose you know that the County Ploughing Match is being held in this village, next month? Why not come over and enter Flower and Captain, just once more?'

And Walter did just that.

Tess and John still have the letter he wrote to them afterwards, which says: 'I only wish you could have been there and seen my horses get their dozen and century! I reckon you'd have been as proud as I was, since we'd never have done it, but for you.'

MARY'S NEW FRIEND
by
Margaret Biggs

Mary Turner stood at the open French windows staring dreamily out across the smooth lawn her father had cut the night before. The garden was neat and tidy. Not a weed could be seen. The room in which Mary stood was equally spotless. Everything was orderly, well-arranged and, Mary thought, just plain dull.

Mrs Turner came into the room and looked at her daughter in faint perplexity. Mary so often stood gazing at nothing nowadays. What could be the matter with her?

'Have you done your homework, Mary?' she asked.

Mary said, without perceptible interest, 'I finished it a few minutes ago, Mother.'

'That's right,' said her mother, in her comfortable voice. 'Well, then, you'll soon be going up to bed — it's past half-past eight.'

'Oh Mother, nobody in my form goes as early as I do!' burst out Mary rebelliously, swinging round.

She was a tall, slim girl, with yellow hair cut in a fringe and curling round her ears. Her grey eyes glowed indignantly at her mother from beneath thick dark brows. She was nearly thirteen, and full of contradictory moods that perplexed her and made her unhappy. She did not understand herself lately, and she knew her parents wondered what was the matter, but she couldn't help it, she didn't know herself. She just didn't feel happy.

Mrs Turner sighed. 'Oh Mary, don't let's have another argument. We have so many nowadays. I tell you what —

211

your father's just going to take the dog for a walk along the front as far as the pier. Would you like to go with him?'

'No thanks,' said Mary, rather ungraciously. As if a walk with her father would be a treat, as if she was a *child*, she thought indignantly.

'Well, then...' At a loss, Mrs Turner decided to withdraw. 'I'm just popping across to Mrs Bruce's with that book I promised her. I'll only be five minutes. You'll be all right, won't you?'

'Oh Mother, of course I will!'

'There's no need to use that tone,' said Mrs Turner, injured. 'Really, Mary, I do think...' But her daughter without waiting to hear the end of the sentence, suddenly marched out into the garden.

'I am a beast to her, but I can't help it,' she thought, pausing to smell a soft pink rose waving in the evening wind.

'Mary — are you coming with me?'

That was her father. Mary turned reluctantly, knowing his feelings would be hurt. Yes, there he stood, beaming fondly at her, which made her feel worse, with Fred, the Sealyham, cavorting excitedly at his side.

'I don't think I will, Dad, thanks,' she said, coming slowly across the lawn towards him.

Mr Turner looked rather disappointed, as Mary had known he would. 'Oh — aren't you? Come on, a walk will do you good — better than mooning about here.'

'I don't want to, thanks,' said Mary, colouring.

'Oh, all right then, please yourself. You used to like coming out with me,' said her father. 'Come on, Fred, we'll be going.'

The gate clicked behind him. Rather guiltily, Mary felt vast relief. Her father was a dear — so was her mother, in a different way, — but oh, how they annoyed her by still treating her as if she was about six! At the weekend, for example, her mother had refused point-blank to let her join the newly-formed Youth Group, half a mile away. Mary had been bitterly disappointed, and had even shed tears, secretly, in her bedroom. She wanted to do something new, something exciting, something different.

The Turners lived in Felpham, a quiet little place just out of Bognor. Mr Turner commuted up to town every day, to work in the City. Mrs Turner was an excellent, efficient housewife. They both adored their only child, but did not understand her in the least.

'Why Mary shouldn't be happy I just can't imagine,' said Mrs Turner several times a week. 'She's got a good home. I'm sure she's got more clothes and more pocket-money than most girls her age, and she gets her own way in almost everything. Why she's so moody and difficult these days I just can't understand!' And her husband agreed, with equally puckered brow.

Mary wandered slowly round the garden, kicking at the ground with one well-polished sandal. Everything seemed dull, she thought resentfully. School, home, everything went on and on in the same tedious way, and never changed. When she left school, her father would get her a job in his firm. It had already been arranged. Mary felt stifled at the thought.

'Oy!'

Startled by a sudden yell, Mary jerked her head up. A thin boy in dirty blue jeans, with blazing red hair, was sitting on the fence staring at her.

'Oh — you!' he called out, as Mary gazed at him in astonishment.

Who on earth was he? Next door lived Miss Spencer, an elderly retired school-mistress. Surely he couldn't be anything to do with *her*? Mary advanced, and saw that the boy was grinning.

'You *were* wool-gathering, weren't you?' he said. 'First I tried whistling, but you didn't take a scrap of notice. You're not deaf, by any chance, are you?'

Despite his disreputable appearance, he had a pleasant voice. 'What do you want? Who are you?' asked Mary, in what she hoped was a dignified manner.

'I'm James Fraser,' said the boy 'I've come over to see my aunt. Yes, Miss Spencer. We've just come to live down here, and I was looking round the garden when I saw you. So I thought I'd talk to you.'

'Oh,' said Mary.

'I suppose you're Mary Turner. My aunt's been telling me what a nice, quiet, well-behaved girl lives next door,' said James with an infuriating laugh.

'Oh, has she?' said Mary colouring, at a loss for anything better to say. 'Where have you come to live?'

'In the next road. We used to live in Hampstead, but the flat got too small for us when we had the twins, so Dad decided to take a chance and migrate down here,' said James. The fence creaked ominously beneath him, but he took no notice. 'Dad's a painter. There are lots of us. I'm the eldest — I'm thirteen. Then there's Judith, she's eleven, John, who's eight, and the twins. They're only two, and a bit of a bind, but not bad sometimes.'

'Oh,' said Mary, letting out her breath in a long drawn-out sigh. 'Aren't you lucky! I'm always wishing I had a brother or a sister.'

'Are you an only, then? I often think *I* wouldn't mind being one!' said James with a chuckle. 'Our house is always full of people shouting and charging about. Can I come over and look round your garden?' And, while Mary was still hesitating, he took a jump, and landed in the middle of Mr Turner's carefully tended lettuce rows.

'They'll bob up again,' he said optimistically, removing his feet from several squashed-looking plants. 'I'm sorry about that.'

'Oh, it doesn't matter,' said Mary without a qualm. What did a few lettuces matter? She was beginning to enjoy herself. Nobody could accuse James of being dull!

'I'm afraid there's not much to see,' she said apologetically, as James looked around with interest.

'Dad never does a thing in our garden. He says he enjoys

a wilderness, but Mum gets furious sometimes,' said James. 'This new house we've just moved to has got an orchard at the bottom, rather fun, and a gate at the bottom of that, which leads down to the beach.'

'It sounds nice,' said Mary.

'You must come and look round. Drop in any time,' said James hospitably. 'People always do with us. It's an older house than yours and it needs painting. Dad says he'll probably get round to it eventually!'

'Is — is your father a *famous* painter?' said Mary. 'No, not a scrap, but he will be one day. He's *good*,' said James with great seriousness, staring at Mary as if she might contradict him.

'Oh yes, I'm sure he is...' Mary began in confusion, when Miss Spencer's rather acid voice could be heard calling, James! *James!*' with gathering impatience.

'I'd better go,' said James. He hitched up his jeans and eyed the fence. 'I think I can get back over there. Well, how about coming to tea tomorrow? Just come any time you like after school, and meet the family. You and I can have a look round the town perhaps. I don't know my way around yet. I knew London, of course, like the back of my hand.' A still more irritated '*James*' sounded from the other side of the fence. 'I'll have to go, or she'll get really livid. See you tomorrow, all right?'

'Well, I would like to — yes, all right!' said Mary eagerly.

She watched James swarm over the fence and disappear from view. She could hear Miss Spencer telling him off, and James sounding very apologetic and submissive. Mary hoped he wouldn't get into trouble — she was a bit scared of Miss Spencer herself — and was much relieved to hear Miss Spencer laugh, after a few moments, and say something that sounded like 'You're incorrigible, James — exactly like your father!'

James appealed to Mary enormously. Into her hidebound, fenced-in life he burst like a rocket, scattering showers of sparks. She knew her parents would take a dim view of him, but she was determined to get to know him better and meet his no doubt fascinating family. Fancy meeting a painter!

So the next day she told her mother casually, as she was going off to school, that she might be a bit late home. She did not actually say so, but she implied that some school event might delay her. Mrs Turner relieved to see her daughter more sunny-tempered, asked no question, but only said, as she poured another cup of coffee, 'I see, dear. Well, you won't be back too late, I hope.' Mary escaped from the house and cycled off to school feeling guilty, but delighted.

When she reached the Fraser's house, just after four that afternoon, she suddenly felt timid and shy, so she was glad to coincide with James, striding in at the battered front gate. He hailed her breezily like an old friend, shoved her carefully looked-after bicycle into the empty garage, which had a door swinging off one hinge, and led her into the garden. 'They'll mostly be out here, I expect,' he said and proved to be right.

Mary found the Frasers bewildering but delightful. After her own careful houseproud mother, Mrs Fraser, placidly reading a book while her two-year-old twins clambered all over her with grimy faces, and her other children shouted noisily round her, was rather a shock. Of Mr Fraser there was no sign and nobody, least of all his wife, seemed to know where he was. 'He never knows exactly where he's going until he's come back,' she remarked to Mary cheerfully. The back garden was choked with dandelions and some of the rooms still had no curtains up, but Mrs Fraser seemed perfectly at ease. She took a vague but friendly interest in Mary and told James to find her something to eat if she was hungry, then returned to her book. Eventually James and Mary picnicked in the kitchen, which was the untidiest Mary had ever seen, with Judith and John leaning against the draining-board eating Ryvita and butter and talking, generally simultaneously. They were all nice, though, Mary decided, and once you got used to the noise and began to shout yourself, instead of being polite and waiting for them to listen to you, it was great fun. Judith was to go to Mary's school the next term, and was eager for information about it, which Mary enjoyed supplying. Then talk turned to swimming, and to her surprise Mary found all the Frasers could swim, expect the twins. Mary was rather sorry. They all seemed so brilliant and unusual that she had hoped to be a better swimmer, at least — but no.

After tea, James and Mary went for a cycle ride round Felpham. Mary, who had been taught to keep well in to the kerb, look both ways at each junction and generally be very cautious and careful, found James's erratic weaving in and out, and darting round corners without the slightest warning, rather alarming. But she soon saw that despite his apparent recklessness he really took no chances and felt better. They rode along by the sea, and stopped to gaze at it. It was a warm evening and quite a number of people were walking on the beach still. The sea was far out, still and grey-blue. James sniffed. 'Gorgeous smell,' he said. 'Have you always lived by the sea?'

'Yes, I was born here,' said Mary.

'It must be funny to live in one place all the time,' said James thoughtfully. 'I've lived in Scotland, and Yorkshire and then Hampstead, before coming here.'

Mary felt alarmed. 'Oh, I do hope you stay,' she said.

'Would you miss me?' said James, laughing.

Mary nodded, unable to express her feeling of sudden dismay. James represented adventure to her, and all the things she had never had. 'Funny kid,' said James loftily. But really he was rather pleased.

The friendship, that had sprung up so suddenly between them, deepened and in a few days they were practically inseparable. James was always dropping in at Mary's house, lending her books or records, wandering about from room to room or lying stretched out anywhere he could find, scanning a book that caught his eye. He was a great reader and he found the Turner's house incredibly peaceful. He genuinely liked Mary and found her hero-worship delightful.

Mary's parents were taken aback by this out-of-the-blue friendship. Who on earth *was* this strange boy with shaggy red hair? Reassured to learn he was Miss Spencer's nephew, they were dubious again when they learnt his father was a painter and that he lived in one the crumbling Victorian houses in Waterton Road. What on earth did Mary see in him? Up until now all her friends had been equally well-brought up girls. They just did not understand this boy.

'I expect in a few weeks they'll drop each other,' said Mr Turner reassuringly to his wife. 'They've nothing in common.'

'His clothes look as if they're never brushed — and his shoes!' said Mrs Turner, sighing. 'I don't know how his parents can let him go about in that state. But Mary gets so cross if I criticise him. I'm sure he's a bad influence on her, Phil.'

'Well, we'll just keep an eye on things. He's an intelligent boy,' said Mr Turner. 'He can't help it if he comes from a beatnik family, I suppose.'

'Miss Spencer tells me that the father is completely unpredictable, but charming when he wants to be,' said Mrs Turner. 'And they have five children — how on earth can his wife cope?'

It was all puzzling, but Mary showed no sign of growing tired of her new friend and she and James continued to spend most of their spare time together. Mr Turner began to enjoy James's company and looked forward to their grave discussions on county cricket, but Mrs Turner remained uneasy. She had always vetted Mary's friends and until recently Mary had always been biddable and docile. But nowadays Mary was so quick to take offence... It was all very difficult, and poor Mrs Turner fretted and worried all the time. She spoke coolly to James, hoping he would take the hint, but he did not notice her snubs and went on cheerfully coming whenever he wanted to.

'Won't your mother be wondering where you are?' she said pointedly to James one evening, when he stayed on and on playing records.

'Oh no. She knows I can look after myself. She probably hasn't even noticed I'm not there,' said James, grinning.

'I expect she's quite dreadful,' thought Mrs Turner.

To Mary, James was the older brother she had always longed for. She followed his lead wherever she could, in books, music and sports. She could not play cricket, unfortunately, but James was also mad on tennis and Mary and he spent many hours, as the summer evenings grew longer, playing on the public courts at the end of Mary's road. Sometimes Mr Fraser sauntered down to watch, bringing John and Judith. He never said much, rather to Mary's relief, but he was perfectly unalarming and would silently hand round chunks of nut-milk chocolate when they were winding down the net and packing up. Mary thought he looked disappointingly ordinary to be a painter, but James proudly showed her some of his father's paintings, and she found them inexplicable but awe-inspiring. She told everybody at school she knew an artist and basked in reflected glory.

About a month after the two had met, Mr Turner had to go down to Devon on business for two or three days. Mrs Turner was always nervous when he was away and when Mary got back from tennis with James a few minutes later than she had been told to, she lost her temper. 'It's always the same when you're with that boy — you don't think of anything else,' she said. 'It's getting absurd. You hardly see any of your other friends. Why not?'

'I like James best,' said Mary, scowling defensively. 'Well, I'm tired of having him always here, and I wish you'd tell him,' said Mrs Turner sharply. 'And all this tennis has got to stop. You come in too tired to do your homework properly — yes, you do, don't argue! I want you to see less of him Mary, do you understand?'

'I shan't, why should I?' flared Mary indignantly, at once up in arms on James's behalf. 'You're unfair to him. He's the nicest person I've ever met and all you do is criticise him. You're — you're horrible to him!'

From this promising beginning they both went on to say more than they meant. In the end Mary shouted at the top of her voice: 'You don't care a scrap about me!' and charged out of the room. The slam of the door made all the ornaments rattle precariously. 'Oh *dear*,' said Mrs Turner unhappily. She felt she had been unjust, but really, if *only* Mary would be the biddable, easy child she had once been.

At breakfast the next morning she was conciliatory, but Mary sat crunching cornflakes and refused to say anything except 'Yes' and 'Pass the toast, please'. She cycled off to school without her usual smile and wave and Mrs Turner cleared the table unhappily. She felt she was in the wrong, yet she did *not* feel James was a suitable friend and surely she, as Mary's mother, could tell Mary what she thought? 'I wish Phil were here. He seems to understand Mary better lately,' she thought as she washed up.

Mary felt cross all day. She raged in James's defence. How could her mother be so unfair on him? 'I wish I was grown-up,' thought Mary bitterly. Years of doing as she was told seemed to stretch ahead of her. 'Grown-ups do exactly as they like and order everybody else about,' she brooded. 'They never listen properly, they just don't bother.' She thought enviously of James's mother, who gave him so much freedom. 'She understands, but Mother just won't try.'

And suddenly, as she was cycling out of the school gates, she thought: 'I know, I just won't go home, at least not for ages. I'll stay out.' She knew her mother would be worried to death, but she felt hard and defiant about her. 'I'll go for a long cycle ride. It'll be light for hours. I can go miles before lighting-up time. And serve Mother right if she does worry,' said a little demon inside her.

She cycled slowly, free-wheeling, down Waterton Road

and met James, as she had hoped, near the corner. James looked hot and tired. He had his cricket-pads and bat dangling from his bicycle.

'Hallo,' he said. 'You look a bit funny. Anything the matter?'

'No,' said Mary. 'I'm going for a ride around. I might even go to Arundel,' she added on the spur of the moment. 'How about coming?'

'I'd want some tea first. I've been bowling nearly all afternoon. I'm famished and worn out,' said James frankly.

'Oh,' said Mary, 'Well...' She fet somewhat rebuffed.

'Something's up,' thought James, eyeing her. 'I tell you what,' he said, 'come and have tea at my house first, and then we can go out afterwards. What time have you got to be back home?'

'Oh, no special time — any time I want to,' said Mary airily.

James was surprised, knowing Mary's mother. 'Well, come on, anyhow,' he suggested. 'Mother's out, she's taken the twins up to town, and John and Judith are having tea at a neighbour's until she gets back, so we can get ourselves something. There's always plenty in the 'frig.'

'All right, thanks, I'd like to, if you're sure your mother wouldn't mind,' said Mary.

'Mother never minds anything,' said James, smiling. 'You ought to know, by now! Come on, then.'

They took ham and tomatoes and bread and butter out on to the lawn and ate, balancing the plates on their knees. James found some ginger-beer and they shared the bottle. After finishing up with biscuits and some apples James found in the larder, they both felt better. 'Now, what's all this about cycling to Arundel?' said James, flopping on to his back in the grass and shutting his eyes against the sun. 'It's quite a few miles, you know.'

'I know how far it is, much better than you do,' said Mary. 'Oh, sorry,' she added, as James turned his head in surprise. 'I'm in a vile mood at present. You're so lucky, James —

your mother never interferes with you!'

'No,' said James, after a pause, 'but she sometimes forgets. Like the match we had at school today. She said last week she'd come and bring the twins, but then she forgot and went up to town instead. Most chaps' mothers came. Not that I minded — I know she's got an awful lot to think of with five of us to look after and Dad as well.'

Mary was silent. James *had* minded, she could tell from his voice. Her own parents always supported her punctiliously at school functions. Still, he obviously did not want her to criticise his mother.

'Yes, of course,' she mumbled.

'Well, what do you want to cycle to Arundel for?' repeated James. 'Just to annoy your mother?' he added shrewdly.

'No, of course not,' said Mary. It seemed so childish put like that. She tugged at a blade of grass. 'Why do you think that?'

'Just a guess. You want to grow up a bit,' said James with a shrug.

'Oh, do I?' said Mary, sitting bolt upright and glaring at him. *James* to turn on her. It was staggering. 'You don't know anything about it. I...'

'Oh, pack it in,' said James. 'I know your mother gets on your nerves. I like her myself, that's all.'

'Well, naturally I'm fond of her myself — it's only that she's so bossy. And...' Mary hesitated.

'Oh, you needn't bother about hurting my feelings. I know she doesn't think I'm a suitable friend for her little well-behaved daughter,' said James, rather wryly.

'You know? How on earth...'

'Oh, I can tell what people think. It doesn't worry me,' said James. 'I don't want to make trouble at home for you,' he added, after a pause. 'It's been fun, but perhaps, if you're really falling out with your mother about me...'

'I don't care *what* she says, you're my friend — at least, if you want to be,' said Mary, suddenly abashed.

James sat up and grinned at her. 'You're nice, Mary.

Then something knocked her sideways

You're my friend too.'

'That's settled, then,' said Mary, feeling better. They exchanged a self-conscious smile.

'I tell you what,' said James — it was a favourite phrase of his. 'Let's have a ride around, but not as far as Arundel, and then I'll come to your home and be very polite. I'll make a good impression on your mother and she'll decide I'm so charming she was wrong about me. How about that?'

But Mary shook her head. She was determined to make some positive gesture of independence. 'She wouldn't change her mind. No, I'm going to show her she can't dictate to me. I'm going to be late home and when she asks where I've been I'll tell her it's nothing to do with her ...'

James shook his head sagely. 'You idiot, you'll make things ten times worse.'

Suddenly, Mary felt cross with him. He was only a few months older, yet there he sat, talking as if she were a half-wit. She jumped up. 'All right, say what you like, I'll go by myself, then.' And she ran across the lawn to get her bike from the garage.

'No, hang on, I'll come — hey, *wait,* you little dope, don't fly off the handle like that,' shouted James after her.

Mary ignored him. She was sick and tired of people telling her what to do and what not to do. She seized her bike and pedalled out of the Fraser's gate, hanging open, as always, propped back with a brick. She rode straight out into the road, too angry and full of passion against the whole world to look round first. 'I'll jolly well go to Arundel by myself,' she thought furiously, 'and I won't get back until I feel like it!' Then, all of a sudden, she saw a sleek, cream-coloured Jaguar looming up in front of her. The driver was wrenching at the wheel, staggered to see the cyclist who had shot out without warning on the wrong side of the road. He sounded his horn frantically, and he was shouting, Mary could see, only above the roar of his engine she couldn't hear him. Everything seemed to be happening at once. She pulled in terror on her brakes but they didn't have time to act. What on earth would happen? The great bonnet of the car was rearing up in front of her when something knocked her sideways, out of the car's way. She fell crookedly on to the pavement, grazing her leg and found herself sitting there, staring stupidly around, feeling dazed. The Jaguar had halted, its front wheels straddling her bike. Mary felt sick and her head was swimming. She began trying to get up.

'Here, come on, Gormless,' said a familiar voice in her ear. 'Sorry I had to knock you sideways like that, but I couldn't think what else to do. You're all right, aren't you?'

It was James, of course. Mary swallowed, fought back her sick feeling, and nodded. She wanted to cry, but she knew James would hate that. 'Yes, I'm all right,' she said shakily.

'Good thing I came out after you,' said James conversationally. 'Of all the idiotic things to do. Oh well, cheer up.' He went over to the driver, who was leaning out of the front window looking relieved, but rather cross. Mary stood by and let James deal with things. James had a charmingly deferential manner with adults when he chose, and in three minutes the driver, mollified, had moved off, with a final warning shake of his head at Mary. James picked up Mary's bicycle and wheeled it over to its owner.

'The front wheel's buckled, but your father might be able to straighten it. Decent chap, that,' he said. 'He might have made much more of it, You were in the wrong, you know — it wasn't *his* fault at all. You frightened him to death, he said, coming out of nowhere like that!'

Mary shivered. 'Oh James, I just never thought — oh, what a fool I am!' Her voice trembled.

'Well, never mind. The main thing is, you're all right,' said James. He leaned the bicycle against the hedge. 'Your leg's bleeding — come and put some T.C.P. on it, and then I'll walk you home. You won't get to Arundel tonight on *this!*'

'I don't want to go, anyhow,' said Mary. 'I feel all shaky. I want to go home.'

So, about ten minutes later, when Mrs Turner looked out of the window because Mary seemed to be very late out of school, she saw her erring daughter, very pale and with a large pad of adhesive bandage on her leg, come limping slowly along the road. Beside her walked the Fraser boy, wheeling Mary's bike — and what on earth had happened to the front wheel? Her heart in her mouth, Mrs Turner rushed to the front gate.

'Mary, what's happened? For goodness sake tell me — you look dreadful!'

'Oh Mother —' said Mary chokily. For once her mother's concern was very welcome, and exactly what she wanted. She leaned against her mother while James stood by in sympathetic silence. 'It was all my fault. I didn't look where I was going... James rushed after me and knocked me out of the car's way... it was awful. But for him I might have been killed!'

Mrs Turner's face was as white as Mary's. James said soothingly: 'It wasn't really as bad as that, Mrs Turner, and anyhow Mary's quite O.K., just a bit shaken up.' And, as Mrs Turner went on looking wordlessly at him, he found himself explaining the incident, minimising it as much as he could. Gosh, didn't Mary's mother look upset! When he ended, Mrs Turner, her arm tight around her daughter, said jerkily: 'I don't know how to thank you, James. But for you, I just daren't think...' She failed to finish the sentence, because her voice gave way. She drew a deep breath, tried to collect herself, and said more normally: 'Come in, both of you. We can't stand out here by the gate. We can talk better in the house.'

'I'll go home. You don't want me,' began James quickly.

'No, please come in, James. I want to thank you properly!' said Mrs Turner. Her mind was in a turmoil, but she was sure of one thing, she had entirely misjudged the boy. 'I'll be fair to him in future, and not so stupid and dictatorial,' she vowed to herself.

So the three of them sat round in the Turner's front room, eating jam tarts and drinking the coffee Mrs Turner had hastily brewed, all talking at once. Mary saw that her mother liked James at last, and her heart grew light as a feather. Her leg ached, and her bike was probably ruined, but what did that matter? She could tell that her mother's attitude to James would be vastly different from now on.

When James got up to say goodbye about an hour later, Mrs Turner said suddenly: 'The vicar called round here today. He asked if you wanted to join that new Youth Group of his, Mary.'

Mary looked in astonishment at her mother. 'I told him I thought you and James might both like to go along. So he's hoping to see you next Wednesday,' Mrs Turner went on.

'Oh Mother, how super-duper!' Mary's face shone. 'But I thought...'

'I know, I didn't want you to, but I've decided I was wrong. It's high time you joined something of the sort. And if James goes along he can keep an eye on you,' said Mrs Turner, smiling at James.

'Mrs Turner, you're wonderful,' said James solemnly. 'Isn't she, Mary?'

'Perfect,' said Mary, jumping up and hugging her mother. And that hug expressed a lot, as they both knew.

FOG

by

Lorna Wood

L etty's elder sister, who went to the Grammar School, often said:
'I can't think how you stand having those kids with you all the way.'

And Letty, who didn't really mind, usually mumbled something about taking no notice of them.

'You can't *not* take any notice when it's a country bus. There aren't so many people on it as all that. Of course, if there were enough of you you'd have a school bus like us.'

'Well there aren't. And anyway I don't like crowds.'

'You'll have to get used to them when you come to our school — if you pass the exam, of course.'

Letty never replied to that because she knew, and Delia knew, that of course she would pass. She had what her father called 'a nose for exams' and in a way that made up for the nose being snub and shiny and crowned with spectacles which the doctor said she wouldn't need when she was older. But it took a long time growing older and in the meantime one just had to put up with being plain and straight-haired and knobbly-kneed and all the things the heroines weren't in the books that Letty was usually buried in.

Now little Margaret was good-looking and Letty always liked to see her when she got on the bus. She was pink and placid and golden-haired with perfectly huge blue eyes. She had a lovely smile too, when she was pleased and in the mornings she was always pleased to see Letty. She was Number One. Then there was young Colin whose teeth were a bit gappy in the front and he wasn't too bright at school, but you couldn't help liking him, he was so affectionate, always bringing you the odd dandelion or offering you a bite of his apple. At the same stop as young Colin, Dennis got on. He was only nine but you always felt he was older, he was so solemn and remembered things like letting you go first and opening doors. Yes, Letty was rather fond of them all. It was nice to have children to look after when you were the youngest at home and really it was a good thing she *was* fond of them, because when they had started school their mothers had all said 'Look out for Letty Bray, she'll see you're all right,' — so they were, in a way, a responsibility.

November mornings were really rather beastly, reflected Letty, as she waited for the bus one Monday. It was bad enough for the trees to be leafless and to have her first chilblain because of the nipping cold, but it was still worse when there was fog in the air. Of course, the Brays lived so near the river that they always got the worst of it. The school Letty went to was on high ground and the air was nearly always clear and bright. She was glad to be going there now, as she stood listening to the slow dropping of moisture from the one sycamore tree at the stop and realised that she couldn't see much further than across the road. Still, a good wind would blow it all away. And the bus wasn't late. She clambered on to it, showing her season ticket to the conductor as she did so and sat down in the seat she practically always had, to wait for Margaret.

'Foggy this morning,' said the conductor, who was one of the friendly ones. 'Shouldn't wonder if it comes down thick. What'll you do if there's no bus home, eh?'

Letty just grinned. He seemed to be talking about something that was quite impossible. She'd never known the bus not to come or to break down and she thought it silly to consider such a thing. She watched Margaret get on, enveloped in an enormous muffler. Her smiling face peeped out, pink and shiny above it.

'Mummy said there was going to be fog. She said if it was thick I've got to put this over my nose and mouth, but I've tried and I can't breathe very well.'

'Well, let's hope it won't be as bad as that,' said Letty. 'Look, there are the boys. *They* haven't got mufflers.'

What Colin had got were two white mice which he displayed with pride. A lady sitting opposite uttered a faint squeak and Letty told him to keep them in their box.

'Anyway, you don't want them to escape.' But they probably would before the day was over, she reflected. Colin always lost everything, he was that kind of boy. She looked out of the window. They were going through a rather drab part of the town now, heaps of little side-streets, all named after Royal Houses. She had never been down any of them but she knew them off by heart: Stuart Street had a broken railing at the end, Plantagenet a sooty lilac-bush, Hanover a milk-bar and Windsor a 'Wayside Pulpit' notice-board. This morning they seemed endless in the heavy haze.

But about a mile further out of the town, the air cleared and the sun shone. Last night's frost still hung on the hedge-rows but was fast melting. 'Good,' thought Letty, 'hockey this lunch-hour.' At the stop for the school she chivvied the children in front of her, stopped Dennis and Colin hitting each other, even though they meant it in a friendly way and, jerking her satchel over her shoulder, set off up the country lane, Margaret's hand clasped in hers.

On the way, there was a Post Office van making repairs to the wires which were all down. The boys showed a disposition to linger but she swept them on. Really, perhaps her sister was right. Kids *were* a bother. She had begun, as she always did at this point, to look forward to seeing friends of her own age, exchanging bits of gossip, discussing hockey prospects. And the moment they all ran in together at the big gates, the children were swallowed up and she never saw them again until it was time to go: not even at lunch, because they ate in the junior dining-room.

At half-past-three, Miss Talbot, the principal, came into the classroom, when Letty was putting away her books.

'Letty,' she said, 'the radio says something about fog covering the south of England like a blanket. But look!' She flung out an arm towards the window, which framed a perfectly clear sky. You could see, not only down to the bottom of the garden but beyond it, over the fields.

'It looked nasty when we left this morning, Miss Talbot,' said Letty doubtfully. 'But it *is* very near. I shouldn't think it could be much.'

'Well, I hope not. The point is, I can't ring up and find out. The telephone isn't repaired yet and I hear they have the wires down in the village.'

'I should just let us go,' said Letty. 'We'll wait for the bus and if it doesn't come we can quite easily walk.'

'You mustn't walk,' said Miss Talbot firmly. 'If there's no bus, come straight back here.'

'But the parents would all be anxious, wouldn't they, Miss Talbot, if they — we — weren't back when they thought we ought to be?'

'Not if there's fog in town. But that's it, we don't know whether there is. Still, I am sure I can trust you, Letty, to do the sensible thing.'

'Thank you, Miss Talbot,' said Letty and resumed sorting her books as soon as the Principal had closed the door behind her.

'Grandma Letty — always so sensible,' murmured Susan Peach, who had the next locker to hers and who lived very near, in the village. 'Fancy having those kids round your neck — rather you than me.'

'Well, you haven't got them so you needn't grouch,' said Letty crossly, slamming her locker door and stalking out. Funny how cross it made you when people said you were sensible! Perhaps it wouldn't, if you had other gifts or were abolutely super-pretty.

She wandered about, collecting her brood. Good little

Margaret was waiting in the hall for her, sorting out the contents of her satchel — at least she said it was sorting out; what it really meant was putting them all in heaps, looking at them and putting them back in again, apart from having to take the biscuits and apple she had at eleven o'clock she really had no need to take a satchel at all.

'Can't think why you like that silly thing bumping on your back,' Dennis had commented.

Margaret always stuck out her lower lip when she was being obstinate.

'It's for my *things*. I need my things.'

And he couldn't very well say her things were daft because they were like the contents of his own pockets. Just now, Letty looking at them absently, took in the same old muddle of a ball of string, a whistle, a china doll without a head, two picture postcards, some old caramels, a pocket mirror and some foreign stamps no one would have because they were damaged and Margaret thought it would be a pity to throw away.

'Get packed up, lovey. Where are the boys?'

'Feeding Colin's mice, I think. Wait for me, Letty, I'm nearly ready.'

Colin was the centre of an admiring group, but Letty was pleased to see the mice were back in their box. Marvellous to think he'd got through the day without losing one of them.

'Come on, we're off.' She and Margaret started off down the drive and soon running feet caught them up.

'Gosh,' said Dennis, 'I'm hungry, I want my tea. Hope the bus isn't late.'

'It never is, or only a minute or two.'

'Well I hope it's early then. Jolly early so that there isn't anyone on it 'cept us and we can sit where we like.'

'That's selfish,' said Letty mechanically, although she was rather wishing the same thing. She looked at the watch she had been given last Christmas. 'It should be coming in exactly two minutes. Colin, if you go round and round the tree like that you'll make the mice dizzy.'

'*I'm* dizzy,' said Colin, sitting down flat on the pavement, 'but they aren't 'cos they can't see the tree.'

The boys began to argue about this, which took all of the two minutes and a bit more, but still the bus hadn't come. Nor did anything else and Colin, who had taken out his car numbers book, began to get irritable.

'Letty, when's it coming, can't we walk on?'

'And lose it? No fear.'

'It'd stop for us.'

'Well, they don't much care for stopping except at the stops. I know, let's all count sixty very slowly and if it hasn't come then, we'll think about walking on.'

So they all started to count sixty at the tops of their voices, but when they got to thirty they were interrupted by someone coughing. It was a man wheeling his bicycle up the road and it was a heavy, persistent cough, the type grown-ups had when they said 'I simply must stop smoking.' As he drew alongside them, he wiped his steaming eyes and said, 'No good you waiting for the bus. They're off the road. It's thick as a bag in town. Never seen anything like it. It'll be like ink when it's dark. You'd best go back to school.'

They stared at him, forgetting to thank him for the information, and he passed on, still coughing.

'Well,' Letty said, 'that settles it.'

Margaret's lower lip came out.

'I want to go home. I want my Mummy.'

'I want my tea,' said Dennis furiously, 'and once when I stayed at school for it it was only beastly bread and syrup.'

'*They* want their tea,' said Colin, pointing to the mice's box. 'Let's walk.'

'It's miles,' said Letty uncertainly, 'and I don't know where the fog begins. He didn't say.'

She was thinking she would like to be home, eating her tea and watching the big, glowing fire. They'd better telephone — oh no, they couldn't. It wasn't mended. But there'd be a call-box on the way, somewhere.

'Has anyone got two pence? I've only got my case-of-emergency five pence.'

Margaret had ten pence and the boys mustered three halfpence and a five pence piece.

'Oh well,' said Letty, 'We'll manage. There'll be a shop where we can get change. Come on and don't start squalling halfway. It's *miles* — three, I think.'

'Squall yourself,' said Dennis rudely. 'Only girls do that. *I* don't mind walking. I once walked four miles with my father when we were on holiday.' Meeting their unimpressed glances and realising he was being a 'big-head' he added: 'Course it was along the shore and it doesn't seem so long with the rock-pools and things.'

'Well, come on,' Letty said, walking rather quickly for Margaret's short legs, but she still felt a bit uncomfortable about the decision. 'Let's do it in three parts — there's here to the *Pony and Cart*, then *Pony and Cart* to the beginning of the town and then from there up to where I live. Let's sing *John Brown's Body* and the time'll go quicker.'

They did and it kept their spirits up, because although the light was going and lamps were being switched on in the houses they passed, they saw no one out, no traffic.

It was just past the *Pony and Cart* that they stepped into the fog. I hung like a white curtain across the roads. It was wet and nasty and you could hardly see a yard ahead of you. Letty's heart sank and she wished they'd ask her to go back, but no one said a word. Only Margaret's hand slid into hers and held it tightly.

'Keep to the kerb,' said Letty. 'If we follow that we'll go straight, otherwise round in circles, I should think — people do when they're lost.'

'We aren't lost,' said Dennis stumping along obstinately.

'If a big wind comes,' said Colin, 'it'll blow it all away and that'll be fun, won't it?'

Letty said it would and recommended the resumption of *John Brown's Body* but they didn't sing as heartily as before because the strange, wet, clinging fog somehow made it difficult and the effort finished up in coughing.

'Better keep quiet,' she said 'and soon we'll come to the shops — not that there are many round here, of course. But if we go single file and follow the kerb we can't go wrong.'

They walked on for about another ten minutes, their feet sounding loud to them. Then Dennis stopped and said:

'You know we jolly well can!'

'Don't *do* that,' said Letty crossly. 'I nearly fell over you. What d'you mean?'

'I mean if we follow the kerb we'll probably go down a side-road. And I believe we have. It went all curvy a few minutes ago. And there aren't any houses on this side. I bet you what you like we've gone on to the waste-ground. We ought to have passed a telephone box and we haven't.'

Letty licked her lips which tasted foggy.

'I'm an ass. We might have telephoned from the *Pony and Cart*. Then perhaps they could have come and got us.'

Margaret began to cry, not loudly, just soft little sniffs. Letty fumbled in her pocket and gave her a handkerchief. 'Never mind, ducky, we're not in the Sahara. We'll go to the first house we come to. They'll take us in. Tell you what, I think this waste-land is behind the 'Royal' roads, — you know, those little ones called Windsor and things. Let's all have a caramel — you've got some in your satchel — and stand and listen for some kind of noise.'

A sweet, however old and squashy, popped into your mouth is pretty good for cheering up. They stood sucking and listening. They heard a train crawl along, not very far away and the explosion of fog signals, then something that might have been a lorry, but they weren't sure; then, far over to the right, a dog barked and went on barking but not excitedly, the way dogs do when they are tied up.

'Let's go towards *him*.' Dennis said, 'and let's hope he

'The mice don't like this fog,' Colin said plaintively

doesn't stop. Gosh, this is beastly, 'specially now it's got so horribly dark!'

'It's an adventure,' said Colin staunchly. 'Got any more sweets?'

Once or twice the dog stopped but the sound came nearer and nearer and presently they saw the faint glow of a street lamp. This was, Letty felt sure, one of the little 'Royal' streets — never mind which one, they'd find that out later. They'd go to the first house with a light in it. Margaret fished out the last sweet each but in doing so dropped her satchel and they had to scrabble about picking everything up. Then they went forward towards the lamp and found the beginning of the street. They went past the house where the dog was barking, because Margaret was a bit frightened of him, and chose one which had a light in the front room, though the curtains were drawn. They could dimly hear a radio so it was certain somebody was in. They opened the front gate and Letty banged the knocker. Suddenly, the radio was turned off and so was the light. There was dead silence. They banged again and there was no response.

'The horrible, mean things!' exclaimed Dennis. 'Shall we shout through the letter-box or what?'

'No,' said Letty. 'Perhaps it's someone in alone and they're frightened. Let's go a bit further.'

'The mice don't like this fog,' said Colin plaintively. 'I think they want some air.'

'Well, they won't get very nice air, you nuggins, if you let them out of that box. Oh golly — that's torn it!'

For opening the box had been fatal. One of the mice was up Colin's arm and then away, as quick as it could go. Its owner burst into tears, soundless ones but he was unable to talk except in gulps. Kind Margaret put her arms round him and the other two went down on all fours but it was obviously hopeless.

'Look,' said Letty, 'we simply must go. Mice are awful to catch anyway, let alone in a fog. Let's find a *nice* house and

240

then perhaps we can come back. But Mummy'll be frantic and I bet yours will be, too. Do come on, I promise you we'll come back. It'll hide all the more if we're stamping round looking for it.'

'And these beasts,' Dennis said vengefully, 'will never come out and help us. I'll jolly well leave all my toffee-papers in their front garden and that will show them.'

'Oh, Dennis,' Letty said, but only half-heartedly because people who wouldn't open their doors when *anybody* might be lost in a fog *were* beasts, when you came to think of it.

The next house seemed blank and the one after that, but they could see a light further on and actually hear the voices of children so they hastened towards it. But before they got there they heard a Tread, a nice, heavy, reassuring one and soon there loomed up a tall figure — could it be? — it was — it *was* a policeman.

'Now then,' he said, switching on a yellow-tinted torch, 'nasty time for you to be out, isn't it?'

They flung themselves on him, even Colin, who was still sadly sniffling about the mouse.

'Oh please, we're sort of lost...'

'...we couldn't imagine the fog would be so bad...'

'...I've lost my mouse...'

'One at a time, please,' said the policeman, 'and anyway you can all come with me, there's a police car about a hundred yards along.'

It seemed wonderful to think of any kind of car being out and they didn't ask why. Letty and Margaret each joyously seized a hand and Dennis began to whistle *John Brown's Body*. Only Colin still wept and Letty's heart was touched:

'Oh please... it's his white mouse... it escaped... I'm going back to have a *little* look.'

And knowing she would be told not to bother, she darted back the way they had come, this time judging her progress by the little brick walls that fronted the gardens. The house they'd tried hadn't had any privet in the front, that much

241

she'd noticed. Anyway, helpfully, the light was on again and
the radio too. They'd left the gate open and she went through:
by the step there was a tiny gleam of white... it wasn't...
it was... it *was* the mouse huddled up! She scooped it into
her pocket and creeping to the window, peeped through a
crack in the curtains. Then she hurried out again to join the
Feet which she heard coming along the pavement.

'Now, young miss,' said the policeman, 'found your mouse
have you? Good, but get along. Funny thing they didn't
open the door to you. The boy's just been telling me — now
mind how you go!'

'It doesn't matter,' said Letty. 'I'm getting used to it in
a funny kind of way. But what funny people they were, not
to open the door — and they couldn't have been frightened,
because there were two or three of them, all men. And you
can't imagine what they were doing — cleaning the silver,
at this time of day!'

'Eh?' said the policeman stopping dead. 'Are you sure?'

'Well, they must have been because it was all there on
a table, ever so twinkling and they were putting it away into
bags...'

'Hurry up, miss,' said the policeman, 'hurry up to the car.
All sorts of things happen in fog and one of 'em's burglaries.
That's Lady Whitelock's silver, unless I'm very much mistaken — went this afternoon. But...' and he stopped dead —
'you're sure you'd know the house?'

'Of course I would! It hasn't got any privet hedge like the
others down here.'

'And all my toffee-papers are in the front garden,' said
Dennis's voice happily from the car. 'I say, can we watch
you make an arrest?'

'It looks,' said the policeman, 'as though you're going to.'

But it didn't work out quite like that. The thieves got
away in the fog, through the back door. Still, as you can't
run for very long with heavy weights they left the silver behind and it was returned that night to Lady Whitelock. When

Letty was happily sitting by the fire, a cup of hot soup at her elbow and the assurance that none of them would go to school the next day if it was still foggy heartening her, the telephone rang. Her mother went to answer it.

'Darling,' she said, coming into the room again. 'Lady Whitelock simply insists on some sort of a reward. She'll talk that over with Daddy but in the meantime she wants to know if there's anything small you particularly want.'

Letty yawned. The strain of the day was telling on her and she wanted her bed.

'I,' she said dreamily, 'would like a big yellow torch like the policeman's. I should think Dennis and Margaret would like simply heaps of sweets.'

'And Colin?'

'I am afraid,' said Letty sadly, 'another white mouse.'

ENGLISH SPOKEN HERE

by

Stephen Mogridge

The rumble of the early train to Paris and the screech of its hoarse whistle woke Fay Richards. She stirred sleepily on her camp bed, then came wide awake with an anxious start. She looked round the tent. It was empty. Her sister, Tess, had already gone.

Something like panic gripped Fay. She sat up, tossing back her fair hair and looking through the mosquito netting of the tent window at the ilex tree under which their washing line was strung. Tess had pegged out a tea towel and the sight of it reminded Fay of the day's chores. For the first time she would be facing them entirely on her own. At the thought another wave of hot-and-cold alarm swept over her. The chores included shopping, which would have to be done in French, and her French was... well, neglected. Also she was shy, and the thought of drawing attention to herself in public made her shudder.

Voices chattering in French, as the occupants of the tent behind stirred, only increased her anxiety.

'*Du lait*, yes, that's milk,' Fay muttered, with a certain desperation in her tone. '*Du pain*, that's bread. Oh, bother, I suppose bread isn't rolls, anyway! I don't want one of those six foot sticks of bread for my breakfast. Bother! Bother! Bother!'

Fay got up, unzipped the tent flap, and emerged to take stock of the table and larder. For a moment she hoped that Tess might have done the shopping and that breakfast, at least, would be there. But of course that hadn't been possible. Bread wasn't delivered to the camp shop much before eight. Nor was milk. So unless Fay plucked up her courage and

247

mustered her French she would have to go without breakfast. The mere thought made her hungry. Besides, it wasn't only breakfast.

Faced with the prospect of starvation her French seemed suddenly miserably inadequate. How did one make *du lait* and *du pain* into a sentence meaning, 'I would like one bottle of milk, please, and a couple of rolls. Oh, and a quarter of a pound of butter and some ice for the ice-box...'

Fay sat down disconsolately on a stool and wriggled her toes in the warm sunlight. For a moment she wished she hadn't come on this holiday, but only for a moment. From where she sat she could look across the terraces of the camp to the blue, blue Mediterranean.

The camp was quite a small one, arranged in terraces under the trees. The railway ran behind, and the road. In front was the beach. It was a delightful site, found by chance, and fortunately there had just been room for their tent — otherwise the camp was crowded with French holidaymakers in their splendid summer pavilions of canvas.

Madame at the camp shop did not speak a word of English, nor did the shopkeepers in the village. Fay muttered, 'Botheration!' at the thought. She'd never really realised that French was *important* until this moment. But her father had been right. She remembered his remarks when she had asked to be allowed to go with Tess and Cherry.

'H'm, please yourself Fay.' Mr Richards had shrugged. 'It beats me why you want to go on this French holiday when your French is so atrociously bad — and don't tell me this trip will help you with your French because I know you won't speak a word of the language while you're out there if you can help it, You'll let Tess and Cherry do all the talking that's necessary.'

Fay's mother had quoted school reports. 'Could do better if she tried... Takes no interest in languages... Lazy and careless... Pronunciation good but does not pay attention to grammar... stubbornly uninterested...'

'I like other things,' Fay had defended herself. '⌐
for instance, and geography, and *people*.'

'Languages are a part of people,' her father had ⌐

'You really ought to *try*, dear,' her mother had said. 'Tess speaks French quite well, and so could you if you tried.'

'But why should I try?' Fay had countered stubbornly, adding ingeniously: 'All the French children are learning English at school, so there's not much point in my learning French, is there? I mean, by the time I can speak it they'll be able to speak English.'

Fay sighed and wriggled her toes again. Her argument had seemed a good one at the time, but now it looked pretty silly. Madame at the shop didn't speak English, and unless Fay spoke French there wouldn't be any breakfast.

Ah, well! In a time of crisis desperate measures were needed. Fay picked up her sponge bag and towel and walked along to the toilet block. The camp was astir now. The hour of her test approaching.

'*Du lait, du pain, du beurre,*' Fay muttered, swinging her sponge bag as she strode along the dusty path with her bathing wrap flapping round her long legs.

Those basic words would take care of breakfast, with a bit of luck, and perhaps she could choose a moment when no other shoppers were present to witness her first real attempt to speak French. But then, heavens! There was the butcher to cope with. Tess had a hearty appetite and had told her to buy some steak.

Up to now the language had been no problem to Fay. As the baby of the party she'd left everything to the older girls, from the moment they drove off the ferry at Calais. Their first camp had been at Paris. Cherry Longhurst, who was a friend of Tess's and the oldest member of the party, had the small car, and drove them about in Paris for two days of sight-seeing before heading south.

Cherry spoke French fluently. She was keen on languages and was ambitious to land a really good job which would involve travelling. At present she was a secretary in London and already doing well for herself.

Tess had no driving licence yet, but a fair knowledge of French. She could at least manage without embarrassment. Cherry and Tess had not brought a phrase book or dictionary along, which now increased Fay's difficulties. With two French-speaking companions Fay had felt secure, and all had gone well as they drove down to the Côte d'Azur.

For nearly a fortnight now they had been happy in the delightful camp they had found on the coast. They had lazed in the sun and enjoyed long swims in the warm Mediterranean. Then, the day before yesterday, disaster had struck. Cherry had been stricken with appendicitis and rushed to hospital for an operation.

Almost at that moment they had been counting their francs and reluctantly deciding that it was time to head for home before their money ran out. Cherry was an orphan, so she couldn't send an S.O.S. home for cash, and Tess and Fay had been told firmly that they must manage on the money they set out with, because there wasn't any more.

As there were still several weeks to go before Fay and Tess started school again it seemed a pity to have to pack up, but money was a hard fact that took no account of sunshine and warm seas. Cherry had a month off, and would have liked to stay one more week. But now she was in hospital, so they would all have to stay, and somehow they must manage.

'I'll get a job, Fay,' Tess had decided. She always remained calm and sensible in moments of crisis, as befitted a girl whose ambition it was to become a nurse.

'That's easier said than done, Tess. We're in France, and you don't speak the language all that well.'

'All the same, I'll try. There may be some holiday job going. I could look after children, for instance.'

Fay had not been optimistic. But by yesterday evening Tess had found herself a job, as nursemaid to two young children whose family were on holiday in a nearby villa. The parents

250

wanted Tess to stay in the villa, but as she didn't want to leave Fay alone too long a compromise had been reached. Tess was to go to the villa early and look after the children until evening.

'I don't suppose I'll be able to see you tomorrow at all, Fay,' Tess had said. 'Not even on the beach. I think we're going out in the car. You won't mind being alone?'

'Not a bit. Not during the day. I'm quite happy lazing in the sun.'

'You'll have to do some shopping for me.'

That was the remark that had made Fay's heart turn a somersault.

'But I can't,' Fay had protested, pleading that her French was too bad and she was too shy.

'Nonsense. It's high time you became a bit more self-reliant,' Tess had retorted in her firmest nursing tones. 'And it will help you to overcome your shyness. You'll get on all right.'

'Oh, I don't know.' Fay had turned hot and cold at the thought of making an exhibition of herself, but Tess had been firm.

After washing, Fay dawdled in the warm morning sun as she walked back to her tent. She looked out over the blue Mediterranean, postponing the embarrassment she felt certain lay ahead. She spent some time dressing and doing her hair. But the sight of other campers, breakfasting outside their tents off fresh rolls and coffee, made her very hungry. She felt sure she could manage three rolls, at least.

She opened her purse and counted her money, then she walked down the dusty path to the camp shop.

Two Frenchmen were buying bread and groceries, chattering rapidly to Madame. She served them briskly and rattled off the prices and the total. Fay's heart sank. She'd never been good at French numbers.

The men gathered up their purchases and Fay stepped to the counter. She'd hoped to be without an audience, but three more Frenchmen turned up with their wives. Fay was hemmed in.

'*Bonjour, Mademoiselle.*' Madame of the dark hair and strong arms looked up expectantly.

'*Bonjour, Madame,*' Fay replied, then stuck. Her carefully rehearsed sentences escaped her entirely. A dreadful silence fell until in desperation Fay blurted out, '*Du pain, s'il vous plait.*'

That, of course, started a torrent of French from Madame, who gesticulated towards a large basket containing fresh French loaves in various lengths, and to other baskets of plain rolls and *croissants.*

Fay tried desperately to assemble a sentence, but failed in the heat of the moment and fell back, on the last resource of the inarticulate, pointing. She felt colour surging into her cheeks, and felt foolish. Her embarrassment wasn't eased by a remark behind her in which she caught the word *Anglais* and which started a ripple of laughter among the waiting shoppers.

'*Trois, s'il vous plait.*' Fay realised she was being asked how many rolls.

Then came the milk, which was much easier. She had yesterday's bottle, and merely put it on the counter and said, '*Encore, s'il vous plait.*'

The ice wasn't too difficult, but the butter landed her in another flood of words. Madame had two kinds of butter but only in large packets. In the end one of the large packets was cut in half, but by then Fay was hot enough to melt the butter if it came near her. Out of sheer cowardice she put a ten franc note on the counter for payment, hoping the change would be right.

By the time Fay gathered up her change and her purchases she felt sure she had been at the shop for an hour! But her French had improved more rapidly than it had ever done, even under the most reproachful teacher. They'd better not write in her school report now that she hadn't tried, she thought grimly. My, how she'd tried!

On the whole she'd done rather well, she thought, as she settled down to eat her breakfast. Tomorrow morning she wouldn't be quite so nervous. But the camp shop was relatively simple. The thought of her encounter with the butcher hung over her head now.

She rummaged in the cardboard box of tinned food, hoping to find a tin of meat to satisfy Tess, who was, unfortunately, a voracious meat eater. But the meagre remainder of their tinned stock was only soups and fruit. Fay sighed. Still, she could put the business of the butcher off for a bit. After breakfast she would go to the beach...

When she arrived on the beach two girls she knew were waiting. They pounced on her, chattering in French. They had made friends with Tess and Cherry and everything had gone splendidly then, because Tess and Cherry could chatter in French. But the girls, who were French, didn't speak a word of English. They were studying German for their second language.

Fay had been content to listen, smiling and lazing in the sun as the others talked. Now she found herself forced to try her halting French. The girls plied her with impatient questions. How was Cherry? Where was Tess? When were they going to visit the hospital?

'*Lentement! Lentement!*' Fay begged.

Somehow she managed to tell them what had happened, but the explanations took a long time. Explaining about the job Tess had found after leaving them yesterday took simply hours, and Fay, exasperated by her slowness, thought enviously that Cherry would have said everything in a few swift sentences and then run into the sea, instead of squirming on the sand and being interrupted by squeals of laughter at oddly constructed sentences.

The morning on the beach turned out to be hard work for Fay. One long French lesson, in fact, though she did get in a swim. But she did have one bright idea, which made her work at her French all the harder so that she could explain to her friends that she wanted to buy some meat. When, at last, they had grasped that fact, Fay sprung her trap.

'*Voulez-vous m'aider?*'

A squeal of laughter greeted the request. The girls weren't going to leave the beach to go to the butcher's. They refused to take Fay's plea seriously.

Buying a piece of meat was perfectly simple, they insisted. Anyway, the experience would be good for Fay. She must learn more French. Come, they would rehearse her! Giggling on the sands, they put Fay's French through its paces and taught her a few useful phrases for the butcher.

But by the time Fay at last screwed up her courage and stepped over the butcher's threshold she'd forgotten the precious sentence. All she could think of, when faced with the long counter of meat and an expectant butcher sharpening his knife, was a feeble bleat of '*Du bifteck, s'il vous plait.*'

'*Ah! Du bifteck, Madamoiselle!*'

The butcher understood at once, to Fay's relief. But he went on, and on, and on, showing her this piece of meat, and that and pointing out differences. There was no such thing as a simple piece of steak. One had to consider the marbling of fat. And what did Mademoiselle propose to do with it? How was she going to cook it?

Mademoiselle Fay grasped the drift of his words, rather to her surprise, but was quite incapable of answering. When, at last, the right piece of meat had been decided upon, she faced the question of how much did she want?

'*Pour deux,*' Fay told him hopefully, adding in a sudden rush of confidence. '*Pour moi, et ma soeur.*'

The butcher looked her up and down and evidently decided that her willowy grace needed feeding up. He put two fat slices of steak on the scales, and would have cut more but Fay stopped him.

He scribbled the price on the wrapping paper, to her relief, so she was able to count out some of the coins which were beginning to burden her purse.

After the ordeal in the butcher's shop Fay found buying vegetables comparatively easy. She returned to camp in triumph and treated herself to another swim before she began to prepare the vegetables, ready for the return of her sister.

'I see you got on very well at the butcher's, Fay,' Tess remarked, the moment she saw the meat. 'You see what you can do if you try!'

'Oh, I *tried* all right, Tess!' Fay adjusted the gas under the saucepan. 'I've learnt more French today than I have in my whole life up to now. Yvette and Marie wanted to know where you were, of course. I hoped they'd help me with the shopping, but they wouldn't. They're lazy.'

Tess laughed. 'They knew it would do you good to fend for yourself. And I certainly don't need to worry about you going to the butcher's now. The steak you bought is going to be delicious.'

'There's an awful lot of it.'

'All the better. I could eat a horse, Fay. You don't know how busy those children have kept me all day.'

'How did things go?'

'Splendidly.'

Tess chatted as she prepared the steak, telling Fay about the new job, but they couldn't talk for too long because they wanted to visit Cherry in hospital.

When they got there Cherry was looking better, sitting up in bed reading a French magazine.

'How's camp life without the cook?' Cherry asked brightly, running a hand over her blonde hair. 'What have you been doing today, Tess? How did the job go? And how are you getting on with French, Fay?'

They told her their news, briefly so as not to tire her. Then she asked how the money was going.

'We'll be all right on my wages, Cherry,' Tess assured her, 'and we'll try to save something ready for when you come out.'

Cherry nodded seriously. 'We shall have to go home the

255

moment I'm fit, Tess. I expect I shall get an extension of my holiday for sick leave all right, but we can't afford to hang on out here — unless I could get some kind of light job.'

'You mustn't think of it,' Tess said. 'You've got to have a spell of convalescence first. I'll try to save out of my wages for that.'

Fay felt rather guilty about being helpless. If only she'd worked at her French at school!

'I wish I could get a job, Cherry, so that I could help.'

'Not much you can do, is there? But don't worry.' Cherry smiled reassuringly. 'I'll see what I can find. A part-time secretarial job, perhaps.'

'You musn't think of it,' Tess repeated, more sternly. 'You've got to recover first.'

Cherry glanced across the ward to a girl in the opposite bed. 'I know, I'll ask Louise.'

'The dark girl?' Fay followed Cherry's glance. 'Is that her mother sitting beside her bed?'

'No, an aunt. Her mother's in Paris. Poor Louise was knocked down by a car a few days ago and she's got several broken bones. But she's been working in her aunt's shop here and knows all that goes on locally.'

When they took their leave of Cherry, Louise was still talking to her aunt, so they did not break in. The next evening Cherry introduced them to Louise, and Madame Gayou, the aunt.

Louise was not optimistic about Cherry's chance of obtaining part-time secretarial work locally. Madame Gayou mentioned that she was missing Louise in the shop and could do with an extra hand, but of course that would be too tiring for Cherry while she was convalescent.

'What kind of a shop is it?' Fay asked, and was glad to find that Louise understood a little English.

'We sell everything for the tourists,' Louise explained. 'You know, souvenirs. Baskets and pottery, and picture postcards, and little things in brass and copper. You know — you must have seen the shop, it's on the corner opposite the church.'

Fay thought it must be fun to work in a shop like that. If only she was a little older, and could speak a little more French. Well... a lot more French.

Cherry did not seem quite so bright, but insisted that she was making splendid progress. She had been up and about during the day.

'And how is your French, Fay?' Cherry smiled. 'Have you been shopping successfully?'

'Oh, it's not so embarrassing now. I didn't blush once, and the butcher was very nice. I seem to be able to remember my French much better.'

Tess gave a sisterly sniff. 'That's because you've been trying, for once. Now I suppose you'll relax, after the first shock of *having* to speak French. You can manage to buy bread and milk and meat, so you won't bother to work on it more than that. You'll settle down to laze in the sun again and in a couple of days you'll have forgotten your panic.'

'Rubbish!' Fay protested indignantly. But in her heart she knew that Tess had hit the nail on the head.

Fay realised guiltily that she was already beginning to relax, beginning to think she needn't bother to swot up more French now that she had mastered a few phrases for shopping. Indeed, she had become very pleased with her French.

Despite Tess's warning, and Fay's own resolution not to let things slide, during the next few days Fay did relax her effort to learn. When Yvette and Marie chattered on the beach she did not really try to learn more French from their conversation. She basked in the sun like an indolent lizard.

At the end of the first week Tess brought home her wages and sat down with pencil and paper, in her most practical manner, to do her budgeting. The answers she came up with shocked Fay out of her lizardly indolence.

'With the charge for the camp site,' Tess said, 'and the cost of food — we have to buy practically all of it now because we've nearly finished the tinned stuff we brought with us — and then the odds and ends, like fruit for Cherry and your sweets, well, we're not going to have very much left over out of my wages to put by for when Cherry comes out of hospital.'

'She'll be out in a few days now.'

'I know. We haven't had time to save, you see. And she really mustn't think of doing any work herself. She's got to get fit for the drive home.'

'Yes, and it would do her good to stay here for a fortnight longer. I'd like to stay, too, Tess.'

'Wouldn't we all?'

Tess sighed. Then for a time they were quiet, and the crickets chirruping in the bushes seemed very noisy.

'I'll have to get a job, too.' Fay said with sudden resolution.

To her annoyance Tess just laughed.

'Nobly spoken, little sister, but what can you do?' Tess dismissed the suggestion without giving it serious thought, and only laughed again when Fay scowled.

'I could help Louise's aunt.'

'In the shop? With your limited French? Don't be silly.'

Fay bristled inwardly, but said nothing more. Tess's calm dismissal of her as the baby sister, too young to be useful, was a smarting blow. It was a challenge!

The next morning Fay lingered for a long time outside the souvenir shop in the village, screwing up her courage to tackle Madame Gayou.

Baskets of all shapes and sizes hung round the doorway, reminding Fay of the amazing basket shops she had seen in the Provençal villages, where hundreds, if not thousands, of baskets were displayed. Then there were metalwork ornaments, and pottery objects of all kinds, and sun hats, and beach balls, and postcards. The shop was crammed with goods for tourists, and it was busy. Fay had to wait a long time for a momentary pause when there were no customers. Then she slipped inside.

'*Ah! Bonjour, Mademoiselle Fay!*' Madame Gayou greeted

her with a smile, and went on to ask what Fay would like.

Fay had prepared her little speech carefully. In fact, she had written it out and had studied the piece of paper again before entering the shop. She explained that she wanted money, so that Cherry could have a holiday when she came out of hospital, and Madame Gayou had said she was finding the shop too much for one person and was missing Louise...

'*Mais, Cherie! Vous ne parlez pas français!*'

Fay explained that she did speak a little and was getting better every day, and was not Louise so useful because she could speak English? There were so many English visitors, surely Fay could help with them, or did Madame Gayou speak English to them?

Alas, Madame admitted that she did not speak English. All the same she did not think Fay would be quite suitable...

Fay said that she was ready to do anything. Dusting. Even housework. It was terribly important to Fay to get the job, not only because of the money but, because, now that she was standing in the shop, she knew that she would love to work in it. She'd always liked playing shops when she was a very little girl, and this would be a real shop! And she would work really hard at her French.

Still Madame Gayou shook her head doubtfully. Then they were interrupted by a group of French people who came into the shop. Fay stood in the background while they were served. She tried very hard to understand everything they said, pretending they were really speaking to her. But this exercise depressed her — she only understood very little and she had to admit that she wouldn't be much use as a shop assistant selling to the French.

But while they were still occupying Madame Gayou's attention three middle-aged Englishwomen walked in.

'Eh, I bet they don't speak English here,' the liveliest of the three said. 'Come on, Betty. Get those cards and we'll leave the other thing.'

'No harm in asking.' The stouter lady also had a North

259

Country accent, and Northern enterprise. Madame Gayou had broken off her conversation to smile at the newcomers, and the lady tackled her. 'I say, do you speak English? 'Cause if you do I'd like that little pot at the back of the window. Seemingly it's only one you've got.'

Madame Gayou, faced with strongly accented English spoken at a brisk speed could only shrug and look helpless.

'What'd I tell you, Betty?' the first lady said. 'You be content with those cards and don't start any fuss and bother over that pot.'

The third tourist nodded. 'Come on, Betty.'

Fay saw her chance. She stepped forward briskly out of the shadows by a column of baskets.

'Perhaps I can help you — I speak English?'

'So you do, love.' All three tourists seemed startled and the one addressed as Betty looked Fay up and down. 'Did you understand what I was saying?'

'Yes. Would you like to show me the pot you want, please?'

'Eh, I'll do that, love.' Betty led the way to the pavement, but instead of indicating the souvenir of her choice she looked Fay up and down again. 'Are you French?'

'No, English. I'm er, working here — just helping in the shop.' Fay hoped her statement would prove true. If she could sell the Northerners something, that would convince Madame Gayou of her usefulness! 'Now, which pot did you want?'

'That blue one with the red markings.' All three tourists pointed it out.

Fay thought it rather ugly, but she said it was a very nice choice and she would get it for them.

The French customers were leaving when Fay entered the shop again. She told Madame Gayou the English wanted *le vase bleu, avec rouge*. This came to her in a moment of inspiration, and Madame Gayou beamed with understanding.

'My word,' Betty exclaimed admiringly, looking at Fay with something like awe. 'You can speak the lingo all right,

'Perhaps I can help you — I speak English'

and you so young, too.'

'Oh, I only speak a little,' Fay said with modesty, but she felt very satisfied.

'A darned sight more than we do,' Betty chuckled. 'We haven't two words of French between the three of us.'

'I know how difficult it is,' Fay replied, with more feeling than they knew. 'But now you're here and there's no language trouble can I show you something else? A basket, perhaps?'

Fay felt that her chances of getting a job helping Madame Gayou were improving, and she went all out to play the charming saleswoman. In the end she did sell them a basket, and half a dozen ashtrays, and a framed picture of the village, and three beach hats, plus the blue pot and a dozen postcards.

They left the shop in high humour. Madame Gayou was also beaming.

Fay tackled her about the job again. Madame Gayou continued to beam. She had to admit that Fay would be useful in the shop while Louise was in hospital. There were so many English visitors. Yes, Fay could have the job. And her first task would be to put a notice in the window. Madame Gayou groped under the counter and handed a card to Fay.

'English spoken here!' the card proclaimed.

Fay laughed with delight and put the card in a prominent place in the window. And almost at once some more English walked in. Fay knew that she was going to enjoy herself tremendously. A shop was fun! And how she would surprise Tess when they met in the evening!

All the same, it was Tess who had helped to shake her out of her lizard-like laziness. She would work hard at French, then perhaps she could come to help Madame Gayou next summer.

And one day, Fay thought dreamily, indulging in visions while her customers chose postcards, one day she would have a shop of her own, somewhere in England and she would put a card in the window — *Ici on parle français!*

DOUBLE IDENTITY

by

Kathleen Mackenzie

The two lanterns bobbed up the field, throwing fan shapes of light on the crisp, rime-covered grass. The frost was so sharp that the feet of the four children crunched slightly, even though they were walking over a grass field. Michael, who was holding one of the lanterns, looked up to the stars crowding the sky and said suddenly:

'I bet you don't know which is Sirius, the dog star.'

'I bet you don't either,' said Peter, but more because he was in the habit of contradicting his brother than because he believed Michael was unable to pick out the star in question.

'Where is it?' asked Monica.

'There,' said Michael. 'Below Orion's belt and dagger and to the left of them. That frightfully bright, rather whitish star.'

Monica carefully set the basket, containing two thermos flasks, a pasty and some cake, on the ground and looked up in the direction of his pointing finger.

Philomel, who knew Sirius by sight, said nothing, but wished the others would get on. It was too cold to stand stargazing. She did not like to go on by herself to the little hut in the corner of the field where her uncle, Michael's and Peter's father, was waiting for them to bring him his supper. She did not know him well and was not sure he would want her barging in on the lambs and ewes. Besides, though her sister Monica had assured her that Uncle Frank was a dear, Philomel, who had not been on the farm twenty-four hours yet, had only seen him when he was very preoccupied and stern. At least, he seemed stern, but perhaps it was only because he was worried over the number of lambs he had lost, not through their weakness or illness, but because they had been worried and killed by a dog.

The boys and Monica were determined, as soon as they had taken Uncle Frank his food, to stay up for a while on guard near the sheep to see if they could catch the dog who was doing all the damage, red-handed. Philomel had not liked to say she did not want to go with them, especially as Aunt Mary had taken it for granted that she would, but if she had had the courage to say what she really wanted to do, she would have preferred to go to bed and read.

It was going to be pretty awful, she felt, if she did not get to like staying on a farm better then she did after her first day's experience of it. She hoped it was just because everything was so new and that when she had been there a fortnight, as Monica had, she would get used to it. Though she was afraid it was going to take more than a fortnight to get used to the animals. She had never realised before, when reading about them (and up to now the only contact she had had with farm animals was through books) how terrifying they would be. The sight of an enormous horned cow made her feel quite sick with fright, she was frightened of two old sows who roamed about the yard, hated the geese when they ran at her hissing with their necks stretched out, and was even alarmed when the dogs rushed out barking. The worst of the dogs was Vulcan, an unusually large collie with a black marking on his back the shape of a hammer. He belonged to the cowman's son, Norman, who assured her that Vulcan was the gentlest creature in the world, but Philomel found this impossible to believe when he rushed out barking and leapt up at her, nearly knocking her over.

She wondered, if she had been as tall and sturdy as Monica, if she would have minded the animals so much — she felt she would not — but she was not only two years younger than her sister, but also very small for her ten years, and rather delicate. She felt that perhaps that was why she never seemed to have the energy the others had and why she felt the cold so much. She thought she might have enjoyed staying on a farm more in the Summer instead of during a very cold February. She was very glad to hear Peter say to the star-gazers, 'Hurry up, you two. Daddy will be ravening for his food.' Though she was sorry to hear him add, 'Besides, we want to get a good place for our look out post.'

The hut, when they got to it, was gloriously warm. There was an oil stove in it, and bundles of straw, and the two or three ewes and their lambs helped to warm it too. In the light from the hurricane lantern Philomel could see their mild, benevolent, but foolish faces and was glad to find an animal of which she did not think she would be afraid. The lambs, with legs too long and sprawly for their bodies and big heads, were not as sweet to look at as she had expected them to be, but her uncle said they would be much more lively and engaging in the morning, when they were strong enough to go out and start skipping about in the field, and that anyway he only had the weakly ones in the shed.

He was much less stern than he had been and Philomel would have preferred to stay talking to him, but the boys and Monica were determined to go to keep watch in case the sheep outside were attacked again. They were very anxious, too, to identify the dog who did it, if possible. Uncle Frank was keen for them to go, although he said he did not think the killer dog would come till later in the night. Again, lacking the courage to say that she wanted to stay, Philomel unwillingly left the warm shed for the icy field.

Most of the sheep were lying under the high, stone-faced bank at the east side of the field, sheltering under it from the nipping wind which, though not very strong, was very cold. The boys chose a spot not far away and, climbing the bank, settled themselves on the lee side of the hedge on top. The girls joined them.

'We mustn't say a word,' said Michael in a low voice as the sheep, disturbed by their arrival, settled down again.

'I hope we don't have to wait long,' said Monica.

'We shan't be able to stay very long anyway,' said Michael. 'Mummy said we were to be in by half-past-nine.'

'And it may not come at all,' added Peter.

Philomel hoped it was nearly half-past-nine already. It was not only that it was so piercingly cold on the bank, but it was also creepy waiting in the silence for some horrible great dog to come bounding down on the huddled sheep to murder them. She supposed that Ancient Britons and shepherds in the Bible must have felt somewhat as she did when guarding their flocks from wolves and wild beasts.

There were a surprising number of rustles near them and she seemed constantly to be seeing dark shapes leaping about and nearly gave the alarm — falsely — several times. But when the dog did come there was no mistaking it.

The sheep suddenly seemed disturbed, there was a frightened baa or two and a black shape darted over the bank and leapt among them. There was a horrible sound of worrying and a cry from a lamb. The boys sprang to their feet and dashed towards the killer, turning on their torches as they did so. Philomel saw two green eyes gleaming in the beam of light, a horrid jaw with dark stuff dripping from it and then Michael's lasso whirled. He was very good with a lasso usually, but this time, in the excitement and the dim light, he missed.

The dog sprang forward out of the beam of light and then turned sideways and bounded away. Philomel had just risen to her feet when something huge and dark leapt up the bank at her, knocked her back into the bushes, made a glancing snap at her arm and was gone.

'It came this way!' screamed Monica. 'I heard it!'

The boys came running towards her.

'Where?' shouted Michael.

'Just here, between Phil and me. Are you all right Phil? Where are you?'

'It's gone, I suppose,' said Michael, scrambling up the bank, followed by Peter.

'Yes, it's gone. It went just past me, Phil, are you all right? I say, she's crying. Phil!'

When, guided by her sobs, the others found her they were appalled to see blood flowing from her arm. Philomel was almost too frightened, at first, to be coherent, but when Monica and Peter escorted her to the farm, and Aunt Mary had comforted her and dealt with the bite on her arm (which proved to be only a graze) she recovered enough to drink some tea and talk about it more sensibly.

'Did it kill another lamb or were you able to save it?'

'It killed it,' said Michael grimly who, after taking the dead lamb to his father, had just joined them. 'And I say, the most awful thing of all — I saw the dog quite clearly and it's Norman's dog, Vulcan.'

No one knew how to tell Norman that it was Vulcan who was the sheep killer.

'You are absolutely certain about his markings, Mike?' his father asked at breakfast the next day.

'I wish I wasn't, but I am. I did see his back quite clearly in my torchlight and that black hammer shape is distinctive. I couldn't have mistaken it.'

'What will happen to Vulcan, Uncle Frank?' asked Monica.

'He'll have to be destroyed. You can never cure a sheep-dog that has started killing sheep. There's just nothing for it but to shoot him.'

'But Norman loves that dog more than anything in the world,' said Peter, horrified.

'I know he does. It's a most miserable affair.'

Norman came to the back door as he usually did with some eggs he had collected just after they had finished breakfast. The four children were doing the washing up and so were present when Uncle Frank, his dislike of what he had to say making him sound very stern, told Norman what Michael had seen. Norman's usually pale, peaky face turned slowly pinker and pinker till it became red, but he did not say a word till Uncle Frank said, still sounding stern, though really he was full of pity: 'You realise what this will mean, Norman? We shall have to have Vulcan destroyed.'

Norman's eyes blazed. 'You can't!' he said. 'You can't! 'Tweren't he. Vulcan were along of me all evening. He weren't out killing no sheep.'

'With you? Are you sure?'

'Course I'm sure. He never left my side.'

'Michael, how well did you see that dog? Could you have been mistaken?'

Michael, a tea-cloth in his hand, had stopped drying the cup he was holding and had been gazing at his father and then at Norman. He, too, turned slightly pinker as he said, 'I don't think so, Daddy. It was a dog awfully like Vulcan, anyway. I'd give anything that it wasn't but it was.'

'It couldn't have been,' said Norman stubbornly. 'He were along of me.'

Uncle Frank looked from one boy to the other, his frown deepening. 'Are you absolutely certain, Norman, he never left your side? What were you doing?'

'I were watching the telly.'

'Was your father with you?' (Norman had no mother; he and his father kept house together.)

'Part of the time.'

'Did he see Vulcan?'

'Dunno. He were asleep a bit.'

'But you will swear that Vulcan was never outside for a moment? And you are telling me the truth?'

Norman gulped and then nodded several times. Uncle Frank did not know whether he believed him, but he realised he could not possibly destroy the dog in the face of his master's insistence that Vulcan had been with him. He looked hard at Norman, who did not return his glance, but stood, one hand on Vulcan's neck, on the red collar he had recently bought him, looking stubborn and miserable.

'Well, I suppose Michael may have been mistaken, but if you are telling me a lie, Norman, it won't do any good. If

270

Vulcan is the killer he'll kill again, and if we find him out we shall have to have him put down.'

Norman stared at Uncle Frank, his eyes getting larger and the pink colour draining out of his face till it looked pinched with misery. Philomel who had been putting the clean china in a cupboard, could hardly bear to look at him and was glad when, without a word, he turned and went away, Vulcan trotting at his heels.

Uncle Frank watched him go and then turned to Michael, who was also looking miserable.

'It was Vulcan, Daddy,' he said.

'Well, we shall have to see. Hurry up with that drying and then you can drive the cows back to Far Meadow. I must answer the 'phone.'

The telephone had been shrilling through the house from the hall and Uncle Frank went out, as he spoke, to answer it. Michael, looking thoroughly dissatisfied, put down the cup.

'It was Vulcan,' he repeated. 'You saw him too, Pete.'

'I thought it was, but I didn't see him very clearly. Anyway, I'd much rather it wasn't, wouldn't you?'

'Of course I would, but it was.'

'How simply beastly everything is,' said Monica. 'I shan't be able to bear it for Norman if it does turn out to be Vulcan.'

'Neither shall I,' said Peter. 'Vulcan's been such a jolly good sheep-dog too, that's the extraordinary part. Norman's been training him for the sheep-dog trials. We all thought he might win.'

'I don't understand,' said Philomel. 'How can it be Vulcan if Norman says he was with him all the evening?'

'He wasn't telling the truth,' said Michael. 'I don't exactly blame him, feeling about Vulcan as he does. But I can't see it will do any good in the long run.'

'You sound as if you wanted it to be Vulcan,' said Monica in an accusing voice.

'I don't. Of course I don't. But the more I think of it the

more sure I am that it was. I did see him awfully clearly and I couldn't have mistaken that hammer shape on his back.'

'Well, I shall go on hoping you are mistaken all the same. Think what Norman will feel like if they have to shoot Vulcan.'

'I do,' said Michael miserably, kicking his foot against the table-leg in his distress as he spoke.

'There! This beastly job's done,' said Peter, emptying the water out of the washing-up bowl with a slosh and hurriedly drying his hands on the roller towel behind the door. 'Let's go and do the cows. Come on.'

Thankful to have something active to do, Michael and Monica stampeded after him to get their rubber boots and coats on. Philomel, always slower, found they had disappeared by the time she was ready, in spite of her repeated cries of 'wait for me!'

She wandered down towards the cowsheds feeling rather cross with them until she realised that she had no real desire to drive cows; they terrified her even when she was behind them. The trouble was she did not know what she did want to do.

She went aimlessly along until, as she passed the big dutch barn, a hen ran out, clucking, from some bales of hay. Philomel wondered if she had laid an egg and went to see. The hay was piled up at one end of the barn in a series of steps made by the bales. Another hen fluttered, squawking and cackling, from a higher step and Philomel climbed upward. As her head came above the top she heard a muffled sob and found herself gazing at Norman, lying with his arm round Vulcan, his tear-streaked face only a few inches from her own.

If he had not seen her she would have crept away; she felt horribly embarrassed and did not in the least know what to say to him. But he had seen her and he looked so miserable that she found herself wanting to help him, though she had no idea how to do it. She could not find the words.

It was Norman who spoke first. Trying to pretend there was nothing the matter he said, 'What do 'ee want?'

'Nothing. I didn't know you were here.'

'Leave me be.'

Vulcan rustled through the hay towards her a little, and then turned and licked Norman's face. Though she was usually so nervous of him he seemed very gentle now and it was difficult to think of him as the savage dog who attacked and killed lambs.

'Are you feeling so miserable because you don't think Uncle Frank believes you?'

Norman stared in front of him, biting his quivering under-lip to keep it still. 'If they kills Vulcan I just about don't know what I'll do,' he said at last.

'But if he isn't the dog who kills the sheep they won't.'

'Vulcan ain't never killed no sheep. Nor lambs.'

'But you don't think they'll believe you?'

'I'll kill that there Michael for saying it were he.'

'Well, he thought it was. He hated saying it. But, anyway, if Vulcan was with you, Mike must have been wrong. Why are you so worried? Unless he really wasn't.'

'Don't 'ee dare say he wasn't with me.'

'I shan't say anything,' but her heart sank as she said it. She was beginning to be almost sure Norman had not spoken the truth.

'But it won't do no good, nothing will do no good. I can't keep Vulcan so he'm never out of my sight, and if any of they lambs gets killed they'll say it were he. But they shan't kill him — they shan't, they shan't, they shan't!'

Norman's voice rose almost hysterically and Philomel knew that though he spoke such bold words he had no idea what to do save his dog. She had no idea either and was thankful to hear the others calling her so she could leave him. She did not mention Norman's name to them.

It was a wretched morning, and after a bit the boys and Monica decided to try to forget the general misery in a ride;

but Philomel could not ride, even if there had been a pony for her. She hung around while they saddled up and then watched them ride out of the yard, feeling more depressed than ever. She had not the slightest desire to go with them, she was far too frightened of horses, but she wished they had decided to do something with her. She wandered into the kitchen where her aunt was baking.

She suggested that Philomel should go for a walk up on to the moor, which rose steeply above the farm. The wind had gone out of the east and it was much warmer, with a gentle breeze blowing from the southwest, and Philomel thought perhaps it was not a bad idea.

In spite of her depression about Norman and her dislike of the farm, she enjoyed the walk. She found a path that ran through rough pastures, just below where the bracken and heather-covered moor lifted to the sky. The path wandered on, sometimes by loose-stone walls, sometimes by little streams, sometimes through copses, and it was in one of these small woods that, turning a corner, Philomel suddenly stopped. On the left hand side of the path rose a steep bank, like a little precipice before the slope of the hill began again. Shrubs and young bushes grew on the top of the bank and from one of these, hanging by his leather collar which had got caught on a strong, sharp spike of wood, was a large collie dog with a black mark on its back exactly like a hammer. There was a little pile of loosened earth below the swinging figure on the path, which the dog had dislodged in its wild attempts to get its footing; but now it was hanging limply, just uttering a little whimper and occasionally twitching its foot.

For a moment Philomel stood still, horror-struck. She recognised that it was Vulcan at once, not only by the marking on its back but by its red collar. She simply did not know what to do; she loathed the idea of doing anything. Not only was she frightened of dogs, but she did not really like touching them, and Vulcan had always seemed to her

For a moment Philomel stood horror-struck

a particularly alarming kind of dog. But she could not let him die before her eyes with no attempt to save him. Not even if he were a killer of lambs; not even if he were going to be shot by Uncle Frank very soon. The sight of that limp, twitching creature was too much for her and she simply rushed forward and seized his swinging body in her arms and lifted it up.

It was most surprisingly heavy and she could not lift it high enough to unhook the collar. Then she managed to clasp Vulcan to her with one arm and with the other reach up for and grab the branch and drag it down enough to enable her to slip the collar off the spike. She had no sooner done so than the dog's weight was too much for her and she fell, with Vulcan on top of her, backwards on to the path.

She was not hurt and scrambled up, afraid that she had been too late and that Vulcan was dead. Timidly she put a hand where she thought his heart would be, as he lay on his side and felt it. She was not sure, but she thought she could feel something thumping faintly. Very gently she began to rub her hand round and round over his heart and he stirred and, to her joy, tried feebly to lick her hand as she kneeled by him. Then he coughed once or twice, rose unsteadily to his feet and shook himself.

Philomel, regardless of the muddiness of the path, sat back on her heels and watched him thankfully. He shook himself again and then gently licked her hand as if to say that he realised what she had done for him. Then he walked a little way towards home and stopped, looking round at her as if to say, 'Come on, we'd better get back.'

Philomel rose to her feet and followed him.

Vulcan trotted on before her, every now and then turning to make sure she was following. He took her a slightly different way and she hoped he was not leading her by a route practicable for dogs, but difficult for human beings, when she saw the farm below her. She crossed a rough pasture, the ground dropping steeply away below her in a series of fields.

When she got to the bank separating her from the first of these she found a way up on her side easily enough, but on the other side the drop was very steep and she had to go some way along the top of the bank, pushing her way past the bushes that made a hedge on the top before she found a place where she could get down. Then she saw a wooden hut in the corner of the field and realised that she was on the scene of the adventure of last night.

There were still several lambs and ewes in the field and the sudden fear struck her that Vulcan had come that way in order to attack them again. He was nowhere in sight for the moment. What was he doing? Lurking on the top of the bank, ready to spring at the lambs below, or had he gone home?

Then she saw him across the corner of the field from where she stood, poised on the bank for a spring on to the lambs below him. He took no notice of her; did not seem to see her. There was a stir from an old ewe, and a baa of terror, and then, as he leapt down among the sheep, Philomel flung herself off the bank shouting.

The noise she made stopped the dog in the act of seizing a lamb; it swung round on her and for a ghastly moment she thought it was going to spring at her. Then something large and tawny shot past her with a growl and then, before her startled eyes had really seen what it was, she was aware of a snarling, whirling mass of fighting dogs. The ewes and the lambs dashed away to the other side of the field and Philomel, feeling very weak in the knees, found herself running down the hill, yelling.

She was not, strangely for her, yelling for fright, but to make someone hear and come to help, but before she got to the farm she saw a skulking shape tearing for its life and then Vulcan joined her, coming quite jauntily up to her, although one ear was torn and bleeding.

Her shouts brought her uncle and aunt as well as Norman and his father into the yard. What with the fright she had had, running and excitement, Philomel hardly had breath to tell them what had happened, but she did manage to make them understand. Her story cleared Vulcan completely, of course, because not only had she seen a second dog, so closely resembling Vulcan that she had thought it was him actually going for the lambs until the real Vulcan drove the killer away, but at the time when he was hanging by his collar another nearby farmer had seen a dark tawny collie with a black hammer-shaped patch on his back kill one of his lambs.

The other dog was traced; it belonged to a queer-tempered farmer right up on the moor. It turned out to be a half-brother of Vulcan's by a different mother who had been a savage, sheep-killing dog herself, and after it was destroyed no more sheep or lambs were killed.

Uncle Frank could never be sufficiently thankful he had delayed shooting Vulcan. Norman, who became Philomel's devoted slave, gave her Vulcan's collar (which he would never let him wear again) as a momento of what she had done. He admitted that though he had said Vulcan had never left his side that evening, he was not perfectly sure that this was so. He had been so absorbed in the television programme that the dog could have gone out without his noticing.

The others couldn't get over what she had done, particularly Monica.

'It really was jolly brave of you, Phil,' she said. 'You're so frightened of dogs, and for all you knew, Vulcan might have bitten you when he was so terrified himself.'

'For all she knew,' said Michael, 'he might have been a savage sheep-killer.'

'I think you deserve a medal for bravery,' said Peter.

Philomel did not want a medal, but she was very glad to have the collar to remind herself that though she was such a wretched coward about so many things, when she had something to do she could be quite brave.

JOB - HUNTING

by

Elisabeth Sheppard-Jones

K atie, hurry up! Breakfast's ready.'
Katie gave her standard reply: 'O.K. Mum, won't
be a minute.' She leapt out of bed and began
to pull off her pyjamas. Dressing was no easy operation, as
her transistor set was blaring forth the latest chart success
and Katie could not resist dancing her way from pyjamas
to pants and vest, and from pants and vest to jeans and
sweater. A final twist, a quick flick through her hair with
her comb, and she was in the kitchen, demanding to know
what was for breakfast.

Her elder sister, Susan, was already seated at the kitchen
table, making toast in the electric toaster. 'Really, Katie,
your idea of a minute! It must be at least ten since Mum
called you and half-an hour since I did. And I don't believe
you've washed now.'

Katie pulled a hideous face at her, one she had spent
a long time practising in front of the mirror.

'One of these days,' said Susan, 'the wind will change and
your face will stay like that — not that it wouldn't be an
improvement, mind you.'

'Katie, haven't you washed?' Mrs Nichols, who was frying
the bacon, turned and frowned at her twelve-year-old
daughter.

'Well, Mum, you see, it was like this. Subconsciously,
I suppose, I knew it was half-term and I must have overslept.
I didn't hear Susan call me so I got a shock when I heard you
say breakfast was ready. I didn't want to keep you waiting...
Katie began to shovel cornflakes into her mouth.

'Katie, have you washed?' Mrs Nichols tried not to smile, but the corners of her mouth quivered. Everyone found it difficult to be cross with Katie.

'No, not really. I thought I'd do it afterwards; plenty of time then and I won't be in anyone's way 'cos you'll have gone to work and Susan will be at College.'

Mrs Nichols was a widow. Her husband had died when Susan was ten and Katie only six. He had left very little money, so Mrs Nichols had gone back to the job she had had before they were married.

'As a matter of fact, girls, I'm not going to work today.' Mrs Nichols joined her daughters at the table.

A worried expression crossed Susan's face. 'Oh, Mum, I quite forgot to ask. What did the doctor say last night? Won't he let you go back to work?'

'No, not for a few months at any rate. It's nothing to worry about. I've been overdoing things apparently, and need a rest, but with two capable daughters that should be easy enough, shouldn't it? Money will be a little tight for a time, of course, so we shall all of us have to be less extravagant — fewer pop records, Katie! Fewer tights, Susan! — and I will give up the hairdresser, and have a home perm. How about that?'

'All right, except for the home perm,' said Katie. 'I've seen some people with terrible home perms. You don't want to look like someone from outer space, do you? I mean, you're always one of the prettiest Mums at the School Sports — don't forget they're next week — and I'm not keen on the idea of you appearing all frizzed up. I'd hate to have to be ashamed of you. Suppose you came with a bird's nest of hair and a hat on top like a blackbird's egg.'

Her mother laughed, and assured her that she would do her best to look presentable. Katie giggled.

Susan, who took life more seriously, frowned. 'I do wish I could get a job,' she said. 'It would help a lot, wouldn't it, Mum?'

'You'll find one when the time comes,' said her mother. 'You're getting on all right, aren't you?'

'Yes, I think so. The shorthand is more difficult than the typing — so many signs to remember — and I don't much like the book-keeping, but, on the whole, I'm managing to keep up with the class. I expect I'll get my speeds eventually, but I'm sure to go to pieces when it comes to an interview. I don't seem to have any confidence. You know how shy I am with strangers, and I do wish I didn't look so much younger than I am. Nobody ever believes I'm sixteen. Now, if only I had Katie's cheek...'

'Ah, but if you were me, you wouldn't be doing a silly business course, you'd be up the Amazon with David Attenborough or orbiting round the world in a capsule or...'

'Doing anything but bringing home the bacon,' Susan finished for her.

'Anyway, I simply can't understand why you gave up the idea of a glamorous course at Art School for something as stuffy as shorthand and typing at a Business College,' said Katie.

Susan glowered at her, but didn't answer. Mrs Nichols got up from the table and told them to clear away the breakfast things while she went to make the beds.

'What did you want to mention Art College for?' Susan demanded after their mother had left the kitchen. 'You must know I chose Business College because the course was shorter and I could be earning sooner. You are the limit. You've probably put the idea in Mum's head that I'm not happy doing this course.'

'Sorry, Sue, I didn't mean it,' said Katie, looking woebegone. 'I just didn't think.'

Susan patted her sister's arm comfortingly. 'Never mind, but it's a pity you don't think a bit more sometimes, isn't it?'

Later, when Susan had gone to catch her bus, and Mrs Nichols was busy preparing dinner, Katie decided to take Susan's advice. She always found the swing in the garden was a good place for thought, and she sat on the little wooden seat, idly swinging herself to and fro, thinking great thoughts until her mother came out to ask her to go shopping. Katie took the list and fetched the shopping basket. She was still deep in thought when she met her friend Gillian Blake outside the front gate.

'Hullo, Katie,' said Gillian, waving a newspaper in front of her nose. 'Have you seen the photograph of the new school block in the local rag?'

'No, I haven't,' said Katie, her eyes lighting up, 'but that paper is just what I do want to see. May I borrow it?'

'Sorry, no can do; Dad wants it back. You can only have a peep. Are you going shopping? Because, if so, I'll come with you. I'll treat you to a coffee somewhere, and you can look at it then. But Dad made me promise not to let it out of my hands.'

So Gillian helped Katie do the shopping; then the girls ordered two coffees at a small café, and sat with the Carhampton Courier spread out in front of them on the table. Katie rustled through the pages until she came to the 'Situations Vacant.'

'Photo's on the centre page,' said Gillian.

'I'm not interested in that at the moment,' replied Katie. 'I had an idea this morning when I was on the swing...'

'Oh, not another,' sighed Gillian, who had often suffered from Katie's ideas before. There was the time she had been persuaded to sing a duet with her at a talent spotting concert when neither of them could sing a note in tune; there was the morning she had been encouraged to accompany Katie to the top of a nearby hill to watch the dawn rise and been caught in a thunderstorm the like of which had never been known before; and the dreadful occasion when she had been coerced into selling bunches of wild flowers on a street corner in aid of a local children's Home, and one of the street vendors had accused them of horning in on his preserves.

Katie let out a squeal of excitement. 'Ah, this is just the

'Ah! This is just thing!'

thing! Absolutely tailor-made. What a bit of luck!'

'I wish you'd tell me what this is all about,' said Gillian patiently. 'I thought your mother said you weren't to do any baby-sitting because you don't do your homework properly as it is.'

'It's nothing to do with baby-sitting,' said Katie scornfully.

'Well, she certainly won't let you do a paper-round — I'm not allowed to either — so if you've got any ideas in that direction, you can drop them.'

'This is a full-time job, you nit,' said Katie.

'You're the nit, not me. You're too young for a full-time job. You can't leave school until you're sixteen, however much you may want to. Remember?'

'Oh, Gil, my dear idiot! This is a job for Susan, not me. You see, Mum's doctor says she mustn't go back to work for months yet, and Susan would like a job but she's too shy to apply for one. She's afraid she'd flop at the interview. You know how reserved she is. So, I thought, I'd apply for her — I mean I'm not a bit shy — and I could tell them how marvellously efficient and reliable she is, and sort of pave the way for her. Don't you think that's a wonderful idea?'

Gillian shrugged her shoulders non-committally.

'And listen to this,' went on Katie, reading out of the paper, '*Wanted Junior Shorthand-Typist for Advertising Agency. Apply Messrs Lowe & Davies, King Street, Carhampton 4.* Where there's advertising, there's art — of a kind anyway — and Susan would love that: she'd be much happier there than in an insurance or a solicitor's office or anything dull like that. And the fact that she would probably want the job so much would make her all the more nervous about applying for it. So, I'm going along there this afternoon.'

'You're mad,' said Gillian, 'Aren't you going to ask Susan's permission? Or tell your mother about it first?'

'Now who's mad? Of course not. I am going to reverse the Nichols family fortunes on my own initiative and you're coming with me.'

286

'Look, Katie, I don't mind coming with you — without me, you'd never find King Street anyway, you know how easily you always get lost — but don't you think Messrs Lowe & Davies will have a good laugh when they see someone as young as you going into their office after a job?'

'Look, Gil,' said Katie, imitating her friend, 'Susan and Mum are worried about our finances, and I must *try* to do something to help. Can you think of anything better?'

Gillian admitted that she couldn't and, with some reluctance, agreed to call for Katie that afternoon.

'It'll be fabulous fun,' said Katie. 'You'll have to wait outside, of course, while I'm having the interview.'

'Catch me going inside,' said Gillian. 'Honestly, I've never heard of anything so daft. Fancy going after a job for someone else.' She got out her purse and paid the waitress for their coffees.

'You won't say that,' said Katie airily, 'when, as a reward, Susan gives me money out of the first pay packet, and *I* treat *you* to coffee — and I might even throw in some chocolate biscuits!'

'Why are you wearing a dress and your best coat?' asked Mrs Nichols when Katie appeared from her bedroom soon after two o'clock. 'I thought you and Gillian were going to cycle to Lark Woods this afternoon. You're certainly not going dressed up like that.'

'Well, you see, Mum,' explained Katie hesitantly, 'we changed our minds. We thought we'd go and look at the shops instead.'

'What? On a lovely day like this? I thought you hated window-shopping. You always make enough fuss when you have to come with me.'

'Yes, I do hate it, but Gillian wants to go and, as she nearly always does what I want, I thought this time I ought to give in to her.' Katie kept her fingers crossed and hoped she would be forgiven for telling so many lies.

'I still don't know why you have to put on your best coat,'

said Mrs Nichols. 'It seems rather unnecessary; and that coat's got to last you a long time, you know.'

Katie pondered for a moment before answering, and then came out with what she thought a most inspired reply. 'You know how this morning I said I didn't want to be ashamed of you, well, neither do I want you to be ashamed of me. I don't want to be downtown, wearing my old jeans, when some of your friends might see me there and say: "Oh dear, look at the poor little Nichols girl, what a sight she is, how her mother neglects her!" '

'Anyone would think you had nothing but your old jeans or your best coat.' Her mother smiled at her. 'May I remind you that you have other frocks, three skirts, a mac, blazer and a school coat, to mention but a few?'

There was a ring at the front door.

'There's Gillian,' cried Katie, 'No time to change now, have I, Mum darling? What a pity!'

'Yes, indeed what a pity,' agreed Mrs Nichols. 'Oh, go on with you, you wretched child!' She kissed her fondly.

'Still, you love me in spite of my wicked ways, don't you?' asked Katie, kissing her back.

'Can't think why!' came her mother's retort.

'What you all dressed up like a dog's dinner for?' asked Gillian, when Katie opened the door to her.

Katie put her finger to her lips. 'Sh! I've just had enough of that from Mum.' She stepped outside and shut the door after her. 'When one goes after a job one must look presentable. First impressions are very important.'

They caught a bus to Carhampton High Street. Katie was quieter than usual and when Gillian commented on this, she said she was feeling nervous.

'You, nervous? Huh, I don't believe it,' said Gillian.

'Well, not very, but just a bit. I've got a wobbly feeling in my tummy, rather like before an exam. Of course, you know what they say about great artists, they can't give a really good performance if they don't feel a bit nervous beforehand.'

'You're not going for an audition,' said Gillian, doing what she often did — bringing Katie down to earth.

They got off the bus, and Gillian led Katie expertly down the road, through an arcade, across the open market, up a side lane, and into King Street.

'Wonderful,' said Katie. 'I could never have found my way here. I don't know how you do it.'

'Natural brilliance,' said Gillian modestly. 'And I looked up Lowe & Davies in the telephone directory, and would guess they're about halfway down.'

The street was a long one, large, light modern office blocks on the left, and some shops and older, grey stone buildings on the right.

'Left or right hand side?' asked Katie.

'It didn't say which in the telephone directory,' replied Gillian caustically.

'Bet it's on this side,' said Katie, 'bet you two pence it's on the right. Lowe & Davies somehow has an old-fashioned ring to it.'

'You owe me two pence,' said Gillian almost immediately. She pointed across the road to a huge glass and concrete building. Halfway down a board outside it, in big black lettering, was written 'Lowe & Davies, Advertising Agency.'

Katie raced over the road; Gillian followed her at a more leisurely pace.

'This is it all right,' said Katie, studying the board. 'Do you want to come inside the building, or will you wait here for me?'

Gillian elected to stay outside.

Katie pushed her way through some swing doors, and walked boldly across the deserted entrance hall. A uniformed porter was sitting behind a reception desk, reading a newspaper. He looked up, when he saw Katie approach.

'Messrs Lowe & Davies, please,' said Katie, hoping she did right to ask him.

The porter nodded. 'Second Floor, lift's over there.' He

pointed to a black and silver monster, which had just opened to let out three men and couple of giggling girls. They smiled at the youngster who, with an air of bravado, walked into the lift they had vacated.

Katie pressed the appropriate button, the great doors slid together silently, and she was on her way. Now she had got this far, she had a momentary qualm. Was she doing the right thing? She comforted herself with the thought that, even if she was thrown out, no harm would have been done. 'Nothing venture, nothing gain,' she said aloud, to give herself courage.

Soon she stood outside Messrs Lowe & Davies's office door. She made sure she was neat and tidy, then she knocked on the door. It was a louder, more imperious knock that she had intended.

'Come right in,' called out a female voice.

Katie went in, and found herself in a light, spacious room, full of girls, desks, typewriters and filing cabinets. There was a hum of activity about the place, and a noisy clatter of typing. A blonde girl, with a file in her hand, was standing near the door.

'And what can we do for you, kid?' she asked.

The typists stopped typing when they saw Katie standing in the doorway. There was a terrible silence. Katie felt their eyes boring into her, and when she spoke, her voice sounded much too loud and over-confident.

'I've come about the job that was advertised in the Carhampton Gazette, the one for a junior shorthand-typist. May I please see Mr Lowe — or, er, perhaps Mr Davies?'

The blonde laughed, and the others joined in. 'Mr Lowe is in London,' she said, 'but I'm sure he'll be sorry he's missed you and Mr Davies is with a client. I don't think we can interrupt him just to interview you.'

'Well, who do I see then?' asked Katie, annoyance with the blonde's manner giving her added spirit.

290

'Surely you're much too young, dear, to see anyone about a job,' said one of the other girls, quite gently.

'Stop wasting our time, kid,' said the blonde. 'Go on, hop it: we've got enough to do here as it is.'

'No need to be nasty, June.' An older woman at the far end of the room got up from her chair, and beckoned to Katie. 'Come over here a minute, my dear, and tell me all about it.' She smiled at Katie. 'And the rest of you get on with your work.' She was obviously someone of authority here.

Katie threaded her way through the desks, noticing as she did so that there was a glass partition on the left of the room beyond which, in another large room, some men and a few women appeared to be sketching at drawing-boards.

'It's about the job,' repeated Katie, when she reached the older woman.

'How old are you? Twelve or thirteen? I think you'll have to wait a few years before you can start applying for jobs,' said the woman.

'I don't want it for myself,' began Katie, and was about to explain about Susan when a door immediately beyond opened suddenly.

'Could you come and take a few letters, please, Mrs Pratt?' A tall fair man with a neat beard stood in the doorway. His eyes caught sight of Katie, and he grinned. It was a nice, friendly grin. 'Don't tell me we have a new client,' he said. 'What do you want to advertise? We could do you a good poster, advocating shorter school hours.'

'She's come about the vacancy for a shorthand-typist,' smiled Mrs Pratt.

'Oh, has she indeed! Well, you know I always deal with that sort of application,' said the man quite seriously, although his eyes were twinkling. 'Won't you come into my office, Miss...er...'

'Miss Katherine Nichols,' said Katie, glancing triumphantly at the blonde who was standing, open-mouthed, by a filing cabinet.

'You'd better go with Mr Graham — he's our General Manager,' said Mrs Pratt.

Katie obediently followed the man into a well-carpeted room, furnished with dark green leather chairs, its walls covered with the originals of advertising posters, many of which Katie had seen before on hoardings and in magazines. Mr Graham sat down behind his dark green leather-topped desk, and indicated a chair to Katie.

'And what makes you think you'd be suitable for the job, Miss Nichols — or may I call you Katherine?' asked Mr Graham.

'You can call me Katie; everyone does.'

'Right, Katie it shall be.'

'I don't want the job for myself,' she explained, 'I want it for my sister Susan.' And she went on to explain about Susan's shyness, and about the Nichols' unfortunate financial position. She found Mr Graham a most sympathetic listener. 'And Susan is really efficient and capable, and artistic, too, which would help in a place like this, wouldn't it?'

'Certainly, some artistic ability is an asset here,' agreed Mr Graham.

'Tell me,' said Katie, 'do girls out there in the office ever move into that other place next door, where the real work's done?'

'Make no mistake, the typists do real work,' said Mr Graham. 'But, to answer your questions, yes, there have been occasions when a particularly artistic girl has asked for and been given a transfer to the other department.'

Katie said no more; she had shot her bolt, and now waited to hear that the job was Susan's. She'd put the case fairly and squarely; she was convinced that Messrs Lowe & Davies would be getting a bargain in Susan, and she hoped she had managed to convince Mr Graham of this fact, too. Mr Graham tapped his pencil thoughtfully on the desk.

'Katie, may I ask you a few questions?'

'Certainly; fire ahead.' Katie was completely at her ease

292

with this delightful gentleman.

'What are Susan's speeds?'

Katie thought this an odd question, and had no idea what he meant. Surely he couldn't want to know how fast she could run or walk or jump?

'Speeds?' she queried.

'Yes, her shorthand and typing speeds.'

'Oh, those!' Katie vaguely remembered Susan talking about tests — and speeds, now she came to think about it — but she didn't know the answer to the question, neither did she know what speeds were required by a juniour short-hand-typist.

'Three hundred words a minute in shorthand?' she hazarded a guess. Then she recalled Susan having once said that you couldn't type as many words a minute as you could write shorthand. 'And about two hundred in typing, I should think,' she added cautiously.

Mr Graham shook his head, and wagged a finger at her. 'Quite impossible,' he said. 'So far as I know nobody has ever achieved such staggering speeds. We ask for about 100 words a minute in shorthand and 35 or 40 in typing.'

'Oh, do you?' said Katie brightly; it all sounded most complicated to her and she didn't think it could be very important.

'And what about references?' asked Mr Graham. 'Have you brought your sister's testimonials with you?'

'What are those?' asked Katie.

'Letters of recommendation from people who know her, telling us about her character and abilities and so on.'

'But I've told you about that.'

Mr Graham grinned his friendly grin. 'Yes, I know but, as a relation, you are what might be called a biased witness. I mean testimonials from people like her former Head-mistress or the Principal of her Secretarial College or the Minister of your church.'

Katie shook her head dolefully, and confessed she had no

such things.

'Now, Katie, one last question,' said Mr Graham. 'How long has Susan been at College?'

'About three months,' replied Katie quickly; this was something she could answer.

'That's what I thought. And the complete course is usually about a year.'

'Is it? I didn't know that.'

'So your sister couldn't possibly be qualified yet for any sort of post as a shorthand-typist. It's not surprising, is it, that she hasn't much confidence? She will have, just as soon as she feels herself to be completely competent.'

He waited for his words to sink in. Katie was dumbfounded; none of this had occurred to her. As she hadn't discussed the matter with Susan, she had assumed that, if a job could be found for her, she would be ready to take it. She felt rather a fool and, near tears, she rose from her chair.

'Then Susan can't have the job,' she said slowly.

'I'm afraid not.'

'Oh well, that's that. I'm sorry I've wasted so much of your time, Mr Graham. Thank you very much for seeing me.'

She walked towards the door. She was deeply disappointed.

'Just a minute, Katie,' Mr Graham called her back. 'There'll be another job going here at the end of the year. June — the blonde girl you saw in the outer office — is leaving then to get married. If Susan would like to apply when she's finished her course, I think she's just the sort of girl we're looking for.'

Katie's face lit up. So it hadn't all been in vain. 'Oh, thank you, Mr Graham,' she said, 'thank you very, very much — that's certainly better than nothing. I'll tell Susan what you say.'

Mr Graham got up, and opened the door for her. 'Thank you, Miss Nichols,' he said, 'it has been a pleasure to meet you.' He held out his hand, and they shook hands solemnly.

Katie felt very grown up.

She almost danced through the outer office, called out goodbye to Mrs Pratt, and even smiled at June. She was glad it was June who was leaving, as she was sure Susan wouldn't like working in an office with such a silly creature.

'You've been an awful age,' Gillian greeted her when she arrived outside the building. 'I hope Susan got the job or, rather, that you got it for her because if she didn't, you've wasted a lot of valuable time.'

'Well, she didn't exactly, and yet, in a way, she did. It was like this...' And she told Gillian all about it.

'Are you going to tell your mother and Susan when you get home?' asked Gillian, more impressed by Katie's description of her interview than she would admit.

'Yes, I think I'll have to tell them. I hope they won't think I've been a frightful idiot — and I do hope they won't be cross with me.'

As it happened, they didn't think she was an idiot, and they weren't cross with her. Katie chose to tell her story after tea when the three of them were in the sitting-room, comfortable and relaxed. Every now and again, Susan interrupted to say: 'Honestly, Katie, you have got a cheek!' and Mrs Nichols stifled a giggle or two here and there.

'So, there you are,' said Katie finally. 'I'm afraid I didn't achieve much. We'll still be in deep financial waters for some time but, later on, the job's there if you want it, Sue.'

'You're a darling, that's what you are!' exclaimed Susan 'It sounds a gorgeous job, and just the sort of thing I'd like best in the world. And now you've described the office and Mr Graham, I don't believe I should even be nervous at the interview.'

'Well, not once you've got your speeds and are completely competent,' said Katie, quoting Mr Graham and sounding very pompous.

'No harm has been done, and probably quite a lot of good,' said Mrs Nichols, 'but I think, Katie dear, it might have been better if you had consulted me in the first place. This business of our finances seems to have been worrying you. Although we must be a bit more careful than we have been in the past, there's no need for panic; we're not paupers. My job is open for me to go back to in a few months, and I am getting half-pay from the firm in the meantime. I'm sorry if I alarmed you at breakfast this morning. I didn't realise you'd take it so seriously.'

'Katie take things seriously? — never!' laughed Susan. 'I bet she's thoroughly enjoyed her romantic role as saviour of the family fortune and honour.'

Katie thought a bit about this, and then admitted that she supposed it had been rather fun while it lasted.

'And I'll tell you something,' she said, 'today has been a day of great importance in my life. I have come to the conclusion that I could do worse than go in for a business career myself. Perhaps Messrs Lowe & Davies will have a vacancy to offer me when the time comes. Did I tell you? That Mr Graham was quite young and looked rather like my favourite pop star — gosh, he was absolutely dreamy!'

WHITE FOR DANGER

by

Rosemary Weir

Soon after three o'clock the snow began again, slowly at first with tiny flakes drifting before the rising wind, then faster and thicker until the trodden, dirty snow in the village street was hidden under a fresh, dazzling blanket of white. Cars, their chains clanking on the icy roads, switched on their headlamps as the short day waned and the snow-heavy sky brought evening pressing in before its time.

Inside the village hall the Saturday Guide meeting broke up early. Snow was an old enemy of this Dartmoor village and everyone who lived in the neighbourhood knew what snow could do, and treated it with respect.

'Home, girls, as quick as you can,' said Miss Lennard, the Guide captain, anxiously. 'It looks as if we might be in for another heavy fall. All you people who live in the village are all right, but what about the rest of you? Anne, how about you and Jane?'

'Father said he'd pick us up with the Land Rover at half past three outside the post office,' said Anne. 'We'll be all right.'

'Then that only leaves Penny and Tessa to worry about,' said Miss Lennard. 'And they've got further to go than you.'

'We're fixed up,' Penny assured her cheerfully. 'We've only got to walk as far as Tor Cross and Dad will meet us there. He's gone in to Tavistock with the tractor and trailer to fetch pig meal because the lorry can't get along our road, and Dad can take the tractor over the moor. He told us to be at the Cross not later than four, and we'll make it easily, if we go now.'

'Then don't lose any time,' said Miss Lennard rather anxiously. 'Is the road to your farm still blocked?'

'It's right up to the top of the hedges,' Tessa said impressively. 'It's been like that for a month now and you can walk on it, it's frozen so hard.'

Penny and Tessa Biddlecombe lived on a farm right out on the moor. It was only four miles from the village by road, and on fine, hot summer days when the heather was out and the air sweet with the honey-scent of gorse it seemed to the tourists, who stayed at the farm, a most romantic and delightful place to live. Penny and Tessa thought so too, even in the winter, but the visitors might not have agreed with them if they could have seen the little grey stone farmhouse isolated in a waste of snow. The Biddlecombes, however, had been bred to the moorland life, six generations had lived at Merrivale Farm. 'Treat the moor right and mostly he'll treat you right,' Mr Biddlecombe said as soon as the girls were old enough to understand. 'Take liberties and you'll find yourself in trouble. Mist that comes down suddenly, that's the moor's favourite trick; bog is always there, so you can learn its ways. But snow is the worst weapon of Old Man Moor. That's the weapon he uses when he's feeling really vicious. Snow strikes and hits the animals as well as the humans. Snow starves the ponies, unless they've got good owners who catch them in and keep them fed. Snow buries the sheep, and snow would starve us out too if we hadn't the sense to be prepared. Still it doesn't last long as a rule. Only twice in my life have we had a real, long freeze up, and I'll tell you this, girls, I don't mind if I never see one again. Why, last time the frost was so bad I saw ponies frozen where they stood, sheeted in ice, like a parcel wrapped in cellophane. We lit bundles of straw around them and thawed them out. You never saw anything like it in your life! As for the sheep — they just disappeared. We were out every day digging for them, and some we found and some we didn't — not until the thaw came and then it was too late.'

300

And now Old Man Moor was up to his tricks again. Penny, as she pulled on her gum boots and helped Tessa to tie a thick scarf round her head and half over her face so that only her bright blue eyes and snub nose peeped out from a fringe of scarlet wool, thought soberly of the tales her father had told and felt a tiny shiver of apprehension at the idea of the walk ahead of them. It was a full two miles to Tor Cross, an ancient stone monument whose top, lichen covered, still stuck out of the drifts like the snout of some hairy antediluvian monster. She did calculations in her head while Tessa struggled to pull on her boots which were proving a tight fit over an extra pair of woollen socks. Three-quarters of an hour to walk to the Cross, half an hour across the moor in the trailer, then the lights of home, and Mother waiting anxiously with dry clothes warming by the kitchen fire, and the smell of baking, and tea laid all ready on the table. Mother hadn't wanted them to come to Guides today, but they had never missed yet, and Penny was working hard for her first class badge and Tessa for her second class, so they had gone, assuring Mother that they would be back before dark.

Everyone had left the hall by now except Miss Lennard, Penny and Tessa. When they opened the outer door the cold struck at them like a knife, but the snow was lighter again and the wind, momentarily, had dropped.

'It's not so bad,' said Penny. 'I'm rather glad we've had a fresh fall, it's tidied everything up.'

'Well, that's one way of looking at it,' smiled Miss Lennard. 'The motorists won't be pleased though. The Council gritted this road yesterday and now it's all covered up. Well, don't stand about, girls. Hurry on home, and give me a ring when you get there to say you're all right.'

'Oh, Miss Lennard!' protested Penny, but the Guide captain said: 'Yes, please, Penny. I shall worry until I know for certain that you're safe at home. Promise?'

'Guide's promise,' said Penny and gave the Guide salute. Then she and Tessa set off briskly along the road to Tor Cross.

They had gone about halfway when the snow started again. Suddenly, and with no warning, the whole world was blotted out in a whirling whiteness. The wind, which had been moaning softly, rose to a scream and seizing the newly fallen snow tossed it into mad shapes, piling it against the walls and hedges, driving it into the faces of the two girls until they were forced to stop and turn round in order to be able to draw breath. Penny looked about her anxiously for shelter, and saw, not far away, a low stone hut, snow piled to the roof. She knew the hut well; it was a shelter for cattle, and now, if they could get there, it would shelter them until the blizzard died down.

Seizing Tessa's arm she lowered her head and thrust through the driving snow to the hut. Something stirred in the gloom and both girls started violently, but it was only a huddle of sheep pressed close together for warmth.

'They're some of ours,' gasped Tessa as they crept through the low doorway and drew breath in the comparative shelter inside. Penny looked and saw the letters H. B. stamped in blue on the sheep's fleece. At once she felt less frightened. It was comforting, in this white wilderness, to find something that belonged to home.

'We can't stay here long, or we'll miss Dad,' said Tessa. 'Oh, Penny, I don't like this much, do you?'

'It's all right,' said Penny with an assurance she was far from feeling. 'We'll just have a breather, Tess, and then we'll go on. I expect it'll ease off again quite soon.'

She went over to the low doorway and peered out. It was dusk now; only the reflected glimmer from the snow prevented it from being quite dark. She looked towards the road and realised with a shock of fear that she could not see it. Everything, every familiar landmark, had disappeared in the last few moments of blizzard, and outside the hut lay a new country of unfamiliar hills, valleys, mountains where before had been well-known walls, hedges, rocky outcrops and the road.

Which was the way to Tor Cross? Desperately Penny tried to orientate herself. The village lay back there — or did it? Which way did the hut face? It stood with its back to the road, surely? But the road had disappeared, and now darkness began to press down in earnest. Penny's heart thumped, she felt dizzy and very, very tired. The cold seemed to drive right through her head, making it difficult to think. With an effort she pulled herself together.

'Tess,' she said, as casually as possible. 'Come here and see if you can tell which is the way to Tor Cross. It's funny, but it's really getting quite hard to tell.'

Tessa joined her in the doorway, and when she had taken one look outside her usually rosy face grew white.

'Gosh!' she said. 'I don't know! Oh, Penny, are we lost?'

'No, of course not,' said Penny hastily. And then her face brightened. 'It's all right!' she said. 'Look, there's a light. It must be Dad, waiting for us at the Cross. Come on, let's hurry. The snow is letting up a bit and I don't think the wind is quite so bad.'

Clinging together for support the girls left the shelter of the hut and struggled over the soft, newly fallen snow. It was an effort, for at each step they sank almost up to their knees, darkness pressed down and only the small, yellow light drew them on.

'D-Dad will be awfully c-cold hanging about on the t-tractor waiting for us,' said Tessa through blue lips. 'L-Let's shout to t-tell him we're coming.'

'Dad! It's us!' yelled Penny, but her voice was blown away.

The wind rose to a howl, and, tearing the snow clouds apart, allowed a brief glimmer of starlight to shine down on the world below. It was only for a second, but in that second the girls saw, not the comforting, familiar sight of the big scarlet tractor with Dad's burly figure at the wheel and the laden trailer behind, but a small grey cottage, through whose window the twinkling light shone out on to the snow.

Penny and Tessa stopped dead in utter amazement. There

was no cottage between the village and Tor Cross! The only cottage of which they knew was right out on the moor, where a young widow lived alone with a little boy of four or five. People thought she was mad to live in such a lonely spot by herself, but she liked it and walked into the village every day to help the vicar's wife with the housework, taking the boy with her.

'That must be Mrs Bright's cottage,' said Penny incredulously. 'We've been walking in completely the wrong direction since we left the hut. Oh, Dad will be worried if we don't turn up!'

The wind screamed again, the gap in the clouds disappeared and the small, twinkling light was once more the only thing to be seen in the cold, dark world.

'Let's get inside,' muttered Tessa with chattering teeth.

The door of the cottage was on the opposite side to the lighted window. The girls felt their way cautiously along the rough stone walls until their questing hands met the smooth boards of the door. Penny knocked, and they waited, longing desperately for warmth and shelter, but no sound came from inside and no one opened the door.

Penny knocked again and then, seizing the knob, turned it impatiently. The door opened and they stumbled in.

'Mrs Bright?' called Penny. 'Are you there? It's us — Penny and Tess Biddlecombe!'

No one answered; no sound came from the lighted room. Penny, her face tense and white, crossed the little stone-flagged hall and opened the door.

It was the kitchen they found themselves in. The light came from an oil lamp hung from the ceiling, and in the well-blacked grate a coal fire glowed red. On the table was a brown tea pot, two cups and saucers, jam, butter, bread. The kettle purred softly on the hob, but no one was there.

'It's like that ship — the Marie Celeste,' said Tessa with a nervous giggle. 'You know — where everything was ordinary, only everyone had gone...'

304

'She wouldn't take little Brian with her,' protested Tessa. 'Not in this cold. Penny, I think we ought to look in the bedroom. Suppose something *awful* has happened?'

'Such as what?' snapped Penny.

'I don't know,' said Tessa lamely. She went over to the fire and warmed her hands. 'Oh, this is lovely! Penny, do you think she'd mind if we made some tea?'

'Honestly!' exploded Penny. 'One minute you say something awful has happened to poor Mrs Bright and the next you calmly propose to make tea!'

'Listen!' demanded Tessa and Penny stopped talking and stood quite still. A child's voice called from the room over their heads.

'Mummy! Mum-mee!'

'It's Brian!' said Penny. 'Give me that candle, Tessa, and I'll go up.'

'I'll come with you,' said Tessa, handling her the candle in a brass candlestick. 'I've got the creeps and I don't want to stay down here alone.'

Penny lit the candle at the fire and led the way up the steep, narrow little staircase which led directly into the room above.

'Mummy?' came the little boy's voice again with a hint of uncertainty in it, and Penny said quickly:

'It's all right, Brian, it's us. You know us, don't you?'

'No,' said Brian and his mouth turned down at the corners. 'I want Mummy!'

'I expect she'll be back in a minute,' said Penny soothingly. 'I'm Penny, Brian. I gave you a ride on my pony last summer at the Vicarage fête. Remember?'

'No!' roared Brian. 'Want Mummee!'

'Oh dear!' sighed Penny. 'Brian, why are you in bed?'

'I'm poorly. I've got a snuffle in my nose. I want...'

'All right, we know,' put in Penny hastily. 'You want Mummy. Well, where is she?'

'Chopping wood in the shed,' said Brian. 'Fetch her, girl.'

'Righto,' agreed Penny. 'Tess, you stay here and keep him company. It's a shame to leave him all alone in the dark and I daren't leave him the candle.'

'Seems funny that Mrs Bright left him at all,' said Tessa. 'But I suppose she had to get wood. All right, I'll stay. Shall I tell you a story, Brian?'

'No,' grizzled the little boy. 'I want my Mum*mee!*'

Penny went quickly downstairs and out into the yard. Dimly, in the light from the kitchen window, she could see the woodshed, black against the snow, but no light shone out from it and no sound of chopping broke the absolute silence of this tiny oasis amidst the waste of whiteness. Penny began to feel creepy and hastily went back to the kitchen to look round for a torch or lantern. The idea of feeling her way in the dark to that silent shed was unattractive, and it was with relief that she found a small electric torch in the dresser drawer. The battery was almost exhausted but even so the glimmer of light was a comfort, and she set out once more with greater courage.

The door of the woodshed was ajar, and inside it was pitch dark. Penny called: 'Mrs Bright — are you there?' and nervously shone the light around. Then she started violently and nearly dropped the torch as the feeble light shone on the huddled form of a woman lying very still on the beaten earth of the floor. Her eyes were closed, her face chalk white, while from a gash on her ankle blood flowed alarmingly. The chopper lying nearby told its own tale.

'I must keep calm, I *must!*' Penny told herself firmly, as she fought off waves of faintness which swept over her. She struggled desperately to remember the first aid she had learnt in the Guides, and then, quite calmly and competently she found herself doing the right things.

She had just finished bandaging the ankle using her handkerchief as a pad when Mrs Bright opened her eyes and said feebly:

'Where — what — has — happened?'

'It was so silly of me to faint,' said Mrs Bright apologetically

'It's all right, Mrs Bright,' said Penny gently. 'You've cut your ankle chopping wood and you fainted, but I've bandaged you up as best I can. Now all we have to do is to get you back to the house. Do you think you could manage to hop if you leant on me? We must get you back into the warm.'

'Brian — ?' stammered the injured woman, struggling to sit up, and Penny said quickly: 'He's quite all right. My sister is with him, telling him stories. Take my arm and don't be afraid to lean on me. I'm not very tall but I'm awfully strong.'

Getting back across the snowy yard to the house was a nightmare. The snow drove into their faces and their feet sank deep, making every step a major operation. By the time the kitchen was reached Mrs Bright was again on the point of collapse, while Penny's breath came fast and her arms felt as if they had been wrenched out of their sockets!

'Mum*mee*!' shouted a furious little voice from upstairs, and Tessa called down anxiously, 'Are you all right?'

Ten minutes later everything, as Penny said, was under control. Mrs Bright, her injured ankle supported by a cushion on a stool, sat before the fire, a steaming cup of tea in her hand and the colour gradually flooding back into her pale cheeks. Brian, well wrapped up, sat on Tessa's lap opposite his mother, sipping hot milk.

'It was so silly of me to faint,' said Mrs Bright apologetically. 'I do feel so stupid. It was the cold, I think, as much as the pain of the cut. My hands were so numb I couldn't hold the axe firmly and then when it slipped and cut my ankle, well, I just passed out. What would have happened if you two hadn't come along I shudder to think.' She paused, and said in a bewildered voice: 'But why *are* you here? It's not on your way home?'

'Lost in the snow,' said Tessa cheerfully. 'We were supposed to meet Dad at Tor Cross.'

'But that's in the opposite direction,' said Mrs Bright. 'Oh, my dears, they'll be half mad with worry about you!'

'I know,' said Penny soberly. 'I've been thinking about that, but I don't see what we can do. I'm afraid we'll have to stay here, Mrs Bright, at least until the morning, if you don't mind.'

'Mind? Of course I don't mind,' said Mrs Bright. 'But I do wish we had some way of getting in touch with your poor parents. They'll be out of their minds with worry when you don't turn up.'

'Tractor!' said Brian suddenly, sitting bolt upright on Tessa's lap.

'Don't be silly, darling,' said his mother gently. 'There can't be any tractors out tonight.'

'Tractor! Tractor! Tractor!' bawled Brian, and Mrs Bright said uncertainly:

'I wonder — he's got very sharp hearing. Open the window a crack, Penny, and let's all listen hard.'

Penny opened the window, shivering as the keen air flowed in. She stood quite still peering out into the darkness and far, far away it seemed to her she could see a dim light moving slowly over the moor.

'Tractor!' said Brian again with great satisfaction. 'I told you so.'

'I can hear it now,' said Tessa, leaning over Penny's shoulder. 'Yes, and there are two lights, not one. It's Dad — I'm sure it is, looking for us. You know he's got those extra strong headlamps on the tractor. He had them put on when he was behindhand with the ploughing and had to work at night,' she continued, turning to Mrs Bright. 'We've got to attract his attention, Penny. What can we do?'

'He'll be searching for you along the road,' said Mrs Bright in a worried voice. 'He'll never think of coming all the way out here. Oh dear, he and your poor mother must be so worried. If only we could think of something...'

'Could we signal with the lamp?' asked Tessa doubtfully.

'Not strong enough,' Penny answered briefly. Then an

idea struck her and she said 'I know! We'll do what ship-wrecked people do when they see a sail.'

'Have you gone potty?' asked Tessa, staring. 'They wave things and the ship sees them, but it's pitch dark and if we waved till we were blue in the face Dad couldn't see a thing.'

'They don't only wave,' said Penny excitedly. 'They light a bonfire. Mrs Bright, have you any straw, and paraffin?'

'In the woodshed,' said Mrs Bright. 'There's a bale of straw there, and plenty of paraffin in the drum. Oh, you are a clever girl! Only be careful with the paraffin. Stand well clear when you throw the match.'

'I'll be careful,' Penny promised. 'Tess, you'd better come and give a hand with the straw bale. Quick now, before Dad gets out of sight!'

The straw bale was soon dragged into the yard. The binder twine was cut so that the straw fell apart and paraffin was thrown liberally over it. Then Penny ordered Tessa to stand well back, lit a match, threw it on to the paraffin-soaked straw and retreated in haste. The straw exploded into bright flame and burnt fiercely, lighting up the white landscape all around. Far away the twin light of the tractor halted, then swung in their direction and soon everyone could plainly hear the engine labouring through the snow.

'We're here, Dad?' shouted Penny as the tractor drew up outside the cottage, and Mr Biddlecombe said quietly 'Thank goodness for that. You've given us all a rare fright.'

'Sorry, Dad,' said Tessa cheerfully. 'But it wasn't our fault. We got lost in the blizzard. What did you think when you saw your shipwrecked mariner's signal?'

'I thought Mrs Bright's cottage was on fire,' Mr Biddle-combe said shortly. 'I was torn in two, I can tell you, trying to decide whether to come and help her or go on looking for you. I never thought to kill two birds with one stone. But now I am here, m'dear,' he went on, turning to Mrs Bright, 'I'm going to take you and young Brian home to Merrivale.

My wife will see to that nasty cut on your leg, and make a real fuss of the lad. We've nothing but girls at home and they're not worth much!'

'I'll not have you say that,' cried Mrs Bright. 'No, not even in joke! The girls have been wonderful. I might have died out there in the shed of cold and loss of blood if they hadn't turned up and known just what to do. It's too awful to think about. I'll come back with you gladly, and many thanks.

'Well, maybe girls aren't so bad,' said Mr Biddlecombe looking proudly at daughters. 'I reckon the Guides teaches them a bit of sense. Now, wrap up warm, and bundle young Brian in blankets. There's a thick bed of straw in the trailer and you won't do so badly.'

'Goodbye to the island!' called Tessa as they jolted away through the snow, but it was Brian who had the last word.

'I *told* you it was a tractor!' he said.

FORGOTTEN ISLAND
by
Elizabeth Coatsworth

The fortune-teller told them both the same fortune. Jane went into the tent first and sat there with her hand held out across a table covered with an Oriental cloth. She felt a little scared, as the woman in the bright-coloured skirt and white waist, with earrings and a handkerchief about her head, looked at her palm for a while. Then the fortune-teller said, 'There is adventure ahead of you. I see it soon, and yet the adventure is connected with something from far away and long ago.'

The fortune-teller said some other things, too, unimportant things that didn't stick in Jane's mind after the sound had left her ears. She paid her quarter and slipped out. John was waiting for her.

'Any good?' he asked.

'I'm not sure,' said Jane. 'I don't suppose she's a real gypsy.'

'The money goes to charity anyhow. I'd better see what she tells me,' John said, and he went in.

'What did she tell you?' Jane asked as he came out a few minutes later.

'Oh, a lot of stuff about school, and being on the football team if I only believed I could make it — a lot of stuff like that. And then she said I was to have an adventure, soon, and that it was connected with a faraway place and things that had happened a long time ago.'

Jane's grey eyes flashed indignantly.

'I bet she says that to everyone! That's just what she told me. I feel like going in and asking for my quarter back.'

'Hold on.' John was more logical than Jane. 'Maybe we might be going to have it together.'

They stuck around the tent. It was part of a church affair on Mrs Sumner's lawn and it was made up mostly of flower and needlework booths and things like that, with a pony they felt they were too big to ride, and a grab bag filled mostly with rubber dolls and rubber balls. After getting themselves another bag of brownies, they had plenty of time to question some of their friends who had had their fortunes told, too.

'Hi there, Bill! What did she tell you?'

They must have asked five or six children, but to none of them had there been promised an adventure of any kind.

'It bet she means our going up to the cabin. That's an adventure, right on Green Pond, in the woods and everything,' Jane said. But John, who was two years older, twelve going on thirteen, shook his head.

'It couldn't be that, Jane,' he argued. 'The cabin's new. Dad just had it built last winter. And it's on land where nothing has ever been before. That couldn't be it. We'll have to wait and see.'

'I can't bear to wait!' Jane cried.

John grinned at her. 'Don't know what you'll do about it,' he said. 'Come on, I've got five cents left. That'll get us a big piece of fudge, anyhow.'

Two weeks later the Lane family were climbing out of their car at the end of a rough Maine wood-road. At the same moment the smell of pine needles and fresh water, the sight of the lake shining between the straight trunks of the trees, and the wild shaking call of a loon struck upon their senses like a welcome to the wilderness. For just a moment they all stood still, feeling happy. Then Mr Lane unlocked the back of the car and they began to carry suitcases and blankets into the new log cabin which stood a little back from the edge of the water. They were as busy as four chipmunks during acorn season.

No one but Mr Lane had ever seen the place. It was his

surprise. He had been travelling up to Maine every week or two since last fall to superintend the building of the cabin. It was made of peeled logs, oiled so they would stay clean and shining. It had a big living room with a boulder fireplace with a fire already laid, which mother immediately lighted as a house-warming. There was a small kitchen, too, with a sink and a new pump painted red under the window, and three bedrooms in a row opening from the big room. Out of John's room a stairway led up into the loft where cots could be placed when the Lanes had friends. Everything was complete; the furniture was in place, simple and strong; the china stood on the china-shelves; the skillets hung behind the wood stove, shining in their newness; and the picture calendar on the wall was torn off to June.

'Jim!' exclaimed Mrs Lane. 'You've thought of everything.'

'You're pleased, Janet?' Father asked anxiously. 'It's the way you thought it would be?'

'Only much nicer!' said Mother.

The Lanes were a family who had very good times together. Their names all began with 'J' and they often called themselves the four Jays, and the bluejay was their totem-bird, so bright and gay even in the falling snow. They loved to go camping together and they all could paddle and fish and swim and build a fire outdoors and flap pancakes on a skillet. So it had seemed perfect when Father found this land on a secluded cove in Green Pond and began to have a cabin built for them. Now that he was a senior member in his law firm, he seemed able to get away from his office a good deal in summer.

'People don't feel so quarrelsome in warm weather,' he used to say — though that was probably a joke. 'They get crotchety in the fall and begin to go to law with each other after the first hard frosts.'

Anyhow, whether he was joking or not as to the reason Father managed to get away a good deal in the summer. Now they had a place of their own, and he and Mother were

317

happy all day long working on the finishing touches. John and Jane tried to help, and did, too, but there were times when there was no need for them. Then they were likely to get into their bathing suits, pack a light lunch, and take to the canoe to go exploring.

They had named the canoe *The Adventure* because of the church fair prophecies, but for a long time their excursions were of a quiet character. Green Pond was about ten miles long, but its shore line was very uneven. Now the pond was a mile or two wide, now it narrowed to a few hundred feet, only to widen once more. Long coves indented its wooded shores, and here and there an island lay like a frigate becalmed. There were farms along the slopes in many places, but only occasionally did their hay fields stretch down to the water. More often there lay a fringe of woods or rough pastures along the lake. Sometimes, these woods were very thick, extending into the wilderness which covers Maine, the great central wilderness on which the farmlands lie like scattered patches hardly noticeable to the eagle flying high against the whiteness of the summer clouds.

There were no towns on Green Pond, no summer cottages except their own, no camps. Paddling along with silent paddles the children came upon many things — a deer drinking, or a fox slipping off into the underbrush, or a fish hawk rising, its prey catching the sunlight as it dangled in those fierce claws.

They heard voices calling at the farms, usually hidden from sight, and sometimes towards evening they came upon a farmer fishing after the milking was done. But the sounds which they heard most constantly were the clank-clank of cowbells and the slow notes of the thrushes. Less often, they heard sheepbells. And of course there were other birds, too — the warblers and white-throated sparrows and, above all, the big loons which seemed to like them and often appeared floating near them, uttering their lonely cries. But when the children paddled too close, the loons would dive, and when

318

they reappeared it would be a long way off, to teach the young humans that they must keep their distance.

One day as John and Jane were eating their lunch on a flat rock under a pine at the opening of a small bay, a curious sound began to vibrate through the air. It was hard to tell where it came from. It filled the bay and echoed back from the slopes above the trees, all the time growing louder.

Jane stopped eating her sandwich.

'What's that?' she asked in a low voice. 'It sort of scares me.'

John squinted his eyes across the glint of water.

'It must be an outboard motor,' he said. 'It sounds near. We ought to see it.'

But they saw nothing that day.

In the weeks which followed, however, they became acquainted with that sound. Sometimes they heard it at night, waking up to raise their heads from their pillows to listen to its passing. It sounded then as though it circled in front of their cabin, like an animal circling a fire. Sometimes they heard it by day, and once, in a thick fog, it passed very close to them. They saw the outlines of a boat and of a figure in an old slouch hat at the stern. They waved, but there was no gesture from the boat, and in a moment it was gone again. Only the coughing of the engine and the rank smell of gasoline fumes were left to stain the ghostly silver of the day.

'There's something queer about that man,' said Jane. 'Why don't we ever see him? And why didn't he wave?'

John sent the canoe ahead with a powerful stroke of his paddle. 'He probably didn't see us,' he answered.

Jane still had her paddle trailing.

'No,' she said, 'it's a feeling. It's as though he were always sneaking around the lake. Whenever I hear him it scares me, but when the engine stops, it's worse. Then I don't know where he is or what he's doing. But I know he's up to no good.'

'That's just because his outboard motor's old and has that stumbling sound,' insisted John. 'He's probably a farmer at one of the farms trying to get some bass for supper.'

'He chooses very queer hours to go fishing then,' Jane said, unconvinced. 'And I don't know when he gets his farm work done, either. You know as well as I do that there's something queer about him, John, so don't keep on pretending there isn't.'

'Have it your own way, Jen,' John said, not admitting anything. But a queer little cold feeling came over him, too, whenever he heard that choking splutter across the water.

Often the children would explore the woods along the shore, following little paths or wood-roads when they saw them. One afternoon towards dusk they were going single file along a trail so faint that they were not sure it was a trail at all. Perhaps the deer used it, or a cow coming down to the pond-side to drink. And, yet, here and there a twig seemed to have been broken off as though by a human hand.

It was hot in the woods and the mosquitoes bothered them.

'I vote we go back,' said Jane at last, stopping. But John peered over her shoulder.

'There's a little cliff ahead,' he said. 'Let's just go that far and then we'll go back.' It seemed wrong to turn around until they'd reached some sort of landmark.

The cliff was very pretty, its seams filled with ferns, while funguses which they called 'elephants' ears' seemed to be peeling in great green-and-grey scales from the granite surfaces. A squirrel scolded from a branch overhead and, far off, a thrush was singing in a solitude of its own.

But the children had no eyes for the woods at that moment. Around the faint bend of the trail something was hanging from a high branch. Jane gave a little scream of surprise and then stood staring. For it was the carcass of a sheep, such as she had sometimes seen in a butcher's shop, but strange and terrifying to come upon here in the midst of the woods.

For once the children said nothing. They stared and stared and then turned, and John made room for Jane to pass him and go first, while he brought up the rear with one horrified look over his shoulder. They crashed through the woods like two runaway colts, and never stopped until *The Adventure* was well out from shore.

Jane heaved a great sigh. 'Well!' she said.

'Well!' said John.

Their father was quite matter-of-fact about their tale when they told it.

'Probably a farmer has killed one of his sheep, and didn't have any way of getting it up to the ice-house just then. So he may have hung it high out of reach of foxes until he can bring down a horse or a wheelbarrow for it.'

'Dad, a horse or a wheelbarrow couldn't get to that place, and it wasn't near any sheep pasture, either,' John said.

'It's the man with the outboard motor!' cried Jane.

'You're jumping to conclusions, Jen,' her father declared. 'You haven't an iota of evidence that would stand in any court.'

'Bedtime,' said Mother.

But after a day or two of inquiry, they heard from the postmaster at the little post office, a mile or two away on the crossroads, that several sheep and heifers had disappeared in the neighbourhood during the spring and summer. Some people thought that maybe a bear had come down from the north, or, worse still, a lynx. If dogs had been running the stock, there would probably have been more noise. People were inclined to think that the killer was a bear. There had been one seen for a while four or five years ago.

'A bear doesn't butcher his meat and hang it up a tree,' said Father, and told the postmaster where the children had seen the carcass. They felt very important for a little while and would have gone on discussing the affair, if something had not happened to put it altogether out of their minds.

About three miles from the Lanes' cabin, across the pond, there was a cove lying between low marshy banks, where the swamp stood thick, with now and then a few pines on a knoll. The cove, too, was very shallow, choked with water plants of all sorts.

Several times John and Jane had forced their way for a few yards into this marine flower garden, but the canoe moved very slowly. John had to use his paddle for poling while Jane peered ahead, alert for the old submerged logs which here and there lay on the shallow bottom, the bark long since peeled away, but the white stubs of branches still thrust out to rake against the bottom of a passing boat.

They had soon turned back, until one day, when pushing in as usual among the reeds, they came upon a sort of channel leading up into the cove.

'It almost looks as though it had been made,' said John; 'anyhow, let's go up it.'

If the channel actually had been cleared, it must have been done a long time ago, for here and there it was completely grown over and once more the reeds would close about *The Adventure*, scraping its sides with their rubbery touch. Yet by standing upright for a moment in the bow, Jane was always able to see clear water ahead, and they would push into a new opening.

The cove was much longer and wider then they had dreamed. They seemed to be moving in a small separate pond surrounded by maple-covered shores; all view of Green Pond was lost now, with its slopes of farmlands and woodlands and the Canton hills along the west. The breeze was lost, too. It was very hot among the reeds, and still. There was a secret feeling, moving slowly along these hidden channels, while the dragonflies darted silently in and out among the leaves and a kingfisher flew overhead.

Deeper and deeper they went into this mysterious place, and as they went they grew more and more quiet. A voice sounded out of place in this silence. First they spoke in whispers, and then they scarcely spoke at all; Jane, balancing herself at the bow when the passage was blocked, merely pointed to the clear water ahead.

It seemed only natural that they should come upon something wonderful, so they were excited but not surprised when

Above the beach stood an old-fashioned house with fretwork scrolls

they saw an island ahead of them. It, too, was larger than one would have expected, and rockier. There were pines on it and tumbled ledges ten or fifteen feet high. The channel led to a cove where a small beach lay between low horns of rock. At a distance it would have seemed merely another knoll in the swamplands, but it was a real island, with water all about it, and the shore of the mainland still some distance away.

It seemed only part of the enchantment of the place that a house should stand above the beach, an old-fashioned house with fretwork scrolls ornamenting its eaves, and an elaborate veranda. One or two of the windows had been broken by falling branches or blundering birds, and the door stood open into the darkness of a hall.

The children exchanged one glance of awed agreement and in a moment the bow of *The Adventure* grated on the sand. Jane jumped to the shore and turned to pull the canoe further up the beach.

Still in silence they ran up the rotting steps, and with a last glance backward into the sunlight, stepped through the gaping door into the house.

'You never saw anything like it in your life,' said Jane. 'It was all dusty and spooky with cobwebs over everything!'

'And the swallows flew out and nearly scared us to death,' said John. 'They had their nests on the top bookcase shelves—'

'One of them flew straight at my head! I thought it was a bat and would get into my hair.'

'And there were footstools made of elephants' feet stuffed with straw, but the rats had got at them, and ...'

'You've forgotten about the chairs and table made of horns, John ...'

'You mean I haven't had a chance to tell about them! And there was a crocodile on the mantel ...'

'Hold on! Hold on, children! Is this a dream or a new game, or what?' Father demanded.

'It's all real as real as real!' the children cried. 'It's the island we discovered.'

'They couldn't make up a house like that,' Mother said. 'You know they couldn't, Jim. What else was there, children?'

'Well,' began John, 'there were lion skins and zebra skins on the floor, but they were pretty well eaten up, and on each end of the mantel there was a big bronze head...'

'Of a Negro girl,' interrupted Jane. 'John thinks they might have been boys because their hair was short, but they looked like girls and they had necklaces around their necks and their heads were held high...'

'And there were ivory tusks coming out of their heads. They were holders for the tusks. You'd like them, Mother. And there was another statue standing in an opening in the bookcase, about three feet high, a chief or a god or something with eyes made of seashells, and hollow.'

'Yes, and tell what was written over the mantel in queer letters—you remember we learned it—"The Bight of..." what was it, John?'

'Oh, the Bight of Benin,
The Bight of Benin,
One comes out
Where three goes in.'

'That settles it,' said Father. 'You two haven't gone mad or been hypnotised or had a dream. Your evidence is too circumstantial. That's the beginning of an old sea chanty of the African Gold Coast. What else was there in this house?'

The children stared at him, their eloquence brought to a sudden stop.

'That's about all, Dad,' John said, wrinkling his forehead, trying to bring back that strange interior with its smell of dust and mice and the stirrings overhead of loose boards. How could he describe how he and Jane had clung together, their hearts hammering, tiptoeing from room to room, ready to run at a moment's notice.

They hadn't gone upstairs. Upstairs had seemed too far from the open door. No one knew where they were. There might be some mysterious person living in this house, after all. They might come face to face with him at any moment. There were ashes in the fireplace. How long would ashes last? And in the dark kitchen into which they had peered for a breathless moment, John had seen fish bones on the sink drain and an old knife. How long would fish bones last? Who had been using that knife and how long ago?

A sudden squawk from a heron outside had raised the hair on their heads. They had catapulted towards the door and then tiptoed back into what had been the living room.

'Do you think we might take the crocodile?' Jane asked wistfully. 'The rats will eat it if we leave it here.'

But John had a very strong sense of law.

'We don't know who owns the house,' he said. 'It would just be stealing. And if the rats haven't eaten it by now, they won't eat it before we can get back.'

For hours the Lanes sat before their own fireplace, talking over the mysterious house and making guesses about it.

It grew darker and darker outside, but Mother forgot to start supper on the stove and everyone forgot to be hungry. Over and over the children described just where they had found the house in its own lost and secluded cove. Then they went over what they had found inside. Now and then Mother asked a question, but Father hardly said anything; he sat looking into the fire, smoking his pipe. It kept going out, and had to be refilled and relighted every few minutes, so the children knew he must be very interested.

'Far away and long ago,' said Jane suddenly. 'This is our adventure, John.'

John was about to answer when the old droning squeal of the outboard motor sounded from the darkness of the lake. Once again it moved nearer and nearer them, and once more it seemed to pass their windows only to turn and pass them again.

'There's that same fisherman,' Mother said, a little uneasily.

Father went to the door.

'Ahoy, friend!' he called into the darkness. 'Ahoy! Won't you come ashore and have a visit?'

The engine seemed to check for a minute as though someone were listening. Then it began to sputter with its sawmill-wheel violence and, after apparently circling them once more, whined off down the pond and at last merged into silence.

'I guess he couldn't hear me, that old outboard of his makes such a racket,' Father said as he came back from the open doorway. 'Anyway, it's of no importance. It's your island that interests me. Now all I can say is that there are several little ports on the Maine coast which once carried on a regular trade with the Gold Coast in the sailing-ship days. Take Round Pond — that's only about twenty miles from here. Fifty years ago, they say, it used to be full of monkeys and parrots and African gimcracks brought back by the sailors. But your house has things too fine for any ordinary sailor to bring home. And why should he build a house on an island in a pond, and then desert it, with everything in it? If he was a captain, why didn't he build a house in a seaport, the way most of them did?'

'Maybe he didn't want people to know where he had gone,' Jane suggested.

'Maybe that's it,' agreed Father. 'But don't you think that's a little too blood-and-thundery? He probably was just a nice old gentleman whose nephew had been on a hunting trip to Africa and brought back a few trophies for his eccentric old uncle. He kept them round for a few years, and then got tired of the place and went out to California to visit his married sister. He liked it so well that he decided to buy a house, and never bothered to send for the African stuff, which he was tired of anyhow.'

John looked at his father indignantly.

'That might be it, Dad,' he exlaimed. 'But how about his writing "The Bight of Benin, the Bight of Benin"?'

"One comes out where three goes in," Jane finished the quotation softly.

Father looked thoughtfully into the fire.

'Yes,' he agreed, 'that has the voice of adventure in it. Maybe it wasn't anyone's eccentric old uncle after all. We'll find out soon enough.'

'How?' the children cried, all awake and excited once more.

'We'll go to the town clerk and see in whose name the house stands.'

'Tomorrow?' begged the children.

'Tomorrow, rain or shine,' promised Father.

'And now,' said Mother, 'what about some scrambled eggs and stewed tomatoes? It's after nine o'clock.'

It took old Mr Tobin over an hour and two pairs of glasses before he found the record of the ownership of the island.

'Here it is,' he said at last in some triumph. 'A man named E.R. Johnson bought it from old man Deering — the Deerings still own the farm back there on the east shore — paid two hundred dollars for it. That was on April 7, 1867. I remember there was talk about him when I was a boy. But he didn't stay more than two or three years, and I thought the place had burned or fallen down long ago.'

He licked his thumb and turned the pages.

'Let's see, here's the assessment for 1877, thirty dollars — that must have been after the house was built, of course. Paid. Here's 1878, paid too, and 1879. After that it's all unpaid. In 1883 they dropped the assessment to five dollars — guess they thought the house weren't worth much by then.'

He went on turning pages with interest, while the Lanes sat about him on kitchen chairs watching his every motion.

'Now here's 1890. I can't find any record of an assessment at all. Guess they thought a swamp island which didn't belong to anyone weren't worth carrying in the books. Kind of forgot about her. Yes, here's 1891. No sign of her in this, either. Well, let's figure her up. Three years at thirty dollars is ninety. And seven years at five is thirty-five, add ninety, and it makes one hundred and twenty-five dollars back taxes.

'Anyone who wanted to pay one hundred and twenty-five dollars would own the island.'

Father rose and shook hands with Mr Tobin and thanked him for his trouble.

'We'll talk it over,' he said mildly. 'Nice weather we're having, but we need rain.'

'My peas aren't filling out,' agreed Mr Tobin; 'just yellowing on the vine. If we don't get a thunder shower soon all the gardens in Maine won't be worth cussing at.'

Mother couldn't stand it.

'Aren't we going to buy the island, Jim?' she asked.

But Father only looked absent-minded.

'Have to talk it over,' he repeated vaguely. 'Come, children, in we get. We ought to drive to town and get provisions. Thank you, Mr Tobin. See you later — maybe.'

In the car all the Lanes began chattering.

'Can we have it?'

'Are you going to buy it?'

'Oh, Father, how wonderful!'

'Look here,' said Father severely. 'You people don't know how to act about forgotten islands. You want to keep them forgotten. Raise as little talk as you can, slip in quietly, buy them quietly, don't start a ripple on the water. You'll spoil it all if you get the whole countryside sightseeing and carrying off souvenirs. So long as Mr Tobin just thinks you kids have run across an old ruined cottage on an island, which you'd like as a camping place, he'll hardly give it a thought, but you mustn't start his curiosity working.'

'But you will buy it?' Jane begged.

'Of course, I will. What's more I'll buy it for you and John. You found it and it's going to be yours. What'll you name it? Adventure Island?'

'No,' said John, 'I like Forgotten Island better. It seems more like the Bight of Benin.'

'What is a bight?' Jane asked. 'I like Forgotten Island, too. Forgotten Island, Forgotten Island. It makes me feel sad and wonderful.'

'A bight,' said her father patiently, 'is a very large bay. Benin was a great city up the river from the Gold Coast. Those bronzes must have come from there, for the Negroes of Benin were famous for their bronze work. They used to trade in slaves and were very cruel. It was an unhealthy coast for whites. They died from fever and all sorts of tropic diseases.'

It was not until late afternoon that the children paddled their parents over to see Forgotten Island. All was as it had been the day before, except that the thunderheads were crowding along the sky to the northwest and there was a little breeze, even across the acres of the water garden. They were lucky in finding the channel again and in managing to keep to it, with Jane as look out. Once *The Adventure* rasped over a flat stone, and for a second they all thought they might be stuck there, but after a moment or two, they pushed the canoe sideways and were able to go on.

But today there was a different feeling in the air. There was a continual rustling among the maples as though they were preparing for a storm. A big turtle slid off a rock at the edge of the shore, and raised its head to stare at them as they went by. It thought itself hidden among the reeds, but they could see its horny nose and two small bead-like eyes as it watched the human intruders from its hiding place. Even the house had a more secret air about it. The door still stood open, but Jane suddenly thought of a trap, and even with her father and mother there, hung back a little before going in.

However, this curious antagonism, which all felt but no one mentioned, was not strong enough to drown their interest once the Lanes had stepped across the threshold. All that the children had remembered was true and more still. There were carvings in wood which they had forgotten, split and

330

stained with age. They found chief's stools upheld by grinning squat figures shaped from solid logs, and hangings of curious woven cloths on the wall. Father and Mother were as excited as the children.

'I can't believe my own eyes,' Mother kept exclaiming.

Father said more than once: 'Now who the dickens was this man Johnson, and where did he come from, and where did he go to?'

This day they went upstairs, testing each step carefully to make sure it would hold. There were three bedrooms on the second floor; only one was fully furnished, and it did not seem to go with the rest of the house. It had a set of heavy walnut furniture and a photograph of a mountain in a gold frame. The matting on the floor smelled of mould and damp, and a hornet's nest hung papery and lovely from one corner of the ceiling. Not a thing in the room suggested Africa.

'It's as though Mr Johnson hadn't wanted to think of Africa when he went to bed,' Mother said, quietly, as she looked about. 'Perhaps the Bight of Benin was something he preferred to think about by daylight.'

Jane was standing near the window, and happened to look out. She had a distinct feeling of seeing something move behind the bushes along the shore. But though she thought 'It's a man,' she really wasn't sure. Things move sometimes in the corner of your glance, half out of sight.

Lightning flashed in the sky, silent, without thunder, and the trees shook their leaves and shivered down all their branches. She could see nothing now but the whitening leaves. Their motion must have been what had caught her attention. She said nothing, but she was ready to go back to the new cabin, which Father had built for them, about which there was no mystery.

The lightning flashed again, brighter this time, like light on copper.

'Goodness!' exclaimed Mother. 'I suppose we'd better be getting home before it rains. But I feel as though we were leaving a foreign land. I expect to see giraffes staring at us when we push off.'

Halfway out of the cove a sound began at some distance.

'Thunder?' Father asked, cocking his head, but the children knew, without waiting to hear it again, that it was the sound of an old outboard motor going about its secret business.

The next day Father bought the island for back taxes and had the deed made out to John Lane and Jane Lane. The children signed it with a sense of awe.

'Now you'll have a place you can call your own,' Father said, for Mr Tobin's benefit. 'You can camp there, if you're able to find a spot where the roof doesn't leak.'

'Yes, Dad,' the children exclaimed dutifully, but their eyes were wild with excitement. Forgotten Island was theirs. They owned its remoteness and its mystery, or it owned them. Anyway, they were bound together for all time.

For two days the words had been going through Jane's head day and night:

> 'Oh, the Bight of Benin,
> The Bight of Benin,
> One comes out
> Where three goes in.'

She woke up with the verse ringing through her mind like the echoes of a gong. It had rained during the night and the air was bright and clear this morning. She was ashamed of the oppression which had overtaken her the afternoon before on the island. The coming storm had set her to shivering like the trees, she thought, and with no more reason. Why had she imagined they were being spied on? If anyone else knew about the island, wouldn't he have taken away the things long ago?

Mr Tobin saw them to his door.

'Jo Taylor, down the pond Canton way, has lost another

heifer. He went out to the pasture lot to give them their salt and he says only four came for it. He had a look around, but couldn't find a sign of her. He's going to report it. There's a man calls himself Trip Anderson came in here last March and built himself a shack on the lake. Jo's suspicious of him, but it's pretty hard to get proof. People have been missing more than usual from their gardens, too, but no one would ever go to law over that. Jo's mad about the heifer, though. He says he could have forgiven a man's taking one of them, but two's going too far.'

'Has Trip Anderson got an outboard motor?' John asked.

'Yes,' said Tobin, 'so they say. They don't know where it came from either. He's taken the old boat Eb Carson used to have before he died and patched it up and Mrs Carson says she don't grudge him the boat. It was just rotting down by the willows. But no one's missed an outboard.'

'We've been all round the lake,' said Jane, 'and we've never seen his shack.'

'I haven't either,' Mr Tobin agreed. 'Don't get down to the pond much these days, though when I was a boy I was there most of my spare time. I'm not sure as anyone's seen his place, but they know it must be there, probably back a piece from the water. He's worked some for people. Told them he was planning to bring his wife and little girl when he got settled.'

That afternoon the children spent a rapturous two or three hours on Forgotten Island. Once more the place had its quiet enchanted air.

Jane had brought a broom and begun the task of sweeping the living room, tying her hair up in her sweater when she saw what clouds of dust she raised. John carried out the more torn and bedraggled of the skins. One of the hangings on the wall was in shreds, but another had held. A zebra skin, too, was in fairly good condition. They put it in front of the hearth and John gathered enough dead wood outdoors to lay a new fire.

'I'll bring an axe next time,' he said. 'And we must have matches in a tin box. Jane, have you noticed? This room seems as though it belonged to an older building. It's built stronger for one thing, and the floor boards are nearly two feet wide and the ceiling is lower. I think Mr Johnson added on the rest of the house to something which was already here.'

They went about examining the place and decided that John's guess had been right. The windows in the living room had many panes, and in the other rooms they were only divided down the middle in a bleak way, and the thin boarded floors swayed under the children's weight. The veranda was askew and the jigsaw work broken along the eaves. More and more, they saw that the living room belonged to something staunch or better.

'Perhaps we might get the rest torn down some day and have this for the house, with a low shingled roof. We could cook over the open fire.'

'And we could have a long window seat built along one wall which we could sleep on —'

'And we'd keep the African things —'

They got very excited making their plans. All the time they were talking they worked, and by mid-afternoon the room looked very thrilling. They had rifled the other rooms for anything sound and strong, and now the old part of the house had the aspect of the sitting-room of some African trader. The children half expected to see Negroes stealing in and out, and a bearded man, dressed in white, sitting in the largest chair.

They had never been so excited or so happy in their lives. They could not bear to go away from their new possession and kept returning to put a last touch here or there. At last the sun had gone down and they knew they must go home. But just then Jane discovered a mass of old rats' nests and rubbish behind the bronze figure which stood on the floor in the niche in the bookcase. The figure was about three feet high and not as heavy as she had supposed. She dragged at it too hard, and it toppled over and fell with a terrifying clang.

'Oh dear!' cried Jane. 'I hope it hasn't dented! But wait, John, till I sweep out the alcove. Then you can help me get him back in place.'

The statue lay on its side where it had fallen and they could see that it was hollow. It had one hand raised above its head. Perhaps it was from inside this hand, or from some corner inside the head that the things had been jarred which they found on the floor when they started to put the statue back in place.

Gold is gold, and does not rust, no matter how long it may lie hidden. The ring, the crude little crocodile, the bird, the figure which looked like a dwarf — all were of soft virgin gold, almost warm to the children's stroking fingers.

'Look,' murmured Jane in awe, 'there's gold dust on the floor, too.'

The children looked and handled and exclaimed, scarcely able to believe their own good fortune. This was 'far away and long ago' with a vengeance.

'I wish I could go and thank that fortune-telling lady,' Jane said at last. 'Don't you feel, John, as though she'd made it all happen?'

'It's getting late,' John's conscience reminded him. 'Mother and Dad will be sending out a search party for us soon. Let's put the treasure back where we found it and bring them over tomorrow and surprise them.'

'Oh, let's take it back with us!' protested Jane. 'You know, John, I've had the queerest feeling twice that we were being watched? Yesterday, when we were all here, and today after the statue fell. Something seemed to be at that window.'

'What sort of thing, Jen?'

'I couldn't see. When I turned it was gone.'

'Why didn't you tell me?'

'I didn't want you to call me a silly.'

John went out quickly and looked under the window. There was a rank growth of nettles there and not one had been broken.

'You've been seeing things, Jane,' he declared cheerfully as he came back. 'No one could have been at the window. Now be a good girl and give me the treasure. Good, those ought to stay put. I've used my handkerchief to help stuff them back in place. Now let's get Mumbo Jumbo on his feet again. There he is, just as we found him.'

All the time she was helping, Jane was protesting and arguing under her breath, but John was the leader and what he said usually went.

'If they've been safe since 1879, they can stay here a day longer,' John declared. 'Wait till Father and Mother see what we've found! We'll invite them here tomorrow and show them the treasure.'

Next day however, it rained hard and the children had to swallow their impatience. They wanted their party to be perfect in every way. In the late afternoon the rain changed into a fog with a little sunlight coming through.

'Can't we go over to the island?' Jane asked.

Father went out and looked at the sky.

'The fog banks are still blowing in,' he said.

'Smell that sea smell that comes with them! It's likely to rain again in an hour or two.'

'Well, can't John and I take a picnic supper and just go to Oak Point around the corner?'

'We'd better let them,' said Mother. 'I've never known children to be so restless. Perhaps a little paddling and picnicking will help you.'

They had almost reached the point, moving through the fog so silently that they startled their friends the loons by coming upon them before they could dive; they had almost reached the point — when they found the man with the outboard motor. Everything about the picture was grey — a shabby boat, and a wiry shabby figure working over the motor at the stern, with the fog dripping from the broken rim of an old hat.

'Good evening,' John hailed. 'Anything we can do to help?'

The man straightened and stared at them.

'No thanks,' he said then, 'I'll be all right,' and he bent again to his work. The children paddled on and reached the point. They had already on another day built a fireplace of big stones there, and John had brought kindling in his knapsack, so that soon the fire was crackling and the smell of frying bacon filled the air.

Jane felt uncomfortable.

'He looks so kind of hungry,' she whispered to John. 'Go on, ask him if he won't come and eat with us.'

'But —' began John.

'I don't care,' Jane broke in. 'I don't care what people say. Ask him or I will.'

The man who called himself Trip Anderson hesitated and then finally paddled his boat into shore with a crudely whittled-down board which seemed to be his only oar. He ate at the children's fire hungrily but remembering his manners. He seemed like anyone who was rather down on his luck, except for the way in which he met a person's glance, staring back hard, showing a thin rim of white all round the bright blue iris of his eyes. They all talked a little about the pond and the weather. The man knew a lot about fish. It was interesting, but the children were glad when supper was over and the rain began again.

'Guess we've got to go,' they said, and he stared at them with fixed eyes which he never allowed to shift the least bit.

'Much obliged, kids,' he said. 'I'll do something for you some day.'

During the night the wind shifted to the north-west and the day came bright and perfect. The children spent half the morning preparing a magnificent picnic. There were whispered consultations and giggles and smothered arguments.

The greatest excitement reigned in the cabin until ten-thirty when *The Adventure*, laden with passengers, baskets, and extra supplies for Forgotten Island, put out into the pond. The way through the water gardens they knew so well that there was no need for Jane to stand up and scan its stretches. Forgotten Island lay deep in sunlight and shadow, welcoming them to its hidden shores.

Father and Mother were much impressed by the changes one afternoon's hard work had made in the living room. John showed Father what the original house must have been like and he caught their enthusiasm immediately.

'It wouldn't be much of a job tearing off the 1870 part,' he said. 'We might be able to sell the old wood, or if we can't it could be burned on the rocks. Then this would be a wonderful little place. Nothing like it anywhere in the country.'

The picnic was eaten in state around the table whose legs were made of horns, while a small unneeded fire crackled in the fireplace to give an added welcome. After the baskets were packed again and the room in order, Father brought out his pipe and sat down, while Mother began to knit.

This was the moment for which the children had been waiting for nearly two days.

'Want to see something else we found?' John asked with elaborate carelessness.

Jane bounded forward to help him.

They tugged out the statue and laid it on its back, and John reached far up its depths into the hollow arm, while everyone waited breathlessly.

Jane saw the look of shock and surprise come to his face and knew what had happened before he spoke.

'Why,' he said rather blankly, 'they're gone! The gold things are gone. There isn't even my handkerchief there.'

'Sorry, Jane,' he muttered to her when she ran forward to help search the crevices of the statue, and she squeezed his hand hard.

'It doesn't matter a bit,' she cried, bravely blinking the tears out of her eyes. 'Think of all we have left.'

They didn't talk any more about the treasure. John felt too badly about it to bear any mention of it. Jane felt badly, too, but it wasn't half so hard for her as for John, who had insisted upon leaving the things just where they had found them.

But for John the crown was gone from the glory if the treasures were gone. They all paddled home to the cabin making occasional conversation about nothing much, and that evening Father brought out *Huckleberry Finn* and read for hours, not saying once that his voice was getting tired.

Mother had glanced once or twice at the clock when they heard a car come down their road, and a moment later a knock sounded at the door.

It was late for visiting in the country, and they all looked at one another in surprise as Father went to the door. Two men stood there whom they didn't know, one of them in uniform.

'Come in,' said Father. 'I'm James Lane. Did you want to see me?'

The older man shook hands first. 'I'm Will Deering, Mr Lane,' he explained, 'from over across the pond, and this is Mr Dexter, of the State Police.'

Mr Lane shook hands with Mr Dexter and introduced them both to the family.

'Mr Dexter has come up here on business,' Mr Deering explained. 'There've been complaints about a man who calls himself Trip Anderson. One man has lost two heifers and another man, with a camp over on Muscongus Pond, missed an outboard motor from his boat. They brought Mr Dexter to me because I know the lake pretty well and had an idea of where his shanty was. I took Mr Dexter there while he was away, and we searched it and found proof he'd been doing a lot of petty thieving hereabouts. Proof wasn't need-ed, because when this Anderson came back, Mr Dexter recognised him as a fellow who'd broken jail at Thomaston a year or so ago.'

'His real name is Tom Jennings,' the other man broke in. 'He was serving a term for armed robbery. No, he ain't got a wife, nor kids. That was just cover. He's been in and out of jail since he was sixteen.'

Mother looked worried, thinking that the children had been having a picnic with such a man only the evening before. But Father knew that, somewhere or other, the business must concern them, or these two men wouldn't have come.

'Did you wish me to identify him?' he asked, but Mr Dexter shook his head.

'He don't need identifying,' he remarked, pulling out his watch and looking at it. 'By now, he's at Thomaston. But just before we took him away he said he had some things he wanted to return. He had them hidden in the flour tin. Said he'd been using the island you've bought, but never took any of the big things because they could be spotted too easy. When you kids began to go there, he kept an eye on you. He's good at that; moves like an Indian. One day when he was hanging round he heard a crash and looked in and saw you find the gold stuff. That was more up his alley. He could melt it down and no one could ever prove anything.'

The State Policeman fished again in his vest pocket, poked about with a stubby forefinger, and brought out first the dwarf, and then the bird, and then the crocodile. The ring came last. He poured them all into Jane's hand, and she quickly brought them to John.

'Think of his giving them back!' she exclaimed. 'Oh thank you for bringing them! We were so bothered when we found they were gone.'

The big man smiled.

'Jennings said you were good kids and had asked him to eat with you.'

'Do you want to see the treasure?' John asked eagerly. He handed it around so that everyone might examine the little

340

objects close at hand.

Mr Deering held up the crocodile.

'We have one at home like this,' he said. 'In the old teapot, I think it is. My grandfather used to say Johnson gave it to him for boarding his horse, after he'd run out of the gold-dust quills he used to get his money from. The day he gave grandfather the crocodile and drove off was the last time he was ever seen around here. "I took one image from that African temple that was chuck-full of gold," Johnson told Grandfather. "It stands to reason the other images I saw there have gold in them, too. Anyway, I aim to go and see."

'But he never came back,' continued Mr Deering. 'I figure he could play a trick on the priests once maybe, but next time they'd get him. We never knew where he came from, nor what vessel he took for Africa, but it wouldn't be hard to find one in those days, when there was still a good trade there. Grandfather said he had the bearing of a captain. Probably no one else ever knew that idol he'd stolen had gold in it, and he came away here on the quiet where no one ever would know it. But he was a reckless spender, Grandfather said. Money just poured out of his hands while he had it, and then he started back to get more. Anyhow, he was never seen hereabouts again.'

'Why didn't your grandfather use the house on the island, or sell it?' Mr Lane asked.

'It wasn't his,' the farmer replied. 'Johnson had bought the island out and out. And Grandma didn't want any of that African stuff around the place. She called it outlandish, and my mother didn't like it either. We just minded our own business and, pretty soon, the island and Johnson were kind of forgotten —'

'That's what we call it — Forgotten Island!' the children cried.

Mr Deering looked at them and smiled.

'Well, it's yours now,' he said. 'It's nice to have neighbours on it again. Glad we found you all at home this evening.'

Everyone got up to see their visitors to the door. Mr Deering stepped out first and, as Mr Dexter turned to say goodbye, Jane asked, 'Is there anything we can do for Trip Anderson?'

The officer shook his head.

'He's all right,' he said. 'Don't worry about him. I guess he was getting pretty tired of his freedom. He said he'd be glad to be back where he'd be taken care of.'

Then the door closed behind the strangers, and, a moment later, out of the night came the roar of a self-starter. Little by little the sound receded, and silence settled again in the woods, and, after a while, even the Lanes' cabin was dark and still, and the Lanes, too, were asleep. But on the mantel, in the silence broken only by the occasional calling of the loons, watched the four talismans of gold, keeping guard, the treasure of Forgotten Island, made by dark hands far away and long ago.

FUNFAIR

by

Penelope Farmer

That evening, going to the fair, Lesley in her pride walked straight as the lamp-posts along the road. The lamps had just come on and lit her bright proud face as she went with Barbie's gang for the first time, with Barbie and Heather and the rest. No one would have known, she only half knew herself how much she wished they had chosen to ask her on another day.

She walked with Judith who was both her friend and Barbie's. Judith was a neat silent girl and went her own way always. She wore tiny gold rings in her ears which glinted in the new lamplight. She said nothing, but Lesley had to prove to herself that she belonged with the gang. When anyone made a joke she laughed the loudest, and when she had the chance she talked all the time. She could talk quite well and even be funny, and the others listened contentedly enough, but in a little while, seeing the scorn on Heather's face, Judith nudged her.

'Shush, chatterbox, — look,' she cried before Lesley could feel hurt. 'Look, we're nearly there!'

Through the trees of the park they could see the fair lights. Some lights were still, in strings and clusters, blue and red and green; others swung through the air like coloured shooting stars. They could hear the fair also, the music thrumming and drumming in the air, the clatter and whirr of machinery.

Lesley did not want to talk any more. How she hated the thought of those machines — the Octopus, the dive-bomber and all the rest of them; she had not yet seen them, but could imagine what they were like, whirling up and round giddily. Why, oh why had she been asked to come with Barbie's gang to this?

The rest of them began to boast.

'I've been on the Octopus *thousands* of times,' said Heather. She had a round spiteful face and Lesley liked her least of all Barbie's gang. According to Judith, Heather did not like Lesley any better, and had tried to dissuade Barbie from letting Lesley come with them. Now she looked at Lesley and continued.

'*Thousands* of times, and I bet no one else has. How about you, Lesley — I bet you haven't?'

Lesley began to burst out a retort, but Judith put a hand on her arm and stopped her momentarily, and afterwards everyone was speaking at once and would not have heard her.

'I'm going on the wheel,' said someone.

'I'm going on the Big Dipper and the Whip.'

'What are you going to do, Barbie?' another asked.

Barbie said flatly.

'I'm going on the Dive-Bomber.' But the Dive-Bomber was the fastest and most frightening thing of all, no one would have dared to say that except Barbie.

'Honestly, Barbie,' they said, 'I don't believe you,' or 'You wouldn't dare, it's terrible,' or 'Fred says it shakes the guts out of you, honest — will you really go, Barbie?'

''Course,' said Barbie airily, 'I've been on all the other things; I've got to try something new, haven't I? How about you, Judith?' she asked to change the subject away from that. 'What will you do?'

'Nothing.' Judith's feet stamped against the pavement, and the straight tall tulips in their straight park beds stood straight and tall as her back, straight and firm as her answer.

'Nothing. I hate them all. I'll ruin my guts some other way thank you. I suppose I might go on the old roundabout, but that's my limit.'

The gang laughed but not at her, no one laughed at Judith, not even Heather who laughed at everyone else from time to time. But then Heather turned to Lesley.

'How about Lesley, then? What are you going to do, Lesley?'

Lesley's tongue would not work. She put her hand into her pocket and clutched her purse. She could feel the roundness of the coins through the cloth and tried to work out how much was there just by the feel of them. But meanwhile someone else said impatiently,

'Well, how about you, Lesley? What are you going to do?'

Lesley made what was meant to be a joke, as Judith might have made it.

'Me?' she said cheekily. 'Me? Oh I'll go on the Dive-Bomber with Barbie of course!' But then she realised, too late, that the others hadn't taken it as a joke.

'Don't be so silly,' said Heather. 'You wouldn't dare.' Lesley, her pride roused, was not now going to withdraw.

'Of course I dare,' she said indignantly, 'I'm not being silly. I-I-I-'ve always wanted to go on it. My brother says it's smashing.'

'Cor,' said someone. 'Well seeing's believing; rather you than me, anyway.'

'You can all come and watch if you don't believe me,' cried Lesley, desperately. 'Can't they Barbie?'

'Of course, they can all watch us,' said Barbie. 'Well done, Les.'

But Lesley, in spite of that, was the youngest and least of them, and soon they lost interest in her again. She did not want to talk any more and she and Judith fell behind the rest and walked silently under the trees that rose tall and dark on either side of the road. Though people crowded beneath them and scooters roared by like angry insects the trees were not changed but remained dark and still. Lesley felt dark and still herself; the quiet trees calmed her panic, and she wished this walking here silently with Judith could never end, that she would never now have to face the fair itself.

But ahead was light; light and sound; the fair music had been one sound among many before, a thrumming and rhythm in the background; but now it was near enough to dance and sing to, rock music, twist music, and bangy, tinny, roundabout music. The lights also before had been one small part of a great scene. Now everything was light; red light, green light, yellow, blue and white light. It was not yet quite dark. The daylight clinging to the sky dimmed these lights a little, but it was dark enough to guess how it would seem later, when the fair lights made the only day and the sky itself was black.

Momentarily it caused Lesley to forget all her fright. She skipped a little because it was so exciting and beautiful, because her ears and eyes were filled with light and sound. For a moment in such excitement she felt she could go on the Octopus, on the Whip, on everything as well as the Dive-Bomber, she wouldn't mind anything. But Judith nudged her and laughed at her.

'Go on then, you'll be flying next,' she said. And her earrings glinted and shone in the light.

By the entrance to the fair was a hot-dog stall with a red and white striped canopy. Behind that was a little jutting platform where people could stand and look over a low balustrade on to the fairground itself. They bought a hot-dog each and stood there eating and watching; hesitating strangely to go into the fair itself as if that would spoil it. But beneath people crowded; there were groups of bright girls not so much older than themselves, boys in jeans holding other bright girls; and there were families with children jigging up and down. Immediately below their platform a tall coloured man clutched the hands of two little girls with white satin ribbons in their hair; they were wide-eyed, and uncertain whether to pull away from the man to see all they could, or to cling tightly to him from fear of getting lost in the crowds.

348

But ahead was light; light and sound

Just behind them the roundabout went round and round
to a wheezy tune; the painted cocks and horses rose up and
down like washing blowing on a line. And next to that was
something which called itself the Fabulous! The All Time
Whirlaround!! Hundred Percent Funtime!! OCTOPUS!!!!
When Lesley made her first bite into the hot-dog, and her
mouth was first full of sausage and pickle and hot, soft
bread, this stood quite still. A man in a peacock coloured
shirt leant on the low fence round it and called out.

'Come on, it's nice! It's fun! Come on folks, come on!'
People hesitated; some looked and shook their heads and
went on. But others took their friends by the arm and turned
back through the little gate, and sat themselves down on the
seats. The seats were on a wheel, on the end of the wheel
spokes and when one couple had sat down the wheel moved
on a little and another seat rested by the steps up which
daring people had to climb. The wheel was neither straight
in the air nor flat to the ground; it was tilted. The girls in its
seats patted their hair and giggled, the boys clutched the
girls tightly. People leant on the fence to see what would
happen, and Lesley, chewing her hot-dog, watched them all.
There was exactly half of the hot-dog left when the wheel
began to turn. It began quite slowly; it was just a wheel going
slowly round, not so bad after all; then the seats themselves
began to swing and turn on the end of the spokes, faster and
faster; they whizzed round quick as a top, quick as light, and
tilted also this way and that, up and down, and the seats
flashed in and out; all at the same time they went round on
the wheel, whipped round themselves in their own separate
motion, the separate motion of each separate seat, and also
flew up and down, dipping down into the earth, then up into
the air and away. The girls screamed, whether in joy or
terror one could not tell. Their hair streamed out; their
hands gripped tightly at the iron bars, at each swing round
their heads and bodies jerked and jerked again till it looked
as if eyes, teeth, tongues must be shaken out of them. Lesley

chewed at her hot-dog without tasting it, until she choked suddenly, a sausage and pickle choke. By the time the last trace of that had gone the wheel was coming slowly, almost gracefully to a halt. The riders climbed out in turn as their seats rested by the steps. Some looked shaken and shook themselves, and hurried out of the gate as if glad it was all over. But others giggled and walked out gaily, and some, even, stayed in for a second ride.

'Well,' said Heather at Lesley's elbow. 'The Dive-Bomber is ten times worse than that. Are you still sure you want to go on it?'

Lesley drew in her breath. 'I-I-I-'

'Changed your mind, Lesley?' said someone else, grinning at her. Then they were all looking at her, great grins spread on their faces, listening for her reply; all but Judith who leant over the wall and looked into the lights of the fair.

Lesley wiped her fingers carefully on the paper napkin which had wrapped her hot-dog.

'N-n-no,' she said, but doubtfully.

'Go on then,' said one of Heather's friends, 'Look at her face, she doesn't want to go on anything like that, do you Lesley?'

'What, are you going to leave me to go on it on my own, Les?' said Barbie. She was a tall girl, and thin as a broomstick with a sharp, friendly face. She was rarely unkind, and she was not laughing at Lesley now.

'Do come with me, Les,' she pleaded, 'None of the others will.'

She sounded as if she really meant it, as if she really wanted company. Lesley was so pleased at the thought of Barbie wanting her to come, and so pleased to be called Les by her also, that she said out sudden and loud, her voice surer than she felt.

''Course I'm coming, Barbie. I said I was, didn't I?'

To Lesley's relief, she found they did not all intend to go round the fair together. They arranged to meet before they had to go home to watch Barbie and Lesley go on the Dive-Bomber, and then passed in turn under the entrance as they paid their five pence. Lesley and several of the others could have got in half-price, but they all paid five pence because it seemed grander. 'Four young ladies, *five* young ladies,' said the man. Lesley felt the iron bars of the turnstile against her stomach, click, click, and she was through. She was there amid the noise and light. She was not outside watching and listening to it any more; she was in it, she was part of it.

Barbie's gang drifted apart in twos and threes, passed into the crowds and were lost. Judith and Lesley stood alone, dazed, at the entrance, clutching their tickets.

'Fool,' said Judith fiercely. 'Fool.'

Lesley sighed. 'I know, I know.' She felt as if one of her mother's old-fashioned kitchen weights lay in her stomach, thinking about the Dive-Bomber cars which swung so high up into the sky. If she looked up now she would see those cars, and their little lights, one red, one white, swinging round high in the sky. From here it was too far to see the frame of the thing, or the cars themselves, there were just the swinging cruel lights of red and white.

'Oh come on,' said Judith fiercely. Lesley had never known the calm Judith so fierce. 'Come on, you don't have to think about the horrible thing yet, come on, enjoy it now.'

She took Lesley's arm and dragged her off, dragged her fierce and fast through the crowd till Lesley was happy and enjoying herself enough not to need dragging, as they went from this stall to that, to everything they could find. Nothing stood still. Lights flashed on and off, the people moved and laughed and talked, but their movement seemed small and quiet compared to the clatter of machines. Engines not people ruled this place; the metal clash and rattle of dodgem cars and locomotors overcame talk and laughter. And above it all rose the beat of music, rocking and crying, that made Lesley's feet dance without her. She jigged up and down and forgot all her fears, 'Come on, Judith, come on, where shall we go

352

next?' And Judith looked at what she had won, playing
shove ha'penny (a glass mug with a picture of the queen
painted on it that had already begun to peel off) and laughed,
in a face first lit and then shadowed again.

Only once did Lesley let herself, or did Judith let her,
stand still again and look up at the Dive-Bomber; and then
her excitement dropped away and the cold weight was back
in her stomach; and she said nothing at all because she was
thinking of what she would have to do later. The wind blew
her hair into her eyes, for the first time she noticed that
there was a wind, and that it was cold. She brushed one hand
up to remove her hair, but it blew back again and she left it
there though it tickled her eyes and face. For high above the
crowds the Dive-Bomber lights red and white flashed into
the sky in turn.

Judith saw her face and took her arm; and said in her
most kind and friendly voice, 'Come on, let's go on the
roundabout. Come on, Lesley, we've got some time.' Judith
was often kind and often friendly but not always both
together, and Lesley in spite of herself was comforted.

She jerked and turned away. The lights and music of the
fair caught her up again. Before there had just been herself
and the Dive-Bomber lights swinging in the sky, and nothing
else mattered but what she and they must do. Now the
crowd and all the other lights came between her and them.
The Dive-Bomber became distant again and quite unreal.
What ever could she be doing to think of going on that? She
rushed with Judith through the people, brushing them by,
who looked up and glared after them shouting, 'Mind out
where you're going, will you?'

So they came back to the roundabout near where they had
come in. It was painted all over with flowers and scrolls, and
its wheezy organ played waltzes and ancient jigs. All round
its canopy in curly script was written, 'Superb Parade of all
British Golden Horses Galloping. Suitable For All Classes.'
But as well as the golden red-nostrilled horses there were the

cocks with painted combs and purple tails; and beaks and
staring eyes. On to one of these Lesley climbed and held
tightly to the twisted pole. And Judith climbed on to a horse
on the outside of her. Even on this, a little chill of fright
came into Lesley's stomach; but such fright, of a mere roundabout, she would not have admitted even to Judith, who sat,
a toffee-apple in one hand, sucking at it, and holding on to
her pole with the other hand. She was looking at Lesley,
mocking at her almost, but saying nothing. And Lesley was
too intent on her pride to notice that once the roundabout
started Judith held on quite as tightly as she did herself;
even her toffee-apple-holding hand gripping hard on to the
twisted pole of her golden, galloping horse.

Round went the roundabout; the speed quickened, the
music thumped out, jig, jig, jig; up and down, up and down
went Judith's horse and Lesley's cockerel. To her surprise
Lesley found that the chill in her stomach swiftly disappeared.
She was not frightened at all. She felt light and free and easy,
swinging up and down. Daringly she took one hand off her
pole and waved it about. But Judith she saw kept both hers
firmly clasped on to the pole. Faster and faster went the
roundabout. Though the music went the same speed whether
the horses moved or were still; it appeared to move faster
with the rising horses up and down; really thought Lesley it
was too jiggy, jolly music for that graceful gracious rising up
and down and round, like a little girl dancing a waltz with
a tall man. The wind was in her face and in her hair, it was
even in Judith's short cropped hair, flying above the winking
gold rings in her ears.

Lesley's feet danced climbing off the roundabout. She was
dazed and dizzy and wildly happy, she cared about nothing
at all; the Dive-Bomber itself had no terrors for her now, she
almost looked forward to it, even when she raised her eyes
and saw the red and white lights whirling in the air on the
far side of the fair.

But then Judith looked at her watch.

'Lesley! We're late, quickly — run!' She seized Lesley's arm and ran with her through the crowds, bumping and gasping 'Sorry — Oh I'm *so* sorry,' so that Lesley, still dazed, had no time to feel fear at all unless it was fear of being late after this wild rush across the fair.

Just before they reached the Dive-Bomber the crowds broke apart; there was a concrete space with sweet and ice--cream papers blowing in the wind; on the far side of it by a low fence, Barbie's gang stood waiting.

'There you are,' said Heather. 'We thought you'd got scared and gone home.'

Lesley nodded dumbly. Her joy had quite gone. There was nothing now to come between herself and the Dive-Bomber. It had come to rest while she and Judith were running across the fair, and stood there quite still and quiet, one car, the one with the white light on it, high in the air.

It consisted, in fact, of a long, thick, pole, standing upright like a flagpole; but thicker than a flagpole, and cigar shaped; and if that was a long thin cigar shape the two cars placed at either end of it were like very short thick cigars. Each had four seats only, placed in two's on either side of the pole; one car now was high in the air, the other placed by the steps, awaiting passengers for its two little cages, for they were just like cages. Each lid which opened to let people in and out was made of tight meshed wire and there were no other windows, nothing to see out from but that tight wire mesh. Two men got in now, and their lid was shut down and they peered out like men from police vans. But the other two seats were empty.

'Are you *coming*, Les?' said Barbie for the second time; sharply, a little edgily; though Lesley did not notice that.

'She's scared,' said Heather, giggling at her friends.

'Shut up, Heather,' said Barbie frowning. 'Coming, Les?'

Lesley moved her heavy tongue. 'Y-yes.'

She didn't look at Judith again but plunged on in, blindly, through the gate.

'Hey, hey, young lady,' said the man. 'Where's your money? You can't go on without paying, you know.' Lesley looked blankly at him; then realising what he meant fumbled in her pocket for her purse. It was nearly empty now but she found enough for the fare. She counted it out clumsily into the man's palm, noticing and yet not noticing the smear of black oil caught between his thumb and first finger.

'It's lovely, *it's* lovely,' said the man. 'None of you other girls coming? You'll regret it *all* your lives if you don't; it's lovely.' Yet he was a kind man for as he took her money he peered more closely at Lesley's face and suddenly said softly so that no one else could hear: 'You're a bit young, love, aren't you? Sure you want to go?'

That determined Lesley. She nodded firmly, marched up the steps to the little waiting car and climbed in through the flap. She sat there on the hard seat waiting for Barbie and trembling, trembling all over, a pit now opened up inside her, she was so scared.

In that light even Barbie's face looked white when she climbed in. But perhaps it was only the light — and Lesley was too much concerned with her own fear to notice properly. Barbie smiled at her.

'Sure you're all right, Les. Sure you want to come? You can always get out, you know. I wouldn't mind, honest.'

Lesley shook her head, though her heart went up and down. But she did not move. Barbie fitted herself in the seat beside her. It was a tight enough fit, even for two thin girls; their knees touched and their shoulders also. Yet that was comforting, Lesley thought. And for a moment the gladness that it was she and Barbie tightly fitted like this, almost broke out of the fear that ringed round her.

But when the man had come and strapped them in and shut down the lid and they were quite alone, jammed in the little cabin, nothing could break out of her fear. She held so tight on to the steel rail that her knuckles were like a little row of white bones; and so were Barbie's. They could only see out through the little chinks in the wire mesh, chinks of coloured light, chinks of staring faces. Barbie talked fast and jerkily on and off about nothing it seemed — Lesley hardly heard her. It seemed an age while they sat there, though it could only have been a few minutes. In the pauses in Barbie's talking they could hear each other's quick breathing and the voices of the men in the other cabin — which seemed quite casual and unconcerned — and behind that the music of the fair.

'I'm scared, Les, I'm terrified,' said Barbie suddenly. 'I'm terrified. Are you?'

'Yes.' Lesley's throat was so dry by now she could hardly say it. But at that moment they began to move and she gasped softly. Beside her Barbie gasped more loudly, once and then twice and their knuckles tightened on the rail. Then, instead of swinging them on their car stopped; now they were perched high above the fairground and could see the sky and darkness and the swinging glitter of lights, in chinks through the wire grill; music floated up to them, but no voices. Other people, they realised, must be climbing into the second cabin; that was why they waited; but they heard no voices in what seemed an age of waiting silently. For even Barbie's chatter had stopped now; though twice she said: 'I wish they'd hurry *up*.'

Then at last they were off again, swinging downwards and this time there was no halting. The pole swung round faster and faster, their cabins swung too, turned like tops on the end of the pole so that they were upside down and then not, then sideways, upside down, sideways and right again, swinging round and round; swinging up — then, pause and down in a sickening swinging lurching rush.

Lesley could hear nothing but the beating engine and the whirr of their twisting cabins; it was so fast she could not believe they could go faster, yet they did; she was breathing faster and faster, louder and louder, then she was crying, her hair in her eyes, tears caught up in hair, swinging giddily on

357

and on and on, crying and gasping out loud in this giddy turning world, lights rushing past in chinks through wire, rushing down and past, from earth up to sky.

Would it never stop, would it never stop? Now she was crying aloud, but no one could hear except Barbie whose warmth and boniness was the one comfort in the whirling world, Barbie clinging beside Lesley.

Then Lesley felt sickness rising. After that the only thought was how sick she felt, and how to concentrate on stopping the sickness coming. She concentrated so hard on that, as the sickness rose uncontrollably in her throat that she barely even noticed the machine slowing down, and at last coming to a halt. As soon as the lid was lifted, still holding the sickness back she fumbled undone the leather strap, fumbled her feet out on to the steps, and down the steps, rushed out and through the waiting gang, not caring any more what they thought, rushed on out of the lights into the darkness of the bushes at the edge of the fairground, where all was still.

There she was sick; never in all her life had she been so sick as this. And afterwards she flung herself on the earth and lay aching and moaning and miserable and after a little while crying again.

She cried because she felt so ill; though gradually less so; she cried because she would never be able to go with Barbie's gang again; because Barbie would never speak to such a little baby as herself again. Barbie had said she was frightened but she had not cried and wailed and rushed off to be sick, at least not as far as Lesley knew; she would not be crying now behind the bushes like a little child.

At last when she judged they must all have gone, she staggered to her feet. There was a gate nearby and to that she went, through the lights and people, pushing on, till she felt the steel bars of the turnstile against her tummy again, heaved once and was through and out from the light and sound into darkness and quiet.

Judith was waiting there. She said nothing at all but went

with Lesley along the road, in silence except for Lesley's loud sobs, which the comfort of Judith's presence somehow made louder. Yet Judith did not even offer Lesley a handkerchief; for which, dimly, Lesley was grateful.

'They'll never speak to me again,' she burst out miserably, at last.

'Mm,' said Judith.

'Barbie'll never speak to me again,' wailed Lesley, louder.

'Sssh,' said Judith. Lesley became aware of people looking at them curiously and blushed and stopped crying because she was embarrassed.

'That's better,' said Judith. 'Barbie told me to give you a message,' she added.

'What, that I'm a baby?' wept Lesley again, but softer than before because of the people.

'It was horrible, wasn't it?' said Judith.

'It was horrible,' cried Lesley.

'Barbie thought so too,' said Judith.

'But she wasn't a crybaby like me,' then realised she still hadn't heard the message. 'What did she say, then?'

'She said to tell you she thought you were very brave coming on that thing, much braver than the others. She didn't realise how scared you were, and that made you braver she thought. And...'

'And what...' said Lesley, impatiently, her tears checked.

'And,' said Judith grinning at her, the little gold rings, almost grinning too in the sudden lamplight, 'and you're to come out with us all tomorrow.'

Lesley cried all the way home. But this was a cleaner cooler cry of relief. And Judith gave her the glass mug with the peeling picture of the Queen on it to comfort her.

ACKNOWLEDGEMENTS

The publishers wish to express their thanks to authors and publishers for permission to include the following stories:

THE LITTLE WHITE ASS by Maribel Edwin from Argosy

THE MONSTER by Janet McNeil from SPECIAL OCCASIONS (Faber and Faber)

THE CHAMPIONS by Monica Edwards from THE WILFRED PICKLES ANTHOLOGY (W. & R. Chambers)